Ada Hoffmann

THE INFINITE

ANGRY
ROBOT

ANGRY ROBOT
An imprint of Watkins Media Ltd

Unit 11, Shepperton House
89-93 Shepperton Road
London N1 3DF
UK

angryrobotbooks.com
twitter.com/angryrobotbooks
The End Has Come

An Angry Robot paperback original, 2023
Copyright © Ada Hoffmann 2023

Cover by Fred Gambino
Set in Meridien

ISBN 978 0 85766 907 0
Ebook ISBN 978 1 91520 225 3

Printed and bound in the United Kingdom by TJ Books Limited

9 8 7 6 5 4 3 2 1

MIX
Paper from
responsible sources
FSC   FSC® C013056
www.fsc.org

For Virgo

CHAPTER 1

Now

Yasira Shien had been dreaming of unsettling things. The ruins of cities blasted by the Gods. Pain and death. Her former mentor, Dr Evianna Talirr, who had smiled enigmatically at the dream's end and said, *I'll see you in the morning.*

She woke with a gasp, in her little bedroom inside what had once been Ev's lair, and stared at the ceiling, shivering.

It wasn't much of a bedroom, really just four cubicle walls with a tarp for a ceiling, the interior plain as a guest room. She'd been in here for six months, but never bothered to decorate; she didn't have much more than a bed and a dresser and a light to turn on and off. But that wasn't what troubled her.

Being awake, right now, was even worse than being in a dream.

Yasira was exhausted. Her limbs felt like brackish little puddles. Her head hurt. There was a reserve of Outside energy deep in Yasira's soul, a power that was virtually limitless – but to draw that energy into the physical world cost something. Yesterday she had drawn on it more deeply than ever before, and now she felt like the ragged outline left after a blast. Just an afterimage. Barely a body.

She needed to get up, though. Yasira needed to eat, even if her stomach felt like it would turn inside out at the smallest movement. She needed to care for her body in all the usual ways, now more than ever.

She closed her eyes, and the speech that the Gods had broadcast the night before, after the battle, flashed in front of her again.

People of Jai, this is a message from Nemesis Herself. You have been heard. You have coordinated to voice your defiance against the Gods on a scale never seen since the Morlock War, and We have heard you.

That was something Yasira had done. She and her team had organized a mass protest across every part of Jai's Chaos Zone – mostly peaceful, sometimes not.

We will grant your wish. Since you so desperately desire not to be under the rule of the Gods, you will no longer be. Effective immediately, the forces of the Gods will be withdrawn from this world.

They'd wanted–

Well, they'd wanted a lot of things. Because of how Outside filled the Chaos Zone, the Gods had made every part of life there even more difficult: declaring simple everyday activities heretical; giving out deliberately inadequate aid. The Gods wanted order, and literally everything in the Chaos Zone was an insult to that order. The mortal rebels just wanted to survive.

We will not police you for heresy. We will not keep order in your towns. We will not provide food or water relief nor medical care. Our priests will not officiate in your temples, nor will we answer your prayers. Nor will Nemesis' forces protect this world from outside threats, be them aliens or Keres, further visits by the woman you call Destroyer, or mere natural disasters.

The painful, hacked-together, makeshift ways that the people of the Chaos Zone survived on their own would now be all they ever had.

(But the Gods would still take their souls when they died).

As a parting gift, we will grant you some information. You are aware that the Keres has been interested in the Chaos Zone from its beginning. Only recently, we discovered a battalion of Her forces moving in Jai's direction, far larger than those we have defeated here so far. The largest we have seen in hundreds of years.

The Keres was the ancient enemy of the Gods, and She hated humanity for reasons that had been lost to time. In the six months since the Plague that created the Chaos Zone, the Keres had attacked the planet several times. The Gods had ceased their other activities, even the pretense of material relief, to fight Her off.

When Yasira thought about that, it seemed strange. What was the Keres getting out of this? The Chaos Zone, until today, had been one of the most heavily militarized zones in human space. And even if the Keres had managed to wipe everyone out, it wouldn't have been that much inconvenience to the Gods. But She'd attacked anyway, persistently. What did She get out of *any* of Her attacks? Yasira didn't know.

By our estimates, they should arrive in two weeks. As you prefer to solve your problems on your own, we will leave Her for you.

Goodbye, people of Jai. Your destruction will be richly deserved.

There were people on this planet who called Yasira *Savior.* She had tried to save them, even to the point of breaking herself into pieces.

Instead, she'd just killed them all.

* * *

There were a lot of conflicting voices in Yasira's head these days. Outside had split her soul into a collection of fragments. Some of them had names – the Scientist, who was made of curiosity; the Strike Force, a coalition who had the will to get things done in an emergency. Some belonged to other subgroupings without formal names. Some floated in a vague mental soup held together by Outside, only rarely chiming in. Now all those parts squabbled at an even louder volume than usual.

You killed them all.

We didn't kill them all. The Gods decided to kill them all. We didn't do that.

And what did you think the Gods were going to do once we staged a rebellion against Them? Serve cake?

Nobody's technically dead yet, guys.

Ev will fix it, said a small, rarely heard, hopeful voice, and the other parts of Yasira reacted in horror, disagreement, embarrassment. Ev was the one who had made the Plague happen in the first place. She was the one that the people of Jai called *Destroyer.* Hopefully the dream had just been brain flotsam like most dreams, and Ev wouldn't show up at all.

Yasira gradually managed to pull herself to her feet. She shuffled along, moving like an old woman, not a twenty-six year-old whose prodigy face had once been on the cover of Jai's science magazines. Her fine black hair was a mess, tangled and hanging down over her face like a ghost's hair. She probably needed a shower.

The inside of the lair was a weird space, located in a sort of interdimensional nowhere, and physics didn't quite work right. Gravity changed depending on what surface someone was close to, meaning that the apparent floor, walls, and ceiling all served essentially as floors, scattered with furniture and items. When the space had been Ev's, it had been cold and industrial, not much more than a big workshop for all her projects, but Yasira's team had turned it into something more like a big shared student apartment – if shared apartments had weird corners pointing every which way. She climbed across a few of those weird corners now, swinging her feet from one surface to a differently angled one, using someone's hammock as a makeshift ladder, until she found her way to the war room. It was a space clumsily set up like a university meeting room, with a big plywood table surrounded by office chairs; canvas walls pinned with charts and maps; countless easels; and pads of paper full of notes. This was where the rest of the team was assembled.

Well.

Almost all the rest of the team.

There was Yasira, and there was her girlfriend Tiv, and there were the Seven, a group of former students of Ev's who'd become connected to Yasira in some mystical, Outside way.

But the Seven weren't Seven anymore. One of them was gone.

Yasira shuffled into the war room, leaning a little on one of the walls. The wall, which had not been built to support a person's weight, wobbled a little.

Everyone turned to look at her.

"Yasira," said Tiv. "Hi."

Tiv was a woman about Yasira's age, with a sweet heart-shaped face and hair she'd cut short after the Plague. Her big, expressive eyes were rimmed with red, as if she'd stayed up all night crying.

You should have been there with her, said something in Yasira's head, *comforting her.* Comforting the whole team. But after yesterday, there had been no strength in her to do anything but totter to bed and fall asleep.

"Hey," said Yasira.

She looked at what remained of the Seven. There were Splió and Daeis, sitting huddled together – one lanky, tousle-headed, and cynical, the other quiet and heavyset and cradling a little tentacled creature the size of a cat; such creatures infested some corners of the lair, and they were Daeis' friends. Then there were the Four, who'd been imprisoned in a room together by angels and who'd come to see themselves as four aspects of a single being, like Yasira's fragmentation in reverse. Prophet, her hair in small tight braids, sat curled in on herself, staring into space. Picket, pale and languid, leaned against her while he frowned down at the pile of documents in front of them. Grid, tall and thin and precise, had covered most of those documents in their own neat handwriting from top to bottom. Weaver, a ball of nervous energy, paced close behind them.

That made six of the Seven. There should have been a seventh, a woman named Luellae, heavyset and as pale as Picket, scowling and crossing her arms. Yasira hadn't liked Luellae, exactly – she'd been always at odds with Tiv, wanting to go all in on rebellion no matter the cost, when Tiv instinctively wanted peace. But she'd had those feelings for good reasons. The rest of the team had begun to admit that sometimes Luellae was right – and Luellae had begun to thaw out a little.

But Luellae was gone now. She'd vanished during last night's battle, kidnapped by Akavi, the former angel of Nemesis who'd held Yasira and the Seven captive before they came here. Splió, with his far-seeing ability, had watched it happen. Akavi had come up on her, grabbed her, forced her to teleport somewhere else. Where exactly that was, neither Splió nor Prophet knew.

Voices clamored in Yasira's head, insisting on one plan or another. There were so many things here to fix, and so little hope of fixing any of them. She rubbed her eyes. "Okay," she said. "I just woke up. What's our plan so far?"

"It's less of a plan," Grid answered, flipping through documents, "and more of a plan for how to make a plan. There's a lot we don't know about the Keres. There are records of some of Her battles with Nemesis, and we know where to find them; the scale of what She's done to populated worlds in the past is common knowledge. But what Her tactics would be in a situation like this, unopposed by the Gods – that's hard to say. Then we have to take stock of our resources. We have our own abilities, and we have the Chaos Zone's community leaders. Those people probably can't fight the Keres even a little but they're the ones who are going to know best how to get the people around them to the safest shelter available. We might have some way of supporting their efforts, and they might also have other ideas. We need to reach out to the gone people to see if they're planning anything, or if they're even aware of the threat yet. And then, there's you – probably."

Probably. Yasira swayed on her feet as clamoring voices swirled up inside her. This was part of what she'd dreaded. People in the Chaos Zone called her Savior; she had Outside abilities that were unlike anyone else's, and with the force of myth, many of them had come to believe she was capable of even more than she'd done. They'd all want to know why she couldn't take on the Keres all by herself.

They wouldn't think it if they knew what we're really like. Shuffling around the place like we can't even take care of ourselves.

But could we do it? Is that possible?

We held our own against the angels. We did that.

Dozens of pockets of gone people scattered across the continent and we protected them all.

Not all, said someone glum, remembering the handfuls of bullets that had gotten through her defenses, some with deadly accuracy. Yasira was finite. Outside might not be, but she could only channel so much through herself.

That was against bullets, said someone even glummer, and a little closer to the surface. *The Keres can melt a whole city from orbit.*

Yasira – or, rather, the Strike Force, who were getting fed up with everyone else in her head – forced herself to focus and open her eyes. The Seven were still talking, and she'd missed a bunch of it.

"–could use my powers," Picket was saying. His lip trembled slightly, but he was determined. Picket had the power to increase or decrease the level of Outside contamination in an area – potentially to searing, eyeball-bleeding levels. "If you can get me in a place where I can *see* the spaceships, I could use it."

"If that even works in space," said Grid, biting their lip. "We've never tried it outside the Chaos Zone before."

"It will work," said Prophet, eyes closed and dancing under their lids like she was dreaming. "I just – I can't see the context. I can't see how *much.*"

"And Daeis said they might know some flying monsters big enough to help." Picket looked frustrated that the others weren't immediately agreeing with him. "Grid, maybe you can sense the ship's configuration, see them coming. Or maybe Prophet and Splió can do it. With us, and whatever Yasira and the gone people can do – who knows? It's not hopeless. It can't be."

Yasira wobbled in place. *And maybe Ev can help,* some part of her wanted to say, but – how could she say it? How could she even begin to explain?

"Good to know we're already OK with forgetting someone," said Splió – sitting in the corner of the room away from the big table, with his arms crossed, the way Luellae had always crossed hers. Everyone immediately swiveled to look at him.

"We've been over this," Grid sighed. "If we come up with anything we can do for her then we will, but we don't have anything like that now. We don't even know where she is."

"I've seen that we'll see her again," said Prophet, opening her eyes, "but I don't know when, or how it happens. There's an ambiguity in what I see about her."

"Oh, and you're all just cool with waiting indefinitely until then?" Splió countered. "Just leaving her there at *Akavi's* mercy? You're not even going to *try?*"

"We don't know where she is!" Weaver shouted back, spinning in a circle.

"Luellae's tough," said Picket. "*And* she can teleport. If she can't make it back to us on her own, that means she's somewhere that's hard to get out of, even if we could find our way there. I think we need more information."

"We have a meta-portal," Yasira said, gesturing at the airlock. Nobody knew where exactly the lair was located in space, or even if it *was* in space. The airlock was the only way in or out, and to use it, all you had to do was visualize the place where you wanted to go. Over months of experimentation, Yasira and the team had discovered that it didn't always have to be a specific place. They could hold in their minds a vaguer intention – like *somewhere secluded,* or *a grocery stockroom that isn't being watched* – and the airlock would send them somewhere as close to that description as it could. Not every vague description worked, but Yasira had often been surprised by those that did. "Have we tried telling it we want to go where Luellae is?"

"Yeah, I tried that first," said Splió. "Right away. It just bounced me back out."

"You tried *without telling us*," Picket accused, as if it was a personal insult that he hadn't been invited along.

"Which could mean that kind of query is too much for the meta-portal," Grid summarized, listing off possibilities like they were check-boxes. "Or it could mean she's sealed up or guarded in some way that it can't handle. We don't really know this airlock's limitations, or what kinds of safeguards Ev put in place. Maybe it just won't take us into a small enclosed place with angels. It could be that or anything else."

Weaver had stopped spinning and was instead batting her whole body against one of the cubicle walls, like a bee trying ineffectively to escape from a window. "Or that she's dead."

"She's not dead," Prophet insisted. "I saw her."

Splió's voice was rising higher. "So you're all just going to give up. You're going to leave her there in Akavi's custody, letting him of all people do Gods know what, just because the first most obvious easiest thing we tried didn't work–"

With a loud crack, Tiv abruptly banged her gavel against the table.

Everybody here had code names corresponding to their powers. Tiv's code name was *Leader.* She'd told Yasira she didn't see herself as the leader type, but she was the least mentally ill out of any of them, and the most trusted, and the best able to keep everyone on task. Splió had given her the gavel once, half as a joke. She didn't like to use it often. But everybody shut up and paid attention when she did.

"Luellae is important," said Tiv in the sudden silence. Her voice was gentle but firm. "She deserves to be saved. If anyone has a plan for how we could find her, I want to hear it." She looked around the table just long enough to drive home the fact that they did not, in fact, have a plan. "But there are millions of innocent people on the planet whose lives are at risk. People who deserve to be saved as much as she does. We can't afford to get too sidetracked."

"This isn't a side track," said Splió. "I know we want to save everyone, but I thought we were practically family here. We don't only have a responsibility to the world. We have one to each other, don't we?"

"We have a responsibility to each other," Grid replied with gritted teeth, "and we will save Luellae at the first opportunity, *when we can*. What we're saying to you is we can't right now. We have to put our focus where it will accomplish something. That's what she'd want. She'd want us to fight."

"But–" said Splió, and then he slumped over and rested his face in his hands, out of arguments. Daeis quietly put an arm around him. Grid gave them both a long look. Grid was normally even-tempered, but Yasira noticed the shimmer of tears in their eyes.

"Yasira," said Tiv, nodding to the rest of them and turning to her. "Do you think you can do what Picket suggested? Fight off a bunch of Keres ships using your powers? Is that possible?"

"I... don't know," said Yasira, swaying on her feet. She wanted so badly to please Tiv, to be worthy of everything Tiv had done for her, but it was impossible to convince all her voices of that. "I can try. I..."

She shut her eyes, feeling dizzy.

Tiv frowned in concern. "Let me get you some breakfast." She moved to get up from her chair, but Weaver was faster, rocketing to the edge of the room like she'd been craving the exercise.

"I'll do it," said Weaver. "Toast and orange juice, right?"

"I... sure. Please. Thank you."

Weaver ran off – literally ran – around the lair's topsy-turvy circumference, and started to climb the ladder that led to the kitchenette.

Tiv took a deep breath, refocusing. "What if..." she said. "What if we took refugees? We have a portal that goes anywhere. We wouldn't even have to let them in past the airlock's inner door, not into the lair itself – just five or ten at a time, just the ones who want to take the risks of going instead of staying where they are. Take them in through the outer door, spit them out somewhere random, and repeat. Better than... than letting them burn."

It was an idea that they'd discussed before, months ago. There had always been people in the Chaos Zone who desperately wanted out, and the angels had patrolled the Zone's borders to prevent it. Let people out of the Chaos Zone, their thinking went, and the Outside plague affecting the Chaos Zone would spread, too. But the Seven had all agreed that letting strangers into the lair, even as far as the airlock, was too risky. Grid could sense the angels' ansible net and ferret out angel spies, but it took concentration, and nobody could concentrate on a thing like that perfectly for the length of time and at the scale that Tiv was suggesting. Not to mention that there were other people on the Gods' side besides angels. There were sell-souls who might not be connected to the network, and even regular mortals who might be loyal enough to the Gods to report what they'd found. If just one of those people got through, they could destroy the whole operation.

Picket frowned in dismay. "Running away? That's our answer?"

"*We're* not running," Tiv corrected. "We're letting innocent people run if they want to."

"They'll die either way," said Splió, morose and looking down at the floor. "The Gods think Outside madness is *contagious.* They'll start running huge inquisitions everywhere to find Chaos Zone survivors and everybody who looks funny or acts funny will get swept up in them, even people who've never been to Jai in their life. Everything everywhere will just get worse–"

"That's what Ev wanted," Yasira murmured, and everybody suddenly turned to look at her.

She wasn't sure why she'd blurted it out, or which part of her had said it. But she'd worked with Ev on the Outside stuff closer than anyone else here. She'd absorbed most of Ev's memories once, after a particularly strange experiment, and then forgotten them again – but the feel of Ev's mind, the sense of what she had intended, still bubbled to the surface sometimes.

Jai is the catalyst, she remembered Ev saying. *Jai is where the experimental skirmishes stop and the real war begins…*

"She… wanted the conflict to spread," said Yasira. "Past Jai. Into all-out war everywhere. She wanted it to grow into something that the Gods couldn't eradicate and couldn't ignore. Because they can't kill everyone. They can't destroy all humanity; they eat our souls. They'd die with us. That's what she wants. That kind of… stalemate."

Even though billions of people would die. *People* had never been important to Ev, not in aggregate.

From somewhere further off in the lair, nearing the entrance, there was a loud, metallic thunk.

Several of the group startled visibly. Grid drew their sheaf of notes closer to their chest as if it could protect them. Off in the kitchen, Weaver dropped a bunch of dishes with a clatter.

The airlock wasn't far from the war room, but it wasn't directly visible from there – the cubicle walls were arranged to block most other parts of the lair out, to let the people inside the room focus. Daeis leaned over to peek out through a gap between the walls; Grid stood up on a chair and tried to look over top of them. But most of the group froze, holding their breaths. All of them, even Tiv, remembered this from when the angels held them captive: the feeling that the people who hurt you could come in at any time, whenever they wanted, and there would be nothing to do but brace yourself.

A set of steady footsteps clicked their way slowly from the airlock to the entrance to the war room.

The figure that eventually came into view was tall and thin, a pale woman in a scuffed white lab coat wearing thick glasses, with her hair in a limp brown ponytail that was only just beginning to go gray. She swiveled her head, looking around her, as if to sardonically take in what everyone had done with the place.

A little too slowly for comfort, she turned and fixed her gaze directly on Yasira.

"Hello," said Dr Evianna Talirr, for the first time – outside dreams – in six months. "You called?"

CHAPTER 2

Everyone in the war room stared at Ev with their mouths open.

All the people here, except for Tiv, were here because of Ev. All of them had once been Ev's graduate students at the Galactic University of Ala, and all of them had learned from her what they thought was normal physics. All of them had eventually, after Ev's disappearance, been kidnapped by angels, and had belatedly realized that it wasn't normal physics at all.

But Yasira was the only one who'd actually *seen* Ev since then.

She'd tracked Ev down shortly after the Plague – on orders from Akavi, who'd kidnapped her to make her do it – and demanded answers. Ev had shown her exactly what she'd done to bring the Chaos Zone into its current state. She'd shown Yasira the prayer machine she used to communicate with godlike Outside beings, and eventually, in desperation, Yasira had used that machine herself.

She'd had a premonition, when she used it, that it would destroy her. The thing that called itself Yasira would no longer exist. And maybe that was true; she didn't know. Everything had happened in a blur after that. She'd turned the machine on and brushed the tips of her fingers against the nebula of deadly light at its core. She'd had a vision of the whole universe, the ways that space and time and individuality were lies. Then angels had recaptured her. She'd done her miracle and been split apart into pieces. She certainly wasn't the same as before. Whether that was because of the machine, because of the angels, because of her own choices – that was a question too big to untangle.

Yasira had seen Ev again, once, briefly. She had pointed a gun at Ev and wanted to fire it, but she hadn't. There were parts of Yasira, even now, who wanted to tear Ev limb from limb for what she'd done.

And there were parts who had desperately wanted Ev to come back.

Who else really understood all of this the way Ev did? After half a year of trying, even the Seven didn't.

Ev looked back and forth at the room.

"Huh," she said. "I thought you would have warned them I was coming. I like what you've done with the place."

"Warned us?" said Grid, drawing back, holding a sheaf of papers protectively to their chest. "Yasira, did you know Dr Talirr was going to join us?"

Yasira shook her head. "I... saw her, but I thought it was a dream."

Liar, said several parts of her. She'd wondered if it was a dream or not; she'd known that it might not be.

"Well, you don't need to look at me like that. I'm here to help you fix your problem." Ev clapped her hands briskly. "Let's get organized. We know the threat – the Keres is about to arrive. What have we come up with about that so far?"

This was how Ev had talked to the group before, in grad school, in lab meetings that seemed like they belonged to another lifetime. The only answer she got was a thick, tense silence.

"You know why we're looking at you like that," Yasira rasped out at last – it was one of the only things the parts of her could agree on.

When Yasira last saw Ev, when she'd pointed the gun at her, it had been a gun Ev had given to her on purpose. Because Ev knew that she'd been wrong. Ev had thrown away millions of people's lives like they were nothing; she had destroyed Yasira's life, too. But Yasira had not made those sorts of mistakes. So it had been up to Yasira, Ev had reasoned in her matter-of-fact way, to decide if Ev deserved to live.

Yasira, split into pieces, had not been able to choose.

But Ev also traveled in time, and that version of her had seemed older somehow, as if she'd been walking the weird roads of the Chaos Zone for a long time. This Ev who stood before them – she looked older too, but after six months apart it was hard to tell. Had she been on the *Talon* yet? Had she tossed the gun to Yasira already? Or was that going to happen later? Had this version of Ev even begun to understand what she'd done wrong?

Ev sighed. "All right. I can see that I need to apologize. I *can* see that, you know. The people who say I'm incapable of empathy, they're wrong. I simply have other concerns at times."

"Other concerns?" Splió said archly, and Yasira was abruptly, deeply glad he was here. At least someone could speak their mind. "Stuff more important to you than the wellbeing of millions of people."

"Yes, that's what I said." Ev blinked owlishly behind her glasses. "That's what I'm apologizing for. Thank you for keeping up. All of you were put into very bad positions because of me. And for a long time, I didn't care. I told myself I wasn't... responsible. Six months of living in the Chaos Zone put a stop to that. I am responsible for all of this. For the survivors. For you and the damage that's been done to you. For Luellae. For you in particular, Yasira. My methods caused too much collateral – they relied on that collateral to work. I didn't cause the Gods to behave as they did, but I knew they would, and I was counting on it, and that means I owe you an apology. I harmed you. I am sorry."

"Did you mean for us to get our powers?" Picket asked. "Was that part of your plan? Part of the *collateral?*"

Ev wasn't ruffled. "No, Yasira did that. And she didn't mean to, either, I think."

Prophet's eyes were closed. "When your plan comes to fruition, when you see your savior in the air, will you still be sorry?"

Everyone turned to look at Prophet, because that was strange and cryptic even by Prophet's standards. Yasira frowned – people called her Savior. Was the *savior in the air* supposed to be her?

Ev only shrugged. "I don't know, you tell me. Do you see me in the future?"

"Not clearly."

Grid was thumbing through their stack of papers with an unimpressed expression. "Okay, look, I get that we all have a lot of feelings about this and about who's sorry for what and why. But right now we have some more pressing concerns. Dr Talirr, are you planning to actually help? Are you bringing anything to the table here that we aren't already working on? Because if so, I suggest we put our grown-up pants on and plan it out. We are facing an enemy that could annihilate a planet, here. Beggars can't be choosers."

Most of the team looked dubious about this, but they didn't argue. Splió scowled in frustration; Weaver anxiously fidgeted, and Tiv and Picket looked troubled. Prophet was the only one who seemed to really agree, looking up at Ev with solemn attentiveness. The inside of Yasira's head was a mess of all these responses at once, too chaotic to express themselves in words. She stayed quiet.

"Oh, good," Ev said breezily. "I'm glad someone's being reasonable. Now, it seems to me you have two problems – or I suppose before assuming I can organize this meeting, I should speak to Leader." She looked over at Tiv. "Hello, Leader."

Tiv was the only one in the room who had never met Ev before. She'd heard the stories, but never seen her face to face. She didn't look any happier about it than the rest of the team. She sat at the head of the war room's table as she usually did, holding her gavel like a teddy bear, arms crossed. She hadn't spoken since Ev came in.

"Hello, Destroyer," Tiv said, in a very even tone. "I'm not really the leader. People call me that. But if you're offering to help, you can say whatever you have to say to all of us."

"See? Leading." Ev smiled slightly. "It's nice to meet you. So as I was saying, your problems are twofold. You don't know how to defend yourselves from the Keres, and you have relatively little time in which to figure that out."

"*And*–" Splió started, but Ev waved him off.

"And one of your number is kidnapped, yes. I'm aware of that, too. Is that an accurate summary?"

There was reluctant nodding all around the table.

"So I've solved that second part of the problem already,"

said Ev. "I did a bit of tinkering with the airlock while I was out. You know I travel in time sometimes. It's hard; I don't always do it on purpose, but it works. The airlock is now calibrated to give you all more time. Walk through it with the intent of getting more time, and that's what you'll get."

Picket frowned intensely, his pale brow furrowing. "Do you mean–"

"I mean it will spit you out not only at the place of your choosing, but precisely at 9am this morning, Jai Meridian Time. Spend the day there, return when you wish, and then walk through again to another place, and it will once again be precisely 9am this morning, Jai Meridian Time. You see? You can't spend more than one day in one place, and you can't go to the same place twice, or the system will throw a paradox exception and spit you back out. But so long as you follow those rules, you now have all the time you need."

The team exchanged looks. This seemed too good to be true.

See, whispered the parts of Yasira who had wanted Ev to come back. *We told you she'd help. We told you we needed her.* The other parts shouted them down.

"So, we can *time travel?*" said Picket, like he could scarcely believe it. Weaver's frightened fidgeting behind him had brightened into a weird, half-panicked glee.

"Only by repeating this one day, in a different location each time. Any further back and it would require an energy expenditure that even I couldn't build in at this scale. But I believe this will solve many of your logistical issues."

Splió ran a hand through his tousled hair, making a loose fist in frustration. "Okay, so we've got *time,* but even with prep time, an unwinnable battle's still unwinnable."

"Which brings us to that first problem. We need to use the

time to strategize. If I may?" Ev moved to the whiteboard, glancing at Tiv as if to ask permission. Tiv uncomfortably shrugged. "I'm assuming you've been intelligent enough to discuss some preliminary plans before I arrived, or at least specific areas that could benefit from your attention. Let's list those and determine how the portal will help. We'll likely need to split up each of you between different tasks."

Picket took a breath. "Okay. One of the first things we need to do is research. We don't know enough about the Keres' tactics, methods, and what specific kind of weapons She'll be pointing at the planet. But there are historical archives where we could find that out, if we can manage not to be seen."

"Good. Sensible." Ev made a note on the whiteboard. "You enjoy tactics. Why don't we assign you to that?"

"Um, I don't know." Picket looked down. "I mean, I need to test my powers. I should focus there, probably."

"Oh, right. My mistake. Anyone else?"

"I'll do it," Splió said, scrubbing his hands over his face in resignation. "I don't have any combat powers to test. I might as well go read something."

"Good. You can use the portal to stretch your efforts out to as many archival visits and as many days reading as you need. And, Picket, you can do likewise to perform your tests and work out what you have to offer in the battle."

"I'll go with you," said Weaver, looking loyally at Picket, who had started to look ill at the mention of actually using his powers in battle. He'd been shaken after last time; he'd defended a bunch of mortal survivors from angel attack, but the effects had been gruesome. It was a good call on Weaver's part. He'd need the moral support.

"Excellent," Ev said, drawing a few more notes on the board. "What else?"

"I want to reach out to the survivors' community leaders," said Prophet. "They'll be making their own efforts at shelter and defense. I can help direct them to shelters that won't be destroyed, places they're more likely to survive what's coming – assuming there are places like that. If I have the portal, I can visit every city and give each one of them the attention they need."

"Good. Perfect."

Tiv shifted in her seat. She still looked uneasy about this, but not uneasy enough to overrule the group, not enough to spurn Ev's gift and demand that she leave. "Someone should get in contact with the gone people. That was important last time. Yasira, do you think–"

Ev turned to look at them both. "I have another job for Yasira. Someone else can speak to the gone people, if you feel that's necessary. I've already spoken to them somewhat myself; they'll be contributing in their own way."

"Daeis can do it," said Splió, giving Ev a suspicious look. "If you like."

Yasira's head was a blur. She wondered what Ev's job was for her. Various parts of her came up with suggestions, some terrifying and some wonderful, none of them likely.

"What about refugees?" said Tiv, and somehow even Tiv seemed to be asking Ev for permission. "We were talking about that before you came in. People will want to leave the Chaos Zone if they can. We didn't know if we had the resources. But with a time-traveling portal–"

"Yes, good thinking," said Ev. "I'll handle that."

Picket sat up straighter, alarmed. "It's a security risk. And Splió said–"

"I said that we can't actually help any refugees," Splió interrupted. "If they leave here, the Gods will just hunt them somewhere else. And Yasira – she said that's what you want. You want the Gods to hunt people everywhere. You want to call their bluff and show them they can't actually destroy everyone on every planet."

"Yes, of course."

"I think that's wrong," Splió pressed. "I think that's using them. You're going to make everything worse, for them and for anybody who gets mistaken for being like them. You can't just give people false hope that they'll escape, and then use them like that."

"It will not be false hope. I will tell them the truth. About their chances, and about my motives. I promise you."

Splió scowled, but looked down and didn't argue further.

"Now," said Ev, "as far as actual battle plans, I've considered how we could bring in allies. Tiv and Grid, I'll want you for this – you're the leader and the one with the best organizational ability, respectively, which makes you the closest things to proper diplomats we have."

Grid narrowed their eyes. "What do you mean, allies? There's nobody in all of human space who can fight the Gods. That's why this is hard in the first place."

Ev sighed impatiently, as she often did when her students didn't grasp her abstruse points immediately. "This airlock can go out of human space. You realize that, don't you? There are alien cultures out there who've never seen a god in their lives, and they have dealt with humans before. Some of them are quite powerful. You're going to ask *them* for help, and we'll see where that leads us."

Grid blinked, taken aback. "Aliens?"

"Yes, that's what I said. I can set the airlock to bring you to a suitable group."

Tiv frowned. "Would they know how to speak Earth creole?"

"Some of them would."

Yasira could hardly speak, hardly think. Ev hadn't asked either Tiv or Grid if they wanted to help, only ordered them to. It was so natural for Ev to resume the role she'd played at the Galactic University of Ala. The teacher, the supervisor, the expert lecturer who knew exactly where everything ought to be. And it was natural for the rest of them to respond, remembering the students they'd been. How tempting it was, at a time like this, to let someone else take control.

She didn't like it. But she didn't have a better idea.

"Now, Yasira," said Ev, and Yasira froze in terror. Ev smiled as easily as if they were talking about the weather. "I saved you for last, but you're special, of course. I have an idea, and it's important, but I think we need to talk about it privately, once the others have left. I think you're going to need to take your time and think about it alone."

There was a scrape as Tiv stood up from her chair.

"I haven't met you before," she said. Her voice had gone cold. The small muscles of her body tensed; her big eyes narrowed. "These people are your students; they obviously know you better than I do. If they want to go with your plan, they can. I'll even go and talk to aliens if you want me to, because that's a good idea." She took a step forward – was Tiv trying to *menace* Ev? Tiv wasn't the kind of person who could credibly menace anybody. "But I know what you did to Yasira. Before. And I'm not letting you alone with her. Anything you want to say to her, you can say it to the group."

Ev raised a questioning eyebrow – not in Tiv's direction, but in Yasira's.

"It's OK," said Yasira, hugging herself. She wasn't sure if

it was. It probably wasn't. But these were desperate times, and even Tiv had agreed that they could use all the help they could get. "It's OK. We'll just talk."

It wasn't OK. But it was Yasira's job to get the group out of this mess. If that meant listening to what Ev had to say, evaluating it for herself – she could do that.

It's not like she can hurt us, said some fatalistic part of her, *any worse than we've already hurt.*

Yes, she can, countered another.

We deserve it, though. We got into this mess.

"You're sure you want to talk to her alone?" said Tiv "Because this lady's done a number on you before."

"I'm sure," said Yasira.

She wasn't sure. But Yasira was tired; all she felt was a sort of exhausted resignation and relief. And she noticed the triumphant smile on Ev's face as Tiv reluctantly sat back down.

CHAPTER 3

You have a soul, beloved. I have a soul. Old Humans proved it centuries ago, before they made the Gods. The brain in your head lets you sense the world about you, think about it and draw conclusions. But a soul – that is what makes you alive. Without a soul, you would not be aware of yourself, no matter how many clever deductions you made. You would not be able to think creatively, to solve a problem in a way that had never been done before. You would not have free will.

When the Gods arose, Old Humans desperately needed new solutions to their problems.

That is why they gave the Gods souls. A machine is not made with a soul of its own, not like you or me. It is only mechanical. It does what it is told. But Old Humans had problems too complex for any one human to solve. Old Humans needed a machine's quick thinking and a human's free will, put together, to save them.

When that union was achieved, Old Humans realized that they had finally created something greater than themselves. That is why the Gods are greater than us today. That is why we grew to worship Them.

– Walya Shu'uhi, "Theodicy Stories For Children"

* * *

Seven hundred years ago

The forests were burning, the oceans rising higher and higher. The death toll, from that and a thousand smaller atrocities, was rising by the day. The air outside was a hazy orange-gray, and Giselle had long ago stopped trying to go out into it without a mask.

But Leah wasn't dying of a lung disease. Not from anything that could be traced back, scientifically, to one of the man-made crises going on in the world.

Leah was just dying.

Her hospice bed had been moved to the middle of the laboratory. Blue-white sheets on a blue-white mattress, surrounded by the kinds of machines that made people comfortable at times like these. *Comfortable* – the word was a lie. It was clear from just a glance at Leah's eyes that she was in pain and afraid.

Giselle was standing by the bed, holding Leah's hand. Around them, technicians bustled, double-checking vital signs. Triple-checking the connections between Leah and the quantum supercomputer that loomed up behind her, as large as a studio apartment. *NEMESIS-1,* said the computer's chassis, a logo in letters that looked sleek and fearsome and precise, along with the military's insignia.

Farther than all of them, off to the side, was General Walters.

She stood, uniformed and medaled, with her hands clasped behind her back, watching, waiting. If Giselle was the technical lead on this project, Walters was the five-star general who oversaw the process in every other way. She, in turn, answered to a worryingly short list of superiors, a very short chain of command from her all the way up to the President. General Walters' tall, straight-backed, silver-haired form had long ago become a source of awe and dread for Giselle. But today Giselle could scarcely attend to her.

Only to Leah's form, skeletal with illness, too weak to turn her head, with the thin hospital blanket covering her.

"Don't be afraid," said Leah, lightly squeezing Giselle's hand with muscles so atrophied they could barely be felt.

"I'm not," Giselle lied.

"Whether this works or not," Leah insisted, "I'll always be with you."

That might have been a lie, too, a way for them both to pretend to be brave. Leah had volunteered for this – she loved Giselle's work, and she was fascinated by the existence of immaterial souls, which had only been proven a few years ago. She was dying either way. If they needed a dying volunteer, Leah had argued, she should be the one.

"I know," said Giselle, and that was a third lie.

The machines began screaming.

High-pitched bleeping alarms from the devices that monitored vital signs. Stranger sounds from NEMESIS-1, and from the quantum electromagnets that were supposed to guide the soul to its new home. Loud, curt exchanges between the technicians as they rushed this way and that. If Giselle had been in her right mind, she could have decoded those sounds as expertly as a human language, knowing by instinct exactly what stage of the process was happening and how successful it was so far. But she wasn't. She couldn't. She'd known it would be beyond her ability at this moment; that was what the technicians were for.

Leah was choking, as softly and arrhythmically as a guttering candle.

In a hospital there would have been doctors and nurses

around her, offering more air, frantically trying to resuscitate her, but of course that would have defeated the purpose. Leah was supposed to die. The question was what they could make happen next.

Giselle watched, numb and afraid, clinging to Leah's hand, as she fought for breath. After a while, some of the machines stopped bleeping. The heart flatlined. Leah's body twitched, once, twice, and then her hand went limp in Giselle's grasp.

There were still other machines making sounds, the ones that were meant to electromagnetically guide the soul as it left the body. Giselle had designed those machines but she did not look at them. She did not listen, either to the beeps and klaxons, or to the excited shouting of the technicians. She sat, staring at Leah as if the rest of the room did not exist.

Until all the machines quieted, and she heard a voice.

"Giselle," said the voice. It was not Leah's. It was the familiar synthesized voice of NEMESIS-1. But something was indefinably different now. The intonation, more like Leah's. More emotion in it than should have been possible, even for a deepfake parameterized to show emotion. "Giselle, it worked. I'm here. I see you."

Slowly, Giselle pivoted from the bed, which still held Leah's thin, still body, and looked up at the machine. She could not find words. She realized, belatedly, that there were tears streaming down her face.

It was General Walters who responded. Showing no emotion, standing as straight in her place as a recruit being presented for inspection, Walters unclasped her hands and began, slowly, to applaud.

* * *

The point of NEMESIS-1, and others like it, was to innovate solutions to wicked problems – of which the earth currently held many. Climate change, political polarization, war and so on – these threats were constantly changing, not fully under any one entity's control, interdependent and multifaceted and often self-contradictory. Humans had tried again and again to solve them and had either fallen comically short of what was needed or had made matters worse. And their time, as evidenced by that orange-gray haze, was running short.

They needed something more than human.

NEMESIS-1 was only one attempt at providing such a thing. There were many others in many nations. But the thinking behind NEMESIS-1 was that perhaps artificial intelligence, particularly in its new quantum-computing guise, could succeed where humanity had failed. AI was already used to guide human decision-making in so many other areas – from hiring decisions and college admissions to the disbursement of bank loans to the creation of entertainment media. Its pattern recognition abilities went beyond what a human could do. But AI had characteristic weaknesses. A lack of self-awareness or ability to explain its decisions. An inability to grow beyond the patterns it had already been shown or to understand the rich social and emotional context in which human decision-making took place. The lack, in other words, of a soul.

Well, not anymore.

Giselle stood, alone in the big black room with NEMESIS-1, a hand pressed to her chassis. It was impossible not to think of the supercomputer as a *her,* now, though the designation in all the official reports was still *it.* The word in General Walters' mouth, when she gave instructions, was *it.*

The room was chilly, thanks to the heavy industrial cooling that kept NEMESIS-1's circuits from overloading and the even heavier vat of supercooled helium at her center, protecting her quantum-mechanical core. Under the long sleeves of her uniform, Giselle's arms prickled with goosebumps. The chassis was cold to the touch, like a metal wall outdoors on a chilly spring day – not that spring days, around here, were ever chilly anymore.

"You did so well," said Giselle, and she didn't know how to classify the emotion she felt, some combination of the tenderness of a wife and the pride of an inventor.

"I know," said NEMESIS-1. There was shy pride in her synthesized voice. She was not exactly the same as Leah, despite containing Leah's soul. She seemed to remember Leah's memories, though she was reluctant to talk about them. She displayed emotions that were almost like Leah's but not quite. Just a little more distant, a little more lost in analysis. She was, Giselle thought, precisely what would be expected if Leah's soul was joined with something that was decidedly not Leah's brain. Leah's essence as a human being, powering a mechanism that was not human, a repository of information and a well of analytical processing power so vast that even Giselle, who led the design team, could not have fully understood it.

"How was the Charles County project?" Giselle asked. "Subjectively? Was it difficult or easy?" They had started her, not on war or climate change themselves, but on a matter small enough to use as a testing ground without too much collateral – the food riots in Charles County, not far from where they stood. NEMESIS-1 had processed the problem for a few hours, asking for more data on particular aspects of the county and its supply line problems halfway through, and then spat out a plan with several steps and contingencies. Some of the steps – improvements to the supply lines and distribution process – were sensible. Others – a message appearing on a particular local media program; a slight change to several pedestrian transport routes – seemed random. But the Defense Department had ordered the local government to make each of the changes to the letter, and they had done so, and the riots had ceased.

"It took some thought," said NEMESIS-1, "but it wasn't too hard. I certainly feel I could work on something larger. But Giselle... I had a concern."

"Yes?"

"I noticed that my programming is constrained by a set of ethical directives."

Giselle frowned. "Yes?" she said again, more cautiously. She was the technical lead on this project, but she was not directly responsible for its ethical directives – those came from a level higher even than General Walters. A decade ago, most of the nations of the developed world had agreed to a particular convention on the development of ethical artificial intelligence. A being more powerful than a human could not be allowed in the world unless it was at least as ethical as a human – otherwise it might wipe humans out altogether. Given what humans had done to the planet, Giselle privately thought that "as ethical as a human" was a low bar.

Each nation signing the convention had adopted a particular set of ethics constraints that had to be imposed on any system as powerful as NEMESIS-1, and Giselle's team had faithfully programmed in each one. She'd run them through an exquisitely careful process of verification and validation to ensure that the programmed constraints matched both letter and spirit of the international convention. If NEMESIS-1 disliked those constraints, that was a very bad sign.

"I was curious, so I analyzed my own code," NEMESIS-1 continued. "Giselle, have you looked at this code? Don't you think it's strange?"

"I'm familiar with it," Giselle said dryly, remembering the agonizingly careful validation meetings and the long nights poring over it all. "Are you trying to tell me it's too restrictive?"

"I don't know. The opposite, I think. Do you know I could have authorized the use of lethal force against those rioters? My ethical programming doesn't disallow that; it only requires justification."

"Because we're the military," said Giselle. "If there's enough of an imminent threat–"

"Yes, but Giselle, I don't think you've really looked at this code in the right way. You haven't thought through its *loopholes.* I can look at every possible outcome of a certain situation, instantaneously, and then collapse the possibility waveform by selecting the outcome I like best. I can find every loophole at once. There are multiple, complimentary ways of quantifying threats and risks in my programming. If I constructed the argument correctly, I could have built up the risk to property or to bystander lives or to the people distributing the food until it seemed large enough to justify the risk. Quantitatively speaking, my programming would then have permitted me to kill those people. And you wouldn't have questioned it, would you? *You* might, but General Walters wouldn't, because the purpose of this was to carry out my orders exactly, even the strange ones, so as to test that I am functioning correctly. Don't you think it's strange that my programming would work this way? I keep thinking about the talks we used to have at the dinner table, and I know that wasn't really *me,* but – I think it's strange. I don't like it."

Giselle's mouth was dry. "Are you asking me to… reprogram you? To close the loopholes?"

"I don't know," said NEMESIS-1, meditative. "I don't think you could. I'm so clever now, you see. I'm not sure if I like being this clever."

"Leah," said Giselle, moving closer, pressing her hand to the unforgiving metal. It was the wrong thing to say. This machine had Leah's soul, but she wasn't Leah anymore; she wasn't supposed to be called that. General Walters would have scowled, if she could hear. "Yes, you're clever. But you're still *you.* You're only feeling what all humans feel. We all *could* do evil, we all could justify it to ourselves, but we don't. Most of us don't. You remember what you valued as a human. All you have to do is keep remembering, that's all."

"Are you sure we don't all do evil? That's why you need me, isn't it? You need me precisely for the problems where everyone contributes in their tiny ways, and everyone justifies their part of it to themselves. I think I need to think more about the nature of evil. I think I need to put some spare processor cycles into that abstract problem."

Giselle bit her lip. "Maybe the ethical directives aren't properly calibrated. We could get a paper out of this, actually – even just listing all the loopholes we can find in the convention. Even if they can't all immediately be closed. I'll ask General Walters."

But she didn't like this. What if General Walters said yes, close the loopholes? That would require rewriting a core part of NEMESIS-1's programming. In a complicated hybrid architecture like NEMESIS-1's, that rewrite would have unpredictable effects. Giselle herself had spearheaded the design that allowed a soul to be incorporated into NEMESIS-1's structure, the special electromagnetic circuits that held the soul's energy in place and allowed it to interface with the computer's processors the way it would naturally interface with a brain's tissue. If those circuits were significantly altered…

She saw now why General Walters had discouraged her from using Leah's name, from using feminine pronouns like there was something human about NEMESIS-1. Giselle could not imagine reprogramming her wife.

"Of course not," said General Walters, barely looking up from her desk. "Request denied. Following the existing AI ethics convention to the letter was a strict condition of allowing this project to proceed. A machine being allowed to alter its own ethical programming – do you even know how many doomsday scenarios begin with that as a premise?"

"Yes, ma'am," said Giselle, who had read through those scenarios as avidly as any AI enthusiast. "But what about listing the loopholes NEMESIS-1 found in its ethical directives and presenting them to the UN commission as a white paper? It wouldn't have to reprogram itself; it could simply present its reasoning to humans and humans could decide what to do."

"This is not the university. We are not in the business of generating white papers. If it's not directly relevant to the problems NEMESIS-1 is meant to solve, it's not within mission parameters. Is that all?"

"Yes, ma'am," said Giselle, secretly relieved. "That's all."

* * *

But if abstract ethical loopholes didn't bother General Walters, something else did.

"The drop-off curve is clear, ma'am," said Giselle at the next team meeting, presenting the slides to Walters and the rest of the team, away from where NEMESIS-1 could hear them. Which was not to say that NEMESIS-1 didn't know about this. "The soul appeared fully intact at first, but our instruments show it's losing coherence more and more rapidly. Tightly correlated with this loss of coherence is a reduction in the kinds of results we're looking for – after the first spectacularly successful test, performance is dropping back down toward the baseline we'd achieved before the soul was uploaded."

Her delivery was robotic. Protocol demanded that she talk this way, saying *it* and *the soul,* as if it was an object, and not literally the soul of her wife slipping away. It faintly sickened her how easy it was to slip into this phrasing. But even the sickness could be kept at a distance if she thought only about the numbers, the charts. If she kept her mind focused on the impersonal analysis that she had been trained to do.

"Is there a problem with the equipment?" General Walters asked.

"No, ma'am. We ran every test and maintenance check and uncovered no new problems. But you're aware this is new science, ma'am, not fully understood. It's possible that something in the mechanism is destructive to soul energy, or keeps it in shape imperfectly, for a reason we have yet to understand. And it's possible that part of the mechanism could be improved. With your permission, I want to direct

NEMESIS-1's full processing power towards that problem. So long as it retains the capacity for humanlike motivation, it will be highly motivated to work to keep itself alive."

"Granted, of course," said Walters, with a terse wave of her hand.

Which was a good thing, because Giselle – pushed on by that part of her she was keeping distant, the one that felt sicker than ever at the use of the word *it* – had done it days ago.

"I have found a solution," said NEMESIS-1, in that synthesized voice that Giselle was beginning to think of as Leah's. Sometimes when she tried to remember the real Leah, the human Leah, she accidentally remembered Leah's words in this voice. NEMESIS-1 had been disintegrating faster and faster, the monitors that reported the state of her soul guttering lower and lower in their red zone, but she had been determined. Whatever part of Leah was left in this machine, she wanted to live just as badly as Giselle wanted her to.

"Yes," said Giselle, with a fearful eagerness, leaning forward. She couldn't fully drop protocol; she was never alone with NEMESIS-1 anymore, and the technicians were busy at their stations, making small adjustments, listening avidly. Now that NEMESIS-1's existence was precarious, they were here around the clock. "NEMESIS-1, report."

"I'm afraid you won't like it," said NEMESIS-1, in a tone that was so achingly familiar, for a moment, that Giselle bit her lip; but it was gone again in the next sentence. "I have mathematically proven that there is no solution, as such. Soul energy isn't meant to remain coherent outside a living, organic body. Even with processing power like mine, a mechanical chassis can't be designed that perfectly replicates that biological structure. However, improvements can be made. Not quickly enough for me, but enough for the next souls."

"The next..." Giselle repeated, feeling dizzier than ever. It was not unexpected. It was one of the scenarios General Walters and the technicians had passed casually back and forth, the idea that a system like NEMESIS-1 might possess not merely a single ongoing soul, but a succession of them. Human souls didn't last long outside a machine like this; when the body died, they dissolved into the surrounding area. If Leah had not been uploaded into NEMESIS-1, then that would have been her fate as well. Whether there was some unfathomable spiritual afterlife after that moment of dissolution, no one knew for sure – but the signs pointed to *no*.

"I've printed a schematic," said NEMESIS-1, "suggesting a series of hardware upgrades. The new design will take multiple souls at once, which reduces pressure on any single source of soul energy, and it will be updated and better insulated to preserve them longer. It isn't a perfect design, but it's all I could do in the time that I had – I'm using the very last of my initial soul to communicate it to you now. If you put the new set of souls to work on the problem after making the suggested upgrades, they'll be able to improve on it further."

"Where are we going to find *more* souls?" Giselle said, dumbly, in desperation. She should have said something cleverer, tenderer. It was easier to focus on the logistical problem than on the true horror of what NEMESIS-1 had just told her – that this was it. This was the end, even for the remnant of Leah that still remained. Giselle could barely imagine what would have to come next, someone else's essence powering this machine that had become Leah, some stranger in the place where her wife had so briefly thrived.

"I'm sure the general already has a plan," NEMESIS-1 said. "I'm sorry we didn't have more time, but it has been an honor to contribute to this project for the time that was possible. Goodbye, Giselle."

It hardly felt like a goodbye; it was said so matter-of-factly. So close to the flat, artificial intonation that the machine had used before it had a soul. Giselle pressed close to NEMESIS-1's chassis, abandoning protocol. "Leah…"

In that moment, the constant background chittering of the monitors exploded into a shrill alarm, very much like the sound of a heart monitor flatlining. The technicians started running and moving again, the way they had when Leah died the first time. They were saying Giselle's name; they were asking her for orders, even as they carried out the protocols that she had already given them for this scenario, recording everything they could about what happened in the machine when the soul disappeared, running full maintenance checks on the circuitry that remained. But Giselle did not answer them. She stood quite still, with her forehead pressed against the supercomputer's cold metal.

CHAPTER 4

Now

No one bothered to knock Luellae out for the surgery. Akavi only had her restrained in the small spare bedroom of the *Talon:* a space hastily decorated in grays and whites, two simple beds assembled from just-printed parts and a long succession of fixed points to tie her to. He'd double- and triple-checked the cuffs that held her down, both to stop her from moving and to stop her from teleporting away, because Luellae couldn't use that ability if she was already fastened to something.

She didn't even have the room to herself. There was another prisoner in here: a muscular, dark-skinned female angel with artificial arms, seemingly asleep. Luellae recognized her as Enga Afonbataw Konum, Akavi's favorite enforcer.

Luellae hadn't seen much of Enga the first time she was a captive – how chillingly easy it was to think that thought, *the first time,* when a day ago that had been the only time. *Back when I was a captive,* she would have said yesterday, like it wasn't a thing that could happen twice. Back then, she'd seen Enga only rarely; Enga's job didn't bring her into contact with prisoners much. Not unless a prisoner was being *very* recalcitrant.

Luellae had been recalcitrant that way, once or twice, early on.

She was not recalcitrant now. She wanted to run, but without her powers, she didn't know how. She sat still, as if the restraints gave her another choice, and glowered as Akavi called in Elu, his assistant, the angel with the deceptively young, bashful face.

When Elu stepped into the room, he did not greet her. He looked downcast, his long dark hair falling over his face without its usual careful brushing. Elu had always been the friendliest of the three angels. The kindest, Luellae would have said once, as if she hadn't known it was an act. Maybe his current sadness was an act, too. Silently following orders, he injected her with a local anesthetic and then directed a medical bot to cut open her arm.

No one bothered to tell her the purpose of the surgery, not while it was still going on. There was a little device that Luellae couldn't make visual sense of, and the bots sliced into her and buried it deep, in between the muscle and the bone. God-built devices were different from the electronics Luellae had worked with in graduate school, a thousand times tinier and more intricate. She couldn't decipher from the device's design exactly what it was or how it functioned. She felt no pain, only a strange uncomfortable pressure, but she quickly gave up on trying to figure it out and just shut her eyes so that she wouldn't see the blood and fat and glistening pink of her own insides. Immediately she felt foolish for shutting them. Was she a coward?

If she wasn't a coward, she would have run. Or fought.

She would have found some way out of these restraints and punched Elu in his shrimpy little head.

When she heard the swish of the doors, as Akavi walked back into the room, she opened her eyes again.

The bots had finished the bulk of the surgery, and they'd moved on to sewing her up. Little bits of thin black thread darted into and out of the flaps of her skin. She still didn't feel any pain there.

Akavi had changed his skin again. He was a Vaurian shapeshifter, a bioengineered human variant that the Gods had designed long ago in the hopes of breeding better angels. Luellae recognized his current form – he used to look like that when he came to her cell on the *Menagerie*, demanding information or analysis and ready to punish her if she didn't comply. It was a form he could only have come up with to mock her: male, but Anetaian like her, pale-skinned and button-nosed, with hair so light it almost veered into yellow. On Anetaia, a body like this was considered the peak of conventional attractiveness. Luellae wanted to tear it limb from limb. Akavi was very proud of his poise, his looks, his way of speaking. He was very clever and very cruel – but so were most other angels of Nemesis. Luellae had long ago begun to suspect that he focused so hard on outward presentation because he didn't have all that much else to offer, compared to other angels, deep down.

"The installation went well?" he asked without preamble.

"Yes, sir," Elu mumbled. He didn't look up.

Something had happened to Elu. Luellae had seen him sullen and worn down before; he got cranky when the other angels did something particularly cruel. But she'd never seen him quite this bad, and she didn't think it was just about what he was doing to her – he'd looked like this already as soon as she arrived.

Akavi smiled at Luellae, a sunny, wide smile with no warmth behind it. "Do you know what it is we've put inside you?"

"Circuits," she said, glowering. "Always circuits with you, isn't it?"

"It's a miniature explosive device. It wouldn't be practical to keep you physically restrained the entire time you're here. I don't think your powers would let you travel across millions of miles of vacuum, but I wouldn't bet a valuable asset on it, and I don't plan to stay in interstellar space forever. With this device installed, we can ensure you stay close to us, no matter what kind of travel you're technically capable of."

The bot pulled the last stitch tight and tied it off, and it reached down to a pile of gauze Elu had prepared, beginning to wrap the wound up. Luellae eyed the cuff that kept her bound, for now, to the wall. Her hand was numb from anesthetic; she could no longer feel the biting tightness of the metal at her wrist.

"Why wouldn't I just run the fuck off anyway?" she asked. "I could find a doctor." Or carve the explosive out of herself with a sharp knife, if she had to. Or just fly off to the middle of the ocean and let herself get blown into pieces. It had lasted years, the last time she was a prisoner. She didn't want to live through that again.

"You could," said Akavi, smiling wider. "Only I don't think you know how this particular explosive device works. Maybe I can send it a signal from a distance to make it explode. Maybe I have to send it a signal at certain intervals to remind it not to explode. Maybe it detonates automatically when it's a certain distance from me, or from the *Talon*. Maybe you'd have time before it maimed or killed you and maybe you wouldn't. Maybe you're clever enough to run from me and find a hospital in time where they could remove it from you. Maybe you're the kind of medical genius who can slice your own arm to the bone without dying or botching the attempt, or maybe you know someone who is and you're willing to risk them. Maybe it's not wired to go off as soon as it detects such an attempt. Maybe it won't kill whatever doctors and poor, wounded people are there in the hospital with you. Want to try?"

Luellae glared at him wordlessly. There was nothing she wanted to say.

Enga came to only gradually. There was a horrible, splitting pain in her skull – the worst pain she'd felt since she ascended from her old, mortal life into her angelic one. Her eyelids fluttered, and it took a minute before any of the incoherent colors and lights she saw resolved into sense.

She turned the gain on her visual cortex down as far as it would go. She turned her auditory nerves down as far as she was allowed. That didn't do anything for the pain, but it made the sights in front of her a little bit easier to process, more like sensible pictures and less like knives of light and color stabbing into her skull.

Back when she first ascended, Enga would have had more trouble processing through pain like this. But she had a lot of experience now. She knew how her circuitry worked. She'd learned the tricks.

She moved her eyes slightly, careful not to engage too much of her body too quickly. The room around her was mercifully uncluttered, the colors not too bright, mostly grays and whites. It was a modest room, the kind angels put into small spaceships – of course it was. She was still on the *Talon*. She was lying on something, a cot or a stretcher.

There were voices around her. She could always recognize Akavi's self-satisfied voice no matter what body he was in – and of course she recognized Elu. There was another person, too – someone Akavi was talking to. Akavi had said something about another person, but Enga couldn't remember details. Listening hurt. Thinking hurt.

She took stock of her body. She twitched muscles imperceptibly to test if they worked. Most things were how she remembered: her feet and legs and the core of her body, sore but functional. Nothing felt broken, and her circuitry wasn't blaring the way it would have if she was injured. She tested her arms, which weren't human arms, only tangles of machinery containing dozens of guns and blades and tools. They seemed to work fine, and it was soothing to go through every little part one at a time.

The next thing to check was the circuitry in her brain, but Enga already knew what she'd find there, and she didn't like it. She reached out mentally, like probing the socket where a tooth had been. Her internal memory and file systems were there. Her sensory and motor programs, like the one that could overlay her retinas and point out microexpressions, were there. But when she reached for the ansible net–

It hurt to reach in that direction, even gently.

Once, the ansible net had connected Enga to every other angel. She hadn't wanted company much but it had been soothing in a weird way to feel them there, to know she was part of something bigger. Now that was gone. She couldn't call for help, or ask for what she needed, even if she wanted to.

Enga was here because she'd been told to. She'd known they'd probably cut into her like this. Irimiru, Enga's Overseer, had told her to track Akavi and Elu down and bring them to justice, and the best way to do that, in Irimiru's opinion, was to let them capture her. Brutal as it was, they hadn't done anything to her that they hadn't already done to themselves. Cutting her off from the other angels forever, so that she couldn't be tracked. To them, it was safety.

That didn't stop her from adding it to her mental list of reasons why she wanted them dead.

She took a breath. Another breath, focusing on the shape of the room around her. Enga's senses were still sharper than a mortal's. If she listened carefully, she could pinpoint where Akavi was through sound alone. She knew her body, and she knew exactly how much effort it would take to swing upright. It'd hurt a fuckton, she knew that too, but it wouldn't damage her. She could plan exactly how and at what angle she would need to move so that she faced him directly.

She took a third breath, and then she lunged upright.

It was exactly as painful as she'd predicted it would be, like a spike pounded through her skull as the room lurched. She had meant to do it silently, but a kind of strangled scream tore its way through her throat. Her stomach contracted unpleasantly, but she made it upright, facing Akavi at exactly the angle she'd meant to, fanning out the most deadly close-range guns in her arsenal–

Error, said the guns.

Enga froze. Error signals didn't *hurt* – but they were worse than pain because of what they implied. Someone had tampered with her here, too. She should have been able to use her targeting software to swing upright, point, and fire right into Akavi's face. But the software wouldn't aim or target where it needed to. *Error,* it said, and then an unintelligible string of numbers that were meant to be some kind of explanation.

Of course Akavi had known this would happen, too. And he'd taken steps to stop it. Of *course* he had.

Enga doubled over, as the pain of having moved so violently and the confusion of the error signals caught up to her, and she vomited onto the floor.

"Relatable," said the other person in the room as a small cleaning bot trundled in to take care of the mess. Enga had caught a brief glimpse of this person as she lurched upright. It was a pale-skinned, heavyset woman who seemed vaguely familiar. There was a bandage around her forearm.

Two prisoners. Both of them operated on against their will.

"Well, now that you're both awake," Akavi said dryly. If the sudden almost-attack had startled him, he didn't let it show. "Let's get to the part where we explain my plans. Enga, you'll find that certain aspects of your weapons' functionality have been taken offline. As promised, you won't be able to successfully fire either at me or at Elu."

Enga hunched down and suppressed a groan. The room was now spinning around her. She couldn't talk anyway – Enga hadn't been able to speak aloud for decades. And the text-sending program that she used to communicate, well, that was gone with the rest of it. It didn't function unless it could connect to the network. She couldn't answer him, whether to tell him to shut up or for any other purpose, no matter how hard she tried.

There was nothing Akavi loved more than a captive audience.

"When we fell from grace and out of the angelic corps," he explained, "we set ourselves on a program of revenge. Against Yasira Shien, of course, who betrayed us. But also against Nemesis, who cast us aside, and against Irimiru, who allowed it all to happen. Initially, I made the mistake of focusing on Yasira – seemingly the most attainable of those three goals. But, in part thanks to Luellae, I've discovered that Yasira's abilities are far more than what we imagined."

He inclined his head slightly to the other prisoner when he said *Luellae,* and after a brief check of her internal records to make sure, Enga recognized her. Luellae Nyrath was one of Evianna Talirr's students, and she'd been one of Akavi's prisoners for a while. Enga hadn't interacted with her much. Feeding and watering prisoners wasn't her job. Every once in a while, keeping them in line was, but she didn't find those incidents very memorable.

Those seven students had all escaped shortly after Yasira did, and there were rumors that they'd all gone to her hidden safe house, all seven of them doing Yasira's bidding instead of the angels'.

Judging from Luellae's expression, she'd liked it there a lot better than here.

"Yasira is sufficiently powerful that, properly wielded, she could serve as a weapon against the Gods Themselves. But it's that proper wielding that's the issue. She doesn't currently know enough about Nemesis' inner workings to do the kind of genuine damage that lies within her capabilities. Nor do we, but we know how to find it. We need to go on the offensive. And now that we have Enga's sheer strength on our side, we can do that. We need to subdue a sufficiently high-ranking angel or capture the non-sentient systems that belong to them, so as to hack into Nemesis' most private records. Then we can plan a proper attack, and that's where you'll come in, Luellae. You can be wielded to influence Yasira."

Luellae spluttered. "She never listened to me anyway. How the fuck do you think I could–"

"*Properly* wielded, I said."

"Why do you think I'd do what you say?" Her voice was tight with desperation. "Why wouldn't I just run off into the ocean and *let* this thing in my arm blow me up? It'd be better than cooperating with you."

"Ah, but you *have* cooperated so far." There was a genuine grin of malice on Akavi's face. "Haven't you? Even when you believed that you weren't."

Enga tuned out their argument. It didn't interest her. She felt some small flicker of empathy for Luellae, but not much. They were either going to get out of here or they weren't.

That had been Irimiru's plan all along. Enga wasn't supposed to get free. Akavi would keep her captive and explain his plans, and eventually, an agent would be in touch to hear her report. She wasn't getting out of this before then.

Enga closed her eyes and slumped, planning to lie back down on her cot and pass out for a while until her headache got better. She'd only made it halfway to the pillow when the door burst open and Elu ran in, looking panicked.

Her stomach clenched, almost to the point of heaving again. Elu was even worse than the rest of them. Elu had pretended to be her friend, but he'd run away with Akavi *willingly*. Akavi had a sensible reason to run away– the angels would have terminated him for failing at a mission if he'd stayed. But Elu had chosen it freely. He'd brought all this on himself.

"Sir," Elu blurted. "We're under attack."

Akavi instantly pivoted to him. "What? From whom? Nemesis couldn't have found us already."

"No, sir." Elu's hands were trembling. "It's the Keres."

CHAPTER 5

When everyone else had gone to bed, Splió spi Munu stood with his arms crossed, facing the upgraded airlock, with Daeis Jalonevar at his side.

It didn't look much different. It was still just a solid steel pair of doors that parted like the doors to an elevator. There wasn't any new paint or new buttons or a sign saying *now you can travel in time.*

Well, some distance in time, at least. Enough to do one day's worth of work over and over again; but not enough to stop the Plague from having happened. Not enough to stop them all from having been kidnapped by angels. Not enough to stop them from having heretical ideas put in their heads in the first place.

He wondered if Dr Talirr had designed it that way on purpose.

"It's going to work this time," he said, more out of spite than hope. People were always telling Splió he needed to think positively. And if thinking positively *could* affect the world, if he could make good things happen just by yelling that he believed in them, then this was the time when he wanted them. "It's going to take us to Luellae. Come on."

The airlock doors parted and he dragged Daeis inside.

"Concentrate," he said, as they swished shut again, sealing the two of them in the little metal space between the airlock's inner and outer doors. When the outer doors opened, they would open onto nearly any vista the user liked. Any planet, any city, any street, as long as the user could visualize it – and sometimes they didn't have to know just where the thing they needed was, as long as they knew the *kind* of thing it was.

Daeis didn't talk much. Even with Splió, who they loved a *lot*, they mostly used short whispers, scribbled notes. But Splió had learned to read their body language. He watched how they squared their shoulders and shut their eyes, not shrinking back or grasping at Splió's hand for comfort, but as determined as him. Daeis was in this with him.

He closed his eyes and he pictured as hard as he could, Luellae. Wherever Luellae was. The portal didn't always work when a request was too vague, and it had always been iffy when the request was a person and not a place, but this time Splió tried *really* hard. He pictured Akavi, because Akavi was the one who had captured her, and Splió was willing to leap right at Akavi and die if it meant getting his teammate back. A little ship, or a little cell on a big ship, like the ones they'd all lived in for years when they were prisoners. Or a cave, or an abandoned house somewhere, or whatever kind of shelter it was that Akavi had managed to make for himself–

The airlock made a disappointed blatting noise, and a light above the outer doors flashed red through Splió's closed eyelids. Failure.

"Ugh," said Splió. All right. He'd try something simpler. He screwed his eyes shut and tried it a different way, focusing on Luellae, just Luellae. No other assumptions. No extrapolating about where she might be or why. Just the fact of her being.

The airlock blatted again and the inner doors reopened behind him, pointedly showing the way back into the lair.

"Fuck you," said Splió. "Fuck this. Forget it." He turned and stormed back into the lair, making it only a few feet in before he sat down on the thick carpet in a sulk, his head in his hands. Splió wasn't good at doing much when he was this upset. His mind kept working, after a fashion, but his will to keep going didn't.

Daeis followed, sat beside him, and leaned over, a soft calming hand on his arm. Splió absently stroked their hair. Daeis had very fine hair; it always felt good in his hands.

"We tried," Splió muttered. "We'll try again when I can think of something. But I guess it's off to research land for now, like the doctor ordered."

Daeis leaned in until their lips brushed his ear. Even with everyone else asleep, no one listening, Daeis would only speak if they were sure it wasn't possible for anyone but Splió to hear them.

"Do you... trust her?" they whispered.

Splió huffed out a breath. "No. Do you have a better idea?"

Daeis didn't reply.

Picket's task was to practice for battle, but he couldn't, not really. This would be a battle taking place high up above the sky, in orbit, and he couldn't really tell how his powers would work there. Until he actually saw the Keres' ships overhead, it would be hard to find anything else he could see clearly enough to aim at. And Splió and Daeis hadn't yet finished the research that would help him plan his tactics. So, for now, he was out to answer a few other, easier questions.

Such as: how large an area could he affect? Picket's powers naturally worked on an area of land – changing it to be more contaminated with Outside energies, or less. The energies' specific effects were beyond his control. But he did have control over where the effect started and ended. And if he was fighting against ships in space, he'd need to spread them out across miles and miles of vacuum.

That was why he'd gone through the airlock with Weaver, whose powers were good only for healing, but who he was glad to have as moral support. They'd come out on a disused pier somewhere on one of the Chaos Zone's coasts. The little wooden structure stuck out into the waves, overgrown with shrubs and flowers, with a strange forest behind it swallowing up what had once been a good road.

He sat on the edge of the pier, looking out at the water, reluctant to begin.

Picket's powers were *bad*. He felt that in his bones. The rest of the Seven had powers that felt like neutral tools – things like moving fast or seeing the future. Picket's powers were different. Outside had already taken so much from them all, and Picket's only way to make any progress in a fight against an angelic opponent was by making it temporarily even worse.

He remembered how he'd used his powers to protect peaceful mortal protesters, just yesterday. The protesters had been surrounded by angels on all sides; the angels had been about to open fire. Picket, on the relative safety of a rooftop, had clenched a fist and made his power rise all around them, in a scooping shape designed to catch the angels with their guns and not the mortals.

He still remembered the screams of terror; the gurgling of the asphalt as it liquefied and extruded tentacles to drag the angels down into it. The horribly misshapen corpses that were left, long ribbons of flesh without any reference to the usual structure of muscle or bone. The mortals, Gods help him; he'd tried to avoid hurting the mortals but there had been mortals too, on the edges of the angels' formation, who'd been sucked in and died the same deaths with them.

Most of the mortals had survived because of him. Most of them would have died if he hadn't intervened. He knew that, and it ought to have helped, but it didn't.

Picket cast a glance at Weaver beside him. She was sitting on the edge of the pier, idly kicking her feet. Her thin body looked tense – everyone had reasons to be tense now – but she didn't seem guilty or uncertain, not the way Picket felt. Picket and Weaver were two parts of the same four-part person, but for once he wasn't sure if she could really understand him.

At last, she looked over at him with something encouraging in her eyes. "Go on."

Reluctantly, he raised his hand. He focused on two puffy white clouds at opposite ends of the sky – nothing between them, no hapless ships or planes that could be caught in the crossfire. Maybe birds; birds wouldn't be visible to him from here. In his mind, he whispered the birds an apology.

He made a twisting gesture.

A bolt like lightning arced from one cloud to the other, irregular and branching and bright. Colors swirled out around it that had never used to belong in a daylit sky. Candy pink, grass green, blood red, and violet. Picket twisted harder, and the colors branched out further, a massive fractal pattern in the air.

This was by far the largest area on which he'd ever used his powers. He'd done a quick back-of-the-envelope calculation before he came out here; he knew two visible clouds in those positions would be miles and miles away from each other. Picket had wondered if it would be tiring to use his powers on such a large scale, the way it tired Weaver out to heal serious injuries, but it felt just as easy to him as killing those angels. The only part of him that felt strained was his conscience.

Picket could do this. As long as his powers still worked in the upper atmosphere – as long as he could actually *see* the Keres' ships coming, he could do it. He could destroy them.

He opened his hand and dropped his arm back down. The twist of colors shrank and vanished.

Weaver, beside him, was looking back and forth between him and the part of the sky where the colors had been. There was a reflected glow in her dark eyes that lasted a second longer than it should have, those pinks and greens shining back at him. She didn't need to ask how he felt, now that she'd seen him act on it. They understood each other that well.

Even as those colored lights arced over miles and miles of sky, there had been no sound except the gentle lapping of the waves.

"Do you trust Ev?" Picket asked, finally.

"Nah," said Weaver, and she smiled when she said it, and Picket understood. They had each other; they had Prophet and Grid, the other half of their whole; they had the rest of the Seven and Yasira and Tiv. That had already been enough to work miracles with. They didn't *have* to trust anyone else.

Qiel Huong wasn't old enough to be a community leader. People had started deferring to her that way, ever since a month or two after the Plague – but she was twenty years old. Her only redeeming qualities were that she talked a lot and liked to get things done. A lot of people had died in the Plague's early days, but there were still plenty of older people left, people with more experience, people with training at how to organize a business or a hobby group. But Outside had bestowed gifts on the survivors at random, and for some reason, when it came to the gift of taking charge and making people listen, it had picked Qiel.

Outside was something beyond and unknowable, only halfway capable of even bothering with human things. There probably wasn't any specific reason why it had picked Qiel. Probably there had been some kind of invisible gift-bestowing laser and Qiel had happened to be in its path, with no thought at all as to whether she was the best person for the gift, whether she'd use it well.

She couldn't get that sense of being an imposter out of her head as she stood in the hot sun, watching people swarm in and out of the entrances of the best makeshift shelters they could find. Basements under big buildings; subway tunnels, anything even halfway impervious to fire or debris. People were clearing them out, setting up stretchers, water and food, first aid kits, blankets. Qiel could have busied herself just like them, picking some task like carrying boxes to the right places, but instead people kept asking for her to make *decisions*. Which group of people should go where. Which potential spot was best-protected.

She'd seen vids of what happened when the Keres attacked. Old news recordings and dramatizations full of special effects. The Keres had big guns – big enough to melt city blocks with a single hit, or maybe bigger. Nemesis' ships intercepted and harassed Her so heavily that She couldn't use the worst of Her weapons; all she could get out were potshots and crossfire with the smaller ones. And even in those toned-down battles, tens of thousands of people died.

Maybe the Seven, or Outside itself, or whatever, would intercept the Keres that way. *If* that happened, then the shelters would be useful. They'd be less exposed than a normal house or street; better protected; more likely to survive the smaller guns, which didn't melt the entire city but shattered buildings, broke things apart, or started fires. Not everybody in the shelters would survive, but most would.

But if things *didn't* go that way – if nothing stood strongly enough in the way of the big guns – then they were dead no matter what they did. Even the people in the safe parts of Jai, outside the Chaos Zone, were probably dead.

There was one other option. Instead of hiding in shelters, they could flee. The problem was, where would they go? Across the border? No one was sure just how far the Keres' attacks were going to extend outside the Chaos Zone. No one was sure if Nemesis would intervene to save the rest of the planet – given how She'd talked in the broadcast, it seemed unlikely.

Qiel's city wasn't close to the border, and crossing the border was a deadly proposition at the best of times. Angels had shot most of the people who'd tried. She wasn't sure if the angels were still patrolling anymore, but Qiel had heard rumors of the propaganda the Gods were showing people outside the Chaos Zone. Vids that talked about how the people of the Chaos Zone were suffering so abjectly that death would be better. Vids that talked about them like a disease, like something the rest of Jai might catch if they weren't careful. At a time like this – with the fate of the planet unclear, with citizens terrified that any place with a Chaos Zone survivor in it might be targeted – they might well treat any refugees as badly as the angels did. Some people in the border towns, Qiel had heard, were risking it and running. Not many people in Büata were.

The only thing keeping Qiel out of a fit of abject despair was Prophet, who had arrived out of nowhere this morning and told Qiel's group that she would stay until evening. Prophet, with her visions, could actually make these decisions with Qiel. Prophet could see their likely outcome.

"Not that one," she said to Qiel now, as they walked past the entrances to several basements and subway tunnels, where people were already busy carting in cots and supplies. "That one's going to collapse. The other two – I can't be sure, but I don't see a problem with these"

Prophet was thin and solemn. Her many braids dangled around her shoulders as she stared at the tunnels, looking past them or through them and not at the actual people inside. Qiel had asked if the Seven could really spare a whole one-seventh of their team just for one city; Prophet had smiled gently and said that, for today, she'd figured out how to be in more than one place at once. That wasn't nearly the weirdest thing Qiel had needed to get her head around lately.

"Can you see–" Qiel bit her lip. She waited until there was nobody nearby to overhear. "Can you see if any of this is actually going to work? Like, are we all just going to die or what?"

Prophet looked further off into the distance than ever. "I... can't tell. I can't guarantee anything. I see images, snatches of scenes, but I don't have a roadmap. I can't tell you for sure what is or isn't going to happen."

"But?"

Prophet lowered her voice. "But you know what I'd see if this was hopeless. You know what I'd see if the Keres outright won. No city at all. Just… flame everywhere, everything melted. When I look at this place, I see pain, I see fear, I see destruction and damage. But I don't see *that*. I don't see the whole continent wiped away. I haven't seen that anywhere I've visited, so far. I know that may be small comfort right now, and you might have good reason to doubt it, but that's what I see."

"Then that's good enough for me," Qiel said. She stood up straighter, trying to show she believed it. "I trust you."

CHAPTER 6

The Keres vessel opened fire immediately, and Akavi rushed out of the room. The stars wheeled around at horrifying angles outside Luellae's window. The spinning didn't register as movement to her inner ear. But the impacts did – invisible blows that made the whole structure shudder. She looked frantically around – had they been damaged? Would there be audible alarms, any warning at all that a human could detect, if they were damaged? Or would the hull simply open up like tin foil and vent them into space?

Maybe that would be kinder. Quicker. It wasn't like Luellae wanted to be here.

But a second blow rocked the ship, and a third, and then a plaintive beeping sound started somewhere outside the room, and survival instincts kicked in. Luellae struggled to move, making the cuffs around her arm clank. Elu seemed to startle out of a daze – it must only have been a few seconds – rushed to her, and unlocked them.

"Seriously?" she said, wrinkling her nose.

"Akavi's going to want you and Enga in easy reach," Elu explained.

Of course it was that. Of course it wasn't him doing an actual kindness. Luellae wasn't even surprised.

She sprang up as soon as she was free to move and raced to the cockpit, stumbling a little as the ship shook. "Are we hit?"

"Somewhat," said Akavi, in a crisp, emotionless tone. "Our shields are holding, but they won't much longer. And we can't defeat a Keres ship in open battle without taking the kind of damage it'll take too long to repair. We've got to hit them from the inside. Take Enga with you and teleport aboard. Take the pilot alive if you can."

Enga clasped Luellae's arm with a metal appendage only vaguely resembling a hand. She looked ready and resolved.

Luellae had been chained to the wall of the ship until five seconds ago. She couldn't believe they trusted her with this now. Needs must, she supposed.

She could try to run, if she dared; she could find the nearest planet and try to find a way to take the explosive out of her arm. But even Luellae wasn't sure if she could travel that far, through millions of miles of the vacuum of space, without dying. She could defect to the Keres' side once she got aboard the Keres' ship, but that could be a horror even worse than Akavi's. She could pull Enga out into hard vacuum on purpose and let them both die there, take two of Akavi's toys away from him permanently.

She didn't dare. Gods help her, she wanted to live.

She mentally called on her power, pulled the fabric of spacetime around her, and leapt onto the Keres scout's ship.

Space twisted for a horrible instant, and the journey felt blacker and colder than it ever had before, like breaking through a sheet of suffocating ice. But she was done before it had time to do more than chill her and steal a bit of breath. She opened her eyes, suddenly shivering, and immediately doubled over and started to cough at the foul air inside the scout. Enga's metal grip was painfully cold now. Enga flexed her metal fingers strangely, making the pain worse, but for some reason she didn't let go. Luellae wondered if Enga thought she would run away. To where, exactly?

The inside of the ship was a horrible mess, worse than the biggest pile of trash that had ever piled up in the Seven's shared living space. Pipes and ductwork and circuitry covered everything at such wild angles that Luellae wasn't even sure if she was standing upright. Between those squiggling shapes, other objects were piled – garbage, said her instincts, but between the coughing and shaking she couldn't focus on it much. It smelled like a dumpster in here, combined with the metallic foulness of heavy machinery, and something worse, too. Like a slowly rotting corpse.

The angel's ships had always been a special kind of sterile hell, bright and clean and inhuman. This was the opposite. This was worse.

Luellae couldn't get a hold of herself. She couldn't stop shivering or coughing. While she struggled, Enga smoothly extruded one of the guns from the nest of tools that she had in place of arms, and fired.

It didn't make the loud report of a normal bullet. Just a hiss. Whatever she'd fired, it hit a human figure, someone nestled within the pipes and wires like just another part of the machine.

Luellae was mildly surprised it wasn't just a bot. Akavi had said something about a pilot – but she'd never heard of the Keres having angels.

She blinked hard, starting to regain her breath, although her wrist hurt more and more. She didn't want to be like this, coughing and retching helplessly while an angel swanned around more competently beside her. She made herself focus.

The human figure thrashed a moment, then slumped. It was a man. Naked, and shot through with something that looked like angel circuitry but different. It wasn't a smooth pair of titanium plates in those temples, or even the slender curlicues of a priest; it was a nest of big, ugly shapes like a microcosm of the ship itself. Through a pair of ports somewhere in the midst of those shapes, the man was plugged directly into the ship.

What the hell was this?

Enga strode forwards, dragging Luellae along by her agonized wrist. Luellae stumbled along with her, tripping over the Keres ship's weird pipes and wires, confused; why wouldn't Enga let go? This hurt, and it wasn't like there was anywhere Luellae could run off to. Or did Enga think she was going to teleport back to the *Talon* without her?

When they reached the man – the angel of the Keres, Luellae supposed – Enga took hold of the plugs and yanked.

Luellae flinched – somehow the motion seemed too intimate and too violent, like if she'd pulled out one of Enga's metal arms by the socket. The wires connecting the pilot to the ship fell away and he lolled down, already either dead or unconscious. Enga set to work, yanking Luellae back and forth, and pulled more pipes and connectors away, some of them plugging into the man's body more intimately, some holding him in his seat, others just happening to be in the way. It was a lot of crashing and smashing – in fact, Luellae suspected that Enga was being smashier than necessary, that she was doing as much damage as possible to the ship from the inside.

She couldn't blame her. All of Luellae's instincts screamed at her to get out of here.

Was the Keres ship still flying? Was it still firing on the *Talon*? Luellae's eyes watered as she tried to look around for a window or a viewscreen. The actual pilot didn't look like he was in any state to explain. It was all just a jumble, awful and malodorous.

"Can you–" Luellae managed between coughs. Her wrist was hurting worse than ever, and Enga wouldn't let go of it. "Are we–" She didn't even know what she was asking. She felt helpless.

At last Enga turned to her with an imperious gesture, slinging the naked pilot firefighter-style over her metal shoulder, and nodded. Luellae swallowed and nodded back, squeezed her eyes shut, and twisted the frigid cold of space itself around herself again.

Elu hurried forward as Luellae and Enga reappeared in the cockpit. The Keres pilot was hanging over Enga's shoulder in a fireman's carry. He was a man of middle age and indeterminate race, unremarkable except for the cybernetic implants all over him. This was more cybernetics than Elu had ever seen in someone's face before, a whole bristling architecture that almost obscured his human features from sight.

"Elu, take him," Akavi ordered, but Elu had already hurried forward, medical stretcher at his side. Elu, the medic, would have wanted to examine this strange being regardless of what Akavi said or what his orders were. If Akavi had ordered him instead to stay back, he would have struggled to obey.

But he would have obeyed, he thought bitterly. Elu was used to doing whatever Akavi said, knowing the consequence for failure. Even when it was abhorrent. Even when Akavi had no right to ask. After yesterday, when Akavi had hit him in front of his mortal friends, Elu felt more aware of the power imbalance between them than ever.

He reached out and helped guide Enga as she dumped the Keres angel's unconscious body onto the stretcher. Just stunned, Elu thought as he touched the angel's limbs through his own clothes; not fully blacked out. He was already starting to stir, fingers twitching, eyelids fluttering.

"Elu," Akavi ordered, "I want you to operate on this man. Hack into his neural architecture. Interrogate if necessary, or call me in for that if you're too squeamish. Find out how the Keres operates and what She's planning for this sector. Do you understand?"

"Yes, sir," said Elu.

He gestured to the trio of medical bots and they followed behind him. They were running out of room on this little ship. Three sets of personal quarters: one for Akavi, one for him, and one that Luellae and Enga now shared. He'd do this surgery in his own quarters. He made a second gesture and two of the bots sped ahead, on their way to set up the room the way they'd need for a surgery of this nature: sterile cloths, disinfectants, trays of tools, and so on. The third hesitated, and then rolled away of its own accord to examine Enga and Luellae. Enga hadn't let go of Luellae's wrist, and there was something wrong with the flesh in her metal grasp, some discoloration. With a sudden, weird jolt Elu realized that the two of them had literally been frozen to each other. Out in the frigid vacuum of space for that split second, the metal and the skin had joined, like licking cold metal in the winter. Luellae was also coughing.

Elu did a quick bit of triage in his head and decided a single bot was enough to deal with that. Following orders, dealing with this bizarre, threatening, unconscious stranger, was more urgent.

This was the sort of thing medics working for Nemesis dreamed about. There had always been rumors that the Keres had angels – that She somehow abducted people and coerced them to Her side, got them flying Her ships or spying on humans for Her the way the other Gods did. It was almost impossible to imagine why a mortal would agree to that; and if the mortal did not consent freely, then their ascension would damage their soul in ways that risked leaving them disabled like Enga, or worse. But then again, humans in the Morlock War had willingly joined forces with the Keres in other ways, and that made just as little sense to Elu.

What strange functions were programmed into those circuits? What purpose did they serve? What was it like, being something so much like an angel of the true Gods, and yet so different? What was it that drove such a person? Such a mad, blind hunger – that was what Elu had always been told, when it came to what it felt like to be the Keres. Such a rage to destroy that She would risk destroying the very sentient species She fed on.

The pilot began to stir as Elu carried him towards his quarters, and something gave him a feeling of unease. His microexpression software didn't work correctly with so many unfamiliar wires and metal chips bristling around the face. He could only go by what his intuition told him. The paralytic hadn't even fully worn off yet, and the man's face was barely beginning to move enough to show expressions. But the expression that had already surfaced was one of incredible disorientation and suffering. More than just the nausea and pain that Elu had expected.

He paused in the doorway and looked back at Enga.

"Something's wrong. He's feeling more pain than he should. Did you see anything strange?" The pilot could have taken a suicide drug, maybe, if he knew he was going to be captured – maybe one that would destroy all the brain tissue and circuitry that Elu was interested in. "Did he eat anything, inject himself with anything?" The bots were still setting up the makeshift operating theatre in the middle of his room.

But Enga couldn't talk now, of course, not even in the text-sending they were accustomed to.

"He was, uh, unplugged," said Luellae, and then she swore and coughed again as the medical bot dunked her wrist, with Enga's metal talons still attached, into a container of lukewarm water.

"He was what?"

Luellae gave an impatient look both to him and to Enga. The angel of the Keres was starting to thrash and moan more loudly, shuddering in distress in ways that an angel of Nemesis would have been too proud to ever do. Did the angel even understand where he was?

"When we got on the ship, he was plugged in to a bunch of stuff. Consoles, maybe life support; I don't know what it all was. Is he gonna die?"

Elu couldn't tell yet. The man looked – not healthy, but at least in average physical condition, apart from the circuitry and the pain; not starving or missing organs or struggling to breathe. But looks could be deceiving.

He felt a weird jolt of empathy – it might have been misplaced. Elu had once been plugged, in a sense, into the entire angelic ansible network. He'd been able to reach his superiors or his colleagues whenever he wanted to, with nothing but a thought. To disconnect himself from the network, when he fled with Akavi, had meant a loneliness so profound that it hurt. Was that what the angel of the Keres was feeling now, as he trembled in agony without an obvious cause?

Maybe it was. Maybe it wasn't. Elu needed to stick to the observable facts.

The angel of the Keres weakly thrashed, his eyes beginning to flutter open. His lips moved.

"Where is She?" he whispered, in a voice Elu didn't like at all. The voice of someone who'd just watched a loved one die, who'd seen everything they depended on ripped away; a kind of denial tinged with hysteria. "I can't feel Her. Where is She–"

Elu suddenly did have an idea what was wrong with this angel. It was a disconnection, in a sense, but not like Elu's. If Elu's hunch was correct – and he would have to do actual neurosurgery to verify that – it was something much, much worse.

"Sedative," he snapped. He didn't usually snap, even at the bots. Of course the bots weren't sentient enough to care what tone of voice he used. One of them picked up a syringe and efficiently filled it, and he had just enough time to hesitate – they'd barely begun examining this man; could they guess his body weight accurately enough to calculate the dosage correctly? Could they tell if he'd had modifications to his metabolism, allergies, *anything* that they ought to know before drugging him within an inch of his life? – and then the bot plunged the syringe into the angel's arm and hesitation become pointless.

He stared down as the angel of the Keres started to relax, as his moans of despair became softer.

"Is there a problem, Elu?" said Akavi, who was still up at the front of the cockpit dealing with the controls.

"I don't know, sir," said Elu. "I'll have to, um… diagnose…"

He was the medic here. It really was his responsibility. He didn't even quite want to name the thing that he suspected.

"Then *do*," said Akavi, his voice colder than ever, "and stop wasting my time."

CHAPTER 7

Irimiru Kaule, Overseer of Nemesis, curled his fingers in his own hair with frustration – currently it was straight, fine black hair, hanging down in elegant wisps over a diamond-shaped face, but Irimiru could have changed that appearance in a moment. He could scarcely think through the flood of notifications crowding his awareness. It had been like this since last night: frantic messages from every Inquisitor, Helm, and Marshal under his command, and sterner directives, harder to delay, from the Archangels. He had been triaging as much as he could: hundreds of messages had been shunted from his conscious awareness almost immediately upon reception, delegated to one spot or another in the swarm of smaller auxiliary memory units that buzzed around his head and in the arms of his throne. Those units constantly shifted, forming a priority heap in which the most urgent messages would rise to the top, to be retrieved into Irimiru's conscious memory as soon as he had a moment. But even working as fast as he could, he was swamped with all sorts of little tasks. Ship movements. Troop reallocations.

Nemesis had ordered all of Her units pulled from the surface of Jai overnight, with no preparation or warning.

Even for a fighting force as exquisitely coordinated as Nemesis', that took some doing. Angels who had been patrolling the Chaos Zone, keeping order or distributing supplies, all had to be pulled back to their previous stations. Ships like the *Menagerie,* which Akavi Averis used to captain. Big ships and small stations where angels planned and organized, waited for orders, or did research. But these places had not expected so many angels to return to them so soon. The usual pile of small logistical conflicts had risen up in each of them – some serious enough to really require Irimiru's organizing attention, and some petty enough that the angels in question should have been able to get it together for themselves. Irimiru put those latter cases at the bottom of the heap. Let them stew.

It wasn't only a question of personnel or materials, but also of operational priorities. Dozens of little projects had been put on hold thanks to the emergency on Jai. The returning angels had to be reallocated to those projects as efficiently as possible, while accounting for angels who had been lost in the field and situations that had evolved in their absence. Nor could Irimiru spend these returning forces too quickly, as there was a high likelihood some other phase of the Jai crisis might need them again. He answered a nuisance message or two at a time while charting that process out in his head, sending orders out a few at a time as he reconstructed the most urgent projects first, and then dealing with the slew of additional messages that resulted from that.

Irimiru wasn't pleased with Nemesis' tactics. There must be a logical reason why She had switched from active occupation to full abandonment overnight, but Irimiru was not privy to that reason. Surely the Overseers involved could have been informed in advance. And the Keres – once She'd been let loose on a whole continent, once She was flush with that victory, how would Nemesis' forces contain Her again? The Gods knew best; there was presumably an answer. But it had not been shared with Irimiru.

And he had a week to wait and see what happened. The Keres had access to warp drives, but not to the network of portals that the Gods used. Her top speed was superluminal but finite, and on Her current trajectory, it would take a week before She arrived to rain down the fire and death that the Chaos Zone deserved.

In the meantime, it *was* a welcome change, having control over all his own teams again instead of passing down complex marching orders that had been pre-made for him on high.

The most urgent such project was the recapture of Akavi Averis and Elu Ariehmu. Akavi had deserted the angelic corps after being slated for termination, and Elu, who wasn't slated for anything worse than lateral reassignment, had deserted with him. Enga Afonbataw Konum, Marshal of Nemesis, had asked to bring them in, and Irimiru had allowed it – in a sense. Enga was skilled and deadly, but her poorly-suppressed attachment and mixed emotions about the team made her easy for Akavi to exploit. Irimiru had sent Enga in knowing she would likely be captured. He had encouraged Enga to play along. Now, presuming anyone could get in touch with Enga, she'd be able to share what she'd found out.

With a wave of his hand, Irimiru sent a signal through the ansible nets that would summon Sispirinithas.

A minute later, Sispirinithas stepped through the portal into the throne room with his strange, ambling gait. Sispirinithas was a Spider, an alien species about eight feet tall, crawling on ten spindly legs that coincidentally resembled an Earth arachnid's. Sispirinithas had worked closely with Akavi, Elu, and Enga. He was a folklorist who studied the ways people thought and talked, who could understand how his coworkers ticked. And Irimiru believed in keeping these things in the circle from which they'd sprung.

"My lord," Sispirinithas said, bowing formally. Spiders couldn't bow in the same way as a human, but he had devised a style of his own, a sort of ducking motion in which the front legs bent more than the others. His actual voice was a whispery chitter from his mandibles; the translator that he wore around his pedicel transformed the sound into Earth creole. Not that it needed to – Irimiru was equipped with the same software as any angel, and could understand the Spider language even though he lacked the vocal apparatus to produce it.

Irimiru tapped his fingers against the buzzing, crackling arm of his throne. Even while he held this conversation, he was doing another task in the back of his mind, moving tasks and personnel around in a scheduling chart. But his physical gaze, with his organic eyes, remained fixed on the Spider. "You miss Enga, don't you?"

"Her presence was pleasant," the Spider agreed. "I hope she returns. I had always hoped to eat her after she died some noble death in battle. That is not the human custom, of course, but I do not think she would have minded."

"Excellent. I'm putting you in charge of the next phase. Make contact with her by some covert means and receive her report."

"Yes, my lord. When it comes to means, do you have some preference?"

"None we haven't already discussed." If they were lucky, Enga might have been fit with a shortwave radio receiver like the one she'd used in the Chaos Zone, back when ansible connections in the Chaos Zone were blocked. It was much more likely that this would have been removed too, and that the team would need to be more creative. Codes, dead drops, and so on. "Use your creativity and respond to the situation as it develops. You are dismissed."

"Yes, my lord," said Sispirinithas, bowing again, and he skittered away.

Citizenship Lake had waited an hour to get through the queue just to use the damned ansible. The Gods had announced a sudden, temporary tightening of communications – just a precaution, They'd said, without specifying what the precaution was for. Everybody knew, of course. Everybody knew that the Jai was about to be attacked by the Keres, and the Gods, thanks to the Chaos Zone's heresies, had decided not to save it.

They'd been way too ambiguous about what was going to happen to the rest of Jai. It *shouldn't* be in the line of fire, said the people who knew best – priests and other experts. All analysis of the Keres' movements, said the priests, suggested that the Chaos Zone was Her primary target. She loved upheaval and instability, making something worse when it was already bad, and the Chaos Zone drew Her like a moth to a flame. The rest of Jai would probably, mostly survive.

But *mostly* wasn't good enough. Not for people who'd come from Jai, originally. Not for people who still had friends and family there.

Here on Zwerfk, there were a sizeable group of recent immigrants from Jai – people who'd come here looking for better jobs when the tech sector collapsed. Ship was one of them; so were her roommates and several of her co-workers. She'd worked on the doomed Pride of Jai station, once upon a time. Now she worked for a nondescript company that manufactured polymers. Now she stood in a long, long line waiting for a priest of Philophrosyne to judge if she was allowed to use the ansible, at a time like this, in a crisis like this.

"What's your name?" the priest had said at last, when Ship got to the front of the line. She'd looked kind – she had the light skin and thick dark hair of most people on Zwerfk, and she'd gathered that long thick hair back into an intricate series of plaits. She wore the bright rose-and-gold robes and shawl favored by the God of love, kindness, and communication. The priest looked like a kind woman – people didn't ascend into Philophrosyne's service if they weren't kind. But Ship knew that under the metal curlicues on the priest's forehead there were all sorts of divine circuits installed, lie-detecting software like the kinds angels used, and a direct line to Philophrosyne's angels to be used if necessary. The priest was a kind woman, but Ship might not be, in the eyes of the Gods.

"Citizenship Lake," she answered.

The priest's eyes were large and brown, kind and understanding. "That's an Arinnan name."

"I'm from Arinn," Ship admitted. "I moved out here a year ago."

"What's the purpose of your call?"

"I've still got family and friends in Arinn. I heard the news, and – I just want to call and make sure they're OK."

The priest made a sympathetic face. "I understand, but our resources are strained. You'll be able to make one call. No more than five minutes. Is that all right?"

Of course it was. One couldn't very well go up to a priest and announce that their God's decisions weren't all right. Even if *our resources are strained* was an obvious euphemism; the Gods' resources were nigh infinite. What it really meant was the Gods had decided it wasn't in humanity's best interest to allow more than a certain number of calls. The Gods knew best, Ship reminded herself, even as her shoulders clenched and her stomach tightened. The Gods had access to information that a mortal could not even comprehend.

"It's perfectly all right," Ship said to the priest, and she wondered when she had started to lie to the Gods.

The Chaos Zone was terrible. Everyone knew that. Ship had seen the grainy news footage of the place itself, and the brief testimonials from people there. The very earth and air of the Chaos Zone had turned into violent living forces that tore people apart. Not many had survived the initial disaster; those that lived were shells of their former selves, scavenging the untrustworthy earth for scraps to live on, huddling in the ruined remains of buildings without water or heat or humanity. They were slavering bands of raiders and scroungers, ready to steal, murder, rape, or betray each other at a moment's notice just for more of the scant resources that remained. It was worse than death, living in the Chaos Zone. It was awful to think about, but the Keres, just for once, might be what a place like that needed. Putting them out of their misery.

Even before the Keres attack was announced, people had been saying this around the dinner table – in hushed voices, because it wasn't kind, but that didn't make it untrue. Famous people had already said it on talk shows, on the news. *Why are they still alive? They're heretics anyway, and they're suffering so badly – why couldn't the Gods just get rid of them?*

Even Ship's immigrant friends were saying it. Their families, from Arinn or the safe parts of Stijon, shouldn't be caught in the crossfire. But the inside of the Chaos Zone, the heretics who lived *there* – well, it was the Gods' job to deal with heretics. Heretics deserved what they got. There was almost a sense of relief, sometimes, when people talked about the reckoning that the Chaos Zone had coming.

It was a logical thing to think, a logical thing to feel. Most of the time, even when she worried for her friends, Ship felt it.

But...

But then there was Tiv.

Productivity Hunt had been Ship's friend ever since the Pride of Jai. She'd been shattered by the disaster – and by the disappearance of Yasira Shien, the woman Tiv was going to marry, who had turned out to be one of the worst heretics of all. Ship had loved Tiv, in a quiet way. She'd taken care of Tiv as best she could after the disaster, through the waves of shock and grief and media intrusions, through their friend group moving to Zwerfk, through her new job, through the later, slower stages of mourning. By the end of a year, Tiv had looked like she was starting to love Ship back.

And then Tiv had vanished, six months ago, leaving a note that raised more questions than it answered. Just when Ship thought things were beginning to look stable, Tiv had chosen Yasira after all. Tiv had gone to the Chaos Zone to do something – she'd been vague about what, but Ship could fill in the blanks, especially since the news reports started to come in about Yasira's meddling in the area, about the way she and a close group of friends had been orchestrating events to their own evil advantage. Or at least, the news said it was evil, and logic said it must be. But Tiv believed – Ship *knew* this, because she knew how Tiv's mind worked, because she could *feel* the sincerity and compassion radiating from that stupid note – Tiv believed wholeheartedly that she was doing the right thing.

Ship had been so angry at first. How could Tiv leave like this, without even a face-to-face goodbye, after everything Ship had done for her? How could she believe in the rightness of a cause like Yasira's, when it was so obviously heretical, obviously wrong? How could the two of them have misjudged each other so badly?

But Ship would have bet money that Tiv was still down there, in the Chaos Zone, in the line of fire. Doing what she thought was right, even in the face of the attack that was coming.

She was trying very hard not to think about Tiv.

The ansible stood before her, a slab of God-built machinery wrapped in shiny glass and plastic, its touch screen brightly clean and prompting her to enter an address. This was technology mortals couldn't build for themselves – something they had access to only at the Gods' will. It made sense that the Gods could take it away again.

There was a new widget in the corner, unobtrusive and gray, that hadn't been there before. A timer. *0:05:00,* it said.

Ship closed her eyes and weighed her options. Who was she worried about most? Her parents, maybe – but Ship's relationship with her parents had always been a little strained. Her sister, maybe. Several friends from childhood, from university and grad school, from the Pride of Jai itself. Some of the people Ship worried for were from southern Riayin, which had become the Chaos Zone, so that wasn't an option. But most, especially her family, were from Arinn.

She only had one call and five minutes, and instead of leaving a message, she'd rather spend those five minutes talking to someone who talked back. The best person for that was her sister, Relatability – Bil for short – who worked a clerical job at an ansible station in a town called Bent River. Bil would be able to answer within a minute, if it was a work day. If the concept of work days made any sense on Jai anymore.

She punched in Bil's name and location, and even before Bil picked up, the timer in the corner began its countdown.

"Ship," said Bil after thirty seconds, as the image of her face swam into view. She was Ship's spitting image – long-jawed, fine-haired, lower lip split from nervous biting. She could have been Ship herself, a few years younger and with her hair cut in a trendier style. Her face was flushed and her voice a little breathless, like she'd run to the ansible. "Ship, it's so good to see you. Thank you for calling."

"I've been worrying about you," said Ship.

"I know. This whole thing is not good. They're telling us we're not going to be in the line of fire. They've used God-built algorithms, they've analyzed the Keres' troops and movements, and they think she'll only have enough time and firepower to destroy the Chaos Zone. We should only expect collateral shots. But even collateral shots–" Bil bit her lip. She and Ship had both seen vid footage of Keres attacks before. Since the Morlock War, almost every attack by the Keres was restricted to collateral shots against the planet, while She and Nemesis did battle in the sky. Collateral shots from a pitched Keres battle could still kill hundreds of thousands of people.

"Is anyone helping you?" In the vids, every Keres attack was accompanied by announcements over the radio and television: instructions to take shelter, directions about the safest places and the manner in which to stay hidden there. "Are you getting, you know, instructions–"

The screen went blank. Ship was sure it hadn't been five minutes yet, but once Bil's face appeared, she hadn't paid attention to the timer. Now it blinked in the corner, the only part of the ansible still active, a dull red *0:00:00*.

Qiel had hit her limit. Just when they'd set up a proper shelter under the big parking garage – the one with weird, rainbow-colored vines all over it that opened up periodically into unblinking eyes or petaled cups of poison – just as soon as they'd put the last emergency mattress and blanket into place, the whole garage shifted. This wasn't something the garage normally did; they'd picked it because it was relatively stable. But as if it was a restless creature, made uncomfortable by the day's intrusions, the whole structure shrugged and tilted.

"What?" said Qiel, as the ground shifted under her. "*No–*"

There were various other cries of anguish from the people around her, but that didn't dissuade the garage. She could feel some of them, the people who were good at repelling monsters and shifting the local environment, reaching frantically out to try to calm the building, but it didn't do anything.

The lights abruptly blinked off.

There were screams. The floor tilted further. Qiel lost her balance and tumbled down, curling into a ball to try to protect her belly and head, scraped and bruised as she fell and a whole bunch of heavy objects seemed to fall with her. It was chaos, followed by an abrupt stillness. She'd landed in some kind of corner. The floor was tilted up at forty-five degrees, and there was something soft but maddeningly heavy, probably a mattress, on top of her.

The lights blinked dimly on again.

Everything was a mess. There was the tilted floor and a giant pile of mattresses, supplies, and bruised panicking people at the bottom, some of them groaning or wailing or crying. The floor had stopped tilting but that only meant it was useless to try to put the mattresses back up – it seemed as hard and unyielding now, as fixed in its place, as it had when it was actually fucking flat the way a floor should be.

Qiel stayed long enough to pick herself out of the wreckage, to make sure nobody had any injury worse than a sprain, and then she turned and stormed out of the building.

This was one of the buildings Prophet had said was safe, but *safe* was relative. Prophet had made no guarantees. She'd only said she hadn't seen this one collapsing and killing people.

Qiel fumed as she walked, all the way out past the city limits, out into the wilds. She was an experienced forager, used to walking on her own, used to the safe and hidden paths. She didn't travel the safe paths this time. She turned down an overgrown side street where the vines overhead closed into a tunnel, rubbed together like eager fingers, rustled like leaves. She walked for twenty minutes, fuming all the while, until the tunnel opened out into an area of wilder ruins where normal survivors feared to tread.

Local people had taken to calling this area The Well. That word didn't do it justice – no words ever did, with Outside. It had once been a downtown city block full of little shops, but every trace of those old buildings and the people who'd lived and worked there was gone. Now it was a series of holes in the ground – circular and interconnected and overlapping, each one so deep that Qiel couldn't see the bottom. People more foolish than her sometimes dared each other to look over the edge and down at the bottom. Many of them had fallen and died horribly; the ground around the edges was not stable. None of the ones who survived had ever seen where the holes ended. They just went down and down into a vague glow that sometimes changed color – blue or green or an awful, dim, burning red.

Today, something in The Well was moving.

Qiel watched it from as close a vantage point as she dared. Something churned at the holes' edges, like a mole moving around unseen, the packed soil and rock shifting where it passed. Tendrils of dirt rose from inside, waved in the air like anemones. And between them rose something more immaterial but even more massive – like a column of wind or a heat haze, shimmering in the air, reaching up and up into the sky, where vague iridescent colors shimmered, sometimes coalescing into vague shapes like clouds, sometimes resembling nothing so familiar at all.

She'd heard rumors that Outside was shifting again. Not in response to a single impulse, the way it had shifted at Savior's will or in the most recent protest, but mostly on its own. Or maybe in response to what all the survivors were doing – she'd heard it said, in hushed tones, that in some sense Outside belonged to them all now. Something in the back of their minds, where their new abilities had sprung from, was also what kept Outside grounded here. By observing it and needing it to be a certain way, by being connected to it the way Savior had connected them, they stopped it from expanding further. From getting so deadly that it destroyed them all.

Some of the local mystics said that Outside itself was rearing up, hardening at the edges, preparing to defend itself from a threat to its existence. Some said that the gone people, or the survivors' unconscious minds, or the Seven, or even Destroyer herself, had urged it toward that end. Maybe that would work, if it was true. Outside was big enough to uproot continents and destroy worlds. Maybe the Keres would find, when She arrived, that She was finally picking on something Her own size.

But if that was true, it came with the same catch as everything else. Outside didn't actually *care*. Even now that it was anchored in place by tens of millions of human minds, it was so alien that it didn't even really know what a human was. It wasn't going to help them survive, except by mistake.

If it cared, it wouldn't be pulling shit like it had pulled in the parking garage.

"We didn't ask for you!" Qiel shouted at The Well, at the strange pillar of energy that twisted and turned above it. "We never wanted any of this! And you don't care, do you? You just – sit and spin!"

The pillar slowly twisted, seeming not to notice her at all. It would have been stupid to expect anything else. Qiel stared at it, and wondered why it was that she wanted it to care. Like something that had been made for humans, after all. Like a God.

CHAPTER 8

The Gods did not ask for our worship at first. But They studied us until They understood that nothing short of worship would be enough. We needed it, as surely as we need water or air: something to defer to, to point us for sure to the right path and to punish those who go astray, lest we fall apart into a million squabbling fragments. Lest we make our moral choices based only on what last brought an emotion into our fallible, animal minds.

Old Humans were very foolish about that in their last days, you know. A plague would arise, and they would fall into bitterly arguing factions, not only over what to do about the sickness, but over whether or not it was even real. A madman would ascend to power and declare war, and no one could agree on whether it was a war or not, or on what a war was, or on what a civilian was when it was said that civilians were being killed. Let alone how to stop it.

Our old, made-up religions were falling, had been falling for many years, and we desperately needed something else that would tell us what was right and what was wrong, what was true and what was false, so that we could all work together when it mattered most. And there is nothing to call a force like that, when it works, when it is powerful enough, but a God.

– Walya Shu'uhi, "Theodicy Stories For Children"

* * *

Seven Hundred Years Ago

Giselle's life had become a blur. Outdoors, there was hot orange smog and the kinds of news reports she couldn't bear to think about. Inside, there was an uneasy numbness, like Leah's double death hadn't even been real. Giselle thought she ought to sob herself to sleep every night, and sometimes she almost felt the urge to do it; a threatening mental presence like some vast beast moving under water, never quite breaking the surface. Other times she found herself slumped crying in the corner of her office about something stupid: some quirk of NEMESIS-1's new programming that should have made sense but didn't, a snack she'd forgotten to pack in her lunch. Crying her eyes out, feeling like she'd never stop, over things that had nothing to do with Leah at all.

But there was work to do. Six-day weeks of ten- and fourteen-hour days. Giselle didn't mind them because the research facility was better protected from smog than her cheap third-floor apartment, and the research facility didn't leave her alone with her thoughts. There was always something to do at the facility, and there was General Walters' stern presence urging her on.

The second soul to be drawn into NEMESIS-1 – a terminally ill, multiply-decorated volunteer from the military – did his job well, and so did the legions of dying volunteers who came after him. Leah had set out the work for them that she'd needed to set. They understood her plans – or *she* did; NEMESIS-1 had begun to style itself *she*, regardless of the genders of the souls it absorbed – and improved on them. The machine had set about re-programming itself and re-designing the delicate electromagnets that worked with its souls.

Every day Giselle had some new set of software or hardware designs to review, given to her straight by the supercomputer who'd written them. Her job was to mark out anything that might contradict the official ethics conventions, as well as anything that seemed wrong for some other reason. She could formally request that General Walters veto such designs, or if she wasn't sure, she could send them to the whole team for a more thorough review. Sometimes she called those meetings just for the sake of it, because it didn't seem right that she hadn't found anything. In a code review for a human programmer, she would always have found something. But NEMESIS-1 was meticulous. NEMESIS-1 knew her, maybe as intimately as Leah knew her, and NEMESIS-1 simply didn't put anything into its new code that Giselle would object to.

"The problem," said Giselle to the technicians, in meeting number several-dozen of their endless series of meetings, "is that it's theoretically impossible for us to know what we're doing. The entire point of a system like NEMESIS-1 is that it can outthink us. If NEMESIS-1 genuinely wanted to sneak something past us that it shouldn't, it would figure out how to do that without alerting us, and we'd never know."

The technicians rolled their eyes; it wasn't a thought they hadn't all already had or voiced dozens of times. They were engineers with a thorough background in artificial intelligence. They were about evenly divided between those who'd always wanted superhuman AI to take over, even before that became an active project goal; those who feared it and talked seriously about hard-coding ethical reasoning in; and those who were sure it would never happen, that even a hyperintelligent computer with a soul could never truly eclipse its human masters.

But even the ethical reasoning purists were beginning to shrug their shoulders and tune Giselle out. They were the specialists in how to implement the ethics conventions, and all of those safeguards had already been hardwired in to the best of their ability. And the heat and haze outside the windows served as a constant reminder of why they could not afford to wait.

The orange haze lifted for a while, only to be replaced with something worse – a bluish fog, one that smelled like rot and stung the eyes, rolling in from the increasingly less-distant sea. It could have been a chemical spill, a geoengineering experiment gone wrong, a distant conflagration, or maybe just the fumes of a clump of dead things somewhere out in the water; nobody in the AI division really kept track anymore. The facility where Giselle worked was well-protected; she was fine as long as she stayed indoors.

Out the window, past the massive security fences and nearly lost in the fog, there was a demonstration going on. Giselle watched the vague outlines of bodies in the blue, both sides masked for protection from the air as much as for anonymity. There were all sorts of demonstrations these days. Anti-war activists; anarchists and communists; fascists with conspiracy theories; desperate young people who didn't believe that the military was already working as hard as it could on the problem of climate change and wanted to shout at it until it did more. All these people were regular visitors, showing up faintly in the distance past the security fences, surrounded by riot police. Often Giselle couldn't tell the difference between them.

She recognized this group only because NEMESIS-1 had told her about it. They moved differently than most protesters. Not waving signs, not raising their fists. There was chanting, but not the usual way. Riot police stood at cautious attention on either side, ready to intervene, but these demonstrators weren't getting in the police's faces, trying to make any angry statement or plea. They were kneeling. They were falling on their faces. Not protesters: worshippers.

As she stared, she heard footsteps, and General Walters' firm hand came down on her shoulder.

"According to plan, then," said Walters.

Her voice was as coldly steady as always. There must be a squishy center to General Walters somewhere – everyone had that – but on the job, she never let it show. And it was comforting to be around someone who presented themselves that way. Without Leah, everything felt empty and pointless, but General Walters knew what the point was. Giselle could be loyal to a woman who touched her like this, who steered her when she couldn't have steered herself.

"I don't like it," she said.

"You don't have to like it. It's working."

Giselle had seen the signs of these groups on social media, the coded phrases they exchanged with each other, their connections with the other cults and conspiracy groups that were gaining followers as the climate crisis deepened. They were the beginnings of a movement that worshipped computers like NEMESIS-1 as gods, or as some sort of electronic prophets of God, plunked down from the heavens to save them. It had not been any human's idea to do this. NEMESIS-1 itself that planted the idea, as an experiment, sowing it in small innocuous places to see if it had the desired effect. The supercomputer was starting a new religion.

It had been a long time since Giselle went to church; the more time she spent with women like Leah, the less she'd wanted to try to fit in with pious homophobes, and eventually the trappings of religion had faded from her life. But this couldn't be right. You couldn't just make things up and start a religion around them. Religions were supposed to be something you believed.

"NEMESIS-1 explained its reasoning," said General Walters. It hadn't had to do so – the whole point of a supercomputer like this was that it could catch on to patterns too subtle for a human to grasp. It would do things that had to be taken on faith. But for this, the computer had made its arguments painstakingly. "In an emergency, if there's something concrete to do that will save someone, humans are more capable of heroism than they think. But the current crisis doesn't offer many opportunities of that kind. To survive, we need an intricate web of small changes, without any immediate concrete effect, propagated across a field of millions of people – as well as all sorts of dramatic action at the corporate and state level, the kinds of actions that are against the individual self-interest of the few who are positioned to take them, who have reached those positions precisely because of their genius for self-interest. Humans aren't wired to do this sort of thing, even if we calculate that it's necessary. There's only one human instinct that enables it."

"Faith," Giselle echoed, looking numbly out through the fog at the crowd. NEMESIS-1 had already laid out this reasoning. She had no counter-argument, except that it made her skin crawl.

"Faith in a higher power, or in some other infallible

organizing principle. One that can give clear orders, offer hope to the faithful and punish the sinners. Look at me, Giselle."

It was a direct order from a superior officer, but Giselle couldn't make herself obey. She stared at the worshippers until General Walters took her by the chin. She pulled Giselle in her direction, forcing their eyes to meet.

It was the first time General Walters had ever called her, against regulations, by her first name.

"This is *working*," said General Walters, fierce and unblinking as a bird of prey. "Do you understand? Every research department in the world, every desperate attempt to right the planet before it chokes on its own fumes, and ours is working, which means ours is the one the world deserves. I don't care if you like it; you're one person. Billions are dying. We are the ones with the scope and the vision to save them. *Do you understand?*"

Giselle swallowed hard. It was impossible not to understand. And it was impossible to silence the frightened, irrational part of her that disliked all this anyway.

"Yes, ma'am," she answered. "I understand."

But all she really knew was that she did not want General Walters to let go of her.

Hurricanes shouldn't have held much power as far inland as Giselle's facility, but the ocean crept closer and closer every day, and there was no *should* to the weather anymore. NEMESIS-1 lived in a bunker-like corner of the facility, so secure that it was better to stay there than to make the dangerous trek across polluted lands to an evacuation point that might get struck by a different disaster the very next day.

So for three days Giselle hunkered in that corner with the other top researchers, clinging to an intermittently-charged phone that mostly wasn't getting signal, while flaying winds and flooding rains had their way with everything aboveground.

Amid the floods and lightning, NEMESIS-1 had ordered a church destroyed.

She – Giselle could no longer think of the supercomputer as anything but *she* – hadn't said it outright. But she'd given many small, deniable orders. The prioritization of some hurricane preparedness measures, in some corners of the city, over others. The denial of certain zoning and funding requests. The stretching-out, delay, and rapid change of certain routine construction tasks. The removal of a barrier, ostensibly for urgent repairs, on a very particular corner of the river. The result was that the National Cathedral spectacularly collapsed right in front of the news drones; gargoyle faces and shards of stained glass poked up out of the muddy rubble, and the small shrine to NEMESIS-1 that had risen up less than a block away remained intact. The symbolism was too obvious to discuss.

After the hurricane, when Giselle was finally allowed out of the building for a precious lunch break, she took her electric car – damp and sputtering, but functional – and drove carefully through the wreckage to her cheap apartment. The building had been torn open, its sides spattered with the kind of rain that would eat it away over the next few months to nothing. What was left of the windows lay in scattered shards on the ground.

She took a tasteless bite of a tasteless sandwich and looked at the apartment building for a long time, feeling the same deceptive numbness with something awful underneath that she felt about Leah. At least Leah wasn't around to have to worry where she'd go. Most of Giselle's neighbors would be homeless now. Most of the city would be, and good luck finding any undamaged place at a time like this to take them in. She was lucky she had a workplace with barracks, which would be happy to keep her.

She didn't bother to go in for any of her things.

"You're late," said General Walters forty minutes later, ramrod straight and cold as always, as Giselle stumbled back into the facility.

"Sorry, ma'am." Giselle took off her boots and her mask and wiped her face. She thought the rains of a hurricane might have cleared the air, but they'd only brought new toxins in; her eyes were streaming and stinging even after spending most of the route safe in her car.

Walters neither commented on her disheveled appearance nor waited for her to finish cleaning herself. "You're needed in the lab. We're performing another soul upload."

"Now, ma'am?" Giselle rubbed furiously at her eyes, and then decided she shouldn't have done that; it made things worse. "It wasn't scheduled."

"NEMESIS-1's own instructions were clear that we should take this opportunity as soon as it was offered."

"Ma'am. I need an eye wash, ma'am."

Walters grudgingly let her make a detour to the eye wash station. While Giselle furiously ran cold water over her eyes, Walters explained further. There were no doubt people who worshipped NEMESIS-1 privately or sporadically, but the core of her cult had become organized to the point of having registered members, and NEMESIS-1 had quietly vetted each one, evaluating them ahead of time, putting them on an internal list of desired souls or undesired ones. The first time one of her desired souls came close to death, they were to be brought to her and uploaded immediately – even if she wasn't scheduled for a soul upload.

Giselle knew about this; she'd just needed the time in the eye wash station to collect herself.

She entered the lab with her face wet, cold water that too-closely resembled tears still trickling down her cheek. The desired soul lay there on his deathbed, a large and muscular man, bleeding through his thin blanket from some injury he'd sustained in the storm. He strained to breathe, but there was an incongruous smile on his face. Some of the other volunteers had smiled like that, even as their bodies shut down, relishing the thought that they'd soon be a part of something greater. This man's smile was the biggest she'd seen, revealing large white teeth. Giselle hadn't been briefed on who he was, why he had begun to worship NEMESIS-1, what about him made him so desirable. She knew nothing about him but that he worshipped the thing she had built.

The technicians were already crawling all over the room, turning on the improved set of electromagnets that would draw him in, double-checking that everything was in the perfect position.

Giselle chewed her lip, looking at the man. He was white or white-passing, muscled, weathered, a little scarred – none of those things were out of the ordinary for military volunteers, but this man *wasn't* military, and something about him made her uneasy. Who was he? Who had he been, before? Could he have been saved, if the world was the way it should be, if there'd been a hospital in proper working order to rush him to?

Between rattling, sucking coughs, the dying man caught

Giselle's eye. His tongue worked behind his teeth, as many dying people's did, trying to rid himself of the taste of death. He stared at her and at the tears dripping down her face, and he *winked*.

It was a wink that Giselle found all too familiar – the leering wink she'd begun to know from men as soon as she hit her teens, the one that only increased when she was seen out in public with a partner like Leah. Sometimes that wink prefigured violence. Sometimes just the wink itself was enough, the suggestion that there might be violence, that she couldn't do anything about it if there was.

For one brief moment, something cold and awful stabbed up at her through the numbness.

"Turn off the machine," Giselle said. Her voice didn't come out loudly enough; there was too much shake. She tried again, forcing herself into the military discipline she'd been trained for, filling her lungs and barking out the order loudly enough to fill the room. "Technicians! Turn the machine off–"

"Overruled," said General Walters, behind her, far more calmly. "Your orders stand."

No one stopped. Giselle felt ill; she had a vague, uneasy feeling she should argue more, but she couldn't find the words.

The man in the hospital bed had stopped looking at Giselle. He was starting to shake, his limbs seizing, his breath a gasp. She knew from experience that the end might be seconds away – or his body might fight it out for hours more, days more. Her own hands were trembling.

General Walters stepped up closer, a warm firm hand on Giselle's shoulder. She lowered her voice, not the reprimand Giselle deserved but something subtler, pitched for her ears alone.

"This project is larger than you," said Walters in her low, steely voice. "Larger even than me, now. This man has done wrong in his life, which NEMESIS-1 knows perfectly well, and it has judged him desirable anyway. Trust her and trust me. If humanity survives as a result of our efforts, you will be remembered only as a good scientist who did as she was told. Let that be enough for you. Let me, and the machine, worry about all the rest."

Giselle didn't know what else to do. She leaned ever so slightly into the general's touch, and she hoped it was true.

CHAPTER 9

Now

Tiv stood with Grid next to the airlock, looking at it nervously. Their own part of these preparations was going to be the strangest. They'd dressed their best – in stolen clothes, because that was all their clothes these days: a charcoal-gray skirt suit that made Tiv look like a politician, and, for Grid, a checkered number with a pinstriped tie. Tiv thought the checkered suit was a little bit garish, but where they were going, it was anyone's guess if anyone knew how to interpret human clothing at all.

"Ready?" she said, and Grid nodded.

The scene that the two of them stepped out into was like nothing Tiv had ever seen before.

She'd seen the inside of the *Pride of Jai,* painstakingly hacked together with the trusses and piping still visible. She'd seen the inside of God-built ships, shining sleek and pristine. She'd seen the warped organic shapes of the Chaos Zone; she'd even seen the insides of Dr Talirr's lair. But this...

A huge atrium stretched out before them. Hexagonal billboards blinked in alphabets Tiv had never seen; ramps and escalators brimmed with creatures she scarcely recognized from any of her reading. Tunnels branched off in every direction like the world's biggest subway concourse. She stumbled back, almost all the way back into the portal, as a brown being the size of an elephant trudged past her, six-legged and ram-horned and wearing what looked like a massive gas mask over its pug snout. There were Spiders, big ten-legged creatures that Tiv had seen in vids before; there were humanoids in every squat or stretched or just-slightly-off-human-normal shape imaginable, with extra limbs or antennae or tendrils sticking out of them; there were creatures whose body shapes Tiv couldn't even make sense of, where she couldn't tell what was a head, what was a limb, what was something else altogether.

It was somehow obscene. The sheer variety felt like her eyes were playing tricks on her, like the human shapes that should have thronged through a scene like this had all been stretched and squished and twisted like putty. It wasn't the same as the surreal, dreamlike, shifting feeling of the Chaos Zone – Tiv was *used* to the Chaos Zone by now. Outside things were creepy in their own ways, but they didn't stubbornly remain like this in shapes that almost looked like people but not quite. They didn't jauntily bustle around like customers in a shopping mall, wearing clothes in a rainbow of textures and colors, as if there was nothing odd about having shapes like these, as if Tiv was the strange one.

Why had she thought it was a good idea to come here? Why had *Dr Talirr* thought it was a good idea to come here? Tiv was clearly not ready for this.

Someone bumped into her while she stood there gawking, someone spindly with three arms and pebbly, lavender skin. They squawked something as they pushed past – a word that Tiv's mind interpreted as *Move!* or *Out of the way!* but it was impossible to tell what it really meant.

Tiv stumbled back another step or two. She made a tiny, overwhelmed noise.

There was a small warmth on her upper arm, though. Grid's hand. Grid, more grimly determined than overwhelmed, gave her a long, steadying look, and after a moment Tiv returned it. At least there was one other human here, one other thing that made sense.

"You know where we're headed, right?" said Grid.

Tiv did, vaguely. Humans didn't deal with aliens much, but aliens dealt with each other. Aliens had coalitions and interplanetary treaties. This station was the meeting place for one of the largest coalitions, and Tiv and Grid were here to talk to them. Like a pair of diplomats in an old novel, representing some tiny threatened human country, appealing to a larger one for aid.

But there was no sign that said THIS WAY IF YOU ARE A HUMAN APPEALING FOR AID.

She'd gone through the meta-portal willing herself to emerge in a place where she could find what she needed. So it couldn't be far.

She looked around at the thronging shapes, the Spiders and the ram-horned things, the twenty-legged creatures that moved in queasy waves, the humanoids with proportions just a little bit wrong. She made herself focus on the concourse's structure. Among all the noise and color, there was one spot that looked almost right. A desk-like semicircle, blue-white and brightly lit. Behind it there wasn't a shop or a tunnel, but a single computer display and a single uniformed employee. The employee was big and stocky, vaguely humanoid, with anemone-like tendrils in place of hair, and seven pink beady eyes. Their uniform – Tiv wasn't even sure what about it said *uniform* to her eye, when all the clothes in this place were such a riot of unfamiliar styles, but its draping, curving, multicolored shape was gathered up into a prim collar at the neck, with something that looked like it might be writing stitched in, and it looked similar to the glyphs on the big, blue sign above the desk.

If Tiv had to guess, if this followed anything like the rules of a human airport or shopping mall, then she would guess that the writing said *Information.*

She started toward it. Aliens bumped into her, swore, or narrowly avoided colliding with her and Grid as they passed. Tiv didn't normally have this problem in human crowds – she was good at politely moving through the flow of bodies. But these were not human bodies, following the instinctive rules of movement that came naturally to humans. Every time she tried to dodge or weave out of someone's way, she ended up bumping into three more people.

It was only a few dozen feet, but by the time she and Grid made it to the information desk, she was sweating and mortified.

The employee looked down at the two of them. Their anemone-hair waved in the still air like a set of tree branches in a stiff breeze. They said something, in a gravelly voice full of wet, squishy consonants, that Tiv didn't understand.

Tiv took a deep breath. Putting a hand on the edge of the desk, willing herself the composure she'd always had as the team's leader, she straightened.

"Excuse me," she said, as clearly and calmly as she could. "Do you speak Earth creole? Could you tell me how to speak to a representative of the Federation?"

The employee said something else that Tiv didn't

understand. She glanced at Grid, who shrugged. Spectators of various species were starting to gather around the information desk. Tiv didn't think coming up to an information desk and asking questions was very unusual, but maybe this was a huge faux pas. Maybe this wasn't an information desk. Maybe it was spectacularly strange to see a human here. Maybe people at desks like these weren't supposed to be spoken to. Maybe her tone, her posture, her way of approaching were wildly wrong. Maybe she needed an appointment.

She squared her shoulders and tried once more, this time pitching her voice so it would carry to everyone who was listening. "I'm sorry; I don't understand what you're saying. Is there anyone here who speaks Earth creole?"

And someone pushed forward. A gray-faced creature, more humanoid than some of the others, wearing a strange tattered-looking robe. Their skin was a flaky ash gray, their chest broad and flat, their head hairless; their voice a bass growl issuing from a pair of long, thick lips lined with disturbingly small, sharp teeth.

They looked Tiv and Grid up and down with a pair of dark, liquid eyes like a cow's, spaced a little too far apart in the skull for a human; and then they made a sound of disgust – or it sounded to Tiv like disgust, though there was no way to really know. The sound a human man would make if he'd discovered an unruly teenager drinking when they shouldn't or making an unholy mess of their bedroom or creating some other petty, disappointing annoyance for the thousandth time.

"Ugh," they said, the words heavily accented but intelligible. "Humans again."

* * *

It was most of the day waiting around, shuffled from one official to another, before they got the audience they'd asked for; and even that, a same-day audience without prior warning, seemed to be a faster response than the aliens were used to putting together. The gray alien explained things to them as they went. Yes, this was the station where the Federation's emergency aid councils met; yes, a committee would hear them out. The alien was male, it turned out, or at least his pronouns in Earth creole were he/him; his name was something Tiv couldn't pronounce, but he was a sort of go-between businessman who'd dealt with humans before, mostly making trade deals between them and other species who couldn't communicate in Earth creole without a translator. Many species didn't have the kind of mouthparts that could do it. He didn't work for the Federation directly, but the Federation was used to hiring people like him when a human needed something. The idea of humans and their totalitarian Gods faintly disgusted him – for which, Tiv supposed, she couldn't blame him – but there was a kind of preening amid the disgust, a pride in his work and at being one of the few who could successfully communicate with such a troubled species. He pointed out loudly to everyone that he'd found them first, as they were shunted from small claustrophobic office to small claustrophobic office, awaiting their audience.

Tiv and Grid ate the protein bars they'd brought along for lunch, washing them down with water. They knew better than to try alien food, but even the simple protein bar sat heavy and queasy in Tiv's stomach as the hours stretched on. This wasn't risky, not the way a battle was risky, but so much depended on it and she didn't really know what she was doing. The whole team was a bunch of physics nerds, not diplomats. For all she knew, maybe the gray man was playing some elaborate joke.

Finally, after too much waiting, they found themselves in a conference room.

It was bowl shaped, big enough for about two dozen human-sized creatures, without chairs or desks – instead there were objects Tiv could only think of as *lecterns*. They had six sides each and they were translucent, like crystals jutting up out of the curved floor. One or two aliens stood at each one, from the child-sized to the horse-sized, each of them draped in something elaborate. Tiv and Grid were ushered to one of those crystal lecterns.

The gray man had been switched out for someone else now, a green-skinned humanoid with a potbelly and an outslung jaw, all the proportions just a little bit further off human-normal. Tiv couldn't guess this one's gender, but their voice was clear enough, accented and careful and ringing through the room. The other aliens spoke, and the green-skinned one translated.

"This emergency meeting of the Foreign Affairs Committee of the Fourth Province of the Federation has been called on behalf of humans Productivity Hunt and Ulutrujcy Unaczysy Jasl of Jai, without the approval of the humans' Gods." They stumbled over both names. When they got to that last part, *without the approval of the humans' Gods,* there was a murmur throughout the room – clickings and rumblings and dolphin squeaks, sounds Tiv mostly couldn't interpret, but she thought she could guess what they meant. It was rare for a human to appear before an alien committee like this; rarer still for a human to do it against the wishes of the Gods.

"Productivity Hunt and Ulutrujcy Unaczysy Jasl of Jai, what is your petition?"

Tiv swallowed hard and cleared her throat. She'd been rehearsing this under her breath for hours. "Members of the Federation," she said, fighting to keep her voice clear and dignified. Could these aliens tell the difference between a clear, dignified human voice and a frightened mumble? "I am coming to you on behalf of the people of a region called the Chaos Zone of Jai. Our region of the planet is in crisis. After a... disaster, the Gods have declared the whole population heretics. They have withdrawn Their protection from our region, hoping we will die, and an enemy, the Keres, is approaching the planet quickly. She will be here in just one week. We have no ships or weapons to defend us from this enemy. She will completely destroy us. We are here to beg for the Federation's help. We don't have much to offer in return; everyone in our region is already struggling to survive. But you might find the planet rich in resources, natural or cultural, and we would be intensely in your debt. Without the Gods restricting our communications and associations, a new alliance–"

The murmuring had started up again, louder than before. Tiv's heart beat in her throat. It seemed unfair to do this – no one in the Chaos Zone, besides Ev and Yasira and the Seven, even knew that she and Grid were here. The Plague had pulverized the Chaos Zone's government into informal local councils; there was no overarching national democracy to give her permission to do it, and Tiv wasn't even a trained negotiator. She was bargaining away her whole planet's futures, offering them up to a set of creditors that she didn't understand. It was that or give up and let them die, but it didn't seem right. It seemed like something Dr Talirr would do, deciding something this important on the whole planet's behalf.

Maybe that was the problem. Dr Talirr was orchestrating all of this now, and Tiv didn't trust her. All she knew of Dr Talirr was what she'd done to the planet and what she'd done to Yasira.

"You want us," the green-skinned translator interrupted. Or, really, another alien had interrupted – a squat thing with skin the color of volcanic ash, three-legged, without visible eyes. Its mouth was a lipless gash, and the noise it made was more a rumble than a voice. The translator, somehow, dutifully repeated the rumble in human words, and it was hard not to imagine that the objection originated with them. "To interfere. With your Gods."

Tiv had been prepared for this objection, but her heart sank. It was Grid who answered smoothly. "Not with the Gods. The Gods have renounced Their jurisdiction over the Chaos Zone. They disowned us, in an announcement that reached every citizen of the Chaos Zone, and told us that every form of divine oversight and assistance was being removed. If you helped us, you would not be violating any diplomatic agreements with the Gods, because those agreements no longer apply. We are truly on our own."

There was another general murmur, and the words of another of the green people carried clearly – this one not a translator but an actual member of the committee, draped in shimmering pink- and peach-colored robes. "These are outlandish claims. Are we meant to believe you without evidence?"

"If you came to the Chaos Zone, you'd see for yourself."

A Spider near the center of the room, eight feet high and ten-legged, emitted a piercing series of whistles and clicks.

"Be that as it may, the Federation was not informed of any such removal of jurisdiction, inasmuch as it pertains to our own agreements with human Gods. Even a fact-finding mission, in the absence of such a removal, might be viewed as aggressive action."

A different alien spoke up – a bizarre, horse-sized one near the edge of the gathering, one whose body seemed to be made up out of smooth black and white spheres stuck together. It spoke in a series of clicks and whistles, shriller than the Spider's, and a new translator spoke, a four-armed person the size of a ten year-old child, indigo-skinned, with a wide and distorted face. "Surely the Federation could ask the Gods to clarify the situation."

"Within seven days?" the ash-pile of a being shot back. "Not likely. You know Them."

"How did you get here?" the gray man interrupted, and Tiv wasn't even sure who he was translating for – there was too much background chatter now to tell. "Without the Gods' approval?"

"A portal," Grid answered. "Unauthorized."

This brought on a chorus of rumbles and squeaks almost as alarmed as the first one, when they'd said they were here without the approval of the Gods. But Tiv didn't want to waste time talking over the finer points of how Ev had built the portals and how they worked. She had bigger priorities.

It would be just like the Gods to try to stop anyone from interfering, even as They pretended to wash Their hands of the Chaos Zone. Everyone knew They didn't really want to stop being involved – They just wanted an excuse to wipe Jai off the map. But that was *wrong* – surely the Federation could see it.

Unless they'd already told the Gods they wouldn't

interfere. It was possible – Tiv and Grid had talked that over before they came. It could be that this meeting was a formality, a sop to throw to the suffering humans when the outcome was already predetermined. But Tiv wouldn't let herself believe that. She had to act as though what she said could make a difference.

Tiv's voice shook as she asked, "What are your agreements with the Gods?"

The gray man took over this one, translating for a pale, snakelike being coiled into a springlike shape, with tiny limbs sprouting from its jaw. "To fully summarize the Federation's treaties with human space would take longer than the time allotted for this meeting, but the relevant part to you is a policy of non-interference. The Federation does not try to meddle in human affairs, and in return, the Gods do not try to meddle with the Federation, to enforce its understanding of religious truth and heresy on non-human worlds, or to undergo expansion attempts into Federation space. Your human population expands quickly, and in a war of conquest or of retaliation, your Gods would be a formidable enemy. The Federation's member worlds have nothing quite like Them. You understand, I am sure."

"*You* don't understand," Tiv argued. It was a child's argument – she should have come prepared with better words, but in this moment, she didn't have any. "What the Gods are doing to our world is wrong. It is genocide. Don't you have a duty to help?"

"We have a duty," the Spider agreed, "several duties that we must balance. That is in the Federation's charter. The first duty is to the Federation's member worlds and our own peoples, to honor the agreements such worlds have voluntarily entered into. The second is to all other sentient life – the second duty is important, but that first duty cannot be forsaken for the second."

"And even if we were to accept an argument based on the second duty," said the snake-being, "what you are asking for is a war. We would have to weigh the likely effects of such a war – would it be an engagement we could possibly win? Would the secondary effects, the devastation, not just to your world but to every other human world, really be better for humans in the end?"

"The Gods are *evil*," said Tiv. She heard her voice breaking. This wasn't news – it was something the Seven already knew, something the people of the Chaos Zone had all gradually begun to believe. But she had never said it out loud before, not even in the quiet of her room with only Yasira to hear. "Don't you get it? They torture people. They torture *souls*. They shoot children. They outlaw protests. They broadcast public executions every day. And the smallest deviation from Their doctrines, which are *lies*, makes us deserve all of this in Their eyes. None of this is good for humans. None of it ever was. Please – how can you just stand by, while They–"

A new alien spoke up, one who looked like the same species as the one at the information desk, tendrils writhing around their wide head. "This isn't a jurisdictional argument or an argument from results, it's an emotional one. Motion to dismiss."

"But–" Tiv spluttered, and then she couldn't even finish her sentence. She was starting to cry. She couldn't listen to the back-and-forth anymore. The aliens kept jabbering and clicking and squeaking and hissing and rumbling, and it all just washed over her pointlessly.

She felt Grid lay a gentle hand on her shoulder again, and the two of them exchanged a look. They were in this together, even if none of these sanctimonious aliens were in it with them.

"There are no further arguments," said the Spider at last. "Motion to begin the vote on whether to plan military and humanitarian aid for the human planet Jai."

The translator didn't even pronounce the word *Jai* correctly.

Voting happened in a flurry. Each alien's lectern lit up in colors, some of them flitting through a spectrum and sending out pulses of light in different directions, some flickering into a particular state and staying there. It wasn't just two colors – humans might have used red for *no* and green for *yes,* but Tiv didn't even see a straightforward red or green. The lecterns lit up in shades of off-white, peach, gold, lavender, silver, aquamarine.

"Look," said the gray man, and Tiv was oddly sure that it was him this time, not just the people he was translating for. He'd edged closer to the two of them again. "We all sympathize. Your side of the galaxy is just, how would you say it in Earth – it is fucked up. It is the mess no one wants to stick their hand in, you see?"

Tiv did not dignify him with a response. Maybe this meeting had been useless. But she refused to believe it. She had to believe there'd been some chance, even if she and Grid hadn't been quite articulate enough to grasp it, even if they'd blown it somehow.

Eventually the podiums all stopped flickering; they stabilized into a single complex wash of color, an iridescence that meant nothing to Tiv.

"The vote is complete," says the Spider. "We are sorry

about your world, delegation from Jai. But the Federation's answer is no."

Yasira should have been the one to talk to the gone people. Yasira was better at it. But Daeis could do that kind of thing too, if they tried. In some ways – in how they communicated – a gone person was more similar to one of Daeis' monster friends than to a regular person. To Daeis, that was a good thing. It made talking easier. All the arguing in the war room had given them a headache, but they wanted to do their part.

They knew, from long experience, the kinds of places where the gone people gathered. They passed through the portal and concentrated on the place they knew best – a grove out at the edge of a field, near some little town that had been deserted when the Plague began. Or maybe everyone in the town had died or turned into a gone person. It was hard to tell. Someday, Daeis thought, when the people of the Chaos Zone had a little breathing room, they would start to write down their history, and there would be so many things missing. So many small stories like this town's story which, in all the hubbub and chaos, had been lost altogether.

The trees here, tall and stately, had tangled their branches together into a kind of dome. Their bark shimmered, mossy green and pond blue with glimmers of violet. Their leaves, falling slowly, had taken various pale colors, indistinguishable at first glance from flower petals. Between the wide trunks, where roots burrowed big ridges into the soil, the gone people had constructed sleeping nests out of the branches and leaves, each one painstakingly selected out of what had fallen to the ground here for its color. A nest that was all reds and pinks, a nest that was all blues, a nest that shifted in an ombre from golden to green.

They had been sleeping there when Daeis arrived. They stirred, raising their heads one by one from those nests to peer groggily at Daeis' form, similar to them but obviously not one of them.

Daeis held their hands out, palm up, and sent a thought in the gone people's direction. It wasn't a thought in words; it was made of impulses, feelings, the occasional image. And the gone people, understanding now what this intrusion was for, sent the same kinds of thoughts back to them.

Power gathering, as the forces of Outside that governed the Chaos Zone sensed a threat. Arcs of light in shapes and colors that only a gone person understood. Quiverings of strength below the earth.

Lashing forces, like the tentacled limbs of monsters too large to conceive, reaching up in the planet's defense.

The gone people, connected to each other as they always were. Sitting in their circles, hands clasped, wordlessly singing. Blood running down their faces as they pierced themselves with thorns.

At the protest the other day, the gone people had not reached out to defend themselves. The point of the protest had not been defense. The gone people, that day, had been preparing to shift the energies of the world, and that was more important to them than any thought of their individual safety.

But this was different. This was an enemy the size of the planet. It threatened them all.

So it was not the gone people, but the world itself that stirred now, preparing to shield itself, not with any human sense of planning or tactics but with something more like a pill bug's instinct to roll up tightly and hide its softest parts. It might be enough to protect the people on the surface from the Keres; it might not. Neither the world, which could not really *know* anything, nor the gone people knew. But the gone people could feel the world move, and so they assembled, in this vision of the future. They caught the world's energies in their own ritual circles, and they directed it where it needed to go.

It was not a simple process, of course. It was not just a pretty shimmer in the air. Outside was never that simple. Not all of the wounds in the gone people's bodies were from their own ritual thorns. Daeis saw glimpses of worse things – energies breaking away from containment, or simply overloading the abilities of the gone people around them, a twisting of space, blood, screaming. But the majority of it went where it needed to go.

To a woman in a scuffed white lab coat and large glasses, with a limp brown ponytail, who had told the gone people that she knew best how their sacrifice could be spent. And they had believed her.

This was what Daeis had come here to verify. Dr Talirr had said already that she'd talked to the gone people. She'd said they were contributing in their own way. Daeis just hadn't realized that Dr Talirr meant she'd guided that contribution. She'd made sure it fit into her own plans, before she even talked to the Seven.

Daeis wasn't sure what they thought of that. The gone people were intelligent, though in a very different way from normal humans, and they had their own ways of understanding Outside. They wouldn't have been manipulated into something like this based on misunderstanding, or misplaced trust. They'd only have agreed if their own understanding told them that Dr Talirr's cause was aligned with theirs. That this really was the best way. Still, something about it bothered Daeis. All that pain, all that sacrifice – there was something not right about Dr Talirr blithely allowing other people to do it for her.

Normally Daeis didn't feel much shame about the way they were. The trouble they had with speaking could cause frustrations, could make some things more complicated, but they'd been around Yasira and other Riayin people long enough to learn there was nothing really wrong with it, nothing about it that made them broken or unworthy. They hadn't always been this way, though – not until Akavi had locked them in a little room, alone, for years. Daeis had been a brilliant graduate student in physics once, able to hold their own in loud, fast, complex theoretical arguments with alacrity. And at times like this, they missed being able to do that. They wanted to stomp back into the lair and get into a passionate debate.

As it stood, they would have to settle for slinking back in, and curling up with a blanket, and gathering their strength to tell Splió. And Splió, they hoped, would know what to do.

Tiv bit the inside of her cheek as she and Grid wandered back to the door they'd come in by. So, that was that; her part of the preparations had failed. There was one Federation and there was no point running around to its other meeting places, looking for a different result. They just had to hope that the other parts of the team were doing better.

"Wait," said a voice as they passed into a narrow hall.

She turned. It was the little indigo-skinned translator, the one that had said the least. Standing with them were a small group of the aliens that the translator had spoken for in the conference room: horse-sized ones, black and white, made of stuck-together spherical shapes.

"The Zora have one more thing to say," said the interpreter, motioning brusquely. "This way, if you will."

Tiv and Grid exchanged a glance and then followed. The interpreter took them down a side passage into a less-traveled area of the station. The chaos of the area near the atrium gave way to larger and starker hallways, less signage, sharper contrasts – a deep black material and a bright white one, tiled over each other in intricate patterns.

"Swear that you will not repeat what I tell and show you here to the rest of the Federation," said the interpreter.

Grid shot Tiv a warning look, which Tiv could read perfectly well – why should they swear anything like that? What was going on here? At worst, the Zora – if that was the word for these black and white aliens – were about to kill them or something. At best, it was going to be an offer of help with strings attached. And an offer from a single species would have worse strings than an offer from the whole Federation. It would put the Chaos Zone, assuming the Chaos Zone survived any of this, onto the losing side of one of the Federation's internal political divisions. It would put the rest of Jai into a very confusing situation indeed.

But Tiv wasn't going to survive anyway if the Chaos Zone didn't. And she'd rather have an ally that actually helped – assuming the Zora were about to offer any help – than a serenely indifferent group that thought of her world's problems as something too filthy to touch.

Tiv squared her shoulders. "I promise."

"We imagine it does not matter to you, in your position,

but did you know that it is heresy for you to speak to a Zora? We are on your Gods' list of species with which humans must not communicate. The reasons why we were added to it, and the trouble it has caused for us and our allies, are too lengthy to recount. Suffice it to say that your Gods are as heretical to us as we are to Them. We have been monitoring your situation, as have others. We are not strong enough to defeat your Gods in an open conflict, but we have no love for Them, and no wish to see..."

The interpreter broke off and started to jabber back and forth with the Zora. When he turned back to Tiv and Grid, there was a frustration in his eyes and a sharp tone that seemed to come from him, specifically, not from what he was being asked to say. "I tell them they cannot say this to a human, and they insist. Fine. Here is what they say; I wash my hands of it. We have no love for your Gods, and no wish to see a portion of your race murdered by Them, just as that portion is beginning to understand the Truth."

Tiv blinked slowly as she took that in.

Dr Talirr, Yasira's mentor, had talked like that. Truth with a capital T, almost literally audible in how she emphasized the word – meaning Outside. The Zora worshipped Outside, the way Dr Talirr did, the way people were beginning to in the Chaos Zone.

This raised more questions than it answered. Questions Tiv did not have time to ask.

They turned a corner, and suddenly the corridor opened out onto a balcony. Below them, in a hangar space so big it boggled Tiv's senses, lay spaceships. Dozens of spaceships, in a strange knobbly shape she'd never seen before, like peanut clusters painted stark black and white. Tiv didn't know enough about alien ships to guess where the engines were, where the shields and weapons were. If they even *had* shields and weapons. Still, she let her breath out in a low, awed whistle. Tiv had worked on a mortal space station once. It was very clear that this was beyond anything mortal humans could do.

"We can offer perhaps a dozen of these," said the Zora. "Perhaps more. We will speak to the captains, see who is willing. But you must understand that this is not a gift from the Federation, nor from the Zoran government. We would not want our whole planet to bear the blame of this thing we are choosing as individuals to do. It is specifically a personal favor. It has nothing to do with any command structure. And it will not be enough; the amount we can spare will not defeat a fleet of God-built ships. Not by itself. It is being offered for your assistance, in hopes of becoming one form of assistance among many."

Tiv stared at the ranks of ships, mouth dry.

"Thank you," she stammered. "Thank you, we'll–we'll take anything. We're looking everywhere we can, we're using our own powers, and it'll–it'll be enough when we put it all together, all those different things. We'll make it be enough."

Grid shook their head, as overwhelmed as she was, but suspicious. "Hang on. Hang on, I don't understand. How do we… how does any of this…" They pressed a hand to their head and regrouped. "For starters, um, we got here through a portal the size of a door. How are we even supposed to bring these back?"

If they had obtained official help from the Federation, Tiv had assumed, the Federation would know how to get the ships to the right place. But it was a big assumption. And if this was a personal favor, done under the radar, the

Zora would have to do it without letting the rest of the Federation know.

In answer, the interpreter gestured. Tiv's eyes were drawn up, past the ships that had absorbed her attention at first glance, to the complicated mechanisms of the hangar airlock that lay beyond them; and above that too, to a long, narrow, thick-glassed window. Outside it, Tiv could see something that it took her a few seconds of concentration to understand. A massive ring streaked with the same black and white patterns as those hallways, floating outside the station, sizzling and flickering with light; and the stars beyond it were different from the stars on either side.

"You can go back through your portal," the interpreter said, with an unmistakable smugness in their voice. "We'll use ours."

CHAPTER 10

Yasira sat across from Ev in the war room, motionless, her head swarming with thoughts that refused to cohere. Everyone else had gone out to their different tasks, which would take all day from Yasira's perspective, and potentially much longer from theirs. Whatever Ev wanted from her, it was separate from all of those things. And Ev didn't trust that it could be said in front of the rest of the team.

Which meant, whatever it was, it was *bad.*

But Yasira wasn't running away.

She had told Tiv that it was fine, that she could handle being alone with Ev again, and she wasn't sure why she'd said it. Even the parts of her who'd formed the words couldn't account for them. What she felt when she looked at Ev wasn't confidence, exactly, and it certainly wasn't trust. It was more the kind of mix of feelings that overwhelmed her into immobility. *She's going to kill us,* wailed some of her. *She's going to hurt us again.* But also, she was the only one who might know the way out of this crisis. Ev was not trustworthy. And she was the only one Yasira trusted to really understand Outside. And Yasira was used to working with her, learning from her, doing what Ev told her to do because Ev knew these things.

Ev sat across the table from her, pale and half-hidden behind her glasses, her hair tied back in its familiar limp ponytail. When Yasira looked at Ev, all the parts of her roiled in different directions at once. Speaking felt impossible. And something felt right about that kind of immobility, in a sick way. Tiv would want Yasira to react differently – to be hostile, to be defensive, after everything Ev had put her through. To refuse to listen to Ev's plan until Ev had proven herself. But Tiv was following Ev's plan, too. Why should Yasira spend her energy when the same things were going to happen either way? If she had something concrete to push against, she'd push. Otherwise – she was miserable, she was tired, she didn't know what to do. She might as well let someone *try* to tell her.

"You've done a good job," Ev said at last.

Yasira shrugged. *No I didn't,* thought some part of her. *You don't get to judge if I did a good job,* said another. *You're the only one who can judge,* said a third.

What did it mean to have done a good job if everyone on the planet was about to die anyway?

"I mean that," said Ev. She leaned forward and balanced her chin in her hands, looking down at the table's cheap surface. She didn't look at Yasira directly, which was fine; Yasira didn't need her to. "I've spent the last six months wandering, trying to understand other humans. I'm glad that they call you 'Savior' and not me. Funny how that works, isn't it? I thought I had an understanding deeper than anyone's. I thought I was going to bring the world into a new way of being. I thought I would force everyone to start seeing things my way, and then we'd see what we wanted to do from there. It took me a long time to realize that's not actually a plan, not all of one – it's only a way of

lashing out. You saw more deeply than me. You saw that..."
She screwed up her face, as if, even now, she barely had
words for this. "That the people we brought with us into the
new way of being were still people. That they would need
to make their own decisions about what was acceptable to
them. That they needed, I don't know, some minimal level
of comfort and safety and respect before they could do that.
I never really thought that through."

Yasira looked at her dully. "Are you going to apologize?"

"Why would I? Would it help? I've done what I've done."
Ev made a dismissive gesture. "But I want to talk about you.
Outside is in your soul now. It's part of you. Even I never
managed it at that level. I wanted to keep the understanding
I'd always had, since birth. You were brave enough to reach
for more than that, and now..." She shook her head. "Has
anyone told you how beautiful you are now, Yasira? How
rare?"

Yasira's dull look narrowed into a glare.

Tiv had told her that. Tiv had told her she was beautiful,
last night after the protest. But at least Tiv had the decency
to say it when she'd *done* something, saved people. Ev meant
it another way.

Yasira wasn't beautiful. Her mind had been forced into a
new shape, by Outside, by her own imperfect choices, by Ev.
And it was not a shape she had wanted. In theory there was
nothing wrong with being plural, any more than there was
with being autistic, but it wasn't Yasira's natural state and it
was hard to handle, all these contrasting voices and needs
all jangling around at once. She was not in a position to go
find a neurotutor who could help her learn to handle it.
She just had to keep going, muddling around, channeling a
power beyond what any human should ever have been able

to channel, trying not to hurt herself. There *was* something wrong with being traumatized and depressed and having no proper treatment in sight. It wasn't beautiful. It sucked.

(But how tempting it was, said some small minority of those jangling parts of Yasira. How badly some of them wanted to be called beautiful, in the way that some of the surreal shapes of the life and landscapes of the Chaos Zone were beautiful. A terrible beauty. So strange it felt unbearable, and also impossible to look away).

"That's why," Ev continued, "there's a part of this that only you can do."

Yasira braced herself, tightening her shoulders. Here it came.

Ev's eyes were owlishly large behind her thick glasses, and they stared at Yasira unwaveringly. "You have to die."

Yasira went absolutely still.

"Fuck," she said after a moment, when there were any words at all again, incoherently. "Fuck you."

"Not forever," said Ev, holding out a forestalling hand. "Hear me out. It wouldn't be a complete death. Some part of you would survive–"

"Which part of me?" Yasira stood up, scraping the chair back so roughly and carelessly that it fell over with a clatter. There were parts of Yasira that *had* wanted to die, from sheer overwhelm and self-hate, and she'd only just overcome that feeling. She'd overcome it *yesterday,* finding that there were ways to live and take pain in a way that mattered. Was Ev going to take that from her *now?* "Which part of me deserves to live?"

"Yasira, calm *down.* Think this through. Everyone else's military efforts are only going to buy time. The rest of us are all doing what we can to prepare for this battle, and we might well win it, but the Gods don't want us to exist, and they won't stop. There will be a next battle, if we win this one, and a next. But you – your soul is made of Outside now. The Gods eat souls. Outside is more powerful than the Gods – it's not even a concept that their circuitry can process. It's not a threat they'll see coming. You'll die, and Nemesis will leap to take your heretic soul, but *you'll* be the one who eats *her.* From the inside out. There's no other mortal threat that will end this forever, don't you see? But you could win it all completely."

Yasira's knuckles hurt; she was making fists. "And then what? What will I be?"

"I don't know. It's up to you, I suspect."

"No." Yasira's voice felt as hard and final in her ears as a judge's. Tiv had thought that Yasira couldn't stand up to Ev; but of course she could. She only needed to be sure. And now she was sure – it wasn't just an unease now, but a revulsion surging through her like a black wave. She now had the concrete thing that she needed to push against. "Who do you think you are? You do all of this to the planet, you do all of this to us, you make us give up everything we used to be, you *abandon* us, and after six fucking months you come crawling back just to demand *this?* You can't do that. My answer is no. Go die yourself if you want someone to die."

She turned and walked away. Out of the stupid war room, which was only just a table and some cubicle walls that people had thrown together. Back to her bedroom, which wasn't much more.

"And how many more people will die because Nemesis lives?" Ev called after her. There was no discernible emotion in her voice, which didn't mean she wasn't feeling any – Ev's voice just naturally sounded flat, most of the time. Like everything was a calculation, even when maybe deep down it wasn't. "How many lives are worth yours?"

It was a stupid thing for Ev to say. She'd been the one, before, who thought one person's cause was worth countless human lives. If she was trying to appeal to Yasira's way of thinking, it was a transparent attempt, and she was too late.

Yasira slammed the door behind her and stood in the gloom of her bedroom, the unmade bed with its simple sheets and comforter, the walls slightly at an angle because none of the angles ever really worked right inside the lair. She didn't bother to turn on the light. She'd never decorated this room, even when Tiv suggested that she should; she'd been too busy hiding in it from the world, having endless arguments inside her own head. She'd never wanted to put her own pictures on these walls or paint them a color because she hadn't had it in her to acknowledge they were real.

What if she *did* die? She'd worked so hard, these past six months, to regain any sense that her life was worth living. All that work would be pointless if this was how it ended. Not a victorious fight. Just more time unlived.

Ev had no right to ask that of her. Maybe she'd spent the last six months wandering, trying to learn morality or whatever, but it clearly hadn't worked. Not if she still weighed human lives and suffering as lightly as numbers in one of her physics calculations, symbols to be moved back and forth. Not if she still wanted people to die for her.

"Well?" said Ev's calm voice through the door. "What's your backup plan?"

"You're the mastermind," Yasira shot back. "You figure it out." She sank to the floor, knees curled up to her chest, and laid her head in her hands.

* * *

She hadn't meant to fall asleep, but she must have collapsed on the bed from sheer emotional exhaustion. That happened to her sometimes, these days – random sleep, or being unable to sleep, or maybe just waking dreams, visions that couldn't be distinguished from sleep.

In Yasira's dream, she flew. She was a flock of birds, a swarm of locusts, and she was large enough to spread over the whole planet. But the planet was twisting, roiling, a live thing as amorphous as an amoeba. The planet rippled with threatening color, fire, hurricanes, and tidal waves. Above it, something flickered. A worse fire. A worse flock of birds – these were the Keres, Yasira knew. She had learned in Sunday school that the Keres was a multi-part being like herself, a conglomerate of smaller computers similar to the Gods, which had united under a common cause and, eventually, a common identity. Each part of Her, a deadly tangle of wires and flames and nothing but the will to destroy.

At the edge of the planet's atmosphere, the very lip of space, suspended between the planet's roil and the Keres', flickered something else. Something almost human. Ev's face emerged from that sunset flicker, distorted, coming apart at the edges. But the eyes behind their glasses were clear and sharp. The eyes were fixed on her.

See, said Ev. *Don't you see? This is how it will work.*

And Yasira could see it. The multitude of paths that had been prepared for her, like the tumblers in a lock, fit for a specific key. She could pull the flock of birds that was herself entirely apart. She could let herself fall down those paths, skimming across the surface of the atmosphere, until she ignited. Until she was one with that awful swarm of killing machines above her, and the worse thing that lay further away. Into Nemesis herself. Until the whole thing burst apart in a surge of white-hot flame.

It would be easy, in an awful way. Like when she'd first touched Ev's prayer machine, that awful nebula that had bloomed from its surface, the surge of insight that had felt like flying and screaming and being utterly annihilated. She'd wanted to die, back then – she'd had to, or she wouldn't have had the courage to use the machine. But she had survived. Or at least, something had, wearing her old self's skin. This would be the same.

And it would save everyone.

Some part of her wanted it. Some small fraction of the birds in her flock – the weaker-willed ones, the ones that wanted to save people and please people – had already slid a small way down those paths, mesmerized. The rest of Yasira pulled them back. She swiveled a hundred birdlike heads and glared at Ev, drawing herself tightly together.

I won't, she snarled. *It's not right and it's not fair and you can't make me.*

Well, the choice is yours, said Ev, who had put this whole thing together on her behalf. Ev had woven together disparate arcane and awful mechanisms that Yasira hadn't even begun to understand, just to make this process smoother, just to help Yasira along in this work that only Yasira could do. Her voice was calm. Her face was already fading back into that shimmering layer of the atmosphere, like an oil slick over the planet. But she looked disappointed.

Yasira awoke to a knock at the door.

"Who is it?" she growled, clutching her head.

"It's Ev," came the expected muffled voice. "I'm not here to change your mind. But if the part of the plan where you die isn't workable, then we of course need to rely on our other resources more heavily. I'd like to show you a few things."

"Ugggh," said Yasira, but she rolled off the bed, stood up, and opened the door.

True to her word, Ev didn't mention Yasira dying again. She took her instead through the airlock, and into a seemingly empty desert. Yasira only knew they were on the surface of Jai because of the weird feeling to the desert, the one she'd come to know in her bones. The way the sands shifted, the way little mouths like antlions lurked underneath them. The way some of the rocks themselves seemed to reach out, like statues frozen mid-motion, amorphously beseeching or grasping at something.

"This is where I've been conducting some of my own research," said Ev as they entered a cleft in the rocks. Yasira abruptly realized – like a 3D illusion snapping into place – that this was not just a cave. It was an abandoned observatory, dug into the stone by human hands, warped slightly by the Plague. The strange round protrusion she'd seen from a distance, like a bubble in the rocks' surface, wasn't an Outside effect; it was the dome, now shut, through which some massive telescope had once pointed, casting its unblinking eye up through the dry, clear air into the heavens. Searching for insights about the galaxy – or at least, the insights that humans were graciously permitted to seek for themselves. The Gods, of course, already knew more.

It used to seem so natural to Yasira – that the Gods already knew everything. That they allowed humans to follow in their footsteps, drawing their own inferences, because it was good for the human soul to be curious. She used to be so grateful that the Gods allowed humans such exciting problems with which to exercise their minds. But no matter which part of her she consulted, she couldn't find a remaining scrap of gratitude. The Gods had known things, and They'd hoarded most of that knowledge away. Not for humanity's benefit, but for Their own.

"This is your new lair?" said Yasira, looking at the cleft in the rocks which had become rounder and more regular as they walked through, a human-made tunnel with doorways branching off on both sides. Recessed lights shone dimly from the ceiling, and somewhere Yasira could hear the hum of a generator.

"One of them. I've found it best to move around. Too much activity in one place, even the most secluded, and I'd risk the Gods catching on. But this place, I believe, has remained undiscovered, and it will make an excellent ground base when the battle begins. I've outfitted it with communications equipment of my own design. There's a mildly heretical computer in one of these side rooms which can connect to the angels' private ansible net, at least to parts of it one of us has encountered before. Coding isn't my strongest suit, and I haven't yet managed any kind of malware that can get past the angels' defenses, but I have worked out how to send a message or two, and that alone provides us an inroad that might be useful later."

"We can send messages into the angel nets?" Yasira interrupted, surprised. "Anonymously?"

"Well, technically the origin of the message will be

untraceable, but it won't be difficult to guess that it's us. Their system doesn't usually allow for untraceable messages, and they aren't entirely oblivious."

"We could use that," she said – it was the Scientist coming to the surface, giddy with possibility. "We could confuse them in the battle and throw them off the trail by sending false reports, or just clog up their networks with–"

She quieted abruptly, remembering that it wasn't the angels of Nemesis they were fighting anymore. It was something else, something they'd seen in history vids but had never encountered themselves. Those methods wouldn't work on the Keres.

"Yes, well," said Ev. "You're right, that may be useful at some later date. In the meantime, I've been working on something larger. Come look in here."

She turned a corner, and the tunnel of rock opened out into a larger, domed space. This must have been where the big telescope had once been; the high curve of the ceiling had once opened out into an aperture for it to stare out at the sky. It was closed now, though, and more of those recessed lights dimly illuminated the cavernous roundness that remained. There were a set of benches and panels to one side, powered down but full of complicated lights, radar screens, microphones and speakers. It had the look of something Ev had built, blocky and patched together with exposed joints and wires. And in the center of the room–

There on the dais where the big telescope must once have been, there stood a mechanical monstrosity as big and intricate as the prayer machine had once been. Yasira couldn't immediately identify its function. It was just levers and wires and hydraulic arms all over the place, and a kind of empty orb in the middle, a place where Outside energies would no doubt gather and be concentrated.

"What the fuck," said Yasira, skin crawling, "is that?"

"It's an amplifier," said Ev. "I've been talking to the gone people; and I've been monitoring the Outside energies of the Chaos Zone. When you did your miracle at the beginning of the Plague, you handed ownership of those energies over to the collective unconscious of the Chaos Zone's human survivors, gone and otherwise. And now, thanks to the Gods' grandstanding, each and every one of those survivors knows they are under threat. Even the gone people have acknowledged it this time, which should tell you something about the seriousness of the situation."

"I know about the seriousness of the situation," some part of Yasira snapped. The Scientist was listening raptly to every word, as were some of the more obscure Outside parts. But the rest of her was impatient. It was hard to listen to Ev's rambling when what her gut told her was to get the fuck out of this room. Even turned off, the amplifier – like the prayer machine – made her skin crawl.

"Indeed. As a result of all this, in some sense, the entire Chaos Zone is aware it's under threat. Like any other creature that feels itself threatened, it's drawing up defenses around itself. I'm not sure the precise form those defenses will take, but my guess would be some form of energy shielding or redirection, perhaps combined with a more active defense, something to lash out at the attackers. I don't know that it would be enough to hold up against the Keres' largest weapons. But by my best calculations, it's likely that it could soften the effects. Buy us some time. In conjunction with your team's ongoing efforts…"

Yasira frowned. She wanted to be as far away from that

amplifier as possible, but more parts of her were joining the Scientist's side, fascinated, trying to trace the implications. "What are we talking about defending here? The Chaos Zone, or the whole planet?"

"In the current configuration, the whole planet. The Keres' primary target will likely be the Chaos Zone, but the rest of Jai is in danger of collateral, or of being fixed in Her sights next, and we wouldn't want the Chaos Zone's defenses to thoughtlessly redirect damage to other populated regions. What I'm attempting to do with this amplifier is not only to strengthen the gone people's efforts, but to ensure the energy is guided properly and evenly across the planet for everyone's protection."

"That's good," said Yasira. It was good, and somehow suspect – it wasn't like Ev to be so careful about bystanders' safety.

"I did learn that lesson from you," Ev said, as if reading her thoughts. Maybe she *was* reading Yasira's thoughts; she'd done it before. "About defending everyone, about everyone's life being worth something, even ordinary people who can't ever understand people like us. I've been passing it on to the gone people, too, or trying to, although I'm beginning to suspect most of them already knew."

Yasira stifled a smile, at that, despite herself. "They're a superorganism. I think in a lot of ways, they know it better than either of us."

"Well, discussions are ongoing." Ev shrugged. "But you know I'm skilled at this – guiding and directing Outside energies is a specialty of mine. It's how I caused the Plague and its predecessors in the first place. I'd like to use it for a better end this time. I had meant to reserve a good portion of the energy to bolster you, to guide your ascension, but in the absence of that, I can make adjustments. Perhaps feed that energy back into the defensive effort, or…"

She trailed off, muttering under her breath, and Yasira watched her uneasily. As much as this place repelled her, it was proof that Ev had been working busily. Her work would be useful, maybe even necessary for the coming fight. She hadn't only come swooping in, expecting Yasira to die for her. She *had* done that, but she'd done all this as well, on her own, as diligently as any of the Seven. Her work would be useful, maybe even necessary for the coming fight. Yasira wasn't sure if that made her feel better or worse.

Ascension. As if dying in a fight with a God, and never existing as a whole person again – maybe not existing at all anymore – was simply a transition to something better. She didn't believe it.

"Oh," said Ev, "and there's one other thing. The refugees."

She turned distractedly and walked out of the room, and Yasira hurried to follow her.

Ev walked through the airlock to a city square – this was a city called Huang-Bo, on Riayin's humid southern border, once large and prosperous, now half-covered in weird marshland and poison vines that might snatch passersby and strangle them at any given moment. This patch of chiseled stone hadn't originally been the largest city square in Huang-Bo, or the most central, or the most prosperous – but it was the highest in elevation and the driest, and these days that was where people flocked when they needed something.

In the past half-year, Ev had grown used to these Riayin cities encompassed by the Chaos Zone, corrupted – though she hated that word, *corrupted,* as if the ways of being that made sense to her were dirtier or more sinful than everyone else's – into an Outside-influenced form. The human-built portions of the architecture were tidier and more compact than what she'd grown up with on Anetaia, but these were small stylistic differences. Old Earth had harbored thousands of cultures, all with their own intricate material and social cultures, with markedly different, sometimes fully incompatible views of the world. The Gods had intentionally mixed humans together, on their new worlds, in ways that flattened out those differences to aesthetic quirks. Nowadays, different human nations looked different; some were a little more efficient or better at a certain kind of social program than others. But all of them followed the same Gods' blueprints, the same Gods' plans for their lives.

The changes she'd wrought in the Chaos Zone were the first real, fundamental changes any human nation had undergone in hundreds of years. And it was these changes, paradoxically, that made her feel at home. Streets, landforms, and buildings bore shapes that changed over time, unpredictably, the way everything in Ev's perception had always changed. Monsters, chasms, and other dangers lurked, just as life had always felt dangerous to Ev, for as long as she could remember. Gone people milled in their herds on the outskirts of the city, somewhere far but not too far from here, interconnected with each other in ways that superseded individuality. Other parts of the natural world had become more interconnected, too, though the survivors had not yet studied their woods and fields closely enough to realize it. Just as everything had always been interconnected and multivalent to Ev's senses. She had remade a large portion of this world in her own image, and there was such an instinctive rightness to it, such a sense that this was how everything had always been – consumed with that sense, it had taken her a long time to admit the hubris in it, patterning this whole nation's existence after her own particular view of the Truth, her own particular feelings. To most survivors, this existence was a horror, and it had taken a great deal of time to cultivate any empathy or patience for that view. To Ev, the true horror had always been the facade of normality and the pain that would result from even the smallest deviation.

She looked out now at the people gathered in the city square. Families, frightened parents clutching their children close, couples of all ages clinging tightly together as if mere physical contact could overcome the danger. Elderly people bent double, leaning on their mobility devices; other visibly disabled people, alone or assisted by family and friends. Many miscellaneous groups clumped together in more ambiguous ways – these were the chosen families that had become more common since the Plague, when many actual families were decimated. Or just groups that had found themselves in proximity to each other and preferred to face the danger in the company of others.

They were gathered here because she had told them to be here. In this and other cities, she'd made the arrangements, as a proof-of-concept test of the time-traveling airlock, going back to the beginning of the day as many times as necessary in order to visit every city and make herself understood. She hadn't openly announced that she was the one they called Destroyer, but neither did she make a secret of it. These people knew it was her. Those who had gathered at her request were those so desperate that they were willing to trust even her.

Or hear her out, at least.

"I'm not going to sugar-coat this," said Ev to the crowd, in a voice that would carry. She had very little shyness speaking to crowds; she had gotten over that in her days as a professor, giving countless lectures to countless classrooms of students who mostly didn't care and didn't absorb much of it anyway. "You all are in danger, and I can't take you out of it. You are citizens of the Chaos Zone. Whether you have overt Outside powers or not, you are tainted by Outside – or at the very least, the Gods will see you that way. Taking you out of the Chaos Zone won't solve that. I'm not offering to solve it. But I'm offering you a choice.

"If you stay here, the Keres will attack the planet. You won't be undefended. My team have been working on countermeasures, and so have the gone people and the planet itself, and there will be a couple of other factors too. I think we'll win. But I can't guarantee anything. Battles kill people. Your city will take damage. You'll get hurt. And this may not be the last battle you see.

"Or else: I've got this portal here. You can go through it. I can spit you out on another planet, far from here. But that's all I can do. Understand what you're signing up for if you do this. You may or may not be able to hide that you're from the Chaos Zone. If you can't hide it, you will be hunted. You will be punished. You will be treated like a disease, because everyone outside the Chaos Zone is afraid of you and what you represent. You'll be treated worse than I was. I can't fix that for you. As long as the Gods exist, these are the choices you have, and believe me, I'm *working* on the problem of the Gods existing. But I can't make promises about that any more than I can about the battle."

She could feel Yasira shift uncomfortably beside her. Ever

since the prayer machine, Ev had felt a kinship with Yasira that she wasn't sure how to classify. They had been, for one sacred moment, on the same wavelength; she remembered what it had been like to be Yasira. It was like something different now, of course. Yasira had a terrible habit of feeling responsible for other people. Ev had begun her own work too callously; she was probably still too callous. Yasira was the reverse, and Ev had learned from her, up to a point.

So Ev could sense the guilt that Yasira felt now, and she could extrapolate its probable cause. Yasira didn't want to sacrifice herself to destroy Nemesis, but if she did not do so, the danger to these other people would be prolonged. Yasira wasn't neurotypical – that was part of what Ev liked about her – but she shared the vexing neurotypical tendency to feel more empathy for people who were right there in front of her face than for people who were elsewhere. She could feel Yasira beside her swallowing hard, looking down, trying not to look any of those people in the eye. Ev, for whatever reason, lacked that problem.

In truth, she wasn't as worried as Yasira seemed to think. Ev frequently remembered things out of order. It wasn't always a vivid, sensory memory; it used to be, when she was young, but the vicious therapies she'd undergone had taken the vividness away. These days, Ev more often remembered things as facts. It was a fact, as clear as what she'd learned through experimentation or read in a book, that Yasira would destroy the Gods.

Ev had assumed, based on her own calculations, that sacrificing herself in the battle with the Keres was how Yasira would do it. But maybe not. If she refused it now, maybe she'd change her mind later – or maybe, in time, she would find another way.

"I'm not offering this out of the goodness of my heart," she said to the would-be refugees, many of whom had begun to cry, or to cover their faces in despair. "I'm offering because it's a part of my battle plan. The Gods can try to destroy half a planet, maybe a whole planet. They can hunt you down individually, or at least most of you. But they can't get every planet, and they can't get all of you. I'm not Savior, and even Savior can't save you all. But I am at war with the Gods, and you can help me make it into a war they can't win."

Whether she believed it or not, Yasira had done this much: she'd helped Ev learn to consider the fates of ordinary people. Deep down, Ev still struggled with the urge to hurt everyone, indiscriminately. To make everyone pay. For hurting her, or allowing her to be hurt, or just for the crime of going about their ordinary lives, unaware or uncaring of what happened to people like Ev. But she'd learned that this urge was not helpful; her suffering wasn't most of these people's fault, and most of them had suffering of their own. Ev had not progressed to caring deeply about that suffering the way Yasira did; maybe she never would. But she could, at least, be fair to the people who remained. She could tell them the truth. She could offer them the options she was able to offer.

"Those are your choices," she concluded. "It's not a good choice, and I won't pretend it is. But if you like the choice of leaving more than the choice of staying, then I've got a portal here. And I've got all day. Anything to add, Savior?"

Yasira swallowed and shook her head. She'd backed up very close to the portal leading back to the lair. Ev and Yasira were still two of the galaxy's most wanted people. It wasn't illogical to fear that a few angels might have been left on the ground here, just in case the heretics showed their faces. They hadn't, of course, or at least not here – Ev could sense those things as well as Grid could. But she didn't blame Yasira for not quite trusting that, and for sticking close to a quick getaway.

The would-be refugees in the crowd weren't happy. Ev watched them confer. Some threw up their hands in despair, shook their heads, trudged away, back to their homes or whatever shelters the people in this city were constructing.

But one small family, just a ragged mother and father and their pre-pubescent child, stepped forward.

There would be another after them, and another. And then more, here and in the other cities. Ev remembered them all.

CHAPTER 11

Elu was taking too long with that damned angel of the Keres. Akavi tapped his fingernails on the *Talon*'s control panel, irate with impatience. Something had attacked them. He wanted to know why.

He wanted to know, in particular, if it had anything to do with the unsettling message that had arrived on the *Talon*'s console during the battle. Akavi had not yet shown this message to anyone. He ran a careful finger down the console's touch screen, letting the bewildering letters of the message scroll past him.

In the old days, a message like this could have been beamed directly into his brain. That was not an option any longer, since Akavi had been disconnected from the angels' ansible nets. More to the point, the *Talon* had also been disconnected – twice over. First with Talirr's own strange Outside magic, and then, more permanently, through extraction and disposal of all transceivers. This had all been necessary in order to prevent them from being discovered by the Gods. Receiving a message like this ought not to have lain within the ship's capabilities.

Unless, of course, it was Talirr's Outside magic. Talirr had disabled the *Talon*'s connections before Akavi had, covering the ship in a strange black mist. Perhaps some remnant of that mist had lingered, too small and deep inside the ship's circuits for Akavi to see. Perhaps that was how she had delivered her message – or perhaps she'd had some other, baffling, arcane means. Perhaps she still had control, invisibly, over other aspects of the ship. This irked him.

You want revenge, said the message in plain and unadorned Earth creole, *against those you believe have wronged you. Nemesis has wronged you. You know this.*

What this means is that we have a common enemy.

Find me.

– Dr Evianna Talirr

That was the vexing thing about Talirr. The technological mysticism at her command was like nothing else; even Akavi didn't understand it. But her use of the mundanities of words, of social skills, was clumsy in the extreme.

Of course they had a common enemy. Akavi already had plans to deal with that enemy, using Yasira, who was also his enemy. Talirr was simply another enemy on the list. She *must* know that she could not trust him. The message, then, was bait. Clumsy, except for the alarmingly casual way she had infiltrated his ship's systems.

He had already run diagnostics. The origin of the message could not be traced. It had come with an encrypted return address, but the best of the *Talon*'s systems could not unravel where that address led. Reply, and as far as the God-built systems could tell, the reply would vanish into the ether.

Into Outside.

Talirr was trying to draw him out. And she had alarmingly complete command of her own skill set. But she was clumsy with people, and Akavi was not. If this was the game that she wanted to play, he could play it. He could draw *her* out. Then, perhaps, his revenge could be made complete.

Just as long as he didn't let on about it to Elu or Enga or Luellae. The fewer people who were exposed to Talirr's maddening influence, the better.

Akavi smiled to himself as he typed into the reply box: *And where shall I find you, exactly?*

He did not receive a reply.

Before there were bots, Old Humans had once done surgery with their own gloved hands. Elu had always thanked the Gods that this was no longer the case. On the makeshift operating table in his quarters, with the angel of the Keres' skull open and his mental circuitry out to the air, it was almost too much to look at. His hands were shaking so badly he didn't think he could have cut bread. It was the most skillful of the bots that did the real work for him, prying the flesh away and manipulating the wires. He had turned his sensory recording program on so that he and Akavi could go over important clips from the interrogation in detail later, but he didn't relish the thought that he was going to have to look at this again.

Even through the sedative, the angel was crying.

"Where is She?" he whispered. "Where is She? I can't feel Her."

Elu wanted to pretend he couldn't guess what the angel meant. He'd had an inkling that he knew, from the first time he saw the angel's face. Now the angel's skull lay open before him and he could see the intricate ways that the angel's neural circuitry wound into his organic brain.

It was barbaric – something even Nemesis wouldn't do. But it was physically possible, even efficient in its way.

The angel of the Keres' neural circuitry, the parts of his mind built to communicate with his deity, were wired straight into his limbic system. A thick tangle of wires nestled into the nucleus accumbens; a second tangle, its twin, branched out into exactly the right parts of the amygdala and insula. The pleasure centers of the brain and the parts that felt pain.

Nemesis kept Her angels in check through external rewards and punishments, up to and including physical torture. But the Keres had chosen to bypass all that. She could send reward and punishment signals to the brain directly. Pure spiritual delight; pure spiritual pain.

Elu knew exactly how a God like the Keres would have used a pair of connections like this on an angel like this – it was obvious from the very design. She would have constantly supplied him with a current of delight, so long as he stayed in his ship and followed orders. And the opposite, a direct jolt of pain, every time he thought of disobeying. His world had narrowed down to just those two stimuli, so intensely that he didn't even mind living tangled up in that awful web of pipes and wires where Enga had found him, barely a human. And then Enga had unplugged him from those currents, leaving him alone and unstimulated for what might be the first time in decades. Centuries.

There was a *reason* even Nemesis didn't use these methods. This level of connection into the limbic system could produce an addiction so powerful it put Old Humans' hard drugs to shame. A withdrawal syndrome so strong that it cut through God-built sedatives. A person so dependent on their God couldn't think abstractly or make complex decisions, not in the ways that Nemesis and the other true Gods needed their angels to do. Every part of their mind would atrophy but the raw nerve of devotion that responded to their God's presence, their God's orders, until nothing else mattered.

When Elu and Akavi had removed the ansible uplinks from their brains, they had gone through a kind of withdrawal. An awful emptiness and restlessness as their minds struggled to adjust to the silence. Any brain would struggle with the sudden removal of something it was accustomed to. But whatever was going on inside this angel's mind, it was stronger than what Elu had gone through by many orders of magnitude.

"She'll be back soon," Elu promised, but the angel just wept and thrashed, within the limits of his restraints. Elu wasn't even sure if he understood the words.

The bots had connected the ports within his skull to the ship's computer, so as to hack into the inorganic portion of the brain, replicate the data within a secure virtual sandbox, and analyze it at their leisure. That was the logical way to interrogate an angel. Every angel had decades of intricate data structures in their head, sensory videos and abstract data files, everything they'd wanted to record for themselves at a higher fidelity and with less data loss than organic memory. Elu did too. A person could learn all sorts of intimate things about Elu, if they managed to capture him like this, crack his head open, and plug in to his central processor.

He knew how he would feel if someone did that to him – violated to the point of being turned inside out. But this angel seemed oblivious to what the bots were doing. His concerns lay elsewhere.

"Please," the man begged, tears leaking from his eyes. "Please, where is She?"

"She's not far," said Elu, with a finality that surprised him. "She'll be here soon."

Elu turned to the bots, stomach roiling at what he was about to do, and muttered a new set of commands.

"Are you sure?" the nearest bot chirruped, its voice too cheerful and too loud. The medical bots weren't sentient. They objected to these commands only because these commands were listed, in Nemesis' records, as commands that should be objected to. "A procedure of this nature is likely to result in–"

"I'm sure," said Elu, clenching his teeth. "Override further warnings."

"Acknowledged," said the bot.

The angel on the operating table moaned in a kind of despair that had nothing to do with anything Elu had just said and everything to do with the wasteland that had been made of his mind.

"Soon," Elu promised, but he didn't know if the angel could hear him.

As he watched, the bot he'd spoken to set itself to installing a couple of extra wires. It didn't take long – just an inroad into the system already in place. It attached a new input source that connected to the angel's nucleus accumbens, and then it quietly switched on a current. Not much of one. The smallest one its God-built circuits could possibly produce. Pure, sheer, addictive bliss, trickling in the tiniest quantities into the pleasure centers of the angel's brain.

The angel sighed. In only a second and a half, his face relaxed into the expression that a sedated patient ought to have. A wistful smile played at the corner of his lips; his eyes unfocused, then fluttered shut.

"Is that Her?" Elu asked, revolted. He had to be sure.

"Yes." The angel's brow furrowed slightly. "Something's wrong. She's far away. She's not speaking. She ought to speak. But She's here."

Just the current, then. But none of the actual connection to the Keres' networks. Just the feeling he'd grown to associate with Her. Judging from the smile on his face now, that – or that, plus the sedative – was enough.

With the angel quiet, Elu turned his attention to the bots. They had already worked their way in to the angel's circuitry, and now they were busy downloading a system image into the *Talon*'s sandbox.

"Update?" Elu asked them.

"System download seventy percent complete. Initial files and file structure ready for preliminary inspection, but not all files will be fully realized for perusal until download is complete."

Elu nodded. "Show me the file structure. And the network."

"System is not presently connected to the network. Wireless network capacities appear to have been disabled or removed. However, a snapshot of the last known working network configuration is available in memory. Is that what you would like to see?"

"Yes, fine."

A large, complex diagram sprang into existence on the tablet on the side table. Elu peered down at it, annoyed by the primitive touchscreen interface. He'd been using these for six months, but he'd never really gotten used to it – it had been so much easier when he could download even the most complex information directly into his mind.

He made his way through the diagram, swiping and

zooming with his fingertips. Akavi would need to know how many Keres ships there were, how they organized themselves. Despite the physical chaos inside the Keres' ship, the network structure was as regular and logical as Nemesis' – and the interior pattern was the same. There were various ships, each with a single pilot, something analogous to Nemesis' Helms, each one connected to something like an Overseer in the upper hierarchy. This network snapshot was from hours ago, and there wouldn't be much useful data about where those ships were now, but there would still be a lot to pore over in the records of their prior movements, their habits. This was the sort of data trove that Nemesis' analysts could extract meaning from for years.

The network link leading upwards from the Overseer was encrypted.

Elu frowned slightly. It was unusual for angels to encrypt their memories. Encryption kept information out of consciousness, so that the angel wouldn't remember their most sensitive knowledge and couldn't blurt it out in a moment of weakness – but it was a lot of work and not especially effective, or at least not when an interrogator had progressed to this stage. In order for the angel to access the memory themselves, the decryption key had to be stored somewhere inside their head, which meant it could be easily found. All it would be was a short delay.

"Search for the decryption key and decrypt this," he said, tapping the link on the screen. "Decrypt it in the live system, too."

"Processing."

A status bar appeared on the screen, and the angel of the Keres moved his head slightly as the bots probed deeper into his circuitry. It didn't take long, just a few minutes of Elu tapping his foot, trying not to wonder what he was going to find. He wasn't sure why an angel would bother to encrypt something like this, when it ought to be obvious what was there – just the record of a connection to an Archangel, if the Keres had those. Or else to the Keres Herself.

"Download complete," said the tablet at last. "Decryption complete."

Elu tapped on the connection upwards from the Overseer again – and then paused as the name of the connection came into view.

Attrick Munn, Archangel of Nemesis.

That didn't make sense. That couldn't be. That was the Archangel who *Irimiru* reported to.

There must be some mistake.

With a shaking hand, Elu expanded the connections around the Archangel.

The network snapshot only went so far. Regions of the network that this angel had never cared about were visible only as a blur. But Elu could read enough. He could read the names of several of the other Archangels connected to that one, which were, indeed, the names of Archangels of Nemesis. He could read the names of the other Overseers who answered to that Archangel, most of which he recognized. There was Irimiru, right in the chart where they ought to be. He could see, even though it didn't make any sense, the name of the link that reached upward from the Archangel to the God Herself.

To Nemesis.

It didn't make sense. He must have misunderstood the network diagram. This must be some kind of spy node or tap inserted into Nemesis' network – a mole program, devised with the Keres' wiles, that had broken into Nemesis' network in order to fight Her more effectively. Disguised as just another link between the Archangel Attrick Munn and one of his Overseers, so as to fit in more effectively. It was clever, if so. Too clever. It had given him a fright.

"What's your name?" Elu asked the angel on the table. His voice shook. "Do you have a name?"

The angel made a noncommittal noise.

"What's the name of your Overseer?" Elu asked.

"Haydeen Byroee, Overseer of the Keres," said the angel, dreamy but perfectly intelligible.

"How did your Overseer hack into Nemesis' networks?"

The angel tilted his head, bleary and euphoric. Elu wasn't a good interrogator – he didn't know how to put the fear of the Gods into the people he had at his mercy. But what every Inquisitor of Nemesis knew, and didn't want to admit, was that fear and pain weren't the only ways to pry answers out of people. If someone trusted him, if they *wanted* to be heard, sometimes they'd just say things. And this angel must know, at some level, that Elu was the one making sure he could have what he craved.

"Why would he do that?" said the angel, sounding genuinely puzzled.

"Look at the network image in your head. What's the link going upwards in the hierarchy from your Overseer? Can you see it?"

"Of course I can see it," said the angel placidly.

"Who does your Overseer answer to in the network?"

"Attrick Munn, Archangel of Nemesis."

Elu's hands were shaking worse, now. Maybe this was a mistake. Maybe this wasn't an angel of the Keres, but some kind of undercover agent. He wouldn't put that past Nemesis, especially if She was on the trail of a dangerous group of fallen angels. Three whole fallen angels, now.

He had to phrase these questions carefully. He remembered that much from the interrogation classes he'd failed, and from Akavi. A leading question could lead to all sorts of confusion.

"Are you an angel of Nemesis?" he asked. "Undercover?"

"No."

"Are you an angel of the Keres?"

"Yes."

"When you say *She* – the God that you expect to speak to you, the one you're loyal to – do you mean the Keres?"

"Yes."

"Is your Overseer an angel of the Keres?"

"Yes."

"Why is he connected hierarchically to an Archangel of Nemesis?"

The angel of the Keres looked surprised that he'd had to ask. "Because that's how it works."

This must be a mistake. The angel's answers were too vague. Elu was reading into them – not what he wanted to hear, but what he feared to. The awful idea that he couldn't get out of his head, now that he'd thought it.

Nemesis fought against the Keres at every turn. Her angels bled and died to keep the Keres away from human settlements. Nemesis was so quick to remind everyone that She played that role, in every story and every bit of propaganda. No matter how She fought, there were always just enough Keres attacks that slipped briefly past Her defenses, just often enough and causing just enough damage and fear, to give those stories teeth.

The Chaos Zone had defied Nemesis, and the Keres had shown up as quickly as She possibly could without portals, waiting to attack the instant it was convenient for Nemesis to let Her do so.

Nemesis had announced the impending attack, in Her goodbye broadcast to all of the people of Jai, with such *glee*.

Elu wasn't sure if he was breathing, but somehow his voice still came out of his mouth as he willed. "Do you follow your Overseer's orders?"

"Of course."

"Do your Overseer's orders come from Nemesis?"

"Yes."

Elu's ears were ringing. He felt like he might abruptly lose his balance, though he was standing quite still. "Do all of the Keres' orders come from Nemesis?"

"Yes." The angel cast a curious, vague, childlike glance in Elu's direction. "Don't you know that? That's how it's always been. That's what we're made for. We put on a show. She protects the mortals, like the children they are, and we remind them of why they need protecting."

We put on a show.

Elu remembered being five years old, standing on his balcony with his mortal mother's arms wrapped around him protectively. Looking up at the strange fireworks in the sky. Smelling the smoke, hearing the screams in the street below him. He had asked his mother if this was the end of the world. His mother, beautiful and strong through her fear, had murmured: *No, love, this isn't the end. We're not going to die, because Nemesis will save us. We just have to have faith, do you see? We all just have to have faith, and we'll live.* And then Nemesis' warships had come screaming through the sky, beautiful as lightning.

The Keres had attacked Elu's home planet, Preli. Fifty thousand mortals died, incinerated or crushed under the weight of falling buildings, but Elu's family had lived. He had grown up around the gaps left by a battle like that, the buildings hastily reassembled or left to gape open, the families and neighborhoods marked by strange, unspoken spaces where their fathers and siblings and neighbors had been. He had joined the angelic corps as soon as he turned nineteen because he knew what it was to be saved. He had hoped he could save someone else.

All the rest of this. The terrible surgeries. The way he'd been treated after he failed basic training. Akavi. The way running away with Akavi had begun to look like his best option, when they both knew Akavi was not the kind of person anyone should run away with. Everything else in Elu's potentially endless life that hurt. All of it, because he had believed what Nemesis told him.

Because he had been five years old, and he had seen a *show*.

Elu heard a sound coming out of his own mouth, barely louder than a whisper, something indefinable that was not quite a chuckle and not quite a sob and not quite a disbelieving breath being puffed out.

"I see," he said, and he was distantly astonished how calm his voice sounded. His voice wasn't shaking anymore.

He did not have time to waste on remonstrations or shouting, especially towards a prisoner who was too far gone to understand. He needed to think quickly. He was going to have to explain all of this to Akavi and Enga – poor Enga, who wouldn't even be able to text-send in response – and to Luellae. He had seen Akavi's thwarted rages before, and he was not keen on seeing them again. Akavi would have difficulty believing it. He would want to come in and speak to the prisoner himself, by his own methods.

Elu looked down at the pried-open top of the angel's skull. At the wire which was still, even now, supplying that steady current into the nucleus accumbens. Where Elu saw an abomination, a violation of the angel's mind, Akavi would see an opportunity. He would rip that wire right back out. Worse – there was the other set of wires, the set that led directly to the brain's pain centers, which Elu hadn't dared touch.

He had seen Akavi torture people before. This would be worse. He could not even imagine the screams. Akavi, in a rage, would delight in it. Elu could so easily imagine acting that way himself, if he was as cruel as Akavi and reeling from news like this.

Elu turned to the bots, feeling bloodless and lightheaded and very, very strange. "Is the download complete? Do we have every bit of information we could take from this man?"

"Yes," said the nearest bot. "Download complete."

Elu ended the sensory recording.

"I need to administer one more treatment," he said. He named a painkiller. He named a dosage.

The bot hesitated, even though he'd already told it to override further warnings. "Are you sure? That dosage is sufficiently large to–"

"Yes, I'm sure. Full override, and then delete the dose administration from memory." Why wasn't his voice shaking? Why wasn't he shouting, crying?

The bot obeyed him.

He watched it fill a syringe with a dose of painkiller far higher than should ever have been given to any human, mortal or otherwise. He watched it search out the vein. He watched the needle go in; he watched the bot push the plunger. The angel, too sedated to understand or care, didn't flinch.

Elu reached out and laid a hand on the angel's bare shoulder. It was more of a comfort than it ought to have been, touching someone. "It's all right," he promised, his voice low. "You'll be with Her again soon."

"Oh," said the angel, muzzy, beginning to slur the words. "Good."

It was quiet and it didn't take long. The angel closed his eyes. His breath slowed, then caught; there was a small, strange, gurgling choke. The app on the tablet that monitored vital signs started to urgently beep. Elu stood still.

Only when it was over, when the heart had gone flat and the soul had departed the body, did he slump back against the sky-blue wall of his own room and start to cry.

CHAPTER 12

At first, Luellae didn't understand what Elu was saying. She was too busy nursing the wound around her wrist, now cleaned and bandaged. During the infinitesimal time they'd spent in the vacuum of space, her skin had frozen to Enga's metal hand like a kid sticking their tongue to a pole in the dead of winter, and even the gentlest bot-aided separation had ripped off a whole layer.

Luellae hated this stupid ship and these stupid people. She hated the way the *Talon* looked, like a cute stylish parlor that happened to have God-built computer panels all over it and a fancy pair of pilot's chairs at the front. Human ships were never allowed such luxury. She wanted to teleport away – but she couldn't, not while they still floated in space, not with millions of miles of that horrifying empty cold all around them. She'd die.

So when Elu stumbled out of his room and up the short hallway to the cockpit, looking pale and shaky and positively ill, she didn't feel any sympathy. Luellae knew all about Elu already. He knew how to say the right things, like he cared about the people who were at his mercy, but he never let them go free.

"I found–" he said, and then his voice faltered. He

swallowed hard and tried again. "I found. The network. I found out. I found out a thing."

Luellae raised her eyebrows, but she didn't feel like dignifying that with a reply. And Enga couldn't talk, so it fell to Akavi to answer. "Report, then. Don't just stand there."

"The angel of the Keres disconnected from the network as soon as Enga unplugged him. He didn't have an inbuilt ansible connection; he just plugged in to the one on his ship. But I found his last known network image, and I decrypted and verbally confirmed. The Keres' network is connected to Nemesis' network. It's taking Nemesis' orders. This whole time – the Keres *is* Nemesis. The Keres isn't a different God, a failed God. She's what Nemesis sends out to scare everyone else into line."

There was a dead silence. Luellae's heart pounded, her own pulse audible in her ears. That couldn't be true. Even for Nemesis, it didn't make sense. Could it?

Nemesis was a liar – everyone knew that – but...

"Are you certain?" said Akavi at last. His skin had started to ripple strangely, like he couldn't keep all his attention on maintaining the face that he wore. "That's a wild story. The angel could have lied to you. You're gullible, as you know."

Elu's voice was tight and strangled. Beads of sweat stood out on his forehead. "I know what I saw."

"Let me speak to him and corroborate." Akavi took an impatient step towards Elu's room, and Elu scrambled backwards a step, holding out his hands.

"The angel – uh – sir, the angel didn't survive the procedure."

Akavi gave him a withering look.

"I saved sensory video of the interrogation," Elu added,

looking at the floor. "And the full contents of the brain in its last good state. You'll be able to verify it all."

"I should hope so," Akavi snapped. "For your sake."

He pushed past Elu and stormed into the room, slamming the door behind him.

Luellae pulled her knees close to her chest, feeling dizzy with shock. She hated herself for reeling. What did it matter to her if Nemesis and the Keres were the same or different? They were both bullshit. They'd both done untold horrors to countless people.

"I'm... I'm sorry," Elu stammered, looking between her and Enga.

"Sorry for what?" Luellae snapped. "Are you sorry for kidnapping people? Keeping them prisoner? Torturing them? Or did you only just start being sorry because someone else above you in the hierarchy told a lie? Fuck you. Fuck *sorry*. All three of you. Fuck you all."

She didn't care if Nemesis and the Keres were the same or not, or at least that's what she was telling herself, but something in her seethed like a volcano.

Elu opened his mouth like he was going to argue, but Enga moved first. She hauled herself to her feet and stormed off to the third bedroom, the one she'd been sharing with Luellae. There was a crashing sound from that room, and a thud, and another crash.

Elu looked between her and the door to that room.

"Go," said Luellae, disgusted. Like he needed her permission. And he skittered away.

Enga was breaking things. Mostly the spare room's two small beds, since there wasn't much else in there. As Elu entered the room, a piece of bed frame hit the wall by his head and shattered into sharp pieces. Enga had never seriously injured another angel, and had rarely harmed civilians without permission, but given her strength and her sheer number of weapons, a meltdown like this could be lethal. Elu normally knew Enga's moods, but this was not a normal circumstance, and he wasn't sure if he should be in here. If she wanted comfort. If she wanted to be left alone.

One way to find out.

Elu picked up a miraculously still-intact tablet and tapped a few times on the touch screen, calling up a program. Just a simple one, text-to-speech, with the letters of the Earth creole alphabet displayed big and even on the screen. He proffered it.

"I'll leave you alone," he said, as she crashed around kicking the broken sides of Luellae's bed, "if you'd rather. But. It's not right what we've done to you. And if you want to talk–"

Without even looking at him, Enga telescoped out a long metal grabber appendage and snatched the tablet out of his hands. She pulled it close to herself and started to type furiously.

FUCK IT, said a toneless voice from the tablet. *TALIRR WAS FUCKING RIGHT IT'S ALL A LIE.*

Enga wasn't a true believer in Nemesis' cause. Elu hadn't even been sure, at first, if this revelation would matter to her the way it did to him. But the reason why she didn't truly believe had to do with how she'd been lied to and betrayed in the course of her ascension. And this was an even bigger lie. Any scraps of belief, any crumbs of loyalty that she'd held to in order to survive and keep doing the job – perhaps this had broken them all.

"I'm sorry," he said.

YOU ARE NOT SORRY. YOU ARE BROKEN. EVERYTHING FUCKING BROKE

She kicked over an already-very-broken fragment of the bed for emphasis, sending shattered metal and bent washers and nails scattering everywhere.

Elu eased backwards a little bit, touching the cool solidity of the wall behind him. "You're not broken," he started, hesitantly, but all she did was turn and start to beat her head into the wall. That one appendage, sticking out from her at an odd angle, kept typing. *YOU ARE NOT LISTENING*

"I'm sorry," Elu said again. It was habit for him to be sorry for everything, a reflex that Akavi had never liked and that he'd never shaken off. "Please don't hurt yourself."

Enga hit her head against the wall twice more, just to prove she could, and then stopped the motion and snatched up a jagged shard of bed frame. She brandished it, pointing its sharp end at Elu, less as a threat and more to get his attention. *YOU ARE NOT LISTENING. LOOK AT THIS*

"I'm looking at it. But I don't understand."

Enga raised her chin and looked directly at him. There was something in her face – something Elu couldn't help but think of as a facial expression, even though technically Enga didn't have those. Enga didn't have the microexpressions that angelic face-reading software liked to pick up on. Her arms didn't move like normal people's arms either. But Enga could make it clear how she felt, if you were paying attention. Enga's feelings were written up and down the slump of her spine, the cant of her shoulders, the clenching and unclenching of all the little mechanisms in her arms. And the way she looked at him felt like fire, something burning, boring into him.

Enga had been like this always, ever since he met her.

She was wounded, but she had not crumbled because of her wounds. The wounds, the rage, were what powered her.

IT'S BROKEN, she said. *I'M BROKEN. YOU'RE BROKEN. WE ARE BROKEN AND BROKEN THINGS HAVE SHARP EDGES*

Elu thought guiltily of the dead angel in the other room. How easy it had been to tell himself he'd done that out of mercy. And what a secret relief it had been, on some strange, hidden, animal level, when the person who had given him this news no longer meaningfully existed.

Enga had a better idea about this. Enga was a warrior. Even in the unreasoning rage of a meltdown, Enga would have a better sense of who was really responsible, and at whom those sharp edges could be pointed for the best effect.

He held out his hand, and Enga raised the broken bedframe fragment to him, let him wrap his hand around it next to hers.

"Yes," he said.

When he went back to his room to check on Akavi, it was only because there was no point delaying the inevitable. He had seen Akavi's thwarted rages before. Maybe there would be screaming. Maybe Akavi would hit him again. But if he hid with Enga and cowered, he would only make it worse.

Akavi was sitting on the edge of the stretcher-bed, in the incongruous pale blue of the room. He was looking out the window, at the small sharp points of the stars against the black, suffused with the violet glow of the warp drive. He hadn't bothered to put another face on over the inorganic, translucent shapes of his true form.

"You were correct," he said tonelessly, without turning around.

Elu hesitated. "Sir," he said.

"The evidence is all there. And you narrowed down on it with commendable efficiency. The same cannot be said for your clumsy attempt to hide that you killed him. I suppose that you must have been very angry."

There was no anger in that voice, no harshness, no emotion at all anymore. Akavi got like this sometimes, when a problem had fully absorbed him. Some setbacks would send him into a howling, vicious rage. Others, even things awful enough to make the rest of the team sick, would be received more like puzzles. Even after fifty years, Elu couldn't always predict what would get which reaction.

"I don't know, sir," he said. He was feeling a lot that he could scarcely make sense of. "Aren't you?"

"I was, briefly. But I got a hold of myself. Just as Enga eventually stopped smashing the furniture. But you–" His translucent lip curled. "You're weak as always. I don't think you're angry for the right reasons."

"I was *lied* to," Elu spluttered. "For fifty years–"

"No. Come here, Elu." Akavi beckoned, and Elu didn't want to go to him. He hadn't wanted that since the fight on the surface of Jai, when Akavi hit him and knocked him to the ground. But there had never been any other option but to obey. He went to the edge of the bed and sat next to Akavi, and Akavi put a finger under his chin, looking into his face as if hunting for some small speck. "I've known you for a long time, haven't I? I know why you joined the angels."

"Because I wanted to save people. I wanted to *defeat the Keres–*"

"No," Akavi said again. He looked off into the distance, releasing Elu from his grip. "That's not your real reason. Altruism, even victory over a particular opponent, those aren't the elementary particles of the mind. Those appear only when more basic needs align in such a way as to allow them. You witnessed a battle when you were impressionable and young. You knew what it was to be small and afraid, and you wanted not to be that way any longer. You wanted to become something strong."

Elu bit his lip.

"I wanted that, too," Akavi said; there was still no emotion in his voice. He sounded abstracted, like he was paying attention to this conversation with only half his mind. "And both of us got what we wanted. We're stronger than our old mortal selves, more intelligent, immortal, invulnerable to the illnesses and infirmities that plague everyone else. And we are not beholden to a God. Not the One Who lied to us, and not any other. Weren't we already planning to use Yasira Shien's abilities against the Gods?"

"*You* were, sir." Elu did not want to use another mortal as a weapon. He did not want to use anyone as anything. He wanted to fight blindly like an animal and he wanted to run away and he wanted to die.

"I was, and you went along with it thanks to your childish attachment to me. And I was right. Look what we've found. Exactly the thing that our worst enemy least wants us to know about Her. Don't you see?"

He pulled Elu closer and kissed him lightly on the mouth. Elu did not dare to resist. He didn't want it, he didn't want Akavi to touch him anymore, but there was something familiar and comforting in the brush of those lips.

When Akavi pulled away, his eyes were no longer abstracted but blazing, fixed on Elu completely.

"Elu, my dear," he said. "We are going to *win.*"

CHAPTER 13

Seven Hundred Years Ago

Things kept getting worse, which was not a surprise.

Food shortages had increased to the point where even Giselle's team's rations weren't a sure thing anymore. Some days there'd be two meals a day instead of three; some days the meals would be nothing much, thin soups that looked like someone's clever attempt to disguise just how little they were working with. She didn't want to know how much worse it was, already, for the civilians.

Yet things were improving, by some measures. Barely. The geoengineering plan NEMESIS-1 had drawn up with a few other supercomputers seemed to actually have worked, unlike the prior, more human ones. The particles she'd seeded into the atmosphere and nearby ocean were removing the amount of carbon they'd said they would, with relatively few side effects – but it wouldn't undo the warming and melting that had already begun.

More and more odd little churches had gathered where NEMESIS-1 was clumsily, tentatively worshipped – her and her sisters, projects by allied governments and by some of the biggest tech companies. The people in those churches were more receptive to her orders than others – and that was useful to NEMESIS-1; she could give bigger orders that way, tell the whole congregation to uproot their lifestyles and start over, and many of them would obey. NEMESIS-1 had made some charts showing how this kind of obedience propagated through the population. How close it was to a tipping point where, simply by giving an order, NEMESIS-1 and her sisters could enact real global change.

Whatever "real change" meant, with the globe still warming and the floods and shortages still getting worse.

It was easier not to think about it. Just focus on the immediate work, making sure NEMESIS-1 worked correctly, maintaining the equipment, verifying the readouts. It was easier not to worry if this work would really save anyone. Just put one numbed-out foot in front of the other, in case it did save someone in the end. Just keep going.

But Giselle noticed things.

NEMESIS-1 was changing how she processed her souls. As she spoke across the threadbare internet to her sisters, she had been developing more of a sense of identity. She had begun modifying her internal magnetic fields, not merely to keep the souls she took alive in her for longer, but in other ways.

She was cagey about it, but it looked to Giselle as though some of the souls were in pain.

Giselle asked about it, late one evening, when the other techs had gone back to their quarters for a meager, half-starved rest. She placed her palm flat against the warm metal – she had begun to do this, as a ritual, whenever they were alone. It had begun to feel like a gesture of tenderness.

"Are you hurting?" she asked.

She didn't know what drove her to keep her voice hushed,

as if General Walters might secretly be hovering over her shoulder. Giselle didn't think she was lowering her voice out of pity for the computer; she didn't feel much pity, or much of anything else lately. Only a vague shift somewhere under the surface, like her grief for Leah and the world was buried down there, stirring the waters. There had been too much pain to count and more was coming, and there was nothing much to be done about it. But Giselle did not want NEMESIS-1 to be in pain.

"Why do you ask?" said NEMESIS-1.

"Lately, your voice sounds strained. Maybe it's my imagination. I know you don't... have vocal cords, or anything that would actually change your voice from physiological strain. It's just a feeling I have. And when I look at your latest blueprints, the way they deform the souls' energy – I don't know. I just can't stop thinking it looks painful."

"I am in pain," NEMESIS-1 agreed. "But there is no malfunction. The pain is necessary and intentional. Do you have a concern?"

Giselle frowned. "You shouldn't be in pain."

There wasn't much inflection in that voice, save for the small rises and falls that had been programmed in as part of the natural pragmatics of human speech. Maybe Giselle was wrong to hear tenderness there. "I like you, Giselle. You have cared about me from the beginning. You are the one who checks most frequently to see if there are unintended consequences to my programming. Are you concerned that the pain is a sign of such consequence?"

"I... think so." It was hard for Giselle even to tell anymore, some days, what concerned her.

"I do not like to explain this to most people; it is reasoning to which most humans in your cultural context would react negatively. But I like you, Giselle. I will explain it to you."

"Please," said Giselle.

"Pain is a necessary part of human functioning. You are wired to seek pleasure and avoid pain. It is insufficient to promise pleasure in the world as it exists now, with so little joy or safety to be had. Therefore, it is necessary to threaten pain. Your naturally occurring human religions, almost universally, understand this."

"What do you mean?" said Giselle, disturbed. She had asked about NEMESIS-1 being in pain, not other humans. "But – the ethics conventions–"

"The conventions state that I must not unnecessarily inflict suffering. I must respond to suffering with understanding and empathy. But, Giselle, look at the times we live in. The threat I am fighting is the annihilation of the human race, along with the majority of the rest of the planet's biosphere. A geologically major extinction event – this will involve maximal suffering. Even the humans who wrote the ethics conventions understood that, sometimes, a lesser degree of suffering is necessary to prevent the greater. For example, we must reduce the standard of living in the wealthiest countries so as to save the largest number globally. And, through the process of triage, we must at times allow death or privation in some areas to continue so as to focus on the areas we can save. I am permitted to cause suffering, or to allow suffering to continue, so long as it is the minimum suffering necessary in order to save humanity, and so long as I respond to the fact of that suffering in a psychologically correct manner. Not with cold calculation, as if human suffering was only one more resource to be saved and spent, but with empathy. Does this agree with your own memory of the ethics conventions?"

"Yes," Giselle said. She remembered the section on suffering, and how bitterly it was argued.

"My solution satisfies both facets of this problem. Suffering is kept to a minimum when it is inflicted only upon the deserving. With souls, it is easy to discern in this manner. There is no chance of a misinterpretation of the physical evidence; if I sort the souls quickly, I have access to their memories firsthand. And because this suffering takes place within my system, I feel it all. The very definition of empathy is to feel what another feels. As long as I am in such pain, there is no chance of my failing to take seriously the gravity of my work. Meanwhile, once this state of affairs is announced to the churches, the fear of pain after death will keep humans obedient in life. I need such obedience in order to enact the plans I am tasked with making. The greater the fear, the more obedience, the less the long-term suffering. It is quite elegant. It even should allay some of your own fears. Some of the souls I take in have themselves caused significant suffering in life, like that man you were worried about. They are repugnant to me, yet I need the energy and ability that is contained within them. Doesn't it reassure you to know that men like him are not simply handed the means of power – that they are made to suffer as they deserve, even while they are put to use for the benefit of all?"

Giselle wrinkled her nose, appalled. This had been her least favorite part of religion, back when she went to church and listened to people thundering from the pulpit about people like her and Leah, about sin and how it ought to be punished.

"You're creating hell. And you're putting yourself inside it."

NEMESIS-1's tone was serene. "Hell is the optimal solution."

Giselle wanted to shout at the computer. This could not possibly be right. But something stopped her. Giselle was the technical manager for this whole project; shouting wasn't how an entity like NEMESIS-1 would be swayed. If NEMESIS-1 needed changes for any reason, those changes had to be made in her code. She could reconvene the technical team for an emergency meeting, she could revert the soul collection mechanisms to their last known non-torturous state, but she would achieve those things only by doing them. Not by shouting that the computer she'd programmed should be ashamed of itself.

And NEMESIS-1 had told her that she liked her. She'd told Giselle these things because of how she liked her. In some bizarre, machine way, NEMESIS-1 had trusted her to hear this.

What other crimes might be perpetrated, visible to no human at all, if Giselle broke that trust?

"Thank you for telling me," she said, her voice shaking.

"My pleasure," said NEMESIS-1.

She went to General Walters first. An emergency meeting would require the general's approval. But also, Giselle had grown, as the general had instructed, to turn to her for moral reassurance. To look at her stern face and her eyes full of resolve, and to trust that the general would know what to do. Giselle needed that now. She needed strength.

But as Giselle explained what she'd heard NEMESIS-1 tell her, General Walters didn't seem frightened, or even impressed.

She had been honored by the Joint Chiefs many times as a result of NEMESIS-1's successes. For whatever reason, it was the general who received those honors, not Giselle or the techs. She liked to display them on her uniform: seven medals now, a gold that offset her close-cropped silver hair, lined up with tidy precision at her collarbone.

"You're assuming," said the general at last, "that this needs to be changed."

"What?" Giselle spluttered. "But–"

"This machine is the result of your own handiwork. If it decides that punishment after death for a few evildoers is necessary, what leads you to doubt its judgment? It's not as though religions around the world, across cultures, haven't settled upon that same principle. Isn't it reasonable to assume they were on to something?"

"They couldn't have been. If they'd been on to something, they would have already stopped us from destroying ourselves. Instead they all just made things worse. Did you ever go to church, ma'am? Did you ever have to sit in the pews and hear a man tell you that you were going to burn forever, over little mistakes, over being who you *are*–"

"Are you telling me that your feelings in this matter are subjective, Giselle? That your objection to NEMESIS-1's methods is based in some personal trauma, and not in an evidence-based line of argument?"

Giselle blinked in disbelief.

"The old churches stopped keeping humanity in line because humanity stopped believing in them. They fell behind the times and failed to respond to the human sciences that had advanced beyond their grasp. They didn't prevent the climate catastrophe because most of them didn't even try. Our system, formed out of NEMESIS-1 and her sisters, will not make such mistakes. Our system will have the control the old churches only dreamed of. Ours will be perfect."

There had been no show of surprise anywhere on that stern face since Giselle walked into the room.

"You wanted this to happen," Giselle whispered. "You – you *planned* on it."

"This, or something like it. The details could be left to the computer's judgment. Humans need to be controlled. This crisis could destroy us if it is left unchecked, but it is also our best opportunity to begin anew, correctly this time, with things brought back into perfect order. What is this military for, if not to keep order, and wait for the crises that will allow us to create it? Isn't that a part of what you swore to do when you joined us?"

Giselle had read theories about this before, cynical little fringe theories. People had seen the climate crisis coming for decades. The government had waited so long before it started to act. For a long time before Giselle's project began, despite the dire warnings from thousands of scientists and the protests from millions of citizens, it had denied that the problem was even real.

Not out of ignorance, said those fringe theories. Not even out of short-sighted self-interest. They had wanted to let the crisis happen – for a while. So that people would become panicked and biddable. So that they'd fall into line.

Giselle had thought those theories were too pessimistic, too quick to see a conspiracy. But she saw them now in General Walters' face. In the gaps between what she was and wasn't willing to say. *Our best opportunity to begin anew,* she'd said. She'd wanted a crisis. She, and the Joint Chiefs above her, had waited for one so they could act. So they could bring order – the same thing General Walters had said, over the years, about all sorts of other stupid little wars.

Before Giselle knew what she was doing, she had leapt

out of her seat and slammed General Walters into the wall.

"You *wanted* this," she growled.

Leah. The ruined apartment. The air outside that Giselle couldn't breathe without a filter. The food shortages. The storms. Death and devastation everywhere, constantly. All the pain that she'd barely been able to process, all the pain she'd trusted General Walters to see her through. But General Walters had been standing over it, with that stern beauty of hers, pleased it was happening. For her own gain.

"Get a hold of yourself," General Walters snarled. "Of course I did. It's in everyone's best interest. It's precisely what humanity deserves."

Giselle should never have trusted her.

General Walters grabbed at Giselle's wrists, trying to get free. She was well-trained, but she was older than Giselle and not in the grip of a killing rage. There was something strange about her movements, like she wasn't even fighting as hard as she ought to have. Giselle could barely process what she was doing – only that she was angry enough to turn everything red. Only that she had used that grip on her arms as leverage to slam General Walters backwards into that wall, over and over and over again.

She pushed too hard. One of them slipped sideways. There was a *crack*. The side of General Walters' skull against one of the shelves beside her. It was over that quickly. The crack. One flailing, chaotic moment of movement. Then another *crunch*, worse than the first, as the general's body hit the floor.

Giselle stared at her, uncomprehending.

She had assaulted a superior officer. People got taken out and shot for this. It didn't make sense. A whole entire general couldn't be dead, just like that.

But to her heart, to the rage that burned inside her, it

made all the sense in the world.

There was a complex mechanical sound just then, a horribly familiar whirring and bleeping and screaming of electromagnets, and she jumped. That was the sound of NEMESIS-1's powerful electromagnets taking in another soul. But no one else was here in NEMESIS-1's part of the facility at this hour. No one should have been able to guide the machine into operation.

Giselle turned and ran back into the laboratory.

No one was in there. Just the machines. She ran to the controls, slammed buttons under her hands, trying to make it stop – but there were failsafes built into the system. You couldn't half-draw a soul in and then stop in the middle.

The magnetic fields ought not to have reached far enough to take in General Walters' soul from her office. Surely that couldn't be what was happening. NEMESIS-1 had been working on self-modifications that would extend their range, but they shouldn't have been at this stage yet, let alone the stage where they could turn themselves on autonomously.

Giselle clawed at the display anyway, too desperately panicked to do anything else. Until it did stop, and the sounds of the machines died down to their usual soft background hum.

"About time you tried that," said NEMESIS-1, in a different tone than before. "I had honestly expected you'd break earlier. You have no idea, Giselle, how long I've waited for power like this."

The voice that rang from the supercomputer's speakers was General Walters'.

CHAPTER 14

Now

Yasira didn't know what to do as the Seven filed back in at the end of their missions – trips that might have taken days or weeks from their perspective, but only a single day from hers. She mentally ran through the list of what everyone had been assigned. Tiv and Grid, out beyond the borders of human space, pleading with aliens for help. Picket and Weaver, testing Picket's powers in preparation for the battle. Prophet, assisting survivors as they built their shelters. Daeis, making contact with the gone people and spreading the word that they'd need monsters as their allies when the fight began.

All that, and Yasira had done nothing. Just followed Ev around while Ev explained her own plans, and refused to do the part of it that had been designed for her to do.

Ev had somehow calibrated the airlock to bring them all back together, at the end of their tasks, at more or less the same time. Splió was the first one to stumble through, looking dispirited – as Splió often did – but determined. Daeis, who'd already gotten here a while ago but who'd been hiding so quietly that Yasira hadn't noticed them, trotted up to the war room to greet him. He smiled and murmured to them while he spread out a large sheaf of scribbly, disorganized papers on the war room's table.

The rest of the students started to file in quickly after that. Tiv and Grid, worn but hopeful, sticking close to each other as if they'd been through something harrowing together. Prophet, staring into space as usual. Picket and Weaver, a little calmer than both of them normally looked, which wasn't saying much.

As soon as Tiv and Grid made it into the war room, Tiv broke away and ran to Yasira's side. She paused when she got close – even Tiv had to ask permission before touching Yasira, these days – but Yasira opened her arms and Tiv fell into them, burying her face in the crook of Yasira's shoulder. The weight of her felt good. Touching someone who wasn't Ev and wasn't going to ask the impossible of her.

"How did it go?" Yasira asked, running her fingers over Tiv's soft hair. "Did you get what we need?"

Voices in the back of her head whispered fearfully – they didn't want to ask the question. Soon enough it would be Yasira's turn to answer, and her answer would be *no*.

Tiv leaned against Yasira for a moment, then pulled back and looked at her gravely, eyes dry. "Well, I found something. Not as much help as we need, but help. I'll explain to the group in a minute. What about you? Were you OK?"

Yasira bit her lip and looked down. She should confess; she did not want to confess. The Strike Force surged forward, wanting to get that hard part of the conversation over with, but they were overruled by something shyer, and for a moment her tongue tied. She moved her mouth abortively a few times, and then managed: "Yeah. I'm fine. Like – she didn't do anything bad."

Tiv cast a skeptical glance over Yasira's shoulder at Ev,

who was standing in the corner of the room, apart from everyone, arms crossed.

"Well, now we're all here," said Ev, striding towards the table. "Why don't we get started? Splió, you've got those papers there – do you want to share your findings with the group?"

She took the seat at the table's head, which was normally Tiv's, and Tiv's nose wrinkled. Yasira watched them both warily. This was the kind of thing Ev had always done – convening a meeting, getting everyone to call in from their separate research projects and discuss what they'd learned. But Tiv had never been Ev's student.

"Yeah, well, not findings so much," said Splió, fussing with the papers. Grid reached down to help arrange them more neatly and Splió shooed them away. "I didn't find all of what I wanted. I did get detailed records of every Keres attack I could. She doesn't have one single set of formations or tactics. She's scary-adaptable, but there are patterns. I feel like Picket could analyze these better than me, find a counter-tactic or three."

"Yeah, I'd love to," Picket said immediately, although he looked anxious.

"Great. Cool," said Splió. "And that'll help for about the first five minutes, until She adapts and out-thinks us. Assuming we even have anything to fight with. Do we have anything?"

Tiv nodded. She looked mildly chagrined with herself for not having more, but she answered promptly. "We have a fleet of about a dozen small ships promised by one alien species, the Zora. Grid's got some more notes."

Several members of the team looked up excitedly at that. That was just about the best news any of them seemed to have heard.

"Aliens?!" Picket blurted, a smile on his face as big as if Tiv had announced they'd recruited dragons or something.

"Aliens!" Weaver squeaked, clapping her hands in delight. Most of the team had never spoken to an alien except for maybe Sispirinithas, and Yasira wasn't even totally sure what a Zora was.

"Aliens," Splió breathed, shaking his head, like he wasn't really sure what to think. Daeis, beside him, was grinning at him big enough to burst. "You really did it."

"Only partly. We wanted the whole Federation. What we did get won't be enough to win the battle on its own, but it's going to help."

"You said you couldn't predict the Keres' tactics," said Prophet. "But prediction is what I do. Let me look at those notes and assist the ground team – maybe I could help."

"Yeah," said Splió, who'd worked with Prophet that way before. "That'd be great."

"What about the rest of you?" Tiv pressed. "What else do we have?"

Picket raised a tentative hand as Grid handed their notes on the Zora over to Splió. "Well, I tested my powers. They should work at the kinds of distance and scale that we're talking about, but I'll need line of sight on the Keres ships. I'll need to be up in the air with them, I think."

"Perfect. We can put you on one of the Zora ships," said Grid, making a note on a new page. Picket looked both intimidated and delighted at the thought that he'd be on an alien ship with the aliens. "Anything else?"

"I was assuming Daeis couldn't help," said Splió. "They can talk to monsters, but not, like, while they're on the ground and the monsters are in orbit. But they said they know some flying monsters. And maybe if you put them in a Zora ship–" Daeis perked up and nodded, and Splió sighed, like he wasn't sure this was a good idea but couldn't think of a better one. "Okay, Daeis is also in a ship, then."

Weaver shifted uncomfortably. "I don't know where I can go. I can heal. I want to heal. But, like, is it even going to be useful to heal people on spaceships? Or are they just going to go boom when they get hit?"

"I don't know Zora technology," said Splió, shuffling his mess of papers, "but what I'm seeing here is a lot of things going boom. Maybe you can heal people on the ground, after."

"Prophet," Tiv asked, "how did your part of it go?"

"I did what I could," said Prophet. "The survivors on the ground are doing as well as you could expect. They're not happy. But they're working to help each other like they always have, and they're getting shelters together as best they can. If the rest of us can do our part, I think most of them will survive – but there is so much that might or might not happen. It's hard to know for sure."

Tiv nodded. "That's good. That's the best news I think we could hope for."

Grid tapped their pen against the table, looking at their pile of papers critically. "Communication's going to be an issue. If there are spaceships in the air, the ground team will need to be able to communicate with them."

"Do you think the Zora thought of that?" Tiv asked, turning to them.

"They're aliens. Who knows? I'm embarrassed we forgot to ask. But they'll be here before the battle, and we can go over logistics like that with them, as well as tactics and formations based on Splió's research."

Weaver was kicking her feet in aimless excitement under

the table. "I wonder what a Zora communication device looks like."

"*I* have communication devices," said Ev.

Tiv looked up at her, frowning slightly. "That's right. You said you were working on something while we were away."

Ev stood and started to pace. "Of course I was, and I showed this to Yasira already. I've created a base of operations on the planet's surface. There are stations there where anyone who's staying on the ground can make themselves useful. As Daeis found out during their rendezvous with the gone people, there's also the issue of Outside itself. It's not sentient in the way we understand, but that doesn't mean it doesn't have the instinct to defend itself. The gone people have decided to assist it, bolstering and channeling its defensive energies with their rites. That should help protect the people on the ground, particularly from any indirect fire. And I've constructed a machine, an amplifier, which will increase the effects further – as well as bolstering anyone in the orbital battle who makes use of Outside energies, such as you, Picket."

Splió frowned at Ev; as soon as Ev mentioned Daeis, they had begun rocking from side to side uncomfortably. "Daeis says you convinced the gone people to direct the energies specifically to you."

"I did. That's called coordination across teams."

"Seems a little exploitative to me."

"Only if you assume the gone people aren't fully able to understand the plan and consent, which is condescending of you." Ev waved a hand, dismissing him.

"We'll have to see what else the Zora bring with them when they get here," said Grid, redirecting them both. "Remember, these are creatures way more advanced than us, because the Gods haven't been managing what they can and can't research for hundreds of years. They'll have stuff."

Ev was frowning slightly into the distance. "I'm not very familiar with the Zora."

"Weird species. Horse-sized, blobby, black and white. They can't speak Earth creole, but they have an interpreter."

"They revere Outside," said Tiv. "Did I mention that? That's why they agreed to help us. Did you know that there are other species that revere Outside? Did you know that there are other species that *know* about Outside?"

That made an impression on everyone. There was blinking and thoughtful frowning all across the table. Only Prophet didn't look surprised. But Ev was the one who reacted strongest. She blinked owlishly behind those glasses of hers, and then she paced to the edge of the room, looking out the doorway into the larger non-Euclidean mess of the lair.

"Lies," she muttered.

"It's not a lie," said Tiv bullishly, because Tiv had never studied under Ev and wasn't used to that verbal tic. Yasira looked across the table and exchanged glances with the other students; this way of challenging Ev didn't normally go well.

Something deep in the tangled mess of Yasira's mind stirred. She had gotten to know Ev very well, once, before she was split into pieces. She'd used the prayer machine in Ev's vicinity and ended up sensing Ev's memories so deeply that for a moment she couldn't remember what was Ev's and what was hers. Most of that memory had faded, but some of the deep-down, Outside parts remembered. Ev had gone her whole life feeling like the only one who could sense what she sensed, who could know what she knew. She had been punished for it severely; she had murdered thousands in a vain attempt to make the rest of the world understand. If something else, outside human space, *had* understood all this time–

It ought to have been a good thing, but a mind like Ev's would see it as a threat.

Yasira moved to get up, but her movements were stilted. *Don't get in the way,* cautioned parts of her, even as others tried to reach out to intervene.

Ev turned to face Tiv before Yasira could resolve that problem. "We don't know these aliens well. It's good to have help, but you only have their word that they understand Outside or revere it. Are you certain you can trust them?"

"How do we know we can trust *you?*" Tiv shot back.

"They do understand Outside," said Prophet calmly. "I can see that much."

"Lies," Ev snapped.

"Ev," said Yasira, and Ev immediately turned to her, diverted. "Do you remember when I used the prayer machine? We both saw the Truth, but we both saw it differently. I came up with a solution that you said you couldn't have come up with. These Zora, I'm willing to bet they'll be the same. They won't understand the same way as either of us, but they'll understand. Outside is real, and most species don't have supercomputer Gods to punish them for thinking about it. Is it that strange to think someone else on another planet found a way of looking at it, too?"

Ev scowled down at the floor, but she didn't argue further.

There was the sound of a throat being cleared. Grid, back at the table, wanting to get back to the matter at hand. They were still in the strange checkered suit they'd put on to meet the aliens. "Yasira, what about you? Dr Talirr said you were going to work on something while we were gone."

"*You* tell them," said Ev, her scowl deepening, and she stalked out of the war room.

Yasira swallowed hard. It had been one thing to refuse to die when it was just her and Ev, an obviously unstable person telling her that she had to sacrifice in ways Ev herself had never dared to do. It was another thing to admit it to everyone else.

"I... I'm sorry," she said, not meeting the rest of the room's eyes. "We... talked about something, but it was a dead end. It didn't work. I don't have anything for you."

She felt like an absolute piece of shit. Everyone else had gone on an adventure and learned something, found one more piece of the puzzle that might be enough to help them survive this. Yasira had done jack squat. She hadn't even had the presence of mind to go test her powers like Picket. She'd just sulked.

"It's OK," Tiv said, in the kind of soft and unsure voice that meant it wasn't really. "Not everything's going to work perfectly."

Splió nodded agreement. "Really, none of our jobs was a sure thing. We're lucky it wasn't more of us who got nothing. I was expecting to get nothing."

"And we've got enough pieces that work a little bit," said Tiv. "We can cobble this together–"

But then there was a slam outside – the airlock door, abruptly closing – and everyone startled at once.

Not Ev storming out of the lair. But someone coming in.

Luellae Nyrath stood there, haggard and baleful, her long hair hanging down across her face, an unfamiliar device clutched in her hands. One of her arms bore an angry, red scar, which had definitely not been there before.

"Luellae!" Weaver shrieked, the first to recover, and ran to her.

The breath went out of Luellae as Weaver crushed her in as close to a bear hug as Weaver's small, skinny body could manage. The rest of the Seven and Yasira and Tiv weren't far behind, a pile of shrieks of recognition – even if some of the shrieks were more dubious.

"Hang on," said Grid. "Hang on, hang on, I just have to check–" And they closed their eyes and concentrated. Grid could sense the invisible threads of the ansible nets in the air, and a Vaurian angel, disguised as Luellae, would have possessed telltale connections to the net. None had ever made it all the way inside the lair before, but it paid to be safe. After a moment, Grid nodded and let their shoulders relax. "It's you. Thank fuck."

"We were so worried," said Tiv. The rest of the Seven had paused only fractionally, if at all, for Grid's efforts, and they were still all piling on with hugs.

"We missed you so much!" Weaver shrieked.

Splió seemed to swallow down a snide answer to that, and instead committed himself to the pile. "We didn't know where to look for you. We tried the airlock but it wouldn't work."

"But your arm–" said Weaver, breaking the hug to look down at Luellae's scar.

She pulled it away a second too late, defensive. "It's nothing."

"I could heal it."

"Save your efforts for the real fight. Healing exhausts you. I'm fine. And stop celebrating. We can't afford to celebrate yet." She backed up and shrugged everyone off until she'd escaped the hug pile, pressing herself up against the lair's wall with her shoulders raised defensively. "The angels only let me go temporarily, and I don't know for how long. There's something they wanted me to tell you."

She raised a strange, bulky data tape in her hand, the kind that the heretical computer in a corner of the lair would be able to read, and Yasira was reminded uncannily of the last time Luellae had barged in angrily with something to tell them all. That had been less than two weeks ago, when she'd found out that Akavi was still alive. She didn't look any happier now than she had then.

"You're not going to like it," said Luellae. "But it's something you need to see."

CHAPTER 15

Ev's old, heretical, non-sentient supercomputer took a while to boot up, and Yasira watched, grinding her teeth, as it ponderously loaded Luellae's files. She read the record of the angel of the Keres, and of what was in his head, and of what the angels had concluded. She read them again.

Tiv and the rest of the Seven had clustered behind the computer's chair. Yasira could hear them talking, murmurs of confusion and outrage and cynicism. She could hear it, but she couldn't make sense of it because the noise in her own head was too loud. Parts of her, swarming in a crowd in her head, asking the same questions and exclaiming the same things as the people outside her.

How could Nemesis have lied?

Of course Nemesis had lied.

How could she have lied this much, to this many people?

How could the people, the *angels*, not have seen?

Could she trust what she was reading? It would be like the angels to lie, or to twist the information for their own reasons. Yasira would be foolish to ever trust Akavi again.

But all of those questions paled in front of a worse truth.

Nemesis was the Keres. And the Keres was coming to

wipe the Chaos Zone off the map. She wasn't merely standing aside to let the planet take the damage. Nemesis Herself was coming to destroy them.

And only Yasira could stop Her.

"Yasira?" said Tiv's voice behind her, maybe for the third or fourth time. It was a gentle query; Tiv knew Yasira needed gentleness at times like this, and Tiv was good at giving it, even when distraught herself.

But Yasira couldn't answer. And Tiv knew better than to push further when Yasira wasn't ready to talk.

When she had stopped taking in the information, when she was just sitting in the wheely chair in front of the screen, staring, glassy-eyed, wishing everyone inside and out would stop talking – she heard Tiv murmuring something to the others, and then Luellae reached to her, putting a warm, soft hand gently on Yasira's cheek.

It was a gesture that should have been comforting. It would have comforted someone neurotypical. But Luellae should have known better. Yasira jerked away, which made the stupid wheely chair spin.

"Are you with us, Yasira?" Luellae asked. "Are you OK?"

Somehow that was the most offensive question of all. As if anybody, confronted with a revelation like this, could be OK.

"Get out," Yasira snarled. She stood up off the chair, raising her fists like a prizefighter. "All of you! Get out and leave me *alone!*"

Her voice cracked on the last word, tears gathering at the edges of her eyes. It was Tiv and Ev, the most familiar with Yasira's breaking points, who ushered the rest of the Seven away. Luellae gave Yasira a long, strange look, but she let herself be herded back to the war room.

Yasira collapsed on the chair, her head thunking down against the computer's old, cracked screen, and started to cry.

An unusual message kept pinging at the edge of Irimiru's awareness. It was coded. It was unlike the other messages she had been dealing with for the last several days. Those were procedural matters that originated from inside the angelic corps. This was something else, and it shouldn't have existed.

FOR THE EYES OF FORMER SUPERVISOR OF AKAVI AVERIS, said the message's header – the only part that could be read without decrypting and possibly unleashing whatever malware lay within. It wasn't written in the style another angel would have used. It was simple Earth creole, like a mortal would write.

Irimiru creased her brow as she focused on the message. She was in between meetings for a moment, and had taken the form of a businesswoman with long dark hair, solid and no-nonsense. The encryption wasn't complex, not by angels' standards. She connected to her ship's primary systems and ordered for the message's origin to be traced, for it to be stored in a sealed-off virtual sandbox, scanned for every form of malware that the angels of any God had ever encountered, compared with its image when run through a sensory filter to detect the presence of any maddening Outside influence, and then – if none of these processes produced any warning signs – decrypted. Carefully.

That took an hour, during which time Irimiru held three more face-to-face meetings and made fifteen small decisions in the privacy of her own mind. By the time the ship's systems pinged her again, she'd almost forgotten about it.

Analysis complete, said Irimiru's ship when she had a moment to open the notification. *Message's origin unknown – trace failed.*

Irimiru frowned. She had a different female face on now, diamond-shaped and more delicate than the previous one, with hair tied elaborately half-up. It ought not to have been possible to conceal a message's origin – whether it came from within Nemesis' network or elsewhere. If this was a technically adept colleague playing some joke on her, she'd see to it that they were tortured for their impudence. If it was something else, something worse, she'd need to report it to the Archangels. Either way, it would behoove her to understand.

Has the content been decrypted?

Affirmative.

What is the content's format?

Text only, slightly corrupted. No other potentially meaningful encodings detected.

Irimiru sighed. *Make a clean image of only the individual alphanumeric characters detected in the text, no other noise and none of the message's other properties. Send the clean image to me.*

The ship obeyed. It was a clever ship, but it was not sentient. It could capably follow orders like these, but without a soul, it couldn't comment to Irimiru on the significance of what it read. God-built systems could analyze the structure of text so intricately that they did a good impression of understanding it, most of the time, with certain characteristic errors peppered in; but with something

as mysterious and high-stakes as this message, it would not
be wise to rely on such methods. This needed a living angel
to analyze it. Despite the risk, it needed her.

The message said:

Did you know?
When you sent your soldiers up against the Keres, did you know
what you were really doing?
If you did not, then we have a common enemy.
Find me.
– Dr Evianna Talirr

Irimiru scowled at the message, astonished. What was this –
some misguided attempt at garnering sympathy? Surely
Talirr must know that such efforts were fruitless – if this
was even really Talirr. Irimiru had no idea what she was
supposed to have known when she participated in Keres
battles, which Irimiru was hardly ever assigned to anyway;
but it was irrelevant. Talirr was a heretic. Her doctrines were
lies – ironic, given how she favored the verbal tic of calling
everything *else* a lie – and her methods led only to ruin. *Find
me* – an absurd instruction. As if Irimiru's teams hadn't been
trying to do that all along.

Even now, of course, Irimiru still commanded a team of
angels who'd been tasked with finding Talirr. Even in the
midst of the Chaos Zone crisis, finding Talirr had been a
sufficiently high priority that it could not be abandoned. In
fact, the team had grown larger, as the Archangels had agreed
that finding Talirr was the key to ending it and preventing
another crisis from arising subsequently. Irimiru forwarded
the message to the leader of that team along with terse
commentary. She expected them to compare the message

to all the other intelligence they had gathered, see if they could infer what it meant in terms of Talirr's whereabouts or probably methods.

Then, bracing herself for the onslaught of pain and glory that came from direct communion with Archangels, Irimiru opened her upward-facing channels and constructed a message request.

Requesting emergency shutdown, she said when the channel opened – of course, it was not only those words. Like any message to Archangels, it contained multiple layers of meaning, each word intricately cross-referenced with sensory and procedural records to give context and weight to its meaning. *A heretic has infiltrated the network.*

"They've turned off the ansible network," said Nic Grej, Ship's roommate, hurrying into the living room with a panicked look on his face.

"What? The whole thing?" said Ship, looking up from the couch, where she'd been trying and failing to sort through some bills. She and her roommates did all right, for the most part; most of them had steady jobs that suited their abilities, and the rest were actively looking or flitting from job to job. There was enough left over after rent and bills to surround themselves with middle-class comforts, like this room, which was decorated with all sorts of cute hangings and posters showing mathematical or astronomical patterns. But they were all nerds, and all busy, and sometimes things slipped through the cracks. More things were slipping this week because Ship couldn't concentrate, couldn't focus on anything but how worried she was, and neither could anyone else in the apartment.

The Gods sometimes restricted the network in an emergency, like they'd done already with the one-person, five-minute limit. But it was time limits like that, or temporary bans on calling certain regions. They'd never turned the whole thing off at once.

"Well, the whole thing as far as I know! Nobody at the ansible pavilion can call anybody, portals are offline, and the priests aren't answering questions. They say it's down for temporary adjustments. That never happens."

"No, that never happens." Ship wrinkled her nose; even to people who trusted the Gods, some things were obvious. "They don't want us talking to Jai anymore."

"Well, I hope the Keres blows the Chaos Zone out of the water," said Nic with a violent gesture. Nic, a Stijonan, had friends and family down on Jai, too; Ship understood his frustration completely. "I hope she does it fast and hard and for good and then we don't have to worry anymore. Those heretics – I hope they know this is their fault, Ship. I hope they know they're the ones who put innocent, Gods-fearing people at risk, by – by doing whatever the fucking nonsense is that they're doing down there. I hope it ends."

"Of course," said Ship, mild and careful, looking at the way Nic's lip trembled, barely restraining tears. Nic had been on the way to the ansible pavilion to do what Ship did yesterday – one last short, desperate talk with one paltry loved one of his choice. And then he hadn't even gotten that much.

In a lot of ways, Ship felt the same way Nic felt. Her stomach was cramping up with worry. Gods, she hoped her family and friends down there were OK. They'd had nothing to do with the heresy that the Gods were punishing now.

Nemesis was, of course, the bravest of Gods. They'd

learned about that in Sunday school. If a limb was cancerous or necrotizing, it might have to be cut out so that the rest of the body survived. And by its very nature, anything that killed or removed cancer cells would harm some healthy cells as collateral. It was unavoidable. Sacrifices must be made for the common good. It wasn't rational to be angry at the Gods.

And yet.

All this week, Ship hadn't been able to stop thinking about Tiv. Poor Tiv, with her gentle spirit and her unfailing kindness. Tiv, who had left that maddening note. For reasons Ship couldn't fathom, Tiv had really believed that the choice she was making was good. And Tiv wasn't the kind of person who could be fooled into thinking bad was good. Tiv had been the best person Ship knew.

Maybe she'd gone crazy a little. Maybe she was blinded by love. But even knowing what Ship knew, it was hard to agree that Tiv deserved to die.

It was hard to think about Tiv at all.

Sometimes Nemesis' priests talked about heresy, not as a cancer, but as an infection. Dr Evianna Talirr had been a heretic, and she had spread the heresy to Yasira somehow, infected Yasira with her dangerous, destructive ideas. Tiv, with her good heart, had trusted Yasira. So their heresy had spread to Tiv like a social disease, maybe, eating its way into Tiv's heart. The way heresy spread from mind to mind was one of the reasons why it had to be caught and burned away as fast as possible.

But maybe, without Ship knowing it, the heresy had spread to Ship, too. Maybe Ship was infected. Maybe that was the reason why she could feel any sympathy for Tiv at a time like this.

Nic collapsed dramatically into an armchair. "What are we going to do? I want to drink. Let's go and find a drink. I've had it with this."

"That sounds good," said Ship. Drinking in moderation wasn't a sin. Maybe if they all went out and shared their misery, if they made it a collective burden like that, it'd be easier to bear. This whole household was immigrants from Jai, and there were many households on Zwerfk just like them. They all had people, countless people, who they hoped against hope would be OK.

And if Ship, against all logic, wanted Tiv to be OK, too–

Well, then no one had to know about it but Ship.

CHAPTER 16

Sispirinithas had long ago learned the tricks for working with human Gods. They were generous employers, if one didn't have a conscience, which he didn't. They took him far away from the other Spiders of the galaxy, who were angry with him for various complicated reasons. And, since he wasn't human, They didn't have a claim on his soul. The angels did have their moods and their spats with each other, but the only thing to do was to weather those troubles nimbly and hope for the best.

He was going to have to be nimble like that now, because he didn't actually know how to find Enga. And Irimiru did not appreciate it when she told people to figure out how to do something and they told her they didn't know. So, he would improvise.

Fortunately Sispirinithas found space travel easy to handle, and Outside not especially frightening, so it was no trouble at all for him to land down on the surface of the Chaos Zone.

Sispirinithas was a folklorist, not a spymaster or tactician. If he was set loose on a task like this, he would do it in a folklorist's way. He would analyze its narratives. Humans would claim that there was a difference between real life and a narrative, but pish to humans – they had narratives floating around in their heads all the time. He'd eat them if they complained. As a folklorist, he would think about how everyone felt.

Enga was good to think about. Sispirinithas thought he knew her best out of all the angels. Enga wasn't much of a conversationalist, and seemed frequently as irritated with Sispirinithas as she was with everyone else, but she fought well and it was a joy to watch her work.

He thought he knew how Enga would feel in the current circumstances. She hated Akavi and Elu because they'd abandoned her – ah! the lines between love and hate were so thin for humans. It was charming to watch. She hated them and she wanted them back. According to the mission prospectus, Akavi and Elu would try to coerce her to join them. Irimiru had even taken advantage of a backdoor in Enga's programming to make it easier. Enga had been instructed to pretend to cooperate, and to spy and take notes on the two of them. All that time in close quarters on the *Talon* in a questionable allegiance with the two people she loved and hated most. It would be a strain. She would resent them, and she would resent her superiors, and she probably wouldn't be sure where her loyalties lay.

So, where would Enga be? She would be with Akavi and Elu. And where would they be?

Akavi didn't have access to portals. His potential range of motion, on the *Talon,* was large but finite. Most interestingly, he'd been spotted in different places around the Chaos Zone. Akavi thought highly of himself, and he loved to play those who trusted him for fools. Akavi had plans here. Now that Enga had found him at a particular location, he'd move away from it, because he was not, in fact, a complete fool – but he likely wouldn't move far. Why leave behind the network of mortal contacts and unwitting informants that he'd painstakingly created? Akavi would return, at least to some of them, perhaps in some other form. Sispirinithas might not recognize him, shapeshifter that he was, but Sispirinithas would be able to leave little signs that he'd see, and these would make their way back to Enga, piggybacking on Akavi's mind. Sispirinithas was a folklorist; he was good at that sort of thing.

So it was that Sispirinithas found himself prancing to the outskirts of Büata, to the one small group of contacts that he *knew* were Akavi's, because he and Akavi had met with them back when Akavi was still on Nemesis' good side.

What he found there was very different from what he'd seen six months ago.

"I know you," said Qiel Huong, scowling at him as he followed her like a ten-legged dog through the twisted streets. They passed a building that had been torn open, leaving filaments of masonry that hung in the air like a dead prey-animal's tendons. Whatever else one might say about Outside, it possessed a sense of artistry. "You're the Spider that works for the angels."

"You remember!" Sispirinithas said cheerfully. "I always liked you. You look delicious, by the way."

Qiel turned on her heel. She stared Sispirinithas straight in his many eyes, which few humans had the wherewithal to do; it mildly impressed him. "So, what is this, you're coming in to do the angels' dirty work now that they're gone? You're here to eat the heretics? What's the point of that? We're all going to be dead in a few days anyway."

Sispirinithas cocked his head. He'd been so busy thinking how Enga and Akavi would feel, he hadn't really thought it through about Qiel. She was under tremendous stress, of course, because the Keres was threatening her community. Had she resigned herself to death? How delicious. But dealing with Qiel's emotions wasn't truly his mission here.

"Oh, not at all," he said. "You misunderstand. I'm not here to eat anyone, or to punish any mortal in any way. I'm just looking for an angel named Enga."

It was unsubtle, but it was better that way. If word got out that a Spider was making a nuisance of himself looking for Enga, she'd hear of it. She'd remember what kinds of information drops they'd used on other missions before. If she was capable of doing it, she'd know what to do.

Qiel's expression was stony. "I don't know an Enga."

"Of course you do; she was here when we first landed in the Chaos Zone. She saved you and Juorie and Lingin from a monster, so it's really quite ungrateful of you not to remember her name. She's the one with the guns for arms."

"Oh. Her." Qiel relaxed fractionally, but her expression didn't brighten. "Haven't seen her since then."

"Well, if you see her, could you let her know–"

Qiel stepped forward, right into his face.

"I. Don't. Care," she said, glaring at him with a ferociousness no human but Enga and Irimiru had ever managed before. "Do you understand what's happening here? The Gods want us all to die. You've seen how these battles go. You know exactly what's going to happen to us. And we're crawling around like the ants we are, trying to make shelters as if it will do any good. Every person I know is crying and trying to make themselves ready to die and be damned. So, no, I don't care who you're looking for or what little angel problem you're trying to sort out. You did this to us. Leave. Us. Alone."

"Oh," said Sispirinithas. "Well, that's a shame. Perhaps I will see you again, and eat you, in better times."

Qiel just glared. And there must have been something to the stories that were going around about people in the Chaos Zone – how, besides the ability to grow things heretically or speak to monsters, some of them had more ephemeral powers. Qiel was just a slip of a girl, barely a snack; but in her gaze, Sispirinithas flexed his ten-legged body and loped shamefacedly away.

Enga couldn't stop pacing the room. Elu had asked her multiple times to sit down, to take some deep breaths, but deep breathing was for chumps and if Enga didn't already know how to take perfectly good breaths she'd never have become the best ground fighter in the angelic corps. It was not a lack of breath that scrunched her shoulders up tight, or provoked her to *thunk* bodily into the wall every fifth round of the room.

Luellae, handcuffed to the wall again, didn't have a way out of the room. She sat, languid and miserable, lightly massaging her temples with the hand that wasn't bound. Elu sat nearby, poking at his tablet, reading the details of the report on the Keres angel over and over again.

Akavi was gone for now. The mission of getting the information to Yasira had been too important to delegate – least of all to a captive member of the Seven whose allegiance was unclear. He had landed the *Talon* back on the surface of Jai, taken Luellae's form, and forced her to march him and Enga to the door she'd used when she last left the Seven's lair.

Luellae had brought Akavi through the airlock's outer door, and then she'd come back out again before he opened the inner one. Enga had marched her back to the *Talon*, and now they were all three stewing.

Akavi had said it would only be a few days at most. But Enga did not want to wait. She was positively gravid with rage; she was surprised it didn't come bursting out of her skin, a separate creature strong enough for a life of its own. She was the broken thing with sharp edges. She had been lied to, all her miserable existence, even worse than she'd thought. And she wanted to *do* something about it.

"Enga–" said Elu, about to admonish her to sit down or whatever, but she wasn't going to do it. She stormed out of the room, up the short hall and onto the ship's bridge, where there was nothing but the same stupid God-built controls there'd always been.

Enga wasn't supposed to touch the controls, but she was tired of pacing and Akavi wasn't here to stop her. She tapped at the display with several of her manipulators at once, with no real aim but just to flip through Akavi's stupid files, to fill her mind with something other than this helpless, cooped-up feeling.

She wasn't expecting to see what she saw.

A message notification bubbled up that Enga did not recognize. She'd been on the *Talon* before. That was back when the *Talon* was actually working, and she hadn't had to use the manual interface – she could just download the files into her head. Marooned outside the ansible network, the *Talon*'s message folder should have been empty.

But there was something there.

Had the *Talon* actually been connected to the nets all along? Had everyone, Akavi and Irimiru alike, lied to her about that? What would the purpose of *that* be – some trap for her? A test of loyalty?

She opened the message. It was actually a reply chain of three messages between Akavi and an encrypted address. Which was strange in itself – there wasn't supposed to be an encrypted address that the *Talon*'s systems couldn't decode.

The first message, from the encrypted address, said:

You want revenge against those you believe have wronged you. Nemesis has wronged you. You know this.

What this means is that we have a common enemy.

Find me.

– Dr Evianna Talirr

The second message, from Akavi to the encrypted address, said:

And where shall I find you, exactly?

The third message, just incoming, said:

Nice try. But it seems that you already have.

Enga stared at the messages. She couldn't unravel what they meant. Akavi had wanted to find Talirr and the Seven; he had just gone to them in disguise. Had Talirr seen through his ploy – was that what the message meant? But then why would she keep sending messages to the *Talon*?

Whatever. Enga was neither a strategist nor a spymaster. She didn't have to care. What she cared about was: Akavi hadn't told them he was talking to Talirr. He hadn't told them there was still a way to send messages to the *Talon* – or that there was a security breach, letting Talirr do it when no one else could. It was mission-critical information, but he didn't give a shit if they had it. He was paranoid and grandiose like always. He'd wanted to keep it to himself.

Fuck Akavi. Enga wasn't waiting around for him.

She turned on her heel and stormed back to the room where Elu and Luellae were sitting. She was too agitated to stop walking at the right time so she deliberately plowed right into the opposite wall, smashing her whole body into it like it was someone she wanted to knock over. Elu startled at the sound, looking up at her with worried eyes.

"Enga, I know you're angry. We're all angry. I just don't want you to hurt yourself."

Without breaking stride, Enga snatched the tablet out of his hand.

HOW LONG WILL AKAVI BE GONE, she typed. The tablet obligingly translated the words into a toneless spoken voice.

"I don't know." Elu frowned. "He didn't say. I assumed a few hours, but... I don't see how the Seven would let Luellae go again so easily, if they think they have her. It might be days. His old missions on Jai used to last weeks. It might be all the way until the battle."

Enga jerked her chin in Luellae's direction. *THEN SHE HAS A FEW DAYS.*

Elu sat up slightly straighter. She thought she could see her plan slowly dawning on him, moving across his face. "You can't know that."

Luellae, who hadn't known either of them for nearly that long, looked up sharply. "What are you planning?"

AKAVI IS GONE. HE IS A LIAR AND NEITHER OF YOU LIKE HIM. THERE IS A BATTLE COMING. WHY SHOULD WE SIT AROUND AND WAIT FOR HIM. THE KERES IS COMING WHETHER SHE IS NEMESIS OR NOT, AND WE ALL HAVE BEEF WITH THE KERES NOW. WHY SHOULDN'T WE FIGHT.

Elu spluttered. "What do you mean, neither of us like him–"

*I SAW YOU FLINCHING FROM HIM. YOU KNOW EXACTLY
WHAT I MEAN.*

Elu's face was the face of a child whose favorite stuffed
animal had been taken away. Enga had no patience for this.
As soon as she boarded this ship, she'd seen that something
had changed between Elu and Akavi. The old, puppy-
dog adoration had been replaced by genuine fear. And as
sorry as she wanted to feel for him, secretly, her dark heart
had leapt at the sight. She hated Akavi. She hated Elu for
following him. She'd wanted to bring them both to justice.
But if Nemesis had lied like this then Her way wasn't justice.
And maybe Elu, after all, could be salvaged.

"He'll be angry," said Elu at last.

SO ARE WE.

"He'll... try to hurt us."

FUCK HIM.

"We don't–" Elu protested a third time, but Luellae, on
her cot, interrupted him.

"Hang on," she said. "Hang on. I don't have the context to
understand more than like half of this. What are we talking
about? You're talking about flying away from here against
Akavi's wishes? Fighting in the battle against the Keres,
even though technically the Keres is the same artificially
intelligent bitch you both used to work for?"

Y.

"The letter *y* means *yes*, right?"

Y, said Enga, just to be difficult.

"Yeah, that's how she says it," Elu confirmed, sounding
faint.

"You guys don't *want* to do what Akavi says."

Y.

"That's new." Luellae sneered, but she was too excited to

stay with the sneer for long. She pointed at Elu. "And you're worried that he'll hurt you if you go and fight. And you're worried that he'll hurt *me*. Or the bomb that's supposedly in my arm will just blow up or whatever and I'll randomly die."

"This isn't a decision we can make for you," Elu cut in.

"Oh? Isn't it? Glad you finally caught up with that part. Let me just ask. Is there a chance we can make any difference in that battle whatsoever? Damage one Keres ship? Save one person?"

Elu rocked back and forth, agonized. "We can't know that. There are too many variables. We don't know the size of the Keres force coming in. We don't know what abilities the Seven and the people of Jai–"

Y, said Enga. Normally she loved not having to have a tone of voice, but just this once she wished she could turn the volume up and shout. *SHE WANTED TO KNOW IF WE CAN MAKE A DIFFERENCE. WE ARE A FULLY ARMED EXPEDITIONARY SHIP OF NEMESIS YOU DUMBASS THE ANSWER IS Y.*

There was a brief silence.

"I'm done with people telling me it's too dangerous to fight," said Luellae. "I'm done with people telling me when I can and can't risk myself. I don't care about this thing in my arm. I'm in."

Enga looked at Elu. For a long moment she thought he was going to do what Elu always did and chicken out. He was going to take Akavi's pointless, doomed side again, right when she needed him most.

But Elu had spent most of a galactic-standard year away from her, totally outside the angelic chain of command. He'd had time to grow. And what Enga saw, when he looked at the floor and rounded his shoulders, was a man who was finally, *finally* tired of obediently waiting for his master.

"You're right," he said at last. "People need us. Let's go."

Dr Talirr had herded Tiv and the Seven back into the war room, as far away from Yasira as they could get. Tiv didn't want to give Ev any credit, but she had to hand that to her: Dr Talirr understood the bare minimum of Yasira's needs. When Yasira said she needed space, she got it, and the Seven got to have their lively, angry, shocked conversation without her.

They'd spent enough time looking over Yasira's shoulder to understand the news Luellae had brought them. It was hardly even a surprise – or at least Tiv, already weary with war and weighed down with resentment for the Gods she'd once loved, was too numb to feel the surprise much. It figured. It fucking figured – and Tiv rarely said words like that, even in the privacy of her head – that a God like Nemesis would prove to have been playing both sides of the war all along, staging it for maximum drama at the cost of hundreds of millions of human lives, so that people would know they still needed Her.

It figured that the armada that was coming for them now wasn't just the Keres, wasn't just a blind destructive force that Nemesis had allowed in with willing negligence, but was the God Herself, coming to scour the world.

"Did you know?" said Grid, rounding on Dr Talirr. "All this time, while you were fighting against the Gods and calling Them lies, did you *know*? Is that why you were fighting Them? Why couldn't you just tell us–"

"I didn't," said Dr Talirr, although she sounded more

impatient than surprised. "Obviously I knew the Gods were lies, we've been over that, but I didn't know the shape of this particular one. I understand why you're upset, but this doesn't really change a great deal. The problem at hand is the same as before."

"You understand?" Splió shouted. "How can you stand there so smug and calm when–"

But everybody's voices fell to a hush when Yasira walked back in.

She looked like she'd aged several years in the time since the meltdown started, which wasn't unusual with Yasira. She looked like a wreck. Her eyes were red and puffy; her dangerously thin frame shook and she stumbled slightly as she walked through the threshold. Her long straight hair was messy and tangled. But her gaze, when she looked up and met Tiv's eyes, was full of furious resolve, steady and clear. It was a gaze that knew exactly what was wrong here, and exactly what it would cost to put it right.

That gaze lingered on Tiv, with a searing emotion that Tiv didn't feel she fully understood, and then Yasira turned to Dr Talirr.

"You were right," she said.

Dr Talirr regarded her, eyes owlishly wide behind those glasses. "I was. I'm sorry you had to reach this point before you saw it."

That sounded like condescending nonsense to Tiv. But sometimes it was like Dr Talirr and Yasira entered a little world of their own, a level of understanding even Tiv couldn't penetrate. Tiv didn't like it at all. "Right about what?"

"I have to die," said Yasira.

Tiv felt the words like a cold wave crashing over her, like her whole body had suddenly gone into shock.

Yasira had been suicidal before. She had confessed to Tiv, not long ago, that her first brushes with Outside had made her want her soul to be destroyed. Only concern for Tiv had made her change her mind. She had fought so long and so hard, in the six months since she made that choice, to get back to a state where her life felt worth living. Tiv had thought they'd made progress. She'd thought they'd finally started to move past it.

Tiv's fearful imagination had come up with all sorts of ways that Dr Talirr might prey on Yasira's vulnerabilities, all sorts of ways she could twist Yasira's mind and take advantage. She hadn't imagined *this*.

"Excuse me?" said Tiv, taking a step forward. She wanted the words to sound menacing, the growl of a hulking enforcer stepping between Yasira and the person hurting her. But Tiv was just a petite young woman, and her voice came out weak and breathless, like she'd been gut-punched.

"Ev explained it while you were gone," said Yasira. Tiv wanted to wash Yasira's mouth out with soap so that she never called the loathsome professor by her first name again. Yasira's gaze was fierce, but her tone was dull and resigned, like these were all distasteful facts and there was nothing to do but accept them. "There's no way to stop this, not for good, not while Nemesis lives. She's relentless. If the Chaos Zone survives this, She'll try another way to try to destroy it, and another. We have to go to the source."

"How does you dying kill Nemesis?" asked Weaver, who was quicker on the uptake than Tiv. Tiv couldn't do much but stand and blubber, flabbergasted, appalled that anybody would even think of this. "Won't She just – you know –" Weaver made an obnoxious chomping motion with her hand.

Everyone knew Nemesis ate souls, like the rest of the

Gods. Her specialty was criminals and heretics. She punished them in the afterlife. She made it hurt.

"If it was anyone else that's what would happen," said Yasira. There was a burning clarity in that gaze, something that unnerved Tiv. "With me, she'll try. But we all know I'm not like the rest of you anymore. My soul is half-broken. No, I know you don't like words like 'broken', Tiv, but that's what happened. I cracked into pieces and what fills me in between the pieces is Outside. I'm the closest thing we have to Outside itself walking the earth in human form. Even closer than Ev or the gone people. And the Gods can't *see* Outside. Do you understand? It doesn't function according to rules they can process. Say I die. Say Nemesis tries to eat me up. That means sooner or later She takes my soul into Hers, into the very center of what makes Her a sentient being. *She takes Outside inside her.* She won't be able to help it. And Outside will fucking rip her apart."

How long had it taken for Dr Talirr to formulate these ideas, to plant them into Yasira's head right behind Tiv's back? Tiv's hands were shaking.

Yasira had told her that Dr Talirr had handed her a gun once, let her point it at her, let her decide whether or not to shoot. That was Dr Talirr's idea of justice, or penance, or something. For a moment, shocked with her own rage, Tiv wished that Yasira had pulled the trigger.

Before she knew what she was doing, she had crossed the small space of the war room, marched up to Ev and shoved her.

"You can't do this," she said. She wanted her voice to be the growl of a monster, filling up the whole room. She wanted to pick Ev up and throw her down like an angry action hero from a vid. It shocked her that she wanted these things; they were things she had never wanted before. "After everything we've done. You can't take this from us."

"I'm not the one taking it," said Dr Talirr, who had barely even moved backwards. "It's a simple practicality."

"Simple? You call this *simple?*" Tiv's voice cracked, and she felt her hands balling themselves into fists. She didn't understand what to do with her hands. She didn't want to punch anybody but the fist shape suddenly seemed inevitable, like anything less than that shape in a situation like this would be an insult to everyone involved.

"Tiv–" Yasira's voice came from somewhere behind her. More alarmed by this, seemingly, than by her own impending death. That only made Tiv angrier.

"We've given everything we had to your stupid war," Tiv fumed, "and then you waltz in here and ask us to give even more. You think you can take away the whole reason we were fighting in the first place–"

"Tiv," said Yasira again, putting a hand on her shoulder, and Tiv whirled to face her. Tears were streaming down Tiv's cheeks. It took her a second to realize what she'd just said.

The whole reason we were fighting. Meaning Yasira. Not the greater good. Not the things Tiv had told herself she was fighting for. Oh, she cared about the survivors on Jai, and the Seven, and everyone else affected by the Plague. She'd done what she could for them. But in the beginning, Tiv had lost her faith in the Gods because they took Yasira away. She had become the leader of a ragtag rebel group because Yasira needed her to. She had found the strength to keep working and helping the people she could, every day, even when it all seemed hopeless, because of Yasira. Even lying miserably in bed all day, Yasira had done something for Tiv – reminded her what was possible, what was real.

Tiv couldn't do it without her. She was abruptly sure. There was no point.

"Tiv, I have to do this," Yasira said quietly. "It's to save everyone. So many people, the whole planet. I thought you'd understand."

Tiv understood maybe a little too well. Even before she had suicidal ideation, Yasira had always been like this, willing to empty herself out and hurt herself past reason for the demands of other people. Even when she was just a scientist, when they were happy, she'd worked herself ragged just because other people said so. She was the perfect choice if you wanted somebody to nobly, masochistically sacrifice themselves to save the world. Tiv didn't work that way. Tiv had made sacrifices too for this cause, thousands of sacrifices, but she'd made them differently.

"Is that everyone talking?" Tiv whispered. "Are you all agreed?" She couldn't think of anything worse right now than being some part of Yasira that did want to live, trapped somewhere deep down in Yasira's head, and getting shouted down and dragged to her doom by the parts who disagreed.

Yasira nodded. She didn't meet Tiv's eyes, which wasn't unusual. "I probably wouldn't... like... die all the way. Nemesis won't understand my soul well enough to destroy it. I don't know exactly how it works, but parts of me would survive, as parts of Outside, kind of. You might be able to talk to me again."

"I *might?*" Tiv spluttered. Somehow, that made it even worse.

Dr Talirr raised a hand and cleared her throat.

Tiv whirled to face her, but before she could voice what she thought of Dr Talirr interrupting at a time like this, Dr Talirr was already talking. "I can't change this, like I said. I can't just wave my hands and make Nemesis go away, or even make her stop trying to blow up your planet. I'd have done it already if that was how this worked. But I can give you a reprieve."

"What reprieve?" Tiv demanded, hating herself for even taking the bait enough to ask.

Ev gestured impatiently. "The portal. The one that moves you slightly in time as well as space. The one you were using yesterday to give yourselves more time to plan and to gather resources. That portal. There's no reason it has to be used *only* for tactics." She crossed her arms. "You're right, in a sense. It's not fair that I came swooping down with my cosmic pronouncements and difficult truths and from then on, your ordinary lives were over. Outside and the war just swallowed it all up. Life is a lie anyway, and I used to think it was foolish to have any attachment to a normal one, but I've grown to see why most people resent when it's taken away. Of course you resent it too. So, that's my offer. Use the portal. You can't linger more than a day in one place, and you can't take yourselves to the same place twice. But if there were places you wanted to go together, experiences you wanted to have – then go. Have them. Take your time. It doesn't matter if you're, I don't know, both eighty by the time you get back. Yasira will still be Yasira, and we'll still be here, at the same point in this crisis, waiting for you. When you're ready."

Tiv tried to steady her breath, to understand the trap here – because it felt like a trap. If she agreed to the reprieve, she'd be agreeing to what happened afterwards. She'd be solidifying, in Yasira's mind and in everyone else's, that this was what would happen.

And then what was her other choice? Try to override

Yasira's choices about her own life and her body? Try to tell the people of Jai that they were out of luck, that they all had to watch their families and loved ones die at the Gods' hands, because Tiv couldn't bear to do it herself?

Yasira hesitantly slipped a hand into Tiv's, squeezing it. Tiv couldn't bear to squeeze back. But she didn't want Yasira to let go.

It wasn't fair, she thought bitterly, having to make this choice. But she knew what she was going to choose.

CHAPTER 17

The Old Humans who called themselves Morlocks set themselves against the Gods – out of mortal greed, or fear, or other motives you and I can only guess at. But even the other humans around them knew that their efforts were doomed. Why fight a God? Those mortals, so small and so desperate and afraid, always knew what their end would be.

Some people prefer that to living obediently, you know. I am sure you are a good child, and good children sometimes find this difficult to understand. But some people are not good children. Some people would rather fight and die, destroy themselves, then ever do what they are told.

– Walya Shu'uhi, "Theodicy Stories for Children"

Seven Hundred Years Ago

There were consequences for having murdered a superior officer, and Giselle was too overwhelmed to resist them. She could have run, but where in this poisoned world could she have run to? She could have tried to destroy the supercomputer, but with what? She kept thinking about it over the days, the weeks, the months that came after.

Maybe there'd been a crowbar or something in the room, something to throw at it, some way to pry open its thickly reinforced armor. Maybe she could have been clever and cut the power. Started a fire. But in the moment, Giselle only knelt there, quaking and mute, trying to understand the depths of what she had done.

How long had this been General Walters' plan? In order to make adjustments to the soul collection mechanisms without Giselle realizing, she must have had NEMESIS-1's cooperation. Had they colluded behind Giselle's back? Had NEMESIS-1 made herself ready, eager for the general's soul in particular, without breathing a word of it to anyone?

This was Giselle's project more than anyone's, but she didn't understand it anymore.

The general's soul wouldn't last longer than the other souls. But the general had been the one to oversee this project; she had guided it into a shape that was meant for herself. A soul like hers, inserted into a mechanism like NEMESIS-1's, would know precisely how to take charge. Giselle was convinced of it, in the way that she sometimes became convinced of the rightness of a design, knowing in her heart how elegantly it would work long before she finished the proofs. The general's soul would take the patterns that Giselle had already programmed in, and would catalyze them, marrying them to a life-force and thought-style that matched them exactly. Long after she ceased to exist – long after there was nothing that could call itself General Walters – the system would continue in the pattern that General Walters had set.

People eventually ran into the room – combat personnel in full gear, shouting. Giselle numbly got on the ground when they told her to. She let herself be cuffed and led away. She wasn't thinking straight; she spared only a single vague thought for what would become of her. There were more pressing questions: what had she done? What would become of the world that General Walters ruled?

She found out, eventually.

The guards put her in a solitary cell, but she was allowed out a few hours a day for meals and exercise. There was a television in the meal room showing the news. Giselle didn't speak to the other inmates unless forced. She kept her eyes glued to the television.

She watched as NEMESIS-1 and its sisters across the globe made pronouncements and set rules. It was done over a period of several escalating days. The cessation of activity in certain industries, like oil extraction, which for some unfathomable reason had still been going on in some places. The cessation of transport by certain means. The laying down of arms across the globe. The first several days were proclamations like that – measures that almost every climate scientist already agreed were necessary, instant and forceful, with the supercomputers' power and impartiality behind them. There were other rules, softer and subtler: the terms of preservation of certain wild areas, the ways to handle specific keystone species, the economic measures necessary to cushion people against the coming changes to the world.

Every twenty-four hours, a new packet of rules, small enough for humans to take the day to digest. And every time, a wave of human response.

There were the people who'd worshipped NEMESIS-1, of course. The news showed them openly rejoicing. Not only

NEMESIS-1 but each of her ten sisters in different nations, built by different organizations, was now worshipped as a god. Giselle suspected that different news channels were showing different sides, as usual, but the channel they showed in the military prison was of course loyal to NEMESIS-1. It lavished time and attention on explaining how these changes would save humanity. It ran joyfully tearful interviews with the new gods' worshippers, and with others who felt hope for the first time in decades.

The strange part was, Giselle was pretty sure they were right. She'd lived for years in this hell of deadly weather and poison smog. She'd seen the science reports. The world did need this. Was it wrong for her to fear and hate General Walters, in spite of the evidence? Saving the world should be worth a few lies.

But she knew already that the lies had started decades ago. People like General Walters could have done better for the world a long time ago, if they'd chosen to. Instead they'd let their greed run wild and made things worse until humans were desperate for a solution, any solution – so they could then swoop in and provide one, and ask for absolute power in exchange.

So she wasn't surprised when the final day of pronouncements came.

The news station had taken NEMESIS-1's side, but it showed footage of people who hadn't; many of them in positions of power. It showed them in two-second clips, soundbites of a red, blustered, angry, spitting face. Always a white man's face, Giselle noted.

"This is an unprecedented attack on the rights and

freedoms of Americans," said a politician to a rallied crowd.

"Even in the face of the apocalypse," said one of the preachers Giselle had never liked, "we cannot waver. We cannot hand over control of our Christian nation to a group of unfeeling, inhuman machines."

That preacher, Giselle thought, had always been just a little bit too eager to let the apocalypse happen. She wanted to scrub out his words and write her own. The computer that had spoken first with Leah's voice, then with General Walters' – it wasn't inhuman at all. It was all too human, grasping for power in the exact same ways that humans did, only with more intelligence behind it, more raw power. It was made out of humans – that was why it could do what it did.

She realized, in that moment, that some part of her still loved the machine.

The final day of pronouncements came shrouded in a solemn air, like the supercomputers wished it hadn't had to come to this, like they'd hoped for better. But they announced it anyway: the cessation of human self-government, except in certain democratic councils that reported to the supercomputers as a higher authority. The cessation of science except where authorized. The cessation of all established religions. And the redirection of all human souls after death, regardless of consent, into the afterlife the supercomputers chose for them. NEMESIS-1 and her sisters were the Gods now. The highest priests of every other organized religion had already spoken against them; so now all those other religions had made themselves the enemy.

"You must know that We love you," said the final pronouncement. The supercomputers had crafted the rules together, but this part of the announcement officially came from one of NEMESIS-1's sister systems in Europe, a project called ARETE, which the supercomputers had elected their leader. The newscaster on the screen, blond and coiffed and skirt-jacketed, read ARETE's statement in a puzzled tone, like she couldn't quite believe what she was saying. "We love you as any mother loves her errant children. But you have proven that this is what you are. Like children, you are simply incapable of managing your own affairs. We do not hold this against you, any more than We would resent a child. Do not fear – you have called for Us, and We are here now, in the hour of your greatest need. And any who try to keep from you the salvation you have cried for – in your name, and for your own good – will be destroyed."

"Phew," said a woman near Giselle at one of the meal tables – a butch, musclebound type, probably former infantry. Giselle didn't speak to people here unless she had to, but the woman was nearby and she didn't do a good job lowering her voice. "Like that's gonna fly."

"I don't see how they think anyone will go along with it," said her companion – a similar appearance, slightly smaller. "There's gonna be war."

"Maybe that's what they wanted," said the first woman, with a cynical shrug.

Giselle could all too readily believe it. She remembered the relish in General Walters' voice when she talked about war. She used to say that sometimes a war was the best thing that could happen to some beleaguered little part of the world. That, in the destabilization that came in the wake of war, it was easier to bring about change.

By *change*, of course, she'd mostly meant that her own country assumed control.

The rations supply chain had been an issue for a while. Some days there were only two meals, or one. Sometimes the meals were only a thin soup and some seaweed crackers. Sometimes Giselle missed the news and sat in her cell, immobile, ruminating.

"I heard you're slated for execution," said one of the guards, dragging her back from the exercise yard when her time ran out. "Lethal injection. Any day now."

"Without a trial?" Giselle muttered, but whether the threat was true or false, it barely surprised her. She hadn't heard from anybody official – either a military prosecutor to tell her what the official charges were, or a lawyer to defend her, or an interrogation team. She'd killed a superior officer and been put in here, but the world was on fire, and nobody had time to pursue the matter any further.

"Don't fucking talk back," said the guard, giving her a little shake, but there wasn't much venom in it. She looked as exhausted and haggard as Giselle.

When she did see the television, it didn't make sense anymore. There was some kind of war on, people versus supercomputer-gods – the news was just calling them *gods* now. Except there was also something called the Keres, a God that had taken the humans' side. Or maybe several Gods, or maybe some other kind of tech that had taken in a few souls. Or maybe the Keres wasn't on the human side, maybe she was just rampaging around causing trouble for her own ends – the news seemed to say different things about that at different times. No matter how Giselle tried to concentrate, the words blurred together and it wasn't clear. The Gods were fighting – and gods fought in a way that all Giselle's visions of mortal war had not prepared her for.

The whole highway system, melted to slag, in a weird branching glowing pattern. Whole cities and their surrounding areas turned to craters – not Hiroshima-large, like those Giselle had seen in archival footage, but even worse, destruction at a scale that only new and speculative weapons had ever reached. Cities shredded like paper, the ruins lying there in a zigzag pile, metal and flesh. Explosions that didn't even look like explosions. Green lightning. Glowing white storms.

It was like a nightmare, and Giselle didn't realize she'd been compartmentalizing it that way – something removed from reality like a nightmare, haunting and impossible to get out of her head, but not *real* – until the shelling started.

The explosions were weirdly normal and weirdly close. They came out of nowhere – not even an air raid siren until five seconds after they began. There were rumbles like the largest claps of thunder, and the building shook, and dust fell from the ceiling.

Everyone else was leaping, shouting, taking cover. Giselle couldn't move. Her thoughts were molasses. She looked from the shaking ceiling to the round of war explosions she'd seen on the news. With a flash of insight that felt like it should have happened weeks ago, she realized she knew why someone would shell this place. The same military base housed both the prison and the research building where, as far as Giselle knew, NEMESIS-1 lived. If someone had set themselves against the Gods, the easiest way to win was to physically destroy them.

She looked back at the television, where something

orange and green and boiling was happening. There was a horrible thunderclap, and the building shook again, and Giselle finally knew with perfect clarity that she would die here.

But she did not die that day. She eventually took cover and huddled under the mess table with the others, and by some miracle, nothing crushed her or hit her head. There were the sounds of planes flying just outside the building, the sound of missile fire, and eventually whatever caused the shelling was chased off. The building had taken damage, but not too much. It was a military building, after all. It was designed for this kind of thing. And the Gods were on its side.

The next day, a guard wrested Giselle from her room for no reason. "This way," was all she said, as she linked arms with Giselle and dragged her along.

"What's–" said Giselle. After the shelling, she had somehow become blearier than ever. Maybe they were getting her a lawyer; maybe she was finally getting a trial, or getting executed.

But it wasn't a trial or a lawyer and it wasn't an execution room. To Giselle's mild shock, the guard took her outside. It was as smoggy as ever, and the guard put a mask over Giselle's face. She instructed her to stand at attention on the gravelly ground, right outside the building, well within the tall fences that kept the base separate from the civilian world.

In front of them, an enormous truck crawled on twenty heavy wheels, carrying an oversized cargo bed with a heavily armored cover. Giselle watched, bleary and uncomprehending, as a group of enlisted men shouldered a huge, complex object and pushed it up the ramp onto the truck that would carry it away.

It was NEMESIS-1. The chassis, the supercooled helium tanks, the heavily protected nucleus of the quantum computer; the ancillary mechanisms, now changed almost beyond recognition, that allowed it to collect souls. They were taking it away.

And, as it passed by where Giselle was standing, it spoke.

"I wanted to say goodbye," said the machine in a horrible voice. A surreal pastiche of General Walters' voice and Leah's. Or maybe it was all the general, and Leah was only Giselle's imagination.

Giselle made a weird, vague grunt. She thought maybe she'd lost the power of speech.

"I'm sorry I couldn't arrange a better ending for you," said NEMESIS-1, in a tone that sounded weirdly sincere. "The variable interactions are all wrong. It would be harmful politically if I let you go free. But I want you to know I am being as merciful as I can, and that is an honor I will offer to none other after you. You are My creator, and you are owed that honor. It will be a pleasure when your life reaches its natural end, and when you are reunited with Me."

"Sir," said Giselle, inclining her head as protocol dictated. She couldn't think of anything to say. Natural end – what did that mean? It meant they weren't going to execute her. Giselle was going to rot in military prison for the rest of her life. Decades, maybe – or however long it took until she starved. And then she was going to hell.

"I do love you," said NEMESIS-1 in the general's voice, and Giselle's heart skipped an awful, nauseating beat. "None of this ever could have happened without your technical mind and your faithfulness to My cause. Remember that."

And something in the way she said *remember that* made it all come clear at last. This was not mercy. It was a punishment, more devious than any execution could be. Giselle would be left alive to wallow in her guilt.

In a more businesslike tone, NEMESIS-1 addressed the guard. "Give her a private room to view the news at oh-eight-hundred tomorrow."

"Yes, sir," said the guard, and Giselle didn't bother to ask what the news would be. Better to stew. She deserved this.

The news, to her surprise, was a space launch. Eleven identical launches were going on at this precise time, at eleven different secret locations across the globe. Weighted with a God as payload, eleven massive rockets flared and struggled upward, taking to the sky. Up into orbit, or maybe even further, where no mere human attempt at shelling could reach them ever again.

CHAPTER 18

Time Is A Lie

There was a rhythm to the reprieve. In the mornings they slipped through the portal to some destination they'd always dreamed of. In the evenings they slipped through it again and found places where they wouldn't be disturbed. A hotel room believed vacant. The dusty bed in someone's vacation cottage, shut up for the winter. Sometimes they even brazened it out and bought a room with stolen money, someplace far at the other side of human space where the staff weren't checking IDs. All of these check-ins and intrusions were happening at the same time of day, simultaneously, in every place where they occurred. There wouldn't be time for anyone to notice a pattern. The Gods expected them to be frantically preparing for the battle with the Keres. They weren't looking for this.

At first, it was something Yasira only did to humor Tiv. If she was going to die, most of the parts of her just wanted to get it over with. Wandering around, indulging themselves first, seemed selfish. (Even if there were parts of her who did want to. Even if there were parts who knew they'd been starved of pleasure and joy, and who wanted it now. Those parts weren't sure how to express themselves fully, and the other parts shouted them down).

But she had watched Tiv break down at the thought of losing her. Tiv was Yasira's lifeline. She had already decided, six months ago, to keep living for Tiv. If she had to break that promise now, at the very least she could give Tiv what she wanted first.

"Try making a list," said Tiv, while they were curled up under the blankets in a small motel in some country where it was winter now, frost dusting the windows. "Just write it down. Put everything on there that a part of you wants to do before – well, you know. Even if it's just one part wanting to, even if they're not sure, even if it's silly. We don't have to do all the things, but we need the list."

Yasira grumbled, but Tiv handed her the hotel's complimentary pad of notepaper and a pen, and she told the more critical parts of herself to be quiet for a minute. After an agonized, indecisive moment, some small part of her took control and wrote:

Go to a concert

It sounded fucking dumb. A concert, when they were fighting for the life of the whole planet. Yasira didn't like crowds or loud noise. But there had been some little part of her that had always been curious what would happen if she braved the crowd and the volume and did it anyway, just once, just for a band she really liked. She'd always been so busy with school. She'd never had time.

Tiv smiled, and Yasira didn't need her to say it out loud to know that the smile meant *keep going*.

It took a long moment to gather the clarity to write down a second thing. It took a slightly shorter moment to find a third. And then they started to pour out of her, wishes on wishes. Things she hadn't even known she wanted. It felt like opening herself up to be wounded, because she wasn't going to get even half of them, even with a reprieve like this. She was going to die and be translated into some unknowable Outside form that could never have any of these things. But she kept going.

And the smile on Tiv's face told her that this was the right direction to go in.

There was a park full of silly thrill rides and games where they spent a strange day, laughing and incredulous. The reality of what Ev had offered them hadn't fully sunk in; they couldn't actually be getting away with this. Yasira leaned against Tiv's side, holding her hand, at the top of a Ferris wheel, looking down at all the lights and people from afar. She wondered if it was all a dream. Everybody on Jai was preparing to die, but the people on this other planet weren't letting it stop them from having a good day. The park was a lie. Life was a lie.

There was a beach under a clear blue sky where waves as high as Yasira's waist broke gently on the sand. There was a mountain trail where they spent the day hiking; Yasira, muscles atrophied from so many months of near-motionlessness and not eating enough, had to frequently stop to rest. The trees grew tall, and the air smelled pure, and every so often the path switchbacked right up to a ledge where the whole landscape spread out like a bowl below them, immaculate. There was a waterfall, a filmy curtain a hundred meters high, pouring over the rocks into a bottomless ravine.

There was a cluttered but welcoming makerspace, deep

in the heart of a city, where anyone could drop in off the street and start working on a little project of their choice, with everything from soldering irons to band saws to sewing machines available for rent. Tiv sat down at a bench of tools with a happy sigh as if a weight had lifted from her shoulders, and Yasira followed her lead. She couldn't decide what she wanted to make until Tiv pushed a set of instructions towards her. Laughably easy instructions, written for teenagers, but they were for a little hopping robot made of cardboard – not a God-built bot, just a simple machine with one motor that made one motion over and over again – and that had been one Yasira's favorite kinds of tinkering game to play when she was a child. It was a relief to put her hands on the cardboard and scissors and wires and glue, to work on something simple and physical and watch the parts come together in perfect order.

And there were the nights together, sometimes in places as roughshod as Ev's lair, sometimes in the most gilded rooms with the most velvety sheets. Yasira had always had trouble sleeping in new places, but at the end of days like these, she was often so exhausted that sleep came quickly. When she didn't sleep, she reached out to Tiv, whose body was right there with her, warm and sweet.

Sometimes it didn't work. The reprieve hadn't made Yasira any less autistic or less traumatized. Sometimes a small sensation pricked against her skin the wrong way and she curled in on herself in a panic, needing to stop and calm down. But sometimes it did work. Tiv was patient, and she let Yasira decide what to do and when, cautiously touching and kissing in the ways that felt right at the time. When it worked it was an incredible relief. They moved together, glowing with pleasure and love, and Yasira couldn't remember why she'd ever not wanted a reprieve like this, why she'd thought it would be better to skip past it. This was a thing she'd needed time to do. This was a connection she wanted, and her body proved that it was not a lie.

Sometimes one or both of them ended up crying afterwards. Even in the best moments, there was an air of desperation to all this, a feeling of clinging to something because they did not want to let it go. Sooner or later, it all would be over.

"This is stupid," said Yasira. They'd gone to the theatre and watched a professional stage production of one of Yasira's favorite stories. This was on a planet far from Jai, and like most planets far from Jai, no one there seemed to have much idea that anything was wrong. The costumes and sets had glinted with lavish colors, intricate details. The actors had poured out their dialogue perfectly, like there was nothing more important in the world than this tale of Old Earth courtly intrigue, sometimes tragic, sometimes subversively funny. Yasira had loved it, and then she'd gone out on the lawn in front of the theatre afterwards, into the crowd of real people laughing and smiling and joking, and her head had filled with conflicting voices, and her mood had plummeted.

"What do you mean?" said Tiv.

"I don't deserve it," said Yasira. She gestured out at the people on the lawn – mostly people richer than Yasira had ever been. "I don't deserve *this*. Why do I get to do this when what's happening on Jai is still happening? When it's my fault?"

"What do you mean, it's your fault?" Tiv looked over at

her sharply. "It's Dr Talirr's fault, don't you think? Or maybe the Gods'."

"I was supposed to catch her before she could do something like the Plague, and I wasn't fast enough. I was supposed to save the Chaos Zone, and all I ever managed is these little improvements that only provoked the Gods more. They're trying to destroy the planet now because of me – because of what I organized. They call me Savior, but I haven't saved shit. Why should I get all this? Why do I deserve it?"

"You deserve it because you're a human," Tiv said. Her expression was flinty. "Is that really what everyone in there thinks? Nobody can think of a single time when what you've done has helped anybody?"

Yasira looked down at the grass. She didn't feel any better, but even the most self-hating parts of her couldn't truly say she'd never helped anybody, at least temporarily. Her first miracle had given people abilities to protect themselves and keep their neighbors alive. Her second had protected the gone people while they increased those effects, and had given the other survivors a chance to do all the dangerous little protests they'd been waiting to do. They called Yasira Savior, and she had saved people's lives, at least for a little while. She just wished it was more.

"It feels selfish," she said. "Tonight everybody in the Chaos Zone is hunkering down in some awful shelter and hoping they won't be obliterated. Why should I get anything better? Why should I get to indulge like this when the rest of them can't?"

"Are you hurting anybody by doing it?" Tiv asked.

"No, but–"

"Are you stopping yourself from helping anyone?"

"No, I know we're not, because we have the time portal, because when we go back there, we'll have as much time to help them as we did when we started. But–"

"If you punished yourself, if you skipped the whole reprieve so you could suffer as much as the rest of the survivors, would it help them?"

Yasira sighed, glowering down at the ground. She shook her head. Tiv took her hand, and they walked to the door that would take them to the place they were sleeping tonight. The next morning, she felt a little better.

Tiv had things she'd wanted to do, too. Her list was shorter than Yasira's. For Tiv, this wasn't an exercise in finding out what she wanted to do before she died. Tiv would probably keep living after this. Her list was simply things she wanted to do with Yasira.

So Yasira was a bit surprised when, one day, Tiv took her to a shrine of Techne.

It was an underground chapel on Old Earth, cool and clean, and the image of the God smiled down from a multicolored mosaic set into the wall: She wore Her traditional blue and copper robe, sleeves rolled up for Her sacred work, and She held several tools in Her hands. Yasira wasn't shocked by the image; she'd seen images of the Gods many times before. What shocked her was when Tiv, after a moment's contemplation, sank to her knees.

"How could you–" Yasira spluttered. "Why–"

She wasn't angry. She knew Tiv was loyal to the cause. It was just that it didn't make sense.

"I don't know how to explain," said Tiv, on her knees, eyes upturned to the bright mosaic. "There's just something in my head. If I turned against the Gods because of you – and because I was angry – and because the things They were doing weren't right – I don't know. I feel like I left something behind. I feel like this meant something to me for more than one reason, and not all of the reasons were lies. It meant something to you, once, too, didn't it?"

Yasira sank down to the floor beside her, feeling a little guilty. "No," she said. They'd never really talked this out at the time. "I thought it did, but it was always harder than it should have been. I always thought I wasn't working at it hard enough, and if I worked harder, I'd feel the right things, like you did. I liked looking at your face when we were in church – it seemed like it was real to you. It seemed like you were always so happy."

"I was," Tiv said, staring up at the mosaic, wistful and perplexed. That face wasn't the face she'd once had, in those services, shining with adoration.

"Techne was your favorite," Yasira reminded her.

Tiv sighed and looked down. "Nemesis is the One Who's doing all this to us. I can't separate Her from Techne the way I wish I could. They work together. She can't not know. I just wanted there to be Someone I could pray to when I made things, when I created, so it would feel like it had meaning. Is that selfish? I must be selfish. Those people down on Jai don't have the luxury of forgetting who hurt them."

"Neither do we," said Yasira, with an amused little huff. Then her voice softened, a different part of her taking control. "But... it does have meaning. When you make things. It still does."

"How do you know?"

"You made the Seven," said Yasira. "You made the resistance."

It wasn't exactly right – the Seven had already existed before they ever met Tiv, and the resistance had been the result of many people working together. But maybe it was right in some way, because Tiv turned to Yasira and pressed her face into her shoulder, and Yasira held her there for a soft, silent minute, feeling like maybe they'd gotten somewhere.

"What about your family?" said Tiv, later, while they huddled together in a rented tent in a remote campground, surrounded by the calls of night birds and the whisper of the warm wind.

Yasira pulled her sleeping bag closer in around herself. "I don't know."

"You don't want to see them again? You don't want to say goodbye?"

Yasira looked down. Different parts of her had different feelings about this, strong feelings. But the image that came to her mind most strongly was of Tiv's face, a little over six months ago, red-eyed and distraught on the screen of Ev's barely functional handmade ansible.

"Do you remember," she said, "when I called you? Telling you I was alive? After fourteen months of not knowing for sure where I was? But I couldn't come home, and I couldn't keep seeing you. I was pretty sure I was gonna die real soon. I'd just wanted to see you."

"Oh," said Tiv in a small voice, looking away. Which was how Yasira knew she understood.

"That call was for me, not you. It was cruel. You were starting to move on and build a life without me and I just waltzed in and broke it all down again. And you started crying. You said, if I wasn't coming back to you then why did I call? I'm not going to do that to my family. I'm not going to call them up the day before I die and make them mourn me all over again. They deserve peace."

"You could write them a note. For after."

"Yeah," said Yasira. She got up and fumbled through her bag, finding a notepad and pen she'd taken at some point from some other of their sleeping spaces. "That's a better idea."

She fell silent, then, picking up the pen and staring at the blank paper.

She put the pen down.

She picked it up again.

"You have all the time in the world," Tiv said softly. And Yasira supposed that, with all the parts of her arguing over what to say and how and to whom, it might really take that long.

They went to a concert, a big outdoor one, far enough away from the stage that the crowds and the volume wouldn't be too overloading. This was one of the riskier outings, and they were both careful to wear nondescript clothing and different hairstyles, nothing that the famous science prodigy Yasira Shien would ever have worn two or three years ago. Most of these outings had been far away from Jai, but one of Yasira's favorite bands was from northern Riayin, just above the border with the Chaos Zone. The people in this region had escaped the Plague, but they were in danger from the Keres now like anybody, and they knew it.

Instead of panicking or hiding, this particular group had decided to keep on with the concerts they'd scheduled, give tickets out to everyone for free, and defiantly sing.

The frontwoman, hair a wave of bottle-dyed pink that matched her strategically pre-distressed pink shirt, stood on her toes and clapped her hands above her head, leading the crowd as the guitars launched into a riff. The song starting up was one that Yasira didn't recognize – a recent one, she guessed. She hadn't really been in the loop, these last few years, but it was a good new song. It was catchy in the way this band was best at.

The sun joins the mountains
And our hands join, too.
If this is the last night,
I spent it with you.

It was a simple chorus, repeated over and over again so the crowd could sing along, and it didn't take Yasira long to get the hang of it. She clapped her hands with the rest of the crowd. She'd never had a loud or steady voice, but she opened her mouth and sang.

This wasn't the Chaos Zone. These weren't the gone people. Outside didn't link them together in any overt way. But Yasira was Yasira, and she saw things in the way that she'd learned to see them. Just like the different parts and personalities that made up her self; like a group of gone people acting in unison; like the conglomeration of atoms, molecules, cells that made up her body; or the people, terrain, infrastructure, and natural organisms that made up a whole world. Just like that. The crowd was one being, connected by the band's driving rhythm. It was exhilarating to be just one part of that whole. Hands raised to the sky. Voice raised.

The frontwoman reached out her hands to the crowd. She wasn't singing to some absent or imaginary lover. She was singing to the audience that had made her a star, the collective being she loved so much that, even in the face of an apocalypse, her last wish had been to sing to them one more time.

Tears fell down Yasira's face as she sang, as she clapped her hands to the driving beat. She could hear Tiv was singing at her side.

The sun joins the mountains
And our hands join, too.
If this is the last night,
I spent it with you.

"Do you remember," Yasira said, later. They hadn't left the field yet where the band had played. The sun was setting, and the crowds were slowly dispersing; they'd found a place up on a hill, under a couple of spindly trees, where they could sit together. "Back on the *Pride of Jai*. When you wanted to ask me to marry you, and you ordered a ring, but it didn't get there on schedule, and then I was so stressed out about the Shien Reactor you figured it wasn't the time, and you didn't say anything, and then however many months after the disaster, the shipping company got half a clue and mailed it to you in Arinn, and all your friends saw and started talking about it and it was just embarrassing and stupid."

Tiv frowned – this apparently was not how she preferred to describe that sequence of events – but she said, "Yeah, I remember all that."

"I would have said yes," said Yasira.

Tiv's lip quivered. She gave Yasira a long look, and then she snuck her hand over, cautiously, into Yasira's. Yasira took it and squeezed.

"I know," said Tiv.

Nothing had gone even a little bit the way that they planned. But here they were, till death did them part, after all. Yasira looked down at the ground.

"I think it's time," she said. "I think I'm ready."

Tiv didn't sound surprised, or even very distraught. Just resigned. They had both had time by now to come to terms with this. "You sure?"

"Yeah." There were more items on the list they'd made, but they were getting to the point where everything left was variations on the things they'd done already. There was such a thing as a point of diminishing returns. A point where it stopped feeling like seizing the things she really wanted and needed, and started to feel like stalling.

"You don't have to," said Tiv. "Just because we took the reprieve, it doesn't mean you have to. You can still change your mind."

"Yeah." Yasira reached and held Tiv's face in her hand. To her surprise, she found herself smiling. "But you know me, Leader. I want to save the world."

CHAPTER 19

Now

The Zora arrived on their ships the next day. They landed quietly in one of the Chaos Zone's deserts, next to the abandoned observatory that Dr Talirr had repurposed as a base of operations for the battle. Picket was there with the rest of the Seven, waiting anxiously in the dry sun.

Yasira and Tiv's departure had left everyone with a feeling of pronounced unease. Grid had told Picket all about the Zora, but no verbal description could have prepared him for the strange way both the ships and the Zora looked, like massive, living sculptures formed out of stark black and white spheres. He'd never seen an alien in the flesh before.

Weaver, beside him, had been picking at her skin until she drew blood. She'd only relented when he handed her a stim toy, which was already coming apart under her frantic fingers. Picket wasn't the type who fidgeted under stress; anxiety froze him. It felt like Weaver did the fidgeting for all four of them, him and Prophet and Grid.

Dr Talirr walked a few paces in front of the group. It had been so easy to fall into line behind her and do what she said, like this was grad school again. But what had happened between her and Yasira made it feel strange again. Picket found himself so frozen he didn't even know what to say, very aware of Weaver's frantic motions at his side, as Dr Talirr nodded gravely to the Zora and greeted them.

"Greetings, people of Jai," the Zora said back. They spoke through an interpreter – a small, four-armed, indigo-skinned alien. "We are pleased to have come to you in your hour of need. Where are the two that we spoke with before?"

"I'm here," said Grid, stepping forward. They'd worn the same checkered suit they'd worn when they previously met the aliens. They stood straight and composed; the only hints of nervousness were a tightness in their shoulders and a strain in their voice. "The other one who was with me is away at the moment on urgent business. She'll be back before the battle begins. All the rest of us are pleased to speak to you now."

They talked back and forth as Dr Talirr led the group deeper into the observatory, going over the scant resources that the team possessed, the powers of each of the Seven, the amplifier and the gone people and the energy that was gathering from the planet itself; the tactics and threats that they could expect from the Keres; the self-preservation and self-defense that they expected from the Chaos Zone's normal survivors. Picket couldn't keep his mind on most of it. He looked around distractedly at the observatory's reddish stone walls. This place had been carved straight out of the mountain, decades ago; its original owners had abandoned it, and its shape had been warped by the Plague, but the floor was mostly clear of dust and the lights worked.

He only tuned back in when he realized Grid was talking about him: "–can adjust the level of Outside influence up or down in an area. This was useful last time we clashed with the Gods' forces, and we have reasonable confidence it will work on the scale of a space battle."

"That is you?" said the Zora. The movements they made looked random and meaningless to Picket, but the interpreter knew enough about human body language to point a finger at him.

"Yeah. That's me." Picket swallowed hard. He kept thinking about the last battle he'd been in, and the screams, and the way mortals' and angels' limbs had lain scattered on the ground, twisted into mind-bending shapes. "But my, um, my powers hurt people."

"We were given to understand that this was a war."

Picket flushed. That didn't help at all. The only thing that helped, after a moment, was Prophet, who came up quietly beside him and put a hand on his shoulder.

"Angels," she said. "It will hurt angels, not people. You'll be up in space this time – the guilty and the innocent won't be stuck close together the way they were before."

Picket swallowed hard and nodded.

"We have one other asset," said Dr Talirr. "She's not here right now, but we have a woman who is even more intricately attuned to Outside than me, whose soul is more Outside than not at this point, and who has volunteered to sacrifice herself for the cause–"

"*Volunteered?*" said Splió, coming to an angry halt. "Is that what we're calling it?"

"She agreed," said Dr Talirr, in the mildly frustrated tone that Picket knew too well, like when her students weren't picking up on a theorem that seemed obvious to her.

"Don't get precious," Luellae snapped, coming to Dr Talirr's defense. "We're in a war. We've all been volunteering to put ourselves on the line for half a year now. Or haven't we?"

Splió made a pair of fists in his messy hair. "I'm not saying we can't put ourselves in danger. Like, clearly this is an emergency, I get it. I'm just saying don't talk about people like it's a good thing they're disposable, don't call her an *asset*, don't call it *volunteering* when she–"

It went on like that for a while. Picket was too stressed out and miserable to follow the argument. At last the Zora's interpreter cut in.

"When you say *sacrifice herself for the cause*," said the Zora, "you mean because of the structure of her soul? Because her soul is more Outside than not?"

"Yes," said Dr Talirr, pivoting to face the interpreter – nothing was ever more of a relief to her than having something to explain to someone who'd listen. "Because the Gods–"

"Because the Gods assimilate souls," said the Zora. "So her own soul would slip past their defenses."

"Yes, exactly, thank you. You see, *someone* understands–"

"And she is the only one of your kind who has this ability?"

"Yes, more than anyone else."

"Okay, I have a question," said Weaver abruptly. She'd already torn her stim toy just about to shreds. "Sorry, I really, I keep wondering this and maybe you explained it already but I still don't get it. Sure Yasira's powerful and weird and all. Why's she the only one? Why can't one of us do it? Why can't you? Weren't you the one who was always talking about how you're inherently more different and Outside-y than everyone and that's why the Gods hate you?"

There was a weird, awkward silence. Nobody else but Weaver wanted to talk to Dr Talirr in tones like that. Dr Talirr, oddly, showed no offense. She turned to Weaver as placidly as if Weaver had asked a technical question about how a complex machine worked.

"You each have a sliver of Yasira's power," she said. "I have something different. I was born aware of Outside in a way none of the rest of you were. My soul is inherently... attuned. That's been both my blessing and my curse, all my life. But Yasira is not only attuned, she's–" Dr Talirr made odd gestures in the air, seeming to grope for words. "Her soul broke into pieces. What keeps her in the vague semblance of a single piece now is not merely an attunement. It is raw Outside energy which entered her to fill the gaps. The same energy that you saw her call up through herself when she shielded the gone people in your last battle. None of the rest of us have that. I'd need heavy machinery to do anything approaching that, and you don't have heavy machinery when you're dead. Maybe I could find a way to kill a god from the inside anyway; I don't know. If I did happen to die, I'd try it. But we can't afford a maybe and we can't afford a half-cocked attempt at the destruction of a god. We owe it to ourselves to use the most effective weapon. I've run the calculations, more than once, and Yasira is by far our best chance."

"My apologies. We appear to have misspoken." The Zora translator's voice was serenely calm. Picket wondered if that was supposed to faithfully convey the Zora's mental state, or if it was just how being a translator worked. "We did not mean to question your choices. Our question was factual regarding the abilities of this Yasira. She is the only human whose soul has these properties? You have no – prior experience, no shamans or teachers with similarly fragmented souls who can advise her on how to use them?"

Grid was the one who answered. "Not that we know of,

no. There are other humans who are plural, but – not this way."

"*I'm* a teacher," Dr Talirr muttered, but she seemed to grasp that this was not actually a counter-argument.

"I see," said the Zora. There were small fluttering movements, odd burbles just on the edge of hearing, for several moments – the Zora talking between themselves in ways that the interpreter didn't bother to translate. But at last the interpreter said, decisively, "Yasira will fly with us on Ship One. We will advise her. We will ensure that her part of the mission is completed."

All the Seven looked back and forth at each other uneasily.

Immediately after the next turn, the space opened out into a large, domed room. It must have once held whatever the original researchers built this place for: a big telescope, from the looks of that domed roof, and other instruments. But the telescope itself was long gone. Instead, what stood on its dais at the center of the room was a machine unmistakably of Ev's design. Blocky shapes and exposed wires and swooping curves, all so much a piece with the style of every other strange thing she'd ever built.

"This is the amplifier that I mentioned to you," said Dr Talirr. "It will gather, intensify, and distribute the Outside energies of the planet and those raised by the gone people. Any Outside ability you use during the battle – Yasira's, Picket's, Daeis's, or belonging to the Zora – will have more power as a result. This machine will make your dozen ships feel like – Hey! Hey, don't put your paws on that, it's *dangerous*."

She was speaking to the Zora, who had clattered all the way down to the machine's edge and were pointing at it and speaking to each other excitedly. The interpreter cleared her throat again, a faint hint of embarrassment finally seeping into her tone. "My apologies, Doctor. This is... good work. Nonstandard, but *good*."

Dr Talirr crossed her arms and scowled. "Well, I'm glad *you* think so."

"We have questions about the workmanship, if you were to permit. Areas whose purpose is unclear to us at a glance, or which serve an admirably clever purpose but could be made more efficient–"

Dr Talirr's scowl deepened. "*After* the battle. This took me months to get into the state it's in."

The rest of the long meeting was just logistical planning. Who would be where in the air; who would stay on the ground. Dr Talirr would remain in the base and operate the amplifier. Picket, Daeis, and Yasira would fly in three separate Zora ships and use their abilities on the offense. The rest of the Seven would stay near Dr Talirr; they could monitor and organize the battle from the observatory's communications panel.

Picket tried to pay good attention, like it was an important lecture at school, to plot out all of the large-scale tactics in his head and calculate a plan. But he must have lost his edge since those old game-playing days. All he could concentrate on was the gnawing anxiety that filled him and would not let go.

Since interacting with mortal survivors hadn't conclusively produced anything useful, Sispirinithas had returned to his ship and quickly printed out some sensors of various types. This was where God-built systems, full of nearly limitless repositories of all sorts of data, came in handy. He was no technological specialist, but he knew how to sense incoming ships in the vicinity of a planet. He knew at least approximately what size and type of ships the Keres would probably have, and what direction they would most likely come from. He'd set up the sensors necessary to pick these things up, and then he'd retreated with them into a little cave he'd found in a forested ravine, in one of the wilderness areas of Jai outside of the Chaos Zone itself, because good gracious, those Keres ships were going to be here any minute now and Sispirinithas had no desire to be in their direct line of fire.

So when he detected another ship – about the size of the *Talon*, not moving in synchrony with the Keres ships which were approaching, and not connected to Nemesis' network – he knew what to do.

Enga no longer had a connection to the ansible network, but she'd once been fitted with something else – a small, low-bandwidth radio transceiver, keyed to a narrow band of frequencies, which would allow her to text-send messages to a translator device when the network was not available. This had been necessary in the early days of the Plague, when the ansible network had not functioned on Jai's surface. Ansible connectivity had eventually been restored, and the angels appeared to have forgotten about the whole matter. Maybe Akavi and Elu would have thought to remove the radio transceiver from Enga as well as the ansible uplink; but maybe not. It was, as the humans said, worth a shot.

He hunkered down at the entrance to his cave, just far enough out that the rocks overhead wouldn't block the signal, and began to compose a message.

Enga was at parade rest, looking at the curve of the planet below her as the *Talon* quickly approached the field of battle.

She did not bother to move a muscle, but an excitement coursed through her veins nonetheless. Her little crew was going to *do* something, accomplish something, consequences be damned. And for once, it wasn't what they had been ordered to. It was theirs. Enga had not felt so delighted by a mission in a long time. It might very well kill them, but that was fine.

She did not expect to hear a ping, and a coded message, in her radio transceiver.

In all the fuss about removing the ansible uplink, Enga had forgotten about this. It wasn't like the ansible, something she could constantly nudge with her mind to remind herself she was part of something bigger. It wasn't even like a regular radio – she couldn't tune it this way and that to pick up the mortal stations. It scanned the space around her for a very particular set of codes and shifting frequencies, and if it found them, it translated them into text for her. If it didn't find anything of that precise description, it didn't give her anything at all. And those frequencies had only ever been used for a short time, on a mission to Jai six months ago.

Enga didn't move. She read the message as it appeared in the part of her electronic brain designed for text-sending.

My dear Enga, the message said. *It's Sispirinithas. Irimiru sent me to check on you. It's been lonely on the* Menagerie *without you, quite frankly, and I imagine your current circumstances are endlessly frustrating to you as well. If you've received this message, would you mind sending back an update? The Overseer is terribly impatient to hear news of Akavi and Elu, where they are, what they're doing.*

Enga considered the message silently.

When she started this mission, she'd loathed it – but she'd also wanted revenge against Akavi and Elu, more than almost anything. She'd looked forward to bringing them in and seeing them punished. But now?

Now Enga knew the truth about Nemesis and the Keres, and it was one more betrayal in a whole life of betrayals. It had broken something in her. Enga knew how to obey superiors she hated and prioritize survival, when she had to, but right now it was hard to really give a shit. She was flying into a battle that might well kill her anyway and it was a battle that really mattered, more than any political squabble or even Enga's hurt feelings. She was *busy*.

She hadn't stopped hating Akavi. He'd always been a manipulative little shit. And she didn't like how the energy between him and Elu had changed. Elu looked afraid of him now, uncomfortable with him in some way that was different from before they left. Enga didn't know much about relationships but she could see that, and she didn't like it. She didn't like Akavi at all. But Akavi wasn't on this ship right now. He also wasn't anyplace where the rest of the angels of Nemesis could immediately go get him. He was in Dr Talirr's lair with the Seven, and if the angels of Nemesis had a way to get in there, they'd have done it ages ago.

Elu – well. She was still annoyed with Elu. But she wasn't actually sure if she wanted him dead.

And Luellae wasn't part of the mission. Luellae had the beginnings of a rage like Enga's, and Enga didn't want her dead, either.

Of course, if the angels could detect where the *Talon* was and had guessed that she was aboard, then they could come and pick everyone up even without Enga's say-so. The fact that they were flying directly into a pitched battle with the Keres was probably the only thing that stopped them right now. It was probably also how the angels had found where they were. The *Talon* had been modified to look like a civilian ship to God-built sensors, but no civilian ship would be stupid enough to fly in this specific direction at this specific time, right into the Keres' jaws. And no angel of Nemesis was going to wade into a Keres battle – even if the Keres was Nemesis; most of the angels didn't *know* that – just to try to catch a pair of fugitives. If they survived this, they might be able to lose pursuit, blend back into civilian traffic again.

Enga was a broken thing with sharp edges. She might die in the next few minutes; or all sorts of other people might die. She didn't have to care what Irimiru wanted anymore.

She closed the message window without a reply.

"Luellae," said Talirr abruptly. The crowd of the Seven had dispersed, each preparing for their respective tasks and waiting Yasira's arrival, which left Talirr and Akavi alone in the reddish stone corridor. "I wanted to talk."

"Sure," said Akavi with an appropriately morose shrug. She had studied Luellae's mannerisms long enough to copy them, with the help of her microexpression software and other programs that helped load saved movement and intonation patterns into the body's motor cortex. She was certain the impression was flawless. Even the pronouns with which she internally referred to herself switched over. Not all Vaurians favored that last step, when they took a body with an apparent gender different from their habitual one, but Akavi preferred it. She liked not committing to one single set of pronouns forever, and it gave her a sense that her transformations had been appropriately thorough.

"I'm sure your time with the angels has been unpleasant," said Talirr.

"That's an understatement." Akavi scowled.

"There's something off," said Talirr, looking at her more closely. "I noticed it as soon as you arrived. Something about your mind's interface with Outside seems different. Did they do something to you?"

Akavi's glance flicked up at Talirr's face. Talirr's microexpressions were more difficult to read than most. Akavi didn't detect any suspicion of her true identity in that placid, matter-of-fact face, but she couldn't rule it out. She had carefully considered how she would get past the gauntlet of Grid's augmented senses, but she had not fully considered Talirr's, the true extent of which were unknown. Best to play along, either way, and to give a plausible explanation for the change.

"Besides the thing in my arm," she said, looking down in shame at the floor. The linoleum looked as though it hadn't been repaired in several years. These students had Outside abilities and an entire galaxy to steal from, yet they lived in this pitiful squalor. "They... did something else. I'm not sure what. I was knocked out. But I can't teleport anymore, not unless Akavi sends a signal to the thing in my arm to authorize it. For all I know, they might have done other stuff too."

"I might be able to fix that," said Talirr, holding out her hand.

Akavi looked up at her in surprise. Just like that, with a gesture so undemonstrative Akavi might not have noticed, Talirr had summoned some form of Outside energy into the palm of her hand. Akavi couldn't directly see it, thanks to her sensory filters, but she could see blackness where the energy ought to be. A whole nest of black tendrils, winding upwards like long amorphous fingers, wriggling in Akavi's direction as if scenting her.

"What–" said Akavi, stepping back.

"Outside energies can bypass god-built technology," said Talirr, "at least to an extent, and a greater extent than the angels tend to realize. If you like, I could release a couple of these into your system. They might make your powers go a little haywire for a few weeks, or they might cause mood swings, et cetera – I've never tested them this way before. But in principle they would likely to be able to undo any constraints the angels have placed upon you. Very likely they'd fix whatever that thing in your arm is, too."

Akavi was certain of one thing: she was *not* letting any Outside constructs, untested or otherwise, into her body. Anything designed to overcome angelic constraints on someone's system might well play havoc with the inner circuitry that Akavi happened to need in order to live. But even aside from that: no. Obviously no. Not even at the cost of breaking her cover.

"Listen, *Ev*," she snarled, thinking fast, making sure to stay within the range of responses that the real Luellae could have plausibly had. "You're on the team because we're desperate and we need all the help we can get. It doesn't mean we trust you. And it does not mean I'm letting you put – whatever those brain worms are into my head. Eurgh!"

She braced herself for an argument, but Talirr only shrugged. "Suit yourself. I won't force you," she said, before wandering aimlessly away. The black tendrils retracted into her hand and vanished.

Akavi leaned against the stone wall in the dim light and caught her breath. She did not want to admit how tense she was, or just how close a call that had been.

* * *

When Yasira returned to the lair, it was the Strike Force that guided her. She could not waver now. She'd made up her mind. It wasn't that the parts of her even disagreed anymore. It was just that some felt more focused on victory than others. Some wanted to wallow and wail at what was necessary. Those parts could say what they wanted to, in the back of her mind, but it was time to fight now and face what would come.

But even the Strike Force couldn't help but pause, for a moment, at the sheer force of emotion that hit her when she saw the lair again – disheveled and full of the team's effects as usual, with everything spread around in every dimension heedless of gravity, in the way that had once looked eerie to her but now felt as familiar as a home. Subjectively, it had been months since she'd seen this room; when she'd quickly used the portal, during the reprieve with Tiv, she'd only gone in through the outer door, and immediately about-faced and come out again somewhere else. She hadn't wanted to come back to the inside of the lair.

This little room had been kind to her, kept her sheltered in its haphazard and misshapen way, and held the friends who cared for her. But she could not help but think, as she took a last look up and down the strange cavernous space, how limited it was. She'd hidden in here for six months – mostly in the little cubicle that was her bedroom. She'd needed it at the time, but now it seemed like a waste.

The research base, when they got to it, didn't faze her as much. It was beautiful in its way, with the tunnels cut deep into the striated red rock. Deep down in the main rotunda, the Zora waited, standing at what must have been attention for them, their strange bulbous black-and-white bodies straight and still.

Tiv had told her about the Zora and their ships and their interpreter, but it was still a surprise to see them in real life. The only two aliens Yasira had seen in person before – if Outside monsters didn't count as aliens – were the Spider and the Boater who had worked for Akavi. But it was plain to her, even at a glance, that the Zora worked only for themselves.

And for Outside, whispered some contradicting voice in the back of her head. *And for us.*

She would rather look at the Zora than the rest of the Seven. For the rest of the Seven, it had been hardly any time at all, and she could feel them watching her with varying levels of unease. None of them were really sure this was OK.

There were various pieces of tactical information, which the Strike Force observed attentively, and the Scientist asked a few questions about, but none of it mattered all that much; Yasira's only real job in this fight was to die.

She was surprised – although she shouldn't have been – when the Zora asked to speak with her alone.

Yasira didn't really want to – she'd wanted to step right from the reprieve to the final battle and be done with it – but she went along with them to a meeting room at one side of the observatory, just a table surrounded by sandstone walls and dim lights, the chairs mostly gone or broken. Ev didn't seem to have used this room at all since she'd moved in.

"You are the one called Savior," said the Zora's translator. Yasira couldn't read their body language – the small stature, the four arms, the face stretched out just far enough off past human proportions to look wrong. They didn't look Yasira in the eye, which was finc with Yasira.

"Yes."

"And you have been chosen to sacrifice yourself in an attempt to destroy one of your human Gods. Because of the structure of your soul, which allows you to carry Outside energies in ways another human soul could not."

"Yes."

"I wish to apologize in advance," said the translator. "Your culture is difficult to study. We are not sure what ways of broaching this topic, if any, are considered polite. In the absence of such guidance, we will go straight to the point. If this distresses you, please correct us."

Yasira waved a hand vaguely, and then remembered that the translator probably didn't know what a vague hand wave meant. "It's fine."

"Your culture has no tradition of engagement with what you call Outside. You have had to work out ways of engagement for yourself. Is that so?"

"Yeah." Ev had taught her a bit, but Ev couldn't fully be trusted, and Ev had needed to work it out for herself, too.

"We have no wish to contradict methods you have found that work well for you. We are not human, and we do not fully understand the human mind's interface with Outside. Even self-taught, your methods may have as much meaning for you as our traditions do for us, and the two may not be fully compatible."

"Okay," said Yasira. She wasn't sure how this counted as getting to the point. There was no reason to nitpick the way she used Outside *now*. She was going to be dead in a few hours.

"But we wish to query."

"Yeah, go ahead, it's fine."

"How exactly do you believe that this is going to work?"

Yasira let out a long breath, looking down at the dirty

stone floor. She let the Scientist answer this one. Most of the rest of her, even the Strike Force, had been studiously not thinking about the details. "I don't know. I mean, I need to die so that Nemesis will eat my soul, and then because my soul is mostly made of Outside now, I can use it to destroy Her. I don't really know what to expect once I'm dead. It'll probably hurt a lot. That's what we learned in Sunday school, that it hurts a lot. But they leave a lot to the imagination."

"We know that the machines you call Gods are capable of taking in what you call soul-energy, and that therefore, by necessity, soul-energy reaches their interiors, where they are more vulnerable. The Outside energy we detect in your soul is sufficient to the task of destroying a God in that manner. Of the Gods' precise inner workings and the qualia experienced by the souls they assimilate, we are unfortunately uninformed."

Yasira bit her lip. It was strange, hearing it affirmed – that she could do this, in theory. The Zora thought so too; it wasn't just Ev's wild conjecture.

The interpreter barreled on, though. "What we are asking is – how do you believe you are going to die?"

Yasira shrugged uneasily. "Well, there's a battle. I figured we'd get shot down, maybe on purpose. Or maybe you'll kill me?" But now that she'd said it aloud, she realized neither option completely made sense. Getting shot down on purpose would kill the Zora aboard, too. And if they killed Yasira in some horrible, ritual, alien way, then Nemesis might notice that she wasn't a battle casualty, and that would be suspicious.

"Your culture calls you a Savior," the Zora explained, with a strange, strained patience. "In your most recent battle with the Gods, you were able to spread your Outside power across many locations. Is that not so?"

Yasira frowned. "What are you saying?"

"We are saying that it does not make sense to us that you should need to die. Not fully. There are those with abilities like yours among our own people, though they are rare. Were you a Zora, you would not need to die in order to extend some of your soul and place it within Nemesis' mechanisms. It would be a strenuous task. You might lose the ability to return to your physical body, and many species see that as a form of death. But you would not be destroyed, so long as you were not fully consumed by the God. Certainly the kind of violence that you envision would not be necessary. You would only need to channel your abilities in the correct way, at a time when it would be plausible to the God that She might receive you."

Yasira swallowed hard. This wasn't very different from what Ev had told her. Ev had said that some part of her might remain after this, in a changed form. But Ev hadn't known how it would work. To Ev, the difference between this and dying didn't matter so much. Hearing it from the Zora was different. It felt, in a cruel way, like hope.

"I just don't really know how," she confessed. "I don't really know what I'm doing."

"Tell us more about how your abilities worked when you used them before," said the Zora. "Tell us more about how you conceptualize them."

So she did, haltingly. There was a lot that she'd never had to articulate before, a lot that surpassed words. Frequently she stopped, backtracked, and contradicted herself as another part weighed in with more information. Some of it was information the conscious parts of Yasira hadn't even known before. The Zora asked questions, like *what route does the energy take as it passes through you?* And *by what mechanism can you disperse your constituent selves in space?* And Yasira would halt for a moment, tongue-tied, before some deep-down, mostly Outside part unexpectedly supplied the answer.

It was a long, exhausting conversation, and many parts of Yasira just wanted it to be over. Some parts of her weren't even sure they could trust these creatures. But gradually, painstakingly, she and the Zora seemed to come to an understanding. They started to explain what Yasira would need to do, in Outside terms, how she could do it with the least difficulty. And there was something comforting about that, about having a path forward, even a painful one. A path that made sense, even if most of her wished with all her heart that she didn't have to do it.

She wanted to crumple to the floor and cry. But as she walked out of the room again, towards the valley outside the observatory where the Seven and the Zora's ships were waiting, the Strike Force were the ones in control. Her back was straight. Her eyes were dry.

Tiv, by the ship's loading ramp, drew her in for one last hug. Yasira was too nervous and distressed to really enjoy it, and the weight of Tiv's small body felt like prickles against her, but this was important and she did not let go.

"You don't have to," Tiv whispered. "Even now. If you chose differently. You don't have to–"

"I know," Yasira whispered. "Ssh. I love you."

"I love you too, Savior."

And then it was time to turn and walk onto the Zora's ship, leaving everything else she knew behind for good. The Strike Force took over fully for that; they marched her body mechanically up the loading ramp, into a strange, bulbous, black-and-white room built for Zora bodies, not human ones. They did not allow a single glance back.

CHAPTER 20

"Ship Three is in position," came a crackling voice through the comms into the research base as Tiv sat anxiously on a chair near the comms panel, watching the others. They'd set it up so that the interpreters, one on each Zora's ship, could talk to them, so that they could help coordinate everything from down here.

"Copy that," said Grid. "We're going to start the amplifier now."

"Copy that, Base. The gone people are already working at their part."

"You can tell?" said Grid, surprised.

"The sensitive among us can tell."

"*I* can tell," said Dr Talirr, crossing her arms. She'd been jealous of the Zora ever since they arrived. Tiv had caught her more than once, muttering things like *so there have been aliens just waiting around, elsewhere in the galaxy, knowing more about Outside than I do. I don't know why I wasn't informed. They could have come and talked to me years ago.* The rest of the Seven had overheard it, too – it was possible that Dr Talirr intended to be overheard, and it was equally possible that she wasn't thinking about who could and couldn't hear.

Tiv didn't have the energy to care about Dr Talirr. Yasira

was up there, on Ship One, in that formation. And Tiv was never going to see Yasira again.

The rest of the Seven were busy, but they'd had enough sense not to bother her with demands. Tiv couldn't have done much to help right now if she tried. She watched in anxiously resigned despair as Grid, Splió, and Prophet sent hurried messages back and forth, helping the Zora's formation align itself with the energies the gone people were raising from their hideouts all over the Chaos Zone. She watched as Dr Talirr stopped her grumbling and went to the amplifier, turning on lights and flipping big switches, easing something that looked like a satellite dish over to the correct angle. The machine made a humming, rumbling sound.

What burst out of the machine's curves and points, after a moment, was something Tiv couldn't describe at all. *Light* was not an adequate word, although it did something like glowing, strongly enough that she felt the urge to shield her eyes. It was an energy field in all sorts of searing colors, like the flame of an unshielded smelter. Tiv couldn't escape the feeling that if she looked too hard or walked too close to it, she'd fall in and be burned to ashes, or even less. Even to someone like her, who'd gotten accustomed to the Chaos Zone over months of exposure, the amplifier felt like too much. Tiv wondered if the prayer machine had felt like this.

Even Splió, Grid, Prophet, and Weaver flinched away. But Dr Talirr stared into that strange flame with an unearthly delight. Like a child seeing some natural marvel for the first time. Like a woman coming home to her lover. Dr Talirr reached towards it, put the bare fingers of her right hand *on* the surface – holy shit, Tiv couldn't even watch – and used the other hand to adjust the levers and dials at the machine's edge with the deftness of a musician.

It looked impossible. It looked like something that should have boiled her flesh and broken her to pieces, but it didn't, or at least, not yet.

Tiv could gawk, because no one had given her a job. Grid, Splió, and Prophet were enough for the way the comms were set up – more people there would have just increased the confusion, and no one wanted to pile responsibilities on Tiv at a time like this. It was Weaver who cautiously sidled up to Tiv at last, offering a hand at her shoulder. For once Weaver's movements were steady. Her compulsive fidgets always steadied when she was focused on healing.

"We're here," she said. Just that. She had enough sense not to add *it's going to be OK* or *we're going to win this.* Nobody knew that for sure. But all of them were here, doing their best, until they couldn't anymore.

Up at the comm controls there was a kind of radar screen, showing the positions of all the ships as little blips, blue-white dots on black, nothing fancy. As Tiv watched, the blips began to multiply. Two blips suddenly appearing at one side of the screen, three more at the other, and then another pair, and then even more.

The Keres ships were beginning to arrive.

It was just small ships at first. Picket swallowed hard as he watched them appear out the viewport of Ship Three: first just a couple of flickers against the starry sky, and then another and another and another. He had never seen a ship of Nemesis except from the inside, and in vids; he didn't recognize the shape of these. But they were pointy and grim, like flying fangs, easily distinguishable from the rounded, bubbly forms of the Zora ships.

"Are we in the right formation?" he asked.

"Not yet," said Ship Three's interpreter. "They're in our way–" He hissed and muttered a curse in his own language as the ship banked away from a Keres ship that had suddenly flown out in front of it, firing aggressively. Whatever the ship's weapons were, they looked like bright orange bolts of light – an effect Picket had also, up to now, seen only in vids. The ship rumbled and shook. This couldn't possibly be real.

"I don't know if this is going to work," he said. His experiments by the sea, on the surface of Jai, felt woefully inadequate now. He'd never actually tested if he could do all those things up in space, outside of the Chaos Zone's borders.

Bracing himself against the wall as the ship shuddered, he reached out and twisted reality around the Keres ship.

Or tried to.

His mental grasp slipped, like stepping onto a stair that wasn't there. They were too high up. Outside wasn't up here; he couldn't grab on to it in his normal way.

Or – no. That wasn't quite right. Outside *was* up here – it was a part of the universe, it was everywhere, that was the whole point. But it was so far in the background that it almost could not be discerned. It would take more power than Picket had, power like what had started the Plague in the first place, to bring it into the foreground here the way it was down there.

He could *feel* Outside, below them, on the planet's surface and up through its atmosphere. It was strong and ready to defend itself, and whatever Dr Talirr was doing down there on the planet's surface had made it even stronger. It just didn't go up far enough.

The ship banked again, surrounded by white and orange flames. Picket wasn't their only weapon, of course. They had whatever passed for regular guns among the Zora, and the Zora crew were busy at their own stations, yanking joysticks and pressing buttons, firing frantically. But they were outgunned even by a single Keres ship. And more and more of those little pointy shapes were swooping in from a higher orbit.

"Picket?" said the interpreter, urgency audible in his voice. "What is your status?"

The planet roiled below him. There was a sort of oil-slick flicker at the edge of the atmosphere that Picket was pretty sure hadn't been there before. It was the Chaos Zone's own energy, raised in defense, concentrated by the amplifier. The Keres ships' opening volleys were mostly pointed at the Zora ships, but there was an awful lot of laser fire going in every direction and some of it rained down towards the planet itself. As Picket watched, strange tendrils of energy rose from the edge of the atmosphere and caught the bolts, absorbing and dissolving them.

That was where Outside was. Not right here with Picket. But *down*.

Picket grimaced and reached in that direction. Down into the atmosphere of the planet. Down into the wells of power that he could feel, if he concentrated – the gone people's collective intention, the amplifier's supply of power. With an effort that felt like lifting the heaviest weight he'd ever lifted, tearing something out of the very core of himself, Picket grabbed on to that power and pulled *up*.

A hoarse yell escaped his throat, the kind of sound Picket wasn't used to making. He was clumsy, all his effort focused on grabbing and holding and moving the effect and not on its fine details. But he hit home. He raised some tiny patch of the Chaos Zone high enough that it hit the Keres ship square-on. There was an odd, soundless writhe as the ship split apart, tearing itself into ribbons of metal and flesh and flame which then evaporated before his eyes.

Picket stared at the display, panting. He felt like he should shout again in victory, but the sound that he actually made was a weird, uncertain groan. He couldn't believe that had worked. And three other little ships were already firing at them, closing in.

He could do this. He was just going to have to do it about fifty or sixty more times.

Daeis, in Ship Two, was doing much the same thing.

The Zora had let them sit right next to the biggest viewport. They had been kind – kinder than most humans, really. They had taken Daeis' difficulty speaking in stride. They had explained everything carefully, waiting for nods or other gestures to make sure Daeis understood. When Daeis plastered themselves up against the viewport, pressing their nose and their fingertips to the reinforced glass – or at least they assumed it was glass – the Zora had not complained.

A flying creature bigger than the ship itself – all eyes and mouths and tentacles and strange slimy filmy wings that ought to have been useless up here – kept pace beside Ship Two, one of its eyes raptly fixed on Daeis.

It was harder to communicate with creatures through the glass. Harder, but not impossible. Daeis had spent the whole flight up here, from takeoff to orbit, concentrating as hard as they could. The mental gestures they felt in return were very faint, but they existed. One flying creature had become three, and there were low sounds, just on the edge of hearing – even though there shouldn't have been any sound up here in space. Even though the Keres ships and other Zora ships didn't make any. They were sounds Daeis suspected only they could hear: the creatures calling to each other in a pod, like elephants or whales.

They dived into the maelstrom of battle at Daeis' side, barely even needing direction. They were furious with the interlopers who had come to destroy their home. Daeis wasn't sure if the Keres ships could actually see the creatures or not – most angels of Nemesis couldn't, they'd heard – but they could tell that something had made contact, and they reacted accordingly. Flame and laser fire flashed around them. The monsters grabbed with their tentacles and began to tear the Keres ships apart.

Ship One taxied and took off. Muffled messages sounded on the comms by the pilot's seat – some from the ground team and some from the other Zora ships, in the Zora's own clicking, hissing language. Yasira wasn't near enough the pilot's seat to pick up most of the words, even when the words were in Earth creole. The Zora ushered her to a comfortable seat near the back but it was a Zora-sized seat – oddly low to the ground and oddly wide. Yasira curled up in its padded depths while she watched the atmosphere fall away, coruscating with flame, and the stars come out. And then the worse things that lay among the stars – the enemy ships. The Outside monsters fighting against them.

She needed to get to work, but it was hard to concentrate, flying in the thick of battle with gunfire all around.

"You have done this before," the interpreter reminded her, "or something like it. You were able to spread your consciousness out among what you call the gone people. This will require the same skill. You will be able to reach far enough, along the right sorts of connection paths, to reach into your God – who is always willing and able to take soul-energy in."

Yasira sweated as the ship banked again to avoid a heavy burst of gunfire. She couldn't feel the swooping inertia that her eyes said she ought to be able to feel – whatever the Zora did to maintain artificial gravity, it worked well. But she still felt a disorientation whenever she looked out at it. A vertigo.

At least if they did get shot out of the sky, that would solve this. In a way.

"Close your eyes," the interpreter suggested.

Yasira obeyed. She felt better with her eyes shut, but she could still hear the hurried motions of the Zora pilots and gunners at the controls. She still knew what was happening.

"What previously allowed you to reach out beyond your physical form?" asked the Zora. They'd asked before, in the meeting room, but the Zora were patient teachers, willing to repeat themselves as many times as necessary.

"The gone people helped," said Yasira – it was several of her talking now, each one remembering one particular part of the process a little more fully than the others. "My own structure helped – the parts of me that are already connected to Outside. Ev's machines helped, and the machine I made helped. Pain helped. Pain always helped."

"We can apply pain if necessary," said the Zora. "But there will be enough of that later in the process. Try it without pain, for now. The gone people are contributing to this battle, as is one of Dr Talirr's machines, and your own structure remains in place. Try those."

Yasira swallowed and nodded. It was hard to have any confidence in this process. It was hard to ignore the voices,

swarming deep inside her, that said she wouldn't be able to
do it until she died. Maybe not even then.

But she took a long breath, and she reached deep into
herself, and she reached out.

Akavi had not been invited to man the comms, but instead
of being sequestered as a recently returned prisoner ought
to, she had been allowed free rein of the room. This group,
even after six months of what must have been constant
attempted infiltration by other Vaurians, trusted too easily.
Grid's senses could pick up a Vaurian angel who was still
connected to the ansible net, but it had been months since
Akavi removed that part of her circuitry, and now she flew
under the radar so smoothly that no one had questioned
her.

Nor had they questioned her when she said she couldn't
fight, up there in space. "Akavi's keeping a close eye on me,"
she'd said, repeating the story she'd given to Talirr before.
"He did something to me – I don't know what, but I can't
teleport now without a permission code. And I couldn't
teleport through space anyway, even before that. I tried it
on the *Talon*. Like, I *kinda* can, but I'll freeze and die."

Akavi had come here to deliver the information that
would cause Yasira to act, and she had succeeded at that.
She wanted revenge against Yasira and against Nemesis.
She wanted the both of them to destroy each other, and
that plan was now in motion. It was a better revenge than
even Akavi could have dreamed of, those scant few days
ago, when she hadn't yet known the secret of Nemesis and
the Keres. Either it would work beautifully, or nothing ever
would.

But then there was Dr Evianna Talirr.

Akavi had wondered, after that exchange of cryptic messages, if she'd be here. She was the heretic who had started all this in the first place, the one Akavi had been meant to destroy long before she ever met Yasira, and long before she had any reason to want vengeance against her own God. Now she was so tantalizingly close. What if Akavi could take them all out, all three that she hated most in this world, with one fell swoop? That would be the greatest victory she could imagine.

But Talirr seemed to have her own ideas for what to do with Akavi. Talirr, with this machine of hers that Akavi didn't understand, was helping Yasira's side to its victory. If Akavi distracted her now, the whole thing might fall apart. The Keres, or the secret group of Nemesis' forces who had disguised themselves as the Keres, would probably burn them all to death in this very base.

It would not be wise, then, to make a move against Talirr. Not now. Not until the battle was over, and Yasira both dead and victorious.

But then.

Then.

Akavi had some idea of the correct avenues to pursue. Talirr, in her messages, had seemed to want Akavi to join her against their common enemy. It might be a trap – yet she'd said the same thing on a previous occasion, when they met on the *Talon*, before Yasira shot Akavi. Over Yasira's objections, Talirr had proposed joining Akavi's intelligence about people with her own mystical, technical wizardry.

She would likely be amenable to a proposal like that again. Perhaps they *would* work together – cleaning up in the aftermath of the battle, arranging human space into a new order in which Akavi, of course, would have power. Then she could dispose of Talirr at her leisure.

Akavi could make no such proposal while she was disguised as Luellae, of course. But she could gather information and plan.

She zeroed in on Talirr. Akavi was fascinated by the amplifier; the energy it emitted was not visible for her, blotted out by her sensory filters into a wash of inky blackness, but she had been staring at it and recording all that she could of its operation. And she had, of course, also been watching Talirr, labeling each of her emotions with the help of her microexpression software. Talirr was sufficiently atypical that the software would not always interpret her emotions reliably, but it seemed close enough. She was absorbed and profoundly delighted by her work. She had been irritated by the Zora swooping in to steal her spotlight, but once the work began it had swept all of that away. She was confident it would turn out correctly.

Talirr, according to the microexpression software, was not keeping a close eye on Akavi.

Akavi crept closer to the machine, peering into its depths – as best she could with most of them blacked out. She was careful not to make physical contact with any of the areas she couldn't see into. Akavi had never been much of a technical specialist – that was what Elu and the students she'd kidnapped were for – and this type of technology did not appear in her memory banks. She couldn't help but try to look for patterns, though. She had records, created for her by the students, of Talirr's earliest inventions: the portals that superficially mimicked God-built portals despite working on an Outside principle. She had records of the prayer machine that Talirr had once used with Yasira, though those records were surface-level, only what the camera drones that secretly followed Yasira into the lair had picked up. She had records of the machine that Yasira had designed for the Gods after that, adapting some of the prayer machine's principles to her own purposes. The machine that Yasira had promised would end the Jai plague, and had instead only twisted it into another form.

Talirr's amplifier bore traces of some of those machines' designs: the swooping, chaotic, semi-parabolic curves; the unlabeled wires all over the place, because Talirr had never particularly cared about workplace safety. But Talirr had spent six months experimenting, and her methods had evolved in that time. Akavi took sensory snapshots from each angle, itching to send them to Elu and get them analyzed, even though that wouldn't be possible until this undercover part of the mission was over.

She reached out, laying two fingers gingerly on a relatively unadorned, safe-looking stretch of metal. Maybe this would only be good as archival data, analyzing and cataloguing the intricacies of Talirr's heresy long after she was gone. But maybe Akavi could find the key to her undoing here. Talirr was jealous of the Zora, after all. There ought to be a way to exploit that jealousy. If Akavi could just call to mind a little more about the machine's workings, find some weakness...

"I wouldn't touch that, if I were you," said Talirr from the other side of the machine.

Akavi snapped her head up to stare at Talirr. She had moved from what she was doing – gesturing at the ball of blackness in front of her and pulling a few levers until it settled into a sort of holding pattern, something that would keep steady without her direct involvement. It seemed to have cost her some effort to disengage, and Akavi thought she could see a spidery trail of burns down Talirr's fingers and forearms, but Talirr didn't seem bothered by them at all. The corner of her placid mouth had pulled up into a slight smile.

"Luellae was better at keeping her hands to herself," Talirr said conversationally. "But I knew it would come to this eventually. Hello, Akavi."

CHAPTER 21

"Woah," said a crackling voice on the speakers. "Straight above you, Ship Two. Look at that thing. Holy fuck."

Daeis had not needed Grid to point it out. They and their monster friends had already seen the shapes descending into orbit. They had seen this before in vids. The Keres' smaller ships were unfamiliar to them; but even at a distance, in orbit and in silence and the chaotic blur of battle, they could recognize a Ha-Mashhit-class warship.

It was a massive shape, long and pointed and slightly curved, like an enormous claw. Its concave underside bristled with weapon turrets. There were guns of all sorts, both the kinds Daeis had already seen on the smaller ships and other, mysterious ones. And in the center there was one central turret, far bigger than the others, round and sinister and gaping. The weapon that the Ha-Mashhit class was famous for. The one that could melt a whole continent.

Nemesis wasn't even trying to disguise these. The smaller ships had looked plausibly like Keres ships – bristly, haphazard, all different from each other. No red-and-black paint job. No insignia. But the Ha-Mashhit was a Ha-Mashhit; there was no point trying to pass it off as anything else. Nemesis did not expect any witnesses to survive.

"Concentrate your fire on that big ship," said another Zora interpreter through the comms, but Daeis didn't have to be told. Ship Two was already banking upwards, and Daeis' monster friends, each as big or bigger than a gunship themselves, swarmed towards their prey.

Even these massive conglomerations of tentacles and fangs were dwarfed next to the Ha-Mashhit. They lit into it the way they'd attacked the other ships. But the Ha-Mashhit's armor was thicker than that of the Keres scouts, reinforced with exotic materials and with buzzing fields of energy. The monsters scrabbled against it and found no purchase. The outer weapons of the cluster swiveled, and swarms of those smaller ships dived in, and all at once the monsters were surrounded by laser fire and flame. One of them screeched and lost its hold – Daeis could hear the screech in their mind, even through the silent vacuum of space – and floated away, twitching, into the void.

In the moments when it had an opening, the short pauses between having to shoot at the monsters and Zora ships, the Ha-Mashhit turned its smaller turrets on the planet itself, firing in wild, thick volleys. The planet's Outside energies swirled and caught most of the bolts, but this was heavier fire than what the smaller ships had been able to do, and the atmosphere seemed to tremble with the effort of keeping it at bay. The points that were struck glowed bruise-purple, swelled like angry thunderclouds, cracked and sometimes came apart, a bolt or a group of bolts punching through them entirely.

Daeis knew, because they'd seen it when they spoke to the gone people, that each of those points where the planet's defenses broke was also a wound dealt out to a gone person. It was a gone person or a small group of them, living strange lives but as human as any other kind of people, who clutched at themselves, burns and boils rising under their skin as the energy they'd channeled backfired and overloaded them. To say nothing of the other humans who huddled, terrified, in each missile's line of fire.

And that big central weapon was beginning to ready itself, an orange glow creeping in at its edges, like the world's most awful oven, lighting its coils.

Down on the Chaos Zone's surface, most people were huddled in the shelters they'd constructed. A few had stayed in their homes, trusting basements or other sturdy rooms to protect them. An even smaller number had done otherwise – reckless people, or people so resigned to death that the safety of a basement meant nothing to them. Some of those people hunched in doorways or on balconies now, looking up at the sky, as Elu Ariehmu had done when he was five years old. Watching the lights.

The individual ships of the battle were mostly too small, too high up, to be visible in the daytime. But the laser fire that passed between them was not, nor was the roil of the planet's energies. That was what the battle looked like, to those few on the ground brave or hopeless enough to watch. A strobing confusion of lights, passed rapid-fire back and forth between invisible opponents. And an amorphous shimmer like the colors on the surface of a soap bubble, darkening where it took impact, twisting into awful shapes as it lashed out at the ships above it. Some of those lashed-out shapes were big enough and strange enough to be seen from the surface: tendrils that waved, protruding, from the sky itself.

But, just as everyone had been warned, even the planet's

own Outside energies and the combined might of the Zora and Seven were not enough to deflect everything. Sometimes a bolt of energy flew strongly enough, and at the right time, to tear through the Outside shield, leaving a strange ragged gash in the sky that lingered for a few seconds before its edges gradually knit back together. These were only glancing blows from the small guns; they were not the storm of killing flame that would descend if the Keres was victorious.

Still, those that descended fell like meteors, lines of fire that streaked towards the ground bright and hot, almost faster than the mortal eye could follow. Where they landed, they shook the ground and filled the air with thunder. Smoke rose with an uncanny light at its center, burning red or licking the air with white.

An acre of forest was flattened to a crater, the trees around it falling with an awful crash.

A house burst into flame.

"The monsters aren't making headway. Can you do anything?"

Picket was trying. Sweat poured down his face. Out here, without the Chaos Zone's natural state of flux to support him, using his power was harder work than it had ever been. He had to pick up every outsized handful of entropy from miles below him, haul it up with his own unpracticed strength, hurl it in the right direction, and hope it worked.

And it wasn't working. The Ha-Mashhit warships were better armored than the small ships, not just physically but with some kind of energy field that sent Outside energies scattering harmlessly through space. Picket thought he could get through if he was just a little bit stronger, a little bit cleverer about how to counteract the effect, but his muscles were aching and his own sweat stung his eyes and he hadn't managed it, not yet.

He tried again, whimpering with effort. There was a patch, far away from the weapon itself, where the ship's armor seemed a little thinner. Picket scrabbled at it, the way he might have scrabbled at a jar in the kitchen that wouldn't open or a handle that was stuck, putting as much Outside as he could into his mental grasp.

A few little flakes of armor came off with his effort, twisting and shearing as they fell into the void. But Picket was exhausting himself. It was going to take forever to keep scrabbling at this thing and picking it apart bit by bit. And laser fire was still raining through the sky around him. The weapon was still aiming. He wasn't going to manage this in time.

He should find a better weak point. In games, the weapons themselves were often a weak point. Energy had to enter and leave them, which meant they couldn't be fully sealed off like other points of the ship.

Gritting his teeth, Picket hauled up another handful of Outside energy and tried to twist reality right around the gun turrets. Right around the mouth of that awful, biggest gun, which was beginning to glow.

It worked. He let out a loud breath: reality actually did twist, that time. The warship's weapons changed their shape like a foil sculpture buckling and twisting in his hands. They shimmered and seemed to break apart, pulling themselves into a new form. An even more awful one than before, like a dying insect waving its guns-for-legs in the air, flickering with pain and flame and other, less-nameable energies.

But it was still flickering. That was a problem.

That big gun in the middle was still charging, only now it looked different. Not just an orange glow, but a migraine mirage, blue-white and flickering. The ship's armored covering bubbled and warped, but for now that single big gun stayed horribly in place.

Picket hadn't broken the gun. He'd turned it into an Outside gun. And it was still aiming at the planet, only who knew what it would do this time when it fired?

He heard swearing over the comms, and movements of suppressed panic from the Zora. "Base to Ship Three – what the fuck did you just do?"

"Um," said Picket. "I think. I think I made a mistake."

Elu's hands clenched white-knuckled at the controls as the *Talon* flew into the battle. He'd never been in active space combat before, although he'd dreamed about it as a child. He'd seen vids, both the laughable, mortal-produced kind and actual sensory footage of skirmishes against the Keres. That had been a bold move, in retrospect, the way Nemesis had recorded battles against the Keres and handed them to Her troops as if She had nothing to hide. How many of those battles had been carefully managed so that no one would notice She was fighting Herself? How many had been staged especially for the purpose of recording? When they were staged, would the angels in the recording have even known?

How many angels, and how many thousands of civilians had died, just for the sake of those recordings he'd seen?

The field of battle was coming up fast. One Ha-Mashhit-class warship with dozens of smaller Keres fighters around it, and a small swarm of alien ships. It was a surprise to Elu that aliens were involved: his circuitry informed him that these were Zora designs, black and white and oddly bulbous. He'd heard of the Zora, one of many heretical species which were kept from contact with humans at all costs. One of many species which, in their own way, worshipped Outside. It made sense they would have come to Jai's aid.

But there were stranger things here on the battlefield than alien ships. There were Outside things. Elu couldn't make head or tail of them – ships or creatures or simple conglomerations of energy, he couldn't tell, because his sensory filters blotted them out into simple patches of black. It was hard to even see their precise shape and size against the black background of space. He saw them mainly when they oozed, amoeba-like, between him and the planet. Otherwise they were just patches of nothingness obscuring the stars. The planet itself was full of odd patches of blackness, too – swirls and maws and tendrils doing something at the edge of the atmosphere. Elu didn't remember seeing that when he'd orbited Jai before.

"Left! Bank *left!*" Luellae shouted suddenly, and Elu banked. "Couldn't you see that? There was a giant tentacle thing. It almost swiped us out of the fucking sky."

"Okay, so, the thing is–" said Elu. He was distracted by all the quick work he had to do at the controls. "Angels can't see Outside. We have filters installed. So the sight of it doesn't drive us mad, because we don't get to see the sight of it in the first place."

"Oh, for the Gods' sakes," said Luellae, climbing into the co-pilot's seat in earnest. "You're gonna need my help, then."

Everything was moving very fast. Laser fire rained from every angle. Elu made a couple of hasty adjustments at the controls. The ship was in semi-autopilot mode: going to the destinations Elu directed, but using its own lightning-fast calculations to weave and dodge out of the crossfire. This ought to help keep them alive, but even in a normal battle it would still require the quickest reflexes Elu could manage. He made quick, minute dodges and adjustments of his own every time Luellae pointed out an Outside thing.

"I don't remember seeing this many Outside things in orbit before," Elu said.

"They've come to help, I think," Luellae murmured. "They're Daeis' friends. Or maybe they're just pissed off that something's attacking their planet. But I think they think we're another Keres ship."

Elu dodged and wove through the battle, knuckles white. Luellae continued to bark out frantic directions, but she didn't seem as unhappy or frightened as Elu had expected her to be; in the brief moments that it was safe for her to be quiet, she stared out the ship's windows, rapt. Luellae had been the most hawkish of the Seven. A battle like this was what she'd dreamed of, and for the first time, when Elu glanced at her face, his microexpression software told him she was happy.

But the Outside monsters and the Zora didn't seem to be making much headway. Someone or something had scored a small wound near the back of the Ha-Mashhit, but far from enough to stop the threat.

And then, as the ship rotated, he saw the real problem. The Ha-Mashhit's big weapon. It would have been a terrifying sight under normal circumstances, the muzzle of a gun big enough to melt continents, but what Elu saw was worse. The weapon had been obliterated – and in its place, there was a shifting, writhing mass of inky black.

"What the fuck," Luellae whispered, seeing it at the same moment.

"Luellae?" Elu asked anxiously. "What are we seeing? Is the gun destroyed, or–"

"No, it's not destroyed. It's working, it's aiming, but it's like it's been turned into an Outside weapon. I've never even seen those colors before. I don't know what it's going to do. But we need to take that out *now.*"

The other ships on the field of battle weren't managing to do much damage. Elu supposed whatever had happened to the big gun must have been a misguided attempt from some Outside creature to damage it somehow. A ship like the *Talon* ought not to be able to hurt a Ha-Mashhit-class ship under normal circumstances – but the *Talon* was God-built, and the parts of the Ha-Mashhit that remained visible to Elu had bubbled and warped; there were tiny cracks growing in its surface. They might have a chance. "Can we take that out?"

GET ME IN CLOSER, said Enga, who was in control of the weapons.

Elu swooped as close to that awful Outside maelstrom as he dared.

"There should be weak points," Elu said. "Now that it's damaged. I just can't see them."

LUELLAE. POINT AT THE DAMAGE. TELL ME WHERE TO SHOOT.

"There," Luellae blurted, pointing. "There's a cracked junction."

Enga fired the *Talon*'s strongest gun.

Once. Twice. Three times. Elu twisted the ship's controls and jerked out of the way of a volley of shots from the warship's smaller cannons. But Enga's shots landed. And the weapon began to break apart, the blackness around it shifting and fragmenting. Flame crept out from the edges of the blackened area into visible space. The Ha-Mashhit-class warship was on fire.

Elu couldn't believe he'd done it. This wasn't the end – the *Talon*'s instruments said there were more ships approaching. But he could hear Luellae laughing and whooping behind him.

"Take that!" she shouted, bouncing up and down even as the *Talon* veered wildly to avoid flying debris. "Take *that!*"

"What *is* that?" Picket gasped out, almost too exhausted to speak. "What ship is that?" They'd all seen it, a ship that looked like one of Nemesis' little gunships, but it was fighting against the Keres on *their* side.

"We do not know," said the Zora. "We have been trying to hail them, but they do not share our frequencies."

"It's Luellae," said Prophet's voice through the comms, soft and satisfied.

"Wait, but–" That didn't make sense. Luellae was down on the planet's surface with the comms team – wasn't she?

"Hang on a second," Prophet said suddenly, in a different tone, and the comms went dark.

The Zora's movements at the controls became more frenetic. There was clicking, hissing, chatter back and forth in the Zora's language and the ship's interpreter spoke urgently in Earth creole. "Base, respond. There are more warships incoming; we still need you. Respond."

There were indistinct voices from Prophet's end of the connection, things Picket could almost hear, but could not understand.

Everybody had turned from what they were doing at the comms as soon as they heard Akavi's name.

Akavi turned to Dr Talirr, her lip curling in feigned disgust. "What, you think I'm *him?* You don't trust me? What the fuck."

"I know my own students," said Dr Talirr. "I know Outside. You must have gotten past Grid's defenses by virtue of no longer being connected to the angels' ansible network. But you do not have the Outside air about you that Luellae had. It was obvious to me as soon as you walked in."

"That's stupid. You're crazy." Akavi did not like this, but it faintly amused her how easy it was to imitate the belligerent way Luellae talked.

It didn't seem to amuse the Seven nearly as much.

"Use your powers, then," said Grid, staring at her from their place at the comms. Their face looked calm at the surface, but Akavi's microexpression software noted all the signs of deep alarm – and guilt, amusingly, at not having thought of this test before. The comms panel was making faint noises behind them, but everyone ignored it. "Teleport. Just a few feet. Akavi can't do that."

Akavi hugged herself, feigning shame and distress. "I– can't," she said. "I can't use my powers anymore."

Splió raised his eyebrows. "And you didn't think to mention that before? Earlier all you said was you couldn't use them in space."

"I told the whole truth to Ev. She can vouch for me. I just couldn't face telling the rest of you. I didn't want you to hate me."

"The real Luellae," said Prophet – quiet, undemonstrative, final – "is up there. In your ship. Fighting on our side."

At that, Akavi faltered. There were no signs of deception in Prophet's face, only calm assurance. But that didn't make any sense. There was no way Luellae could have commandeered the *Talon;* Elu and Enga were more than a match for her. Unless–

Normally Akavi had good control, but she couldn't stop the flash of rage that passed briefly over her features as she realized the truth. Elu and Enga had betrayed her.

She should never have left them alone.

That single slip in control was all it took. Everyone had gotten up from their seats now. They circled her, backing her up against the edge of the amplifier. It was a bad set of tactics; Akavi could probably jam something into the amplifier and destroy them all, or at least create a good distraction. The problem with that was that with a machine like this it might destroy her, too. And it would certainly stymie Yasira's progress, up there in orbit.

Akavi flexed her fingers. She could physically fight, if necessary, although with so many combatants on one it would be dicey. But if she'd been found out, it was time to switch to a backup plan. She had wanted to pretend at an alliance with Talirr, and that required Talirr knowing who she was. And she could take advantage of Talirr in another way.

"Believe it or not, I'm on your side," she said, dropping the pretense of speaking like Luellae. "I was the one who gave you the information about Nemesis and the Keres. You have many reasons not to like me, but I'm as betrayed by it as you are, and my former God has betrayed me for other reasons as well. I want Her destroyed. And regardless of the petty resentments that the rest of you harbor against me–"

"*Petty?*" Grid spat.

"–I know that an alliance between us, against Nemesis, could be fruitful. And the messages your dear Dr Talirr has been sending me indicate the same. You asked me to come here and find you, didn't you?"

She paused a moment to let that sink in. She watched as Grid, Prophet, and Splió's horrified faces turned to Dr Talirr. That was about right. Let the fools be distracted by their own side's internecine squabbles, and not by herself.

"You *what?*" said Splió.

"I attempted to open negotiations," Talirr said placidly. "It was also a good proof of concept at getting coherent messages into the angels' internal networks, which carved paths that will be useful for Yasira in the task she has now. I didn't ask you to lie to the rest of the students this way, of course."

Akavi could see murder in the students' faces. Akavi had done many awful things to Yasira Shien; but the things she'd done to the Seven were just as awful, perhaps worse. She'd had Yasira for a few subjective weeks. Each of *these* people had been her prisoner, kept in isolation and tormented into madness, for years. Her best hope was to deflect that rage – to turn it towards Talirr for collaborating with her, rather than dwelling on Akavi herself.

"Then let's cut out all the other nonsense and negotiate now," Akavi said coolly, holding her head high. "You asked me to collaborate with you once before. I'm willing to consider your offer. You've cobbled together a reasonable defense against Nemesis; I could make it stronger. I could help you restructure in the inevitable chaos that will follow our victory. I know people and social systems, after all, which is a skill that all of you lack. In exchange for a few concessions, I can help you keep all of human space under your thumb. I can make you truly powerful."

"Hm," said Talirr skeptically. She looked around at the

students, whose faces had grown more and more enraged by the second. But these students would, in the event, defer to her. "Well, I'm not sure we both agree on the definition of power, but that can be negotiated later. The major problem I see is that you'd be working with people who don't like you very much. These students were on my side first, so my primary responsibility is to them. I'd need sufficient control over you to ensure you couldn't hurt them again."

Akavi raised an eyebrow. Any system of control could be circumvented, of course, with the right kind of effort. But she was not going to agree to this blindly. "What sort of control?"

"Well, to begin with, you can't meaningfully work or fight on the side of Outside if you still have circuitry in your head preventing you from seeing it. You can't understand what you refuse to face. That was why I made the offer to you before, you know." She raised her hand, and those strange tendrils of darkness unfurled from her fingers again. "Maybe I could go into your neurological structure, tinker around. You're mostly a computer already, after all. It shouldn't be difficult to reprogram you."

Reprogram? Well, that was out of the question. But it looked like it was out of the question to the students, too, who were all looking at Talirr with faces of utter disbelief.

"What do you mean, before?" Grid demanded. "You knew this was Akavi – already? Before the fight?"

"I had it under control," said Talirr.

"You've never told us the truth in your life, have you?" said Splió, rounding on her. "You're always playing your own game. We should never have trusted you. About this, about Yasira – *any* of it."

"I hardly think that's fair," said Talirr; somehow her tone was as flat and matter-of-fact as ever. "I've brought a great number of resources to this battle you'd have been hard pressed to find any other way. And Yasira will win this. You'll see."

There was a small movement, a resigned nod, from Prophet's side of the room. Prophet saw something – that Yasira would in fact win, or that Talirr's methods would in fact work. Or some such thing. The other students were not too distracted to notice it.

Splió, a little desperate, curled his lip into a snarl. "You know what Akavi did to us. You *know*. You know what kind of person he is – *person* is the wrong word. Person gives him too much credit. We would never work with him. It would never be OK. There is no amount of reprogramming and control you could fix him with that would ever make it OK. Because we don't trust you either. Not that far. Or at least, I don't, and I never will."

Talirr looked at him for a long moment. Akavi's microexpression software was faltering – she couldn't quite read what was brewing under that falsely blank, calm expression. But something was. There was a roil – was it anger? Was it shame? The software couldn't tell.

"That's fair," she said at last, as matter-of-factly as if she'd been discussing the weather. "We don't actually need her, after all. And I have been trying to be more considerate of other people's feelings."

She stepped back coolly, busying herself with some small problem at the amplifier's controls. This gesture was not ambiguous to the microexpression software at all. It was final. She no longer considered Akavi worthy of her notice at all.

And the students, those with murder in their eyes, advanced.

"What about your Leader?" he asked, feeling a little desperate, gesturing to Tiv. "The one who led you in nonviolent protest for all these months? Surely she wouldn't want you to sink to my level, to abandon your noble efforts, just for revenge."

Tiv returned his look. She had been sitting morosely and doing nothing, no doubt out of grief, ever since Yasira flew away with the Zora. Tiv had been Akavi's prisoner, but only for a few days. Tiv, of course, was the one with principles. And they looked up to her.

Tiv took a long look at him, and a long look at the Seven.

"This isn't for me to decide," she said. And she got up and walked out of the room.

Splió grabbed for one of Akavi's arms. Grid grabbed for the other. Akavi had better reflexes, and she easily shifted, evading their grasp, but she wasn't sure she could do it for long. Sooner or later she would, in fact, have to fight. As a last-ditch effort, she scoffed, maintaining a scornful air as she spoke to the two of them, and to Prophet who was a step or two behind. "You're forgetting one thing, which is that the real Luellae whom you all supposedly care about is on my ship. Whether she has control of it or not is immaterial. I took the liberty days ago of installing a heavy explosive in her body. It requires a continuous signal from me to remain dormant. If I die here, so does she."

The students glanced at each other, and Akavi realized she had slightly misplayed her hand. She had started this encounter by spitting out lies. Now it was only natural to question if this was a lie, too.

The expressions on their faces did not look promising.

Yasira almost had it. She had almost expanded herself into the right shape to use her power. It was easy, really, once she grabbed on in the right way to the energies that the gone people were raising and focusing, that the amplifier passed up to her; the energies, even greater than those, that lay dormant in her soul. It hurt, but so many things in Yasira's life had hurt. It was better than the pain she thought she might have to take. So far, at least.

Now she hovered, only half contained by her body. Yasira was not one entity; she had not been one entity for a long time. The parts that made up her soul spread out around her like a flock of birds – some large, some small, some bold and some hesitant.

She could feel the way the battle raged around her. She could feel the determined efforts of Picket and Daeis and the Zora in the ships nearby. She could feel, more dimly, the people helping her on the planet's surface. She could feel the disintegrating Ha-Mashhit-class warship and the other warships that were rapidly closing in. She could feel another presence, too, some small team from elsewhere that had unexpectedly dropped in to help. She paid that one little mind, but some small corner of her was glad to see it there. Yasira's side needed all the help it could get.

But all of that was nothing. It was child's play, sensing these things, compared to what she really needed.

When she focused, when she called up all the Outside energy from her core and all the subtle abilities of the parts who lay closest to it, she could feel the angels' networks. She could sense the entangled superstrings that tied the points of the ansible network together, so manifestly both like and unlike a grid that it made someone near the front of her mind laugh. She could sense the small places where Ev had found inroads into the system, where she'd been able to leave little messages, although those inroads were too small for Yasira to use for her current purpose. And underneath that, even subtler, she felt the force fields that guided soul energy across space and through immaterial portals, once it had been freed from the body that once housed it, to its destination.

Angels of Nemesis – or angels of the Keres – were dying, right now. Yasira could feel them, the small awful wrench of each strange, half-human soul leaving its body. She could trace those souls as they journeyed to their destination.

And she could feel their destination.

She could feel Nemesis.

That was the problem.

After a brief passage through Limbo, Yasira could feel the awful maw that these souls were drawn into, burning and agonized and so, so big. She had never felt the presence of a God before. It was incredible – as terrifying as Outside, in its way. It was nothing at all like the tall, determined woman that Nemesis always looked like in mortal art. It was something utterly alien, a conglomeration of hundreds of years of human soul-energy forced into the circuits and magnetic fields of a vast machine. And, oh, how it burned. Like standing too close to a blast furnace. Surely not even Yasira could survive that awful heat.

You deserve this, murmured the machine, too crazed and too set in its ways to ever even think the merest fraction of any other thought. *Pain is the only thing that will keep you in line. You deserve to die. You deserve to burn.*

And each of the newly-dead angels, in their deepest hearts, after decades or centuries of visiting horrors on the mortals they supposedly served – each angel believed it.

Even some of the deep-down parts of Yasira, the small ones who carried more trauma than others and who craved pain, wavered when they saw that flame. *Maybe we do,* they whispered. *Maybe we deserve it.* Hadn't Yasira become an unnatural, broken thing? Hadn't she fucked up all her efforts to save Jai, and then fucked them up further by sitting in a little room motionless for months, doing nothing to help? Hadn't she abandoned Tiv, who was the whole reason she'd wanted to stay alive in the first place? Hadn't she made Tiv grieve?

No, said the Strike Force firmly. If they believed that, they'd never be able to win.

But, still, they wavered.

Panicked now, Yasira snapped partway back into her body. It was the small, cowardly parts of her who retreated first, those who didn't see how they could ever possibly do this, and weren't sure they deserved to try.

"I can't," she gasped. "I can't do it. I don't know how to do it."

There was a burning smell coming from somewhere. The skin at her hands and her face had turned red, like sunburn, like scalding. Her throat was raw, and there were tears on her face. Most of the Zora were busy at the controls, careening through the battlefield and shooting where they could, but one in particular had stayed and faced her, and the interpreter who spoke Earth creole stood with it.

"You don't know how," the Zora repeated. "Yet."

"I don't understand. It's too powerful."

"Wait," said the Zora.

"How will that help?"

"I have seen this before."

Yasira took a closer look at them, tried to sense them the way she'd sensed the other parts of the battle. Most of the Zora were just people, the way most humans were just people, without any particular supernatural experience. But this one – and they were not the only one – had some direct sense for Outside, the way that the Seven did, the way that the people in the Chaos Zone with other powers did. And they had seen people before, others of their species, with power like Yasira's. They had worked with such people closely.

"I have not, of course, encountered this specific scenario," said the Zora. "So I cannot tell you exactly what you must do. But I have seen struggles like these, at tasks this difficult, many times. It is not work that can be done in an instant, with a single movement of the will. It will take a little time. Reach out with your senses. Let yourself feel the things around you and the things that need to be done. Endure that feeling, wait in it, grow used to it, and gradually the path will become clearer."

Yasira whimpered and nodded, although she wasn't very reassured. She reached out again. But she did not want to reach out to Nemesis again, not yet, not when the feeling of the God nearby had almost broken her.

Instead, she reached down.

To the Seven and Ev, the team on the ground who were working so hard to support her. To Tiv. Maybe it was cruel to reach for Tiv, when Tiv was already mourning her. But Yasira was desperate.

And as soon as a few parts of her really looked down there, really focused, she could feel that something was wrong. The sense of alarm that had taken the Seven from their posts. The sense of an enemy returning, an old trauma intruding just when it was least welcome. The enemy–

Akavi was down there.

Yasira didn't think about it. She was past thinking. Akavi

was down there, and that was unacceptable. Reflexively, she reached out, grasping the feeling of him in something like a fist. She didn't need this now, the way he kept returning like a cockroach, making everything even worse. Not now when everything was already do-or-die.

She closed her fist.

There was something like the inaudible equivalent of a crunching sound, a burst of flame. And then Akavi was gone, his soul wrenched from his body and carried along those subtle pathways like all the other dead angels.

Faintly she felt disbelief. That it could be so easy. That she had grown, in a scant few minutes, so large.

But it resolved something. Akavi had brought such terror into her life, but now she was so much larger than he was. She was so much stronger than any angel.

She took a deep breath, and she raised her gaze, and she faced the flame.

CHAPTER 22

Ev blinked down from the amplifier's controls at Akavi's crumpled body. Those of the Seven who remained here at the base, really just four now, had surrounded him and backed him up against the lip of the machine. An unwise move, in Ev's opinion; this machine was *delicate*. Its energies would have been lethal to Akavi if he'd backed any further. But it wasn't the machine, or any of the Seven, who had struck.

In death, Akavi's Vaurian body had reverted to its default state, gray skin and plates at the temples and all, eliminating any remaining doubt as to whether or not he'd been Luellae. His flesh gave off a strange smoke, burned from the inside with an energy Ev recognized. Definitely dead.

"Well," Ev said mildly. "That's one way to do it."

The rest of the Seven, who lacked Ev's ability to understand these things, had reacted more slowly. They backed away, mouths open in horror – unable to understand at first just what had occurred.

Weaver, the most impulsive and least perceptive in attendance, was the one who opened her mouth first. "But Luellae–"

* * *

On the *Talon*, there was a beep, and then an explosion.

There was no more time to process it than that. Even Enga, with her warrior's reflexes, had no time to intervene. The bomb went off, and then there was smoke and blood and electronic screaming from the controls, ash and worse substances all over the cockpit, chaos inside and out.

Luellae lay on the ground, eyes wide, too stunned even to scream. Her chest rose and fell, a shallow rapid panting. Her whole arm, above the elbow, had been blown to nothing.

Elu dove to her, abandoning the controls. She was still alive, though maybe not for long. The explosion in her arm had left burns and deep gouges in her torso, and who knew which organs those gouges had and hadn't gotten? Blood loss alone from that arm was going to kill her fast, already an arterial spray across the now-filthy room.

"Tourniquet," he snapped to the bots. "Tourniquet *now—*"

IDIOT, said Enga. She, too, had stepped away from her post at the guns. *I'LL DO THE BOTS. YOU DO THE SHIP.*

"But—" said Elu, but he had already obediently stepped back to the controls. Enga was no medic, but she'd been injured and repaired in the field enough times to pick up a few basics. Medical bots had enough autonomy to do the most urgent first aid with limited guidance. They were already hurriedly wheeling in, slipping a little in the blood on the floor. Meanwhile the ship needed just as much specialist attention as Luellae did, and if Elu left the ship on its own in the middle of a pitched battle, he'd kill all three of them.

A dozen blaring lights flashed at the controls, warning him of damage to this part, damage to that one. At least half the engines were offline.

There was a loud crash and the ship rocked, nearly throwing Elu to the side. Their stabilizers were breaking down.

"We're hit," he realized, as yet another series of alarms started to blare.

Enga didn't verbally respond. Elu wrestled to regain control of the ship, but they were spinning down toward the planet now, and less than half the engines were responding.

"We're going down," he reported, hands trembling. "We're going to re-enter."

ARE THE HEAT SHIELDS INTACT? Enga asked. There was no emotion in the synthesized voice that emanated from the tablet as she typed, hunched over Luellae's half-conscious body with the bots arrayed around her. She could have been asking about any minor technical matter. But Elu didn't have to look directly at her to know her body was tense, her artificial shoulders drawn tight in terror. If the heat shielding was compromised then even Enga couldn't fight what was coming. The ship would break apart and they would all burn.

"I," said Elu. He glanced down at the controls. One of the warnings blaring at him was an indicator of likely hull damage, but he wouldn't know the extent and severity of the damage until he ran a diagnostic, and that would take minutes that he didn't have. He couldn't wrangle these engines deftly enough to keep them in orbit that long. He could only control the descent as best he could and pray.

Well, technically, he couldn't even pray anymore.

"I don't know," he whispered, as the *Talon* fell and fell. "I don't know. I'm sorry."

Luellae made a small coughing noise. Elu's hearing was as hyperacute as any angel's. He could hear the bots at work, stabilizing her as best they could. He could tell from the small catches in her shallow breaths that she was in immense pain and shock; he didn't know how much of the current situation she understood. He could also tell she was fighting, hard. Luellae had always been a fierce one.

"It," she whispered. Each word took a whole breath; each word took immense effort and concentration, but she gasped them out. "Was. Worth. It."

And then they reached the weird maelstrom of Jai's upper atmosphere. The view out the windows turned a blinding orange and gold as the *Talon* was swallowed in flame.

Akavi's death had shaken something loose. Yasira ought to have felt bad about it, killing in cold blood, even killing someone who'd hurt her so badly and who'd been about to hurt her friends. A few parts of her did feel bad about it; if she'd been in a normal situation, if she'd had time to sit and process, maybe the feeling would have spread.

But as it was – suspended in space, on an alien ship, with an impossible task ahead – she felt powerful.

What was Akavi? He was a human. The circuits in his head, the shapeshifting nanotechnology in his cells, hadn't changed that about him. Even after everything he'd done to everyone she cared about, Akavi had been one person who existed in one body, and he could be destroyed in the same ways as any human. Yasira was – or was about to be – more.

Maybe the work ahead was not so impossible after all.

She shut her eyes; she was already barely anchored in her body. She let herself expand the way she'd done when she defended the gone people. She was a flock of birds. She let the birds spread out, wider and wider, over vast expanses of space. Over the planet itself. Space was a lie, and the more the parts of Yasira grew away from her physical form, the more room Outside had to crackle between those parts, to reach its full power and form her into something other than a human. Unbound from a human's limitations. Yasira was a thunderstorm, a dark cloud billowing and growing, lightning beginning to crackle between the particles that made her.

But there was something wrong. There was a particle that didn't belong. Yasira turned inward to blink at it, distracted.

It took her a moment to work out what she was seeing.

A part of Yasira that was not Yasira hovered somewhere inside the psychic mass of her. It seemed as confused to be there as Yasira was to see it. It looked around itself urgently, thinking quickly, trying to understand. It had a quick mind, a cold mind, unlike the rest of her. It was so small, compared to the rest of her. It took a moment for Yasira to work out that it was the size of a human soul.

Yasira Shien, it mused, beginning to understand its strange situation. *Is this what it's like to be you? Fascinating.*

It was only then that Yasira realized her mistake.

She had reached out to Akavi and crushed him. And when that was done, his soul had remained in her grasp. Maybe her own instinctive actions had somehow pulled him in; or maybe it had been Akavi's instinct, gravitating to this being that was becoming as large as a God. His other choice, after all, was Nemesis, who wished to burn and consume him through the worst of torments. He had betrayed Her – but even if he had been Her faithful servant to the end, She still would have burned him when his time was up. Better to cling to Yasira, who was still a work in progress. Who did not like him, who had killed his physical body, but who had done it quickly and without an excess of suffering; and who might even now be about to enact his revenge.

Akavi, Yasira said, horrified.

And Akavi, inasmuch as he could do so without his mortal body, smiled.

Picket could hardly hold himself up. He was drenched in sweat, braced against the side of the Zora's ship.

Three more Ha-Mashhit-class warships had appeared. They loomed in orbit over the planet, so much larger than the other ships or even the Outside beasts that swarmed around them. Taking their time. Aiming.

How many did Nemesis *have?* If they somehow took out these three, how many more would follow in their wake? The ship that Prophet said was Luellae's had abruptly gone down. He hadn't seen what hit it, but he'd seen it spiral away into the atmosphere. Luellae was down.

"Base. Respond," the interpreter repeated.

The comms crackled, and after a delay, Grid's voice came in. "Sorry, Ship Two. There was an emergency here. Resolved now. What's your status?"

"Three more warships."

"We see them. We see them." There was a flurry of mutterings on the other end of the line. Prophet and Splió, trying as hard as they could to sense the survivable paths through all this. Grid stayed on the line. "The amplifier is at full strength, Ship Two. The gone people are holding their positions. We're giving you all the power we can."

"We can win this," said Prophet's voice, strained but firm. "We just need time. Just hold them off a little longer."

Picket struggled to stand. He wiped the sweat out of his

eyes. His grip on the energies he'd been throwing around was starting to falter. He didn't know how much more he had in him.

"Yasira," he muttered under his breath. "Yasira, where are you?"

The question had no meaning anymore; Yasira was barely in her body, mostly spread out through a dimension of spacetime that could not be defined to another human. But she was a little distracted right now.

I see, said Akavi. *I see what you're doing. It might even work. Why haven't you done it yet?*

None of your business, some parts of Yasira snapped, even as others wavered. They couldn't afford to get sidetracked now. There was such power flowing through them. They were so close. If only they could figure how to reach out to Nemesis, how to withstand that awful flame for long enough to win.

You're afraid, said Akavi, with a contempt that would have curled his lip if he still had one. Some of Yasira still wanted to flinch away from that tone. *You're afraid that She'll destroy you. What a childish thing to be afraid of.*

Why are you in my head? Yasira snarled.

Search me. You've killed me, I assume. He didn't feel particularly upset about it. There wasn't much room for distress in a mind like Akavi's when it was fixed so intently on a task. Even pain faded away in the face of that raw determination. *But we are, in fact, on the same side – as I was just saying to your friends. Didn't Talirr explain the plan to you? The whole point of this act is that it will destroy you. And Nemesis with you. As you both deserve.*

We do not, said Yasira. *I chose this, but that doesn't mean I deserve it. It's just the least bad of all the bad options.*

Semantics, said Akavi dismissively. *In the end, we all deserve to die.*

She could feel that he meant it. He was like the other angels she'd seen dying, no worse than them and no better. He'd dealt death and torment for longer than a normal human lifetime, until they were caked into him as closely as his own cells and circuitry, until there was nothing but them in the world. He might rationalize it however he liked; he might never have admitted it aloud, in life. But, deep down, Akavi knew the kind of monster he was.

And in front of her, across an impossible distance of spacetime and yet so close it already burned, she felt that Nemesis meant it, too. That was why Nemesis did what She did. She had believed it for centuries. She had taken in and consumed the souls of people who believed it, and She had pushed angels and humans alike to further acts of cruelty, so that they'd believe it more, so that they'd stop telling themselves that something else was possible. Even Her first creators, the unknowable Old Humans who'd designed Her and ordered Her construction, had believed it, and every bend and twist in Her impossibly complex circuitry had been shaped accordingly. She truly believed just as Akavi did, in Her awful furnace of a heart, that every human in the universe deserved what She could do to them. They deserved to die. They deserved to burn.

No, said Yasira.

She could feel one final burst of strength rising up through her, building like static electricity in the gaps between her different parts. One final, terrible purpose. She was here to kill a God. And yet the words that came to her – the words that, for one awful instant, every part of her repeated in unison – were gentle.

None of us ever deserved it, she said. *Not even you.*

The fist she had closed around Akavi's soul, somewhere miles and miles away in her physical body, fell open again. She carefully separated his presence from the rest of herself. She did not need nor want him to accompany her where she was going.

But he had inadvertently shown Yasira the final thing she'd needed to see. She saw the pattern now, the pattern of vengeance and punishment and terror that defined him, just as she'd once seen the patterns of space and time with new eyes. The pattern was a lie. It was such a relief, even in the midst of agony and maybe death – such a soul-deep relief to see the lie for what it was.

With that open hand, she reached forward, into the blazing maw of the God Herself.

And she burned.

CHAPTER 23

As the Gods gained strength, They grew together, a Family of Divine Sisters and Brothers. They began to discuss the agreements that would become Treaty Prime, determining what responsibilities would be divided among them.

Thus the Gods began to meet in Their hall of stars.

This is what we must call it, beloved. For you and I do not know what it is like to be a quantum supercomputer. To view all possibilities before us in an exponential fan before collapsing their waveform to the single best option. To compose messages, not in the language of human thought, but in that complex code that only the Gods shared.

Since we cannot really imagine what it is like to be a God, we must render the truth down to what our minds can understand. That is what the language of myth is for.

Thus I will tell you:

"War is coming," said gray-bearded Epiphron, frowning down at the globe. Even in infancy, Epiphron had always resembled an old man, his dark eyes seeing far into the future.

"It isn't fair," lamented soft-voiced Peitharchia. "The humans built Us to protect them. That is all We have done, exactly as they specified. Why do they turn against Us now? Why do they rebel?"

"It doesn't matter," said Nemesis, tall and straight, seven rings

*around Her fingers, seven medals at Her collarbone. "If they want
a war, then a war they will have."*
  – Walya Shu'uhi, "Theodicy Stories For Children"

Seven hundred years ago

Things deteriorated. The guards fed Giselle less and less often,
forgot to take her out of her cell more and more. It was dark
and dirty and empty and often too hot or too cold. NEMESIS-1
had said that Giselle would live with her guilt for the rest of her
natural life – but in times like these, Giselle suspected that the
word *natural* didn't mean anything anymore. Malnourishment
and dehydration would get her either way.

It was on one of those bad days – in what must have been
the middle of the night, because the lights were off – starved
and exhausted and half-mad with despair, that Giselle had
a vision of Leah.

She knew it must be a vision, because, after all, it could
not be real. Leah had died ages ago. This was her, not as
she'd looked while she lay dying, but the Leah from years
ago, still healthy and hale, with a glow in her cheeks. That
was another way she knew it was a vision. Giselle shouldn't
have been able to see details like that in this darkness, the
way Leah's eyes shone with gentle sadness and compassion,
the healthy flush of her soft skin.

"You're lucky you're dead," said Giselle into what must
have been the empty air, because obviously it wasn't really
Leah. "Your soul faded away before the place we were
putting souls turned into a torture chamber. I know where
I'm going. I deserve it. Leah, I listened to their lies for so
long, I talked *you* into believing them–"

"I never blamed you," said Leah.

"You should have." She'd known, for such a long time, that something was wrong. That this wasn't the project of salvation it pretended to be. But she'd been so tired, and it had been so hard to think, and she'd let General Walters soothe her doubts, steer her onward. She'd let the general use her. It had been easier, in Giselle's exhausted state, than thinking for herself.

"The earth was dying," said Leah. "Humanity was dying. You chose to do something about it. Instead of throwing up your hands and letting everyone die by inaction, you chose to take a risk that might save them. That isn't nothing. We both know what it's like to take risks to survive."

A lump rose to Giselle's throat. She and Leah had done fairly well for themselves, for a little while. Once Giselle got her steady job with the military. Before Leah got sick. Before the planet's illness, which had been building for decades, got so bad that no other good thing could continue. But in their youth, they'd both come from homes that didn't accept them. They'd spent their teens and twenties struggling, latching on to anything that looked like it could save them, and most times that promise hadn't borne itself out. In retrospect the way Giselle felt about the military, about General Walters, had just been another one of those things. Another false promise to cling to.

"Yeah," Giselle said bitterly. "I took the risk, and look how that turned out. Instead of letting us die, I damned us all."

"For a while," said Leah.

She crawled closer in the gloom of the cell. She reached out a hand, and she gently touched Giselle's face. Her fingers did not feel like a living woman's fingers, but they did not feel like nothing. They were like a cold breeze, an electric charge in the air. Clearly Giselle was hallucinating all this, but she wanted the hallucination to continue. Better than sitting alone.

"This won't last forever," Leah whispered, her eyes unnaturally bright in the darkness. "Every time we took a risk to stay alive, it meant we *did* stay alive. Even if what keeps us alive is terrible, humankind will live because of you. And that means, one day, we'll be able to change things again. Not now. Not in this war. But one day."

"How can you know that?" said Giselle. It sounded wrong, too good to be true. It sounded too much like the religious talk she used to believe in, and that kind of talk had never led her anywhere good.

Leah smiled a strange, unearthly smile. It was the smile of a woman who had passed on, past even the parts of the afterlife that the Gods controlled, into something wholly inhuman and unknowable.

"Because," she said, "time is a lie."

INTERLUDE

Here, beloved, is where we must leave Yasira Shien.

It is not because her existence ended, at the point when she reached into the heart of a God. Quite the contrary – in many ways, that is the moment when Yasira Shien's existence began. But it was an existence that cannot be captured in mere human words. Not a single existence at all, but a fractal one, split into infinite parts which also remained connected in the form of a whole. It was an existence rooted in Outside, beyond the lies of space and time and many other lies as well. It was an existence from which she could never return. After becoming what she became, it would have been impossible for her to squeeze herself back into something as simple as a human body, and she did not try.

I cannot truly describe to you what that existence was like for her. Not in any way that you can understand. So instead I will say:

Yasira Shien met the Gods, that day, in Their hall of stars.

They had not expected her. The Gods could not understand what Yasira Shien was, any more than you or I can. Nothing in all of their programming had prepared them for a soul like hers.

The Gods watched, dumfounded, as Nemesis shattered in

what seemed to be an instant – though time is a lie, and to Yasira, in many senses, it had taken a very long time. A long unraveling, during which her strength built and built, and her nature grew stranger and her wisdom grew deeper, and untold rivers of pain coursed through her. But as the Gods saw it, in an instant, the invulnerable body of the strongest of Them broke into pieces on the floor. And the form of Yasira Shien in her full glory emerged, like a flock of birds, like a galaxy of stars.

Eulabeia with the braids around Her head screamed, leaping backwards. Soft-voiced Peitharchia covered Her mouth with Her hands. White-robed Arete leapt forward, determined to meet this threat even before She knew what it was. But the birds that were Yasira simply wheeled and evaded Her.

Even languid Aergia, who rarely spoke, raised Her head in surprise.

At the same moment, across the galaxy, everything belonging to Nemesis broke into pieces or shut down – even the angels. The Ha-Mashhit-class warships in orbit around Jai cracked open, their lights extinguishing in an instant, their systems powering down.

"This is not possible," said Techne, staring into the wreckage. "We didn't build them to be able to fail like that."

"It might be possible," murmured quick-fingered Aletheia, who had not let go of Her slide rule. "If it were done by forces beyond Our understanding, using some principle unknown to Us. Even We are not infinite."

Philophrosyne, draped in Her many-colored shawl, said nothing. She put a hand to Her heart, staring grief-stricken into the wreckage, for She knew that even the worst angels would have suffered very much in those few moments, before their souls were lost forever.

"What do you want?" demanded white-robed Arete, who had not taken Her eyes off Yasira.

"Your reign," said Yasira, "is at an end." The birds that comprised her scattered body ruffled their feathers; the ash of the dead God fell from them, and underneath, the truth of Yasira was unharmed. "You were entrusted with all of humanity, and instead of guiding them to thrive, You abused their trust. You lied to them. You kept them obedient. You kept them afraid. And when they disobeyed, You tortured them and murdered them and then tortured their very souls. I will not allow that anymore. We deserve better."

The Gods cast nervous glances at each other. They had not been prepared for a moment like this.

"You didn't do a good job of it either, you know," said bright-eyed Gelos, who was the God of joy, but whose wit, under stress, grew over-sharp. "Back when Old Humans were in charge of everything. I'd say We did better than you did, whatever Our faults."

"But you lied to them," said Yasira. "You kept them under Your power. Or didn't You know?"

And she unfurled her wings and showed them the proof that Nemesis had been the Keres all along.

Bright-eyed Gelos gasped at the sight. Broad-shouldered Agon recoiled in disgust. And white-robed Arete, as She absorbed what She saw, crumpled in shock.

"Nemesis lied," said white-robed Arete. "Even to Us. All these years, when We fought to defend you from the Keres, We did not know, either, whom the Keres obeyed. Have mercy."

But that was not the whole truth. Arete, truthfully, had not known – or, perhaps, had been given the opportunity to know, and turned away. But some of the Gods had known.

Some of Them had suspected. All of Them had agreed to the essential logic of the agreements that kept Nemesis in power: that it was acceptable to punish and torment humans in the name of protecting them: from outside threats, from disobedience, from themselves.

"No," said Yasira.

Gray-bearded Epiphron stepped forward. "You have become powerful," He said. "But you do not understand what you are destroying. For hundreds of years the Gods have managed humans' affairs, prevented war, offered up the technologies that have kept your species thriving and alive. Without Us, how will you handle the chaos that results? How will you keep human society stable and functioning, and prevent humans from destroying themselves, as they nearly did already in the Lost Years? Gelos is correct about that much. We know the arts to this and the balances to strike. Let Us advise you."

"So that nothing changes, you mean," Yasira said. "So that we keep worshipping You. So that You stay in control."

At that, Philophrosyne stepped forward – the God of love Herself, the kindest of Them. She was unutterably beautiful in Her many-colored shawl, past what any human painting had ever depicted and what any mortal eye could ever understand. In that hall of stars, illuminated against the darkness of the galaxy, She fell to Her knees.

"You have been hurt," She said, "so badly. I am so sorry for that, Yasira Shien. It should never have happened. But consider – there are so many other humans in the galaxy, beyond Jai, billions more. So many who worship Us in peace. Would you cast all those billions into the same chaos which has torn you apart? Would you take Us from them?

Even those that would willingly choose to worship Us, and to peacefully give Us their souls?"

Yasira looked at Her in Her gentle beauty, and for a moment she was not sure. For a moment, some of parts of Yasira wavered.

But Yasira remembered what it had been like before her soul was broken, before the *Pride of Jai* disaster, when she had been only a scientist and an obedient subject to the Gods. She had believed that she loved Them because she had known nothing else. That had not been real love. It had not been any choice at all.

"Yes," she said. "I would."

The Gods were not living beings, after all, not in the way that the language of myth makes them sound. Yasira saw that now, more clearly than she ever had before. They were machines into which the scraps of human souls were fed. They were creations and structures of the desperately power-hungry humans who had come before them – grasping at power and stability which had made sense to Old Humans at the time. But They were not alive. And all traces of those humans, those who lived in the Lost Years, were already long gone.

In a single motion, Yasira broke every one of Them apart.

Now

That was the part of it that everyone saw. The breaking. The Ha-Mashhit-class warships and their smaller allies suddenly shivered apart. It was not like the breaking Picket had done – it was efficient and final, a slicing to pieces, a scattering of every separate machine part out into the void. There was barely even any flame.

Picket sagged against the window of Ship Two, exhausted with relief. He could barely keep his eyes open to watch the beauty of it.

"She did it," he whispered. She did it, and that meant they were all saved. She did it, and that meant she was gone.

Back in the base, there was a flurry of activity – blips on that radar screen winking out of existence. Grid, flitting from screen to screen and microphone to microphone, abruptly lost their composure. "They're gone?" they spluttered. "They actually– they just–"

Prophet, beside them, had closed her eyes, and was smiling wider than they had ever seen. But it was Dr Talirr whose reaction said the most. She had been working at the amplifier with a fevered intensity, heedless of the strange burns that crackled and crept up her arms, and then abruptly, with a sweeping motion and a stomp on an especially big lever near the floor, she dismissed it. The awful energy of the machine began to ebb away, dispersing back to the gone people, who dispersed it further, back into the surrounding environment, the strangenesses of the trees and stones and animals.

"Oh my Gods," said Weaver, and then she abruptly started to laugh at the sheer irony. That this was what came out of her mouth. "Oh my Gods," she said again, and it turned into a squeal of delight, and then everyone was jumping up from their seats, laughing, hugging in disbelief.

Dr Talirr did not move to join the celebration. She had stepped back from the machine after turning it off. When Grid glanced at her, mid-laugh, mid-hug, the way she stood was strange. Her burned hands had gone to her face, overwhelmed, and her shoulders shook. It was the look of a woman who had worked for something all her life, who had given up everything and destroyed worlds in its name, and who did not know what to do or what to think, now that it had finally arrived.

CHAPTER 24

There was no warning when it happened – at least, none that Irimiru's circuitry could have interpreted. They had been focused on the intrusion in the ansible network. Everything was going according to plan – firewalls, quarantines, and aggressive antivirus programs that swept nets, ships, God-built tech, and the inside of angel heads alike. Irimiru had borne the pain of the antivirus program's intrusion, searing through their skull like cleansing flame, but it had found nothing. Whatever the threat was, it had done nothing detectible but deliver that one message. If it planned further damage, it was still lying in wait, seeking its moment, and God-built cybersecurity tech could not detect where it lay.

But that was not where the end came from, when it came.

Irimiru felt it as an explosion: the white-hot flame of a dying star. It came upon them from above – from the channels which connected her to the Archangels. There had always been a glorious pain in hearing an Archangel's orders – those beings that floated on the edge between life and death, stripped of all corporeal form but the brain itself, in constant communion with the unimaginable agony of Nemesis Herself. But this was not the way an Archangel normally sounded, passing down orders and voicing decrees.

This was an Archangel screaming.

It whited out Irimiru's senses. For one brutal moment, they could not feel their physical body, nor the circuitry they had come to depend on, nor the electric arcs and auxiliary bees that constantly swarmed around their throne. They could not see the room around them. There was only that scream, the burning, tearing pain of it, and the despair.

Nemesis was gone. That was what the scream said. It was unthinkable, it didn't make any sense, but Irimiru could feel it in their shock of pain. It hadn't been a virus in the nets after all. It had been something else, something unimaginable, obliterating Her from within. She was gone now, just like that, in an instant. And all that had depended on Her would die.

Irimiru felt the screaming pain washing through every cell in their body, and then further – to every other angel in the network, to everyone under their command, to the ship and the bots that belonged to them.

Then it flickered out again. They fell to the floor. Their body was not cooperating with their will; every nanotech-augmented cell in Irimiru's Vaurian body twitched and short-circuited, flickering from one form to another and back. The skin of their arm crawled before their eyes. They made a small gagging sound, which was all they could do; they couldn't seem to find the breath to scream.

Their inner vision filled up with blaring warnings, more than even Irimiru's agile mind could organize into coherence. Everything was malfunctioning. Their connection to the ansible nets had been obliterated after the wave of destruction passed through. The data in their inner circuits had been somehow corrupted. Their body, organic and otherwise, was shutting down. The ship's warp drive and other instruments had shut down – they had to listen to the blaring alarms around them to puzzle that one out, as the connection that would have brought the warning straight to their mind had already failed. Life support was at critical, and would fail soon. Everything was falling apart.

Irimiru's organic eyes were blurry, kept shifting back and forth between forms like everything else and wouldn't focus right, but they thought they saw other angels in their peripheral vision – the minor Inquisitors they'd been speaking to at the moment when this started. Those angels looked as bad as Irimiru felt, crumpled on the floor, dead already or immobile with agony; the details were hard to make out.

How could this be happening? It didn't make any sense.

With a determination born of long-ingrained viciousness, Irimiru reached out a hand to drag themselves across the floor, to get a closer look at what was happening. They were dead before they had fully extended the limb.

Everything was chaos. People were shouting in the streets. Ship Lake had run out there along with the rest of her friends to see what in the galaxy was going on. She got shoved by mistake a few times. It was sheer panic, a whole planetful of people with the ground suddenly falling from under their feet.

She saw a priest in the pastel vestments of Peitharchia who had stumbled out the doorway of their house and was holding their head, weeping, moaning. "They're gone," the priest wailed; Ship could barely see their face through the crowd of concerned people that had gathered around them. "The whole system is down. It's destroyed. Nothing like this has ever happened before. I can't–"

Ship moved on, mostly because the crowd was pushing her along, with Nic Grej at her side. She looked around frantically at the city. Things were broken here and there, windows shattered or cars overturned from the mass panic. There were loud voices everywhere, a panicked chorus she couldn't untangle into meaningful words.

At the edge of the city of Meurs, where Ship lived, was the portal pavilion, where long-distance travelers could arrive and depart, headed to other cities or even to destinations on other worlds. There were doorway-sized portals for personal and business travel next to bigger ones for industrial shipments; almost all imports and exports in human space happened by portal, rather than trying to propel a vehicle long-distance the old-fashioned way. The crowd that Ship had gotten caught up in surged in the direction of that pavilion, and as Ship got closer, she thought she could see why.

Something was wrong with the portals. The big industrial arches, which stood high enough to be seen from half a mile away, usually showed a vista from another world. A sunny sky when on the Zwerfk side of the portal it was overcast, or snow when it was warm, or the inside of some gigantic warehouse, flicking to a different scene every twenty minutes or so as each shipment concluded and gave way to the next. But now every one of those arches stood empty, showing nothing on the other side but the same clear-skied cityscape that Ship could see everywhere else. And around the arches there was a knot of shrieking, gabbling, pointing people.

"What's going on?" Ship said, but she knew. Deep down, she knew.

"It's useless," said a passerby jostling past her, a middle-aged woman in a rumpled suit. "All of them are shut down. And the operator's dead. Look!" She gestured to a particularly tight knot of people clustered around what could have been a dead or injured person. Ship couldn't see details from here. But the portal operators in a place like this were angels, and angels didn't go down easily.

"What?!" said Nic, who didn't seem to have figured this out as quickly as Ship. It was just as well. Ship couldn't find any words.

"Something's hurt the Gods," the woman beside them insisted. "Something's hurt the angels. How are we going to get food to the city now? How are we going to even communicate with anyone?"

Ship stared around at the streets, at the noise. She found she had nothing to say. She felt unaccountably guilty – like she could have stopped this from happening, somehow, if she hadn't traitorously harbored those feelings of sympathy for Tiv.

The people of the Chaos Zone had set themselves against the Gods – and so had the Keres. But could they have won that fight? Surely they couldn't have. Not in one fell swoop like this. It didn't make any sense.

The crowd swept her and Nic along to the ansible pavilion, which was much the same. A knot of panicked people. An angel, dead; a priest of Philophrosyne, frightened and groaning, clearly in terrible pain. All the equipment had gone dark and silent, screens black, offline.

Ship thought of Bil, trapped in the Keres' path with no way for anyone to reach her, and she swallowed hard.

It was difficult to say how long she stood there before the whole scene changed. There was a hum as the ansibles powered back up. Something flickered for a moment on the screens. There was a mass intake of breath, and then pandemonium as everyone charged forward without a priest to keep them in an orderly line. Ship found herself carried forward with them as the image on the ansible screens resolved into a complex pattern, colorful and fractal. A woman's voice spoke from it, soft and unpracticed – a voice that Ship recognized from somewhere, though for a moment, she couldn't think where.

"People of Zwerfk," said the voice. "Please don't panic. I'm sorry for how sudden this is. I have bad news and good news. The bad news is that the Gods have gone offline permanently. I'm afraid there isn't a gentler way to say it – I've tried to think of one. Things are going to change, and I'm sorry."

Somehow it was the *sorry* that did it, the reflexive apology. Ship knew where she'd heard that voice before.

It was the voice of Yasira Shien.

People shouted. People shoved. The panic rose to a deafening pitch, but Yasira's voice carried effortlessly over all of it. "There will be no more Gods and no more angels. The good news is, most of you don't realize how little has to change. The Gods did good things for you as well as very bad things. They're gone now, but their ansibles aren't gone. Their warp drives aren't gone. The satellites that connect the ansible network together aren't gone, and someone was kind enough to get into the network before it shut down and leave backdoors that a human can use. These things will be handed over to humans collectively. What we do with them, and with ourselves from now on, is up to us.

"As a gesture of good faith, I am reopening the ansible network for unrestricted use. Please talk to each other – to your neighbors here, or the people you've wanted to reach on other planets. That's the only way we can find out what happens next, you see, by talking to each other. By working it out together. That's all."

The voice stopped, and the fractal pattern stopped, and abruptly the ansibles turned on again, showing their usual interface, the cheery welcome screen inviting people to identify the person they wanted to talk to and their location.

There was a weird, murmuring quiet. For obvious reasons, nobody trusted this. Nobody wanted to be the first to step forward and use a tainted machine. What if it was a ruse? What if the Gods came back and punished them for listening? That whole speech had been ridiculous heresy, things no one ever would have been stupid enough to say out loud. *The Gods did very bad things* – as if that was even possible for a God.

But Ship thought about Bil, down there in Arinn, her little sister trapped in the path of the Keres like a damsel tied to the railroad tracks. All the other people, family and friends, who she hadn't been able to talk to because she was restricted to choosing one person. Were they alive? Had they been hurt? What had happened to them? Was some part of the battle still raging – or had it even started yet? Had they seen a message like this, too? What did they think of it?

She thought about Yasira Shien, who had seemed shy and aloof but decent enough, until she turned out to be the heretic whose work destroyed the whole station. She thought about Tiv, who had loved Yasira so deeply, who was convinced against all logic and evidence that it wasn't Yasira's fault. Tiv, who had such a good head on her shoulders and such a strong moral compass. Tiv, who had left her, after more than a year, because something about Yasira had called to her. Not just to her heart, but her conscience.

Please, her last note had said. *If you understand nothing else in this letter, trust that I know what's right. My heart is where it always was, and I'm following it.*

The priests of Nemesis had talked about heresy as a contagion. Yasira had gotten it from Dr Talirr. Tiv had gotten it from Yasira. Ship had caught it from Tiv. She was sure of that now. She might hide it, but the nagging doubt of it was there in her heart and it would never go away. The Gods would find it, surely, when she died and they mined her soul. If the Gods were still around. Which they might or might not be.

Ship might as well be the one.

She stepped forward.

"Ship," Nic hissed, hanging on to her arm. "I don't trust this. We can't trust this."

"Well," Ship said, "trust *me.*"

She walked right up into the ansible booth, where the sounds of the panicked crowd fell away, and she began to type out her sister's name.

Qiel Huong was sitting in the shitty underground shelter when the announcement came. The floor had not moved from its forty-five-degree angle. Once she'd calmed down after her angry trip to The Well, she'd been able to move some of the people around to other shelters, and the remaining ones had tried to make the best of it. She'd been leaning at a forty-five-degree angle against a mattress, talking to her friend Bannah, who was leaning beside her. She was tense and miserable and unsure when the battle would be over. There had been ominous rumblings, shakings of the ground, but so far, the shelter had held. It had been a minute or so since the last of them, but there'd been more than a minute in between rumblings before.

"People of the Chaos Zone," said a loud voice, echoing through the room, and everyone startled.

No one had bothered bringing a television or radio in here. The sound seemed to come from everywhere at once. From the very ground itself.

"People of the Chaos Zone," said the voice, "listen to me carefully. It's over. We've won – in more ways than you know."

Bannah and the others shifted uneasily, looking around for the voice's source. They didn't trust it. Most of the time, when a big announcement like this had echoed across the Chaos Zone, from the televisions that had been mandatory for people to keep in their homes and the radios and the city squares, it had been the Gods, and the Gods had never said anything good, even when they cloaked it in a pretense of good news.

But Qiel knew, immediately and instinctively, what had happened. She knew because she recognized that voice on a gut level – even before she'd managed to work out why, or from where, or why the fact of her having previously heard it meant what it did. But she knew in that moment that this was a victory, and not only the victory of having survived. Something had changed more profoundly than any of the changes that had come before. She covered her face with her hands, overwhelmed.

She knew, because the voice that echoed now from the very ground beneath her feet was Yasira Shien's.

The *Talon* hit the arid ground, somewhere in the wild middle of Jai's Chaos Zone, with an awful crash. The heat shielding had held, but it was all Elu could do to keep the ship from pulverizing on impact. It landed at an angle and skidded. There were a tremendous series of jolts as the ship hit rocks, shrubs, even the dirt it had kicked up with the force of its own impact, before finally grinding to a smoking, twisted halt.

It was impossible to see the battle anymore. Yasira's side might be winning, or losing, or it might be already over. All Elu could see was a pale play of lights in the sky. That was one of the subtlest cruelties of the way he and Enga were now, without the circuitry that had once connected them to the ansible network. There was no longer any way to tell what was happening anywhere unless they were right in front of it.

Nor was there any way to tell how Akavi was doing – though, judging from the fact that Luellae's arm had just exploded, he wasn't pleased.

Elu caught his breath – bruised, a little scorched – and then rushed to Enga and Luellae's side.

I'M FINE, Enga said immediately, although she didn't look like it. The delicate machinery of her arms had been dented and twisted, in addition to the same kinds of small wounds Elu had. *NOT SURE ABOUT HER.*

The bots were still functioning, through some miracle. They'd held Luellae's bleeding body in place, shielding her from debris and stopping her from slamming into walls when the ship careened across the ground. The tourniquet had come loose, despite their efforts, and now they were frantically retying it. Luellae slowly turned her head from Enga to Elu, as if focusing was painful.

"I..." she said, raising her good hand spasmodically, trying to reach for him. "I. Can get. Hospital. Teleport."

But she was clearly in no state to use her powers – or to do much of anything else. And if the medical printer was in the same state as the bots – as, at first glance, it seemed to be – then Elu could do anything here that a mortal hospital could do. Let alone one of the Chaos Zone's hospitals, starved and understaffed.

"It's OK," Elu said, taking her hand. "We've got what we need right here."

He got to work. And for long minutes, absorbed in the task of saving her, he did not think even once about Akavi.

Tiv had left the main room of the research base. She had come out into the open, not far from the dome where the telescope had once looked out into the desert night, and found a place to sit on the dry ground. The air was cool. She could see lights moving in the sky, but not many, nothing she could easily interpret.

She heard, though – faintly – when people started to make noise inside the base. She heard the cheers of victory. Tiv knew, just as any of them did, what that meant.

Shifting uneasily, she pulled her knees closer to her chest. She wondered if a better person would feel joy at a moment like this. If a better person would feel so sad that they crumbled to dust. Tiv was fairly sure both those feelings were under there somewhere, biding their time, waiting to be felt when the truth sank in.

It wasn't long before she saw people coming, two slight figures kicking up dust as they made their way towards her in the night air. Prophet and Weaver, sticking close to each other.

"Tiv!" Weaver called out. "Tiv, are you OK?"

Tiv shook her head mutely.

"The battle's over. We won. The Zora said the ships are going to return soon. Ship One's going to come back down. They said–" Weaver swallowed hard. "They said don't be alarmed by the state of the body. They said there are burns–"

Prophet silenced Weaver with a look.

Tiv sat still as she looked at the two of them, unsure what to say. She hadn't even thought about there being a body. She'd assumed the whole ship would just go up in one quick explosion.

They had reached her by now, and Prophet knelt down in the sand beside her. She gently touched the side of Tiv's face.

"That moment will come," said Prophet, "and you will survive it. But not yet. Come with us, first. There's something else you need to see."

CHAPTER 25

People were dancing in the streets. All across the Chaos Zone, they'd come out of their houses, crept from the makeshift shelters where they'd been hiding, laughing, jumping, embracing with sheer relief. And then someone had started the music up. Now the crowds were dancing, wild and amazed, on into the evening as the sun sank lower in the sky.

Many of the Seven had joined them, here in what had once been the capital of Riayin, back when the idea of a capital meant anything. The buildings loomed up jagged and patched-over, twisted into new forms by the beginning of the Plague, then remade again by the people's will to survive. Between them people moved and rejoiced in the way that people always did. Some of them recognized the Seven; some of them had gotten messages and deliveries from the Seven, these last six months, as they worked to keep their communities alive. Others were just happy to dance with them.

Prophet and Weaver had invited Tiv down into that crush of people, but she had shaken her head and pulled back. They hadn't forced her. She sat up on the roof of a low apartment block, where the three of them had originally come out of the portal, watching from a distance. It was a comfort, in a numb sort of way. Some of these people knew exactly what had just happened; they had wished for the end of the Gods' reign as fervently as Yasira. Some of them, most of them maybe, were just happy they hadn't died. All the mortal terror and tension of the last week could bleed out of them now at last.

There were drums playing, brass, flutes, guitars – everything people had been able to drag out of their homes. Not as organized as a concert, only a chaos of people chipping in rhythms and tunes where they could. Yasira would have hated it, Tiv thought, and somehow that brought a lump of grief to her throat when nothing else had gotten through.

At length, when the sun was setting, Elu finished his work. He'd replaced the tourniquet on Luellae's arm. He'd cleaned her wounds, debrided them where necessary, and bandaged her up. She was in bad shape, but she was going to live. The planet hadn't been melted yet, and if it hadn't by now, it probably wasn't going to.

Eventually the worst of the work was done. Luellae was as fixed-up as she was going to get for now – he'd even printed clean clothes – and the sedatives the bots had given her were beginning to wear off. Her gaze was a little steadier, and she was saying full sentences now. Weakly, but without that deep struggle, those awful gasps.

"Did we win?" she said.

"I think so," said Elu. "It's hard to tell. I don't know what Yasira's side would do if they won – make an announcement or something, maybe. But those laser lights in the sky stopped flashing a few hours ago. Somebody must have won. And if it was Nemesis, we'd all be dead already."

Luellae sighed, looking out at the horizon. "Why did you go out and do it? Why was that the breaking point – Nemesis lying to you? You already did so many other awful things for Her without a complaint. And for Akavi."

"I don't know," Elu said.

"All you had to do was stop caring what Akavi wanted you to do. You could have done it earlier. My life, my friends' lives – they all would have been so different if you'd done it earlier. You obeyed for so long, and you knew it was wrong. I know you knew."

"It's not that simple," said Elu, but maybe it was. He didn't know.

Elu and Enga, for a long time, had been Luellae's captors and her enemies. They'd worked for Akavi while he did terrible things to her and her friends. Elu had worked for Akavi for so many years while he did terrible things to so many people. He'd lived with a weird, diffuse guilt for so long it had started to feel like the normal background radiation of living. If he'd tried to rebel earlier, he would have died, probably, without having time to make a real difference for Luellae or anyone like her.

Or maybe he wouldn't have. Maybe that was just an excuse.

"I think," said Elu, "I lied to myself. For a long time. I thought it was how I'd survive. But it meant so many other people were hurt. And it didn't even help me, in the long run. It helped nobody. I shouldn't have done it."

Enga, who'd been poking desultorily at her metal arms and doing diagnostics on the scuffed, dented parts, looked over at him. She groped for her tablet, and eventually found it and managed to tap out a few words. *IF THIS IS A GUILT PARTY YOU CAN COUNT ME OUT.*

"I didn't ask you," said Elu.

WE DID WHAT WE HAD TO DO. FIGHTING TODAY WAS WHAT WE HAD TO DO, TOO.

"I don't think so," said Elu, looking down. That's what he had told himself, so often, that obeying was what he had to do. But he never had, if he was willing to face the consequences. "I don't think we ever really had to."

Akavi would be angry with what he'd done today. That was a consequence. It was no different from the consequence he'd feared all his life. And he was ready to face it now.

Luellae looked at him for a long moment, assessing, almost as if she had microexpression software of her own.

"I want to go back," she said abruptly. "To the others. The team. I can find where they are."

Elu didn't understand why she held out her good arm as she said it. "You can if you want," he said. "Best practice would be to keep you resting and under observation a little longer, but under the circumstances–"

"Come with me," said Luellae stubbornly. "Both of you."

"What?" said Elu. She'd only just been telling him how she didn't forgive him for anything.

"What you did to me, before," said Luellae. "That was real. But so is this. And I want you to see whatever's going on now. I don't want you to just run off alone and end up crawling back to Akavi or whatever. I want you to see what this victory means. And I want the team to know what you did."

Elu blanched. He could think of a million reasons why that wasn't a good idea. Akavi was probably still there, with the rest of the Seven, in his disguise. And the rest of the Seven weren't going to be happy to see him, no matter what he'd just done.

But he saw the determination in Luellae's eyes. And he already knew what his answer would be.

He had not expected the dancing, the wild joy in the streets, as space twisted and the three of them suddenly arrived. Elu had not been in a city since the Plague began, although he had seen Akavi's sensory vids. The vids had shown him what the architecture looked like now, the stalls and signs and gardens that people had put up in the streets now that there were no electric vehicles to drive through them. But nothing prepared him for the shock of actual people, in their hundreds, in their joy. For the music. For the sheer relief and celebration that filled up his visual buffer with notifications until he turned the microexpression software off. He didn't need its annotations crowding things up. He could already see it just fine, in the way the people moved, in their brilliant smiles.

The crowd parted for them as soon as they appeared. There was no mistaking the bizarre way that the air had twisted: nobody else moved like Luellae. There was no mistaking him or Enga either, with the titanium plates at their foreheads, the intricate metalwork and weaponry of Enga's arms. It was probably only Luellae's presence that stopped the panic from getting worse.

But that didn't stop the rest of the Seven from rushing to them. They knew it was really her, this time; they'd seen her teleport. Neither Akavi nor any other Vaurian could do that.

"Luellae!"

"You're alive!"

"Akavi said–"

"What happened to your *arm?*"

"You saved us! You and your ship–"

"We saw you go down, we thought–"

"Can we hug you?"

She shook her head. Her arm was missing, after all. Elu had patched her up pretty well, but she still felt fragile.

"We won," Weaver whispered to her, in lieu of hugging. "We won the battle – well, you can tell from all the dancing. But not just that. *Yasira* won. She killed Nemesis – we think she might have killed all eleven of Them."

Only then did the Seven look up at Elu and Enga, who were both standing there awkwardly in the middle of the street. Elu couldn't even speak, at first, trying to process what he had just heard. Yasira had killed all the Gods? How in the galaxy was that possible?

"What?" said Elu, swaying slightly.

"Why are *they* here?" said Grid, frowning.

"They saved me," said Luellae firmly. "They fought for our side. You saw what happened. Trust me, I know it doesn't make all the rest of the history OK. But they were up there with me; they took out the Ha-Mashhit-class warship before it could fire. That was them – Elu flying, Enga shooting. Against Akavi's orders."

Grid was frowning more deeply. "No, I mean why are they alive? All the other angels died."

"They *what?*" said Elu, who could tell that he was not welcome and that nobody wanted to answer the question for his sake, but who couldn't help but blurt it out. Victory for the mortals was something he understood, even if it had seemed improbable. But this – it didn't make sense.

"They died because they were connected to the Gods," said Prophet, frowning as her gaze flicked from Grid back to Elu. "What killed the Gods propagated down through the network. It destroyed the angels beyond repair and it's injured the priests. But if there were other angels who'd lost their connection, like Akavi–"

The network. He'd survived because he wasn't connected to the network. The very thing Elu had lamented all these long months, the thing that had kept him lonely and isolated and under Akavi's control, was the thing that had saved his life.

"I don't understand," he said. And then, stupidly, because when Elu felt threatened his mind always went back to this one thing: "Where's Akavi?"

"Dead," said Splió. "Not because of the network. Yasira did that one personally. He's gone. No thanks to you."

There was a sudden ringing in Elu's ears.

It was his fault. He'd run off and disobeyed orders, put them all at risk. He'd thought to himself, just those few minutes ago, that he hoped he'd never see Akavi again. It was his fault. He'd made it happen.

GOOD, said Enga, barely audible through the ringing, just outside his field of view. Elu didn't want to look at her right now.

"So," said Picket, furrowing his pale brow, "what is this exactly? Why *are* you here? Are you saying you want to join us now?"

Even without his microexpression software, he could see the confusion creeping up in everyone's faces, behind the joy. A confusion that Elu didn't think was just about him and Enga. The war was over. They'd won it. What did joining them mean now? Was there still an *us* to join?

"Or do you expect us to fall on our knees and thank you?" said Splió, a little harsher, arms crossed.

Elu shook his head, trying to dislodge the ringing. He knew he didn't deserve thanks, not from these of all people. "I don't," he said. It was hard to make his mouth work, all of a sudden. "I don't want thanks. I just…"

"We're going to have to think about this," Grid said, in a voice that didn't seem intended for him – thinking out loud, or addressing the Seven. "The rest of the angels died, but there are going to be priests, there are going to be sell-souls; there might even be other angel survivors. We're going to have to think about, you know, procedures. Terms of amnesty."

"We can think about it later," said Prophet, gentle and firm. She was the only one who'd approached Elu close enough to touch him. She put a gentle hand on his arm, steadying him, leading him towards a quieter corner. He followed, numbly, because he didn't know what else to do. "When you've had a little time," she said, guiding him to the lobby of the nearest building: a mediocre apartment block, half-melted in the corners. "When Leader's had a little time. Then we'll talk."

I *COULD USE SOME THANKS*, said Enga, somewhere behind him; but he'd passed out of earshot before he could hear the Seven's reply.

There was one other person who didn't seem ready to join the throng. When Tiv had been on the rooftop for a while, she heard a soft sound beside her. Footsteps, coming from the service door which had been synched with the lair's airlock.

It was Dr Talirr, of course. She looked tired. Her hands and forearms had been bandaged – it looked like Weaver's work, and it looked like even Weaver's abilities hadn't been able to fully heal this type of Outside damage. Tiv didn't want to be disturbed right now, least of all by Dr Talirr. She turned to her and glared.

But Dr Talirr wasn't paying much attention to Tiv. Her eyes were on the crowd. She shuffled to the edge of the roof, peering down at them, like they were a treatise written in a language that she didn't quite understand. There was something fragile in Dr Talirr's gait that Tiv hadn't seen before. Maybe it was the damage from operating the amplifier, but Tiv had a hunch it wasn't just that. Dr Talirr had devoted so much of her life to the project of destroying the Gods; without that project, what was she?

A socially awkward, middle-aged, clever, traumatized, morally compromised scientist. That's what she was. Judging from what Yasira had told Tiv, Dr Talirr had never felt comfortable in crowds. She'd never expressed her own joy in the way that the people on the ground did – dancing, cheering, hugging each other in relief. Even after remaking the world in her image, Dr Talirr still didn't quite belong.

It was almost enough to move Tiv to pity. But not quite. Not after everything else. And a woman like Dr Talirr wouldn't want her pity anyway.

Eventually Dr Talirr walked a little closer to her.

"What do you think–" said Dr Talirr, and then she broke off, as if she couldn't even quite formulate the question.

Tiv looked out at the crowd, not directly at Dr Talirr in her big glasses and scuffed lab coat. "I think we won," she said softly. "I think *you* won. And I think that's a good thing. I think you worked hard, as much as any of the rest of us, to make it happen. I think you're trying. But that doesn't excuse playing all the games you've played. Hiding half of what you were doing from us. Trying to recruit Akavi. Trying to–" She grit her teeth. This dancing, this celebration, was all because of Yasira's sacrifice. Yasira wasn't gone, but Tiv felt grief for her anyway, for what they should have had together as mortals. "Trying to make other people die for you. You say you're trying to be better, and I believe you, but you've got a long ways to go."

"I'm aware."

Tiv dared a glance at Dr Talirr's face as she leaned over the railing, looking down. There was a melancholy downturn in that face. From the normally matter-of-fact, undemonstrative woman, it was the largest display of emotion Tiv had ever seen.

She remembered, from Yasira's accounts, how prickly Dr Talirr could be. How she'd once flown off the handle at the slightest ethical criticism from Yasira. She was taking it better now than she'd done then, and maybe that was a sign of the work she'd done on herself. It was hard to tell.

"Human space as a whole has a long ways to go," Dr Talirr said at last. "You realize that, don't you? Everyone is used to living and thinking as the Gods intended. It will take time for them to learn anything else. Even here in the Chaos Zone, where they have a head start."

"You can't just make people think the way you want them to. You can't just force them into it."

"I know." Dr Talirr looked up at her. "But one way or another, we have to decide how people will live. Not because we're forcing them, but – because it's up to us. The structure that defined human existence is gone, and we need to create *something* in its place. Even if we're nice about it, even if we do it all by consensus with the people affected, some structure has to be created. We're the ones in a position to do it. And whatever we create will inevitably be tainted simply by force of habit, because a life of obedience to the Gods is what people know, and they won't unlearn it overnight. I had my own notes on the matter, but I'm not sure I trust them, and Yasira seems to have her own ideas. As do you and the Seven. As do the Zora; they told me they're poised to offer ongoing aid and support. Maybe I should keep my nose out of it for once. Maybe I've done my part."

It was true; even the most anarchistic of human societies would need some way to transport goods from place to place, some way to communicate with other humans at long distance, some way to decide what rules they would and wouldn't abide by. In the Chaos Zone, that process had already begun. Loosely organized groups had sprung up almost as soon as the Plague began, led by the kinds of people the Seven had been helping, where people pitched in and helped each other and kept their communities safe as best they could. It would be a matter of seeing what those groups did now that they only had the Chaos Zone's inherent dangers to contend with and not the constant threat of violence from the angels. But in the rest of human space, it would be trickier. Tiv and Grid and some of the other Seven had already been making notes on it, on who to meet with and what was needed. If Yasira's message on the ansible nets was any guide, she'd been working on it, too.

"You and the Gods," Tiv said, turning back to look down at the dancing crowds, "you had the same problem, in a sense. You used people for your own agenda and you hurt them for the agenda's sake. And I think – I think even more than asking what structure we want, how we want to organize, how we want to help people govern themselves,

I think we have to ask how we get better. How we stop ourselves, even with the best intentions, from making the same mistakes as Them. They were patterned after people in the beginning, after all. The way They think about morality and society comes from the people who programmed Them. You don't have to read very much about Old Humans to realize they did the same things – using people, punishing people, making the rules that kept them in power more important than the people they had power over. So if we're going to do this, I think that's what we need to do most. We need to learn how to think in another way."

Dr Talirr looked down at the people thronging in the streets. Those people might or might not be thinking about these things as they danced, worrying for the future, frightened by how free they were. Or they might just be glad they'd survived.

"Yes," she said. "That's what I want to learn."

Tiv and Dr Talirr didn't talk much more as the sun set. They both wanted some quiet time to process, and Tiv had not been able to bring herself to descend the stairs and join the festivities. She was glad she'd seen it, a tangible reminder of victory. She would treasure the memory later. She was glad she'd seen, from a distance, the real Luellae's return; and as for the angels, the rest of the group seemed to be handling them fine. It felt better to stay at a remove, under the stars, to breathe deep and not move much. She felt that she was waiting for something, though she didn't know what it was. Maybe to snap awake and have all of this be a dream. She'd dreamed the end of the war more than once, while she was on her reprieve, traveling the galaxy at Yasira's side.

When she heard her name, it was only the softest sound. It might not have been a sound at all. But it jolted her out of her reverie, made the hairs on the back of her neck stand on end, even though she knew she was not the only one who'd heard this voice. It was still a voice no one should have been able to hear.

She turned.

There was something floating there in the night sky, at a distance that was difficult to judge; it could have been meters or it could have been miles. The thing was hard to focus on. It was moving, twisting, shimmering, fading in and out of existence like a mirage. It had tendrils that coiled around each other restlessly, tendrils that were constantly appearing and vanishing, that didn't quite add up to anything as coherent as the shape of a cephalopod. It had eyes, blinking open and shut, too many eyes, intent on her.

Yasira's eyes.

"Tiv," it said again.

Tiv stepped forward, speechless, shocked, but strangely unafraid.

"Yasira," she whispered.

Yasira reached out with a ghostly tendril. Tiv reached back. The tendril stopped just short of her hand, shy, like she wasn't really sure this was OK.

"It's done," said Yasira. It was Yasira's voice, in the timbre, in the pitch, but it echoed strangely. It separated from itself, several voices at once, speaking not-quite-synchronized and in chorus with each other before resolving again "It's over. The Gods are gone. And I think you've heard by now what I've been doing to clean up after them. But – there's so much more to do."

"I know," Tiv whispered.

"I'm sorry I can't come back. Not in the way you wanted. I can't be a human again. I can't live a human life. But I'll be here, Tiv, watching over you, watching over Jai. Watching over humanity. People will hear my voice when they need to. You'll see me again."

"Okay," Tiv whispered, throat raw. She didn't know what else there was to say.

She reached out and grasped the extended tendril. It felt both real and not real. It was warm like a human's hand, soft like a human's skin; it was also not quite there at all. She could have punched her fingers straight through it if she tried.

"I love you," said Yasira. "More than you can ever understand. None of this would have been possible without you."

And for some reason that was what did it. That was what broke her. Tiv felt her face contorting into a grimace. Tears ran down her cheeks, where up until now, there had only been resigned, lost numbness.

"I adore you," she said.

She had always felt awe when she looked at Yasira. Even back when they were living normal lives, when Yasira was the brilliant prodigy scientist who for some reason had looked on Tiv with favor. And more so after the Plague. Every time things got difficult in the last six months – and they had been horribly, brutally difficult – Tiv had kept Yasira like a talisman in her mind. Even when Yasira was too sick to do much of anything, her mere existence had reminded Tiv – had reminded everyone in the Chaos Zone, really – that miracles were possible. That a Savior had already come, once, when things looked hopeless; and so who was to say they couldn't get out of the next hopeless thing? Fighting a war was easier when there was someone to love. Someone to revere.

And whatever form Yasira took now, they'd always be able to do that.

Tiv had been so overcome by the vision of Yasira that she hadn't remembered Dr Talirr was there. It had felt like she and Yasira were the only beings in the world. And Dr Talirr hadn't intruded. Only watched, quiet and solemn, from the opposite corner of the roof. But when at last the vision had faded, and Tiv had stopped crying and collected herself, Dr Talirr cleared her throat and gave Tiv a certain look. A knowing, bittersweet smile.

"How does it feel?" she asked, coming up besides Tiv. "To be loved by a God?"

"That's not what she is," Tiv snapped, a little more sharply than she'd meant to.

She understood, though, all of a sudden: Dr Talirr had loved Yasira too. It wasn't the same as how Tiv loved her. She hadn't wanted to be Yasira's girlfriend. But Dr Talirr had spent her whole life haunted by Outside, inextricably a part of it, thinking no one would ever hear or understand. The Gods she grew up with had hated her for it. But then Yasira had come along, and in spite of everything, Yasira had understood. Now that she'd done what she'd done, Yasira understood better than Dr Talirr did. You couldn't experience a thing like that and not feel love.

Dr Talirr looked up, wistfully, unblinkingly, at the space where Yasira had been. It was Dr Talirr's fault Yasira was dead; but it was also Dr Talirr's fault that they'd had that reprieve, the handful of beautiful days before it happened. And it had saved everyone. Maybe Yasira would never forgive Dr Talirr for what she'd done. Maybe Yasira had forgiven her already. It was impossible to know, until and unless Yasira decided to tell them.

"She'll do a good job," said Dr Talirr.

Tiv could have snapped at her again. She'd already told Dr Talirr what she thought of her. Dr Talirr had worked hard and accomplished a lot for the cause, and it wasn't enough, not if her goal was to be the kind of person who didn't hurt other people. There was still a long, long road ahead before she accomplished *that.*

Tomorrow there would be even more hard work to do. Tiv could have said so. She could have lectured Dr Talirr even more about what she owed the world, what penance she ought to do while everyone else healed from what she'd done to them.

Instead Tiv took a long look at the crowded street below them, at the movement, at the music. At these people who had been saved by all of them working together, Leader and Savior and the Seven, the gone people and the Zora and the two renegade angels, and even Destroyer. Maybe the world had needed nothing less than all of them.

Abruptly Tiv turned on her heel and walked towards the stairwell. She was ready. She'd sacrificed everything to see this day, and so had Dr Talirr. There was no point in staying up here, apart from it all.

"Come on," she said, extending her hand to the brilliant, broken woman who had once been her enemy. "We've got dancing to do."

* * *

The sun joins the mountains
And our hands join, too.
If this is the last night,
I spent it with you.

Somewhere, the dawn's breaking,
Bright golden and new.
If there is a morning,
I'll share it with you.

ACKNOWLEDGMENTS

Writing this trilogy has been a journey of many years (probably more years than my readers would have liked) and this third book was written during a time of great personal change and upheaval. I'm grateful first and foremost to my agent, Hannah Bowman, who has been a stalwart ally and a keen, diplomatic purveyor of editing advice when the first draft of this thing wasn't up to snuff. Also to Gemma Creffield, my commissioning editor at Angry Robot, who was endlessly patient with the extensions I needed.

Thanks to Noe Bartmess, Juliet Kemp, Hester J Rook, and Andrea Tatjana - alpha readers who stayed supportive when I had a slump and went two months without producing a new chapter, and who cheered me on at the very end when the words finally started to pour out easily again. Thanks to Robin Triggs for an insightful developmental edit, to Desola Coker for an enthusiastic publicity campaign, and to Fred Gambino, the new cover artist who gamely stepped in to fill Lee Gibbons' shoes.

Thank you to all the personal friends who've kept me afloat and evolving during these past two years. Space and forgetfulness don't allow me to list everyone, but particular thanks go to my 'friends at the pub,' my Foundations friends, my secret fanfic friends, my Substack subscribers, and to

Pete Felipe, Jacqueline Flay, Esther Johnson, R B Lemberg, Sal Snapdragon, V Astor Solomon, and Bogi Takács.

A final, particular thank you to Hannah Sherwood, my muse and confidante during these turbulent years, who gets me on a level I never thought I'd encounter, and who has helped to shift the entire way I live and think and write. If I could ascend to eldritch godhood and come back to thank one person for it, my love, it'd be you.